The front door banged and their feet came up the stairs. April's voice called goodnight to Eileen, then the bedroom door opened.

'Hannah, look what I've got for you.'

She squeezed her eyes shut and kept very still, pretending to be asleep.

'It's chocolate. I brought it home for you.' April knelt by the mattress and gently shook her daughter's shoulder. 'Wake up.'

Hannah rolled over, away from her mother.

'Wake up or I won't be able not to eat it.'

Hannah went stiff. She'd rather die than take that chocolate and please April, who wanted her to die. They both wished she was dead, Daddy had said so when she'd crawled under the carpet, his face white and pinched and broken-looking, and April was on his side, taking her away from Granny.

'Goodness, that child sleeps like the dead!' exclaimed April, picking up the chocolate and turning away.

Hannah looked at her betrayer in the dark, as she crept out of the bedroom.

'I hate chocolate. I don't want it.'

April turned, startled. 'You are awake. But you love chocolate.'

'I hate chocolate,' repeated Hannah.

'That's not true.'

'It is true now,' said Hannah.

Also by Christine Thomas

Bridie
April

Hannah

Christine Thomas

HEADLINE

First published in 1991
by HEADLINE BOOK PUBLISHING PLC

First published in paperback in 1991
by HEADLINE BOOK PUBLISHING PLC

10 9 8 7 6 5 4 3 2

ISBN 0 7472 3641 0

Typeset in 10/12¼ pt Times
by Colset Private Limited, Singapore

Printed and bound in Great Britain by
Collins, Glasgow

HEADLINE BOOK PUBLISHING PLC
Headline House
79 Great Titchfield Street
London W1P 7FN

This story is for Keith Muscutt

Prologue

Hannah Holmes' small pink tongue stuck out at one corner of her mouth, her baby face puckered into a frown of concentration. Fine chestnut hair fell over her nose as she bent forwards, her father's gold-nibbed pen clutched foursquare in one pudgy fist. The soft nib splayed on the surface of his best printed notepaper. Hannah scribbled happily, love letters to Daddy. "I love you," wrote Hannah, using a fresh sheet for each lot of squiggles and circles. Several sheets fell to the floor, looped all over with love and a big "H" at the bottom, though Hannah knew how to print her whole name when she was less absorbed in her own delight.

The pen blotted and trailed wet ink off the paper and on to the desk. Hannah's sleeve dipped in it, ink everywhere. She sat back on her heels, on Daddy's chair, in grave satisfaction. There were no envelopes to be found, so she left the untidy sprawl of notepaper for Daddy to find when he came home from work. April, her mother, scolded and clucked irritably between her teeth at the ink on her jumper when it came to bath time, but preoccupied with counting clothing coupons, still scarce after the war, didn't ask how it got there.

It had been a long day and David, Hannah's father, was weary. He'd worked all the previous night as well, since they'd been too busy on the wards to let him go home. The wanton spoiling of his best and only notepaper, so hard to get hold of in 1947, turned exhaustion to dull, frustrated anger. He rifled the pile, finding every sheet marked, with a grimace of exasperation flinging all Hannah's precious love letters into a disordered heap.

'Hannah's scribbled all over my desk,' he muttered to April as he slid into bed beside her. 'Why can't you keep an eye on that child?'

'I do,' murmured April drowsily. 'Why are you home so late?'

'Woman on the ward had an asthma attack and we thought we'd lost her. There was an almighty flap. I couldn't get away.'

She turned over and slid her arms under his, warm and soft and comforting.

'I left you some supper.'

David yawned hugely. 'I had a sandwich. Too tired.' He felt dog-tired, he thought, achingly tired. You had to be a houseman to know what exhaustion was, and then to come home and find his wife hadn't looked after things . . . His eyes closed despite himself and he drifted immediately into troubled sleep. A child called "Daddy, daddy, daddy", calling and calling, and then the sound turned to shrill, mocking laughter and somewhere a dwarf danced on a stool. Hannah appeared, head lolling, a price tag fluttering from her neck, a pretty doll for sale, a pretty doll that danced with the dwarf, pirouetting out of sight as David groaned and sweat beaded his sleeping face. The nightmare faded. His expression was peaceful when April woke him at six with tea. There was bright sunlight as she drew back the curtains.

'It's a lovely day,' she remarked, looking out over the

newly tiled roofs opposite on houses recently built to replace those destroyed by the same bomb that had obliterated their own in 1944. David squinted in the bright light, looking at the clock, groaning.

'It's going to be hot, I should think.'

'Where are my glasses?' He peered myopically at the outline of his wife's slender figure, hazy against the window. He found them and put them on. As usual, she was dressed, fresh and cool and ready for work before he was even awake. Last night's irritation rose sourly, spoiling all sense of a fresh new day.

'I need a bath. Is your mother around?' he asked, picking up the cooling tea she'd left beside him.

'She's downstairs with Hannah.'

April tilted her head slightly in front of a mirror on top of a chest of drawers and began to stroke red lipstick on to her full, curving lips. She pouted, wiping off a tiny smear with her little finger.

'I came home last night to find my desk in a mess and Hannah's scribble all over everything. I've asked your mother to keep her away from my things, but she doesn't. Will you say something to her? She must know that it's almost impossible to replace what Hannah's spoiled.'

'I think it was my fault. I let her in there. I'm sorry, I was busy and you know how she's into things before you turn round. I'll ask Sam if he can get you some writing paper. It's not the end of the world.'

'No, but it's annoying.'

April turned, her bright lips smiling and golden eyes shining with amusement. 'I think she was writing letters to you, anyway. She said at teatime she'd been doing letters to Daddy. I thought it was sweet. Why are you so grumpy?'

Without waiting for an answer, she took his empty cup and he heard her clatter it into the sink in their tiny kitchen. A door opened downstairs and he heard Hannah's voice, calling April imperiously.

David listened to his mother-in-law's footsteps follow the child up, scraping on uncarpeted stairs still bare from rebuilding. He flung back the blankets and shot into the bathroom opposite, avoiding them.

'I'm going,' he heard April say. She banged on the bathroom door. ' 'Bye,' she called, not hearing him answer above the running taps. 'Don't let her near his things, will you?' she said to her mother, standing on the landing behind her. 'He's in a pet because she wrote on his stationery yesterday. You know what he's like, Mum, so do keep her well out of here.'

Eileen sniffed. 'I do my best. I'm not young, dear, and I can't run after her all the time.'

April glanced at the clock. 'I must run. Thanks, Mum.' She bent down and kissed Hannah. 'You be a good girl for Granny, and don't touch Daddy's desk.'

Hannah nodded cheerfully. 'Yes.'

April sighed. She could mean yes she would, or yes she wouldn't. At that age, one never knew.

'Just be good,' she repeated, and ran down the stairs, out into the morning sunshine that carried on it the smell of dew drying on builder's dust and roses from half restored gardens. She hurried up the slight hill to the end of the road where the bus to the station passed punctually at ten past seven every morning. Finding a seat on the train for the journey into the centre of London, where she worked as a secretary, April did sums in her head and concluded that, if they were careful, when David finished his houseman's stint in a couple of months, and could get a better job, she'd look into sending Hannah to private school. That should use up some of her energy, give Eileen her days back to herself again and teach Hannah to read and write, which she was quite ready to do at the age of four.

April sighed and settled back to look out of the window. London's bomb sites were colourful with early summer flowers. Neat prefabs stretched in all directions. David had nearly finished his training, Hannah was nearly ready for school, London was rising from the ashes of war and all was well with the world. The future was rosier than she had ever dared to hope and she was looking forward to it with joy. To the delight of two businessmen sitting opposite, April smiled, radiant with pleasure at her own thoughts and quite, quite lost in them until the train stopped at her station and it was time to come back to earth.

'If you're stopping at home for a bit, I'll pop down to the Belgrave and do a bit of shopping,' Eileen told David, who was damp and flushed from a very hot bath, towel round his waist, ice blue eyes blinking blindly at her without his glasses.

'I've got a couple of hours, that's all. I didn't really want to spend it babysitting.'

'Nonsense,' said Eileen shortly, 'you don't see much of that child and now's your chance. I shall leave you to it. She's had her breakfast.'

Her feet stomped down the wooden stairs determinedly. She was going to leave him to look after Hannah whether he liked it or not. He sighed. He'd planned a pleasant hour's reading, a rare luxury that he missed in his long hours on the wards where there was no time for *Diary of A Nobody* because he was nobody. Or as good as nobody, until he'd finished and could look for a position that would make him somebody. He began to whistle at the prospect; it wouldn't be long. If he went into surgery . . . he picked up an imaginary scalpel and drew it through the air delicately. "Mr" Holmes again, after all the years spent becoming "Dr". Ironic, that. MRCS . . . Mr . . . or general practice, probably more practical . . .

'Daddy?' Hannah swung on his knees, head tilted right back to look up at his face. He could make out that she was grinning.

'Wait while I find my glasses.'

She let go and he fumbled among the books by the side of his bed and found gold-rimmed spectacles. He put them on and stared round, as he always did, while the world came once again into focus.

'What?'

'Can we go to the park?'

'No.'

Hannah's grin vanished. 'Granny does.'

'I can't help what Granny does, I haven't got time for the park. I'm only staying until she gets back from shopping.'

Hannah watched solemnly as he pulled on his clothes and combed his hair before April's little mirror. When he was dressed she clung to his knees again, tugging and begging for the park.

'I can't take you. Ask Granny when she gets back.'

'You take me.'

'I haven't got time.'

'Daddy . . .'

'I haven't had breakfast.'

He felt sorry for himself. Everyone else had come and gone, leaving him hungry and pestered by a bored child.

He picked her up and started for the kitchen. He and April lived in the half-decorated top part of Eileen's rebuilt house, just as they had during the war until it was bombed. They'd felt they had no choice but to come back when it was rebuilt, for they were poor and housing was scarce and expensive. 'Mum's all on her own, David,' April said, when he objected, 'and if it hadn't been for me, Dad might still be alive. And she'll look after Hannah for me.'

'She's strong as a horse, and your father died because a bomb fell on him,' David had pointed out reasonably, but there had been no real choice.

'We're leaving here the minute I'm fully qualified,' he'd temporised.

'Of course we will,' April had said.

David's eye caught the scatter of paper lying on his desk in the corner of the bedroom, where it should be sacrosanct.

'What do you think you were doing at Daddy's desk yesterday?' he demanded, shifting her weight to his other arm and pointing.

Hannah beamed and threw her arms around his neck. 'Letters,' she announced proudly, 'for you. Lots.'

'I haven't got lots of paper, Hannah, for you to scribble on. You don't understand. Since the war, it's hard to get things. It was naughty.'

Hannah hugged him harder. 'Not naughty.'

David felt her weight on his chest and her chestnut curls caught his unshaven chin, soft as silk.

'Yes, it was naughty.'

Hannah shook her head, enjoying the game, hiding laughter. 'Not naughty.'

Confused, David held her away from him and glared at her behind his spectacles.

'You've been very naughty, Hannah, and you're making it worse by telling fibs. You'll apologise.'

Surprised, she stared back, open-mouthed.

'Say sorry.'

She simply stared, nonplussed, her head on one side, like the doll in last night's dream.

The exorcist's words came back, as they had a hundred times and more. They'd sat, that soft summer night after VE Day, exhausted by David's confession. He'd told of his bargain with evil, how he had sold his soul for the sake of ambition. Mice rustled in the rhododendron leaves around them as the moon sank towards the edge of the peaceful Earth.

'It is finished,' the exorcist had said at last, 'go, and sin no more.'

'There's still something . . .' David had forced himself to admit his greater shame.

'Yes?'

'My daughter. It wasn't just me – I promised her, too. Can I save my daughter?'

The exorcist thought for a long time. 'She is compromised,' he'd said and his voice had been bone weary, 'and you will have to help her when the time comes. She is not yet lost, that is the most comfort I can give you.'

'I can't break the bargain for her?'

'No. It is for her to do.'

David had cried in anguish: 'I'd do anything to undo it for her.'

The exorcist had shaken his head. 'Be vigilant and help her. This will be part of your penance, so pray for your soul and hers and sin no more.'

'That may be beyond me,' David had told him.

Now Hannah was subdued by his anger, but unrepentant.

'For a start you have to learn the difference between right and wrong. It's crucial.' He put her down on her feet none too gently. 'And since your mother doesn't seem to be teaching you, I'd better.'

Hannah went to the door and looked back at him. 'I'll go and find Granny.'

'She's gone out, I said.'

Hannah kicked her foot rhythmically on the door jamb.

'Stop doing that, Hannah. It's only just been painted.'

She kicked harder, watching him out of the corner of her eye.

'I said stop it.'

One small sandalled foot hung half way to the next kick.

'You've got one more chance to stop, come here, and say you're sorry for being a bad girl.' David's voice was dangerously reasonable as her foot landed softly on the doorjamb, flaking off a fleck of paint. With glasses, David's sight was excellent; he saw the scratch as clearly as if it were etched on the very flesh of his own body and the exorcist's words made sense at last. He had to teach the child he had corrupted the meaning of right and wrong, to save her. Indeed, it was his sacred duty.

Eileen stood in her hallway, which smelled of paint and varnish and freshly sawn wood, and listened. 'Hello,' she called up the stairs.

No one answered.

'Must have taken her out, but he could have left a note . . .'

She put away her shopping, put the kettle on, drank two cups of strong tea and wondered how long they'd be.

When they weren't back by lunchtime she felt annoyed. They'd been gone at least two hours and Hannah would be a terror if she didn't have her rest.

The sun rose straight above the rooftops, baking shadowless earth, wilting newly planted gardens and bringing out a strong smell of fresh paint. Eileen opened her windows for a breath of air, fanned herself with one hand and climbed to the flat above to close April's curtains and stop the sun fading her carpets. She opened top and bottom windows as far as they would go in the kitchen, where curdled milk stood in a jug and flies clustered round the metal meatsafe.

'Shoo!' she shouted angrily, flapping at them with a dishcloth. 'Get away.'

The little black cloud buzzed loudly and circled dizzily by the window, avoiding the flypaper hung over the cooker.

'Out!' threatened Eileen, swatting furiously. 'That you?' she called, out of breath, hearing a movement. 'Well, about time . . .' Holding the dishcloth, flushed and perspiring, she went to the kitchen door to give them a piece of her mind. No one appeared.

'I thought I heard . . .' Uneasy, she went to their bedroom and peeped in. Nothing there. She put her head round the sitting room door, just to be sure. The big bay window faced due south and sun streamed in, casting brilliant yellow streaks on to the Indian carpet, turning its gorgeous red shades orange and purple. Eileen went in to close the curtains when half way across the room, her foot caught and she nearly tripped.

'Whatever's that?' She found her balance and stared at the hump in the middle of the carpet. It moved and a small, dry sound came from the floor.

'What is it?' she repeated.

The carpet heaved. Someone small.

'Hannah?'

It couldn't be . . . a cat got in?

The carpet moved again.

Eileen rolled it back as fast as she could until she uncovered Hannah crouched, folded upon herself like a rag doll, right in the centre of the room.

'Whatever are you doing?' gasped Eileen.

Hannah shrank away.

Eileen reached across the folded carpet. 'Come on, pet.'

Hannah, feeling her grandmother's touch, looked up. As she lifted her head, Eileen saw the bruising: red finger marks on her neck.

'Whatever did he do to you?' she whispered.

'Daddy . . .'

'Oh, my God.'

That evening April insisted they should call the doctor. He suggested a man-to-man talk alone with David, and the women went down to Eileen's flat.

'I wanted to strangle her,' said David in a low voice, 'because she wouldn't apologise. It seemed she'd never learn right from wrong. She had no sense that she'd done wrong, you see.'

Dr Sheridan said sharply, 'You feel a four-year-old should be capable of that? And that this was an appropriate way to teach her? Good heavens, man, what did you think you were doing?'

'I'm not used to children, and she's been away almost since she was born. I hardly know her.'

That's an exaggeration, thought Dr Sheridan. 'Has

anything like this happened before?' he asked brusquely.

'No.'

'Do you think it might happen again? Your wife and mother-in-law, I should tell you, are frantic.'

'I doubt it.'

Dr Sheridan rubbed his chin. 'Is there anything I can do for you? I would like to refer you to a psychiatrist, if you'd agree. You say it's overwork and worry and a bit too much enthusiasm for discipline, but you can't go on like this you know. I think we have to put your family's mind at rest, and I have to say that I think you should go into this a little more.'

'If you like. I think you'll find it's just worry.'

'What, exactly, are you worried about?' The GP looked down at his notes and frowned. 'You've no record of poor health yourself and you've finished your medical studies, I gather, in a way that does you great credit. Your family are well, and April seems happier than I've ever known her – and I've known her all her life,' he reminded David. 'Yet you say you are worried about Hannah? She's a splendid little girl, you know; absolutely no cause for concern there unless there's something I don't know . . . is there, Dr Holmes?'

'No.'

'Well, that doesn't get us very far.'

David struggled for words. 'She is, I suppose you'd say, high-spirited. I'm afraid it could get her into trouble unless she has careful discipline. With April at work, my mother-in-law isn't always as strict as I'd like.'

Dr Sheridan disguised his astonishment. 'I believe it's generally held that high spirits in a four-year-old are to be commended. I'm sorry to hear you feel they are morally threatening.'

12

David held his tongue, feeling the hopelessness of it all. Then he smiled bleakly and said, 'I've done paediatrics, but I don't seem to know much about children.'

'Your own child is always different.'

'I'll go and see someone, if you really think it necessary.'

'I'll drop a line to old Fisher, shall I? Already know him, don't you, so he'll cut through the red tape and see you quickly.'

'As you like.'

Recalling the fiasco of his last interview with Fisher, David saw no reason why it should be any different this time.

It was. Dr Fisher listened gravely to what Dr Sheridan had to say on the telephone, and then to what David had to say in his consulting room.

"Paranoid ideas of religious persecution," he wrote on his notepad discreetly, and offered to send David to a psychoanalyst.

David shook his head. 'Can't possibly afford it.'

'As fellow medical men, I think some arrangement could be reached,' suggested Fisher carefully.

David's heart sank. There seemed to be ways round everything except the real problem itself. He wondered what Fisher would say if he told him. Last time it had been, "Help me, Doctor, for I have sold my soul to ambition." And Fisher had told him to go and enjoy himself more, get out and about and stop brooding on the war. Now it was, "Help me, Doctor, for I have sold my daughter's soul to sustain that same ambition from disgrace," and this time the panacea was Freud. Laughter quivered at the corners of his mouth, the bitter joke evident only to himself.

'Yes?' asked Fisher, seeing a fleeting smile cross David's face in a curious kind of spasm.

'No, thank you.'

'May I ask why?'

'I don't think it would help.' David fumbled for an excuse. 'I don't believe it will happen again, and psychoanalysis seems rather extreme for one moment of admittedly violent anger. I have the measure of it now, and I shall watch myself carefully. Dr Sheridan suggests trying to spend more time at home and I shall, to try to get to know my daughter. We're still relative strangers, you see, because she was away during the war. But thank you for your kind offer of help, I shall remember it.'

'No one can force it upon you,' said Fisher curtly, 'but I suggest you give yourself time to consider.'

'I will. I'll be in touch if I decide to go ahead.' David tried to sound bright and appreciative, succeeding only in sounding insincere.

'I'm sorry I can't do anything else or offer something more to your taste,' said the psychiatrist, rising to indicate that the interview was at an end.

'No magic wands for family problems, are there?' said David. 'At least I'm learning something useful.'

Fisher stared after him as he went to let himself out of the consulting room and swung the heavy panelled door open on soundless hinges.

'David?'

He turned, his hand on the doorhandle.

'Should this or anything like it occur again, we couldn't overlook it, you know. Not a second time.'

Their eyes met across the shabby room, over the back of the worn leather chair in which Dr Fisher's patients sat. It had gone with him to Surrey for the long years of evacuation and war, and afterwards returned to London with him – as battered, he sometimes observed wryly, as most of the people who sat in it. The psychiatrist felt something that haunted him long after David had gone, but couldn't quite put a name to it.

'There will be no second time, I promise you,' David had told him.

Fisher felt deeply uneasy, but the chap had committed no crime and there was nothing further to be done. Picking up his pen, he unscrewed the top and began, in a small, pedantic script, to write a note to that effect to his old friend Sheridan.

"We can do nothing unless he wishes to help himself. As he has rejected this suggestion, all we can do is wait and see." Then a peculiar impulse made him add, "And pray." He stared at the words thoughtfully for several moments, felt foolish and gently scratched them out again.

'It would help,' David shouted at April when she asked him what they were to do about it all, 'to get away from here. Altogether.'

On the mattress that served as her bed, on the floor of her parents' bedroom, Hannah listened to their muffled voices through the wall. She caught her name from time to time, always spoken in tones of anger.

'Back to your mother's?' asked April. 'You mean, we should go back there?'

'No, right away. I've been looking for jobs for months and there's some research being done in the Midlands on radioactivity in red blood corpuscles. There's a chance there, if I apply at once.'

'Blood? I thought you wanted to be a doctor. I mean, in a hospital.'

'Post-graduate research isn't a bad way of kicking off, and the effects of radioactivity on humans are of pressing interest since Hiroshima and Nagasaki. It might be a good move. I'd love to get away from London, you've known that all along.'

April held her protests and tried to consider calmly. 'What would it pay?'

'You mean, could we do without your working? Yes.'

She picked at her thumbnail and found she didn't like the idea.

'Isn't that what you've always wanted,' he cried, frustrated by her doubts, 'to stay at home, in your own house? Isn't that what all the rows were about, during the war?'

'Would we have our own house?'

'I'd have a proper salary. We'd have enough to start in somewhere of our own. I thought you'd be keen, and as pleased as me to get away.'

'I am, but I'm scared of being all on my own again,' finished April. 'I could manage while you were in Surrey because I was out at work, and there was my family, and Rachael, and your family, and Lizzie and everyone. We were so busy trying to find something to eat and just keeping going that I never had time to brood. I loved them, David. They helped me cope. I don't ever want to be all on my own again. I don't know anyone in the Midlands.'

'You'll make friends. It'd be a fresh start, on our own at last.'

April started to say something and changed her mind.

'What?' he pressed her.

'Dr Sheridan said you shouldn't be alone with Hannah for a while. Here, there's Mum, or your mother if we go there. In Birmingham, there's no one at all. No one even knows us.'

David came across the room and put his arm on her shoulders, turning her to him.

'Can't you see, that's what we need? What we always dreamed about. Now we just have to go and get it for ourselves.'

'I like living here. The problem is, I like the things you want to get away from, David.'

He let her go, pushing her abruptly from him. 'Fat lot of help you are,' he said bitterly.

'I didn't mean that. Of course I'll come with you and we'll find a nice school for Hannah, and maybe a little brother or sister for her. That'd keep her too busy to mess up your things.' She scanned his face anxiously and to her surprise, he smiled. She had offered him the way to persuade her.

'Right you are.'

'Do you mean that?'

'If it keeps you busy enough not to pine.'

'All right.'

'Now let's see if your mum will babysit, and I'll take you to the pictures.'

My mum won't be there to babysit in Birmingham and I don't think you realise what that will mean to us, thought April worriedly, but she held her tongue because she knew that to protest would be futile and if Eileen agreed, which she always did, they only had twenty minutes until the picture started. They just got to the cinema in time.

The streetlamp outside their bedroom shone through the curtains and made patterns on the wall above Hannah's mattress. She lay, her eyes closed, wide awake since Eileen had crept in to look at her and crept out again, thinking her asleep. Outside in the street she heard her parents coming home.

'I feel so virtuous,' she heard her mother exclaim. 'I could have eaten it a dozen times over, and I haven't.'

The front door banged and their feet came up the stairs. April's voice called goodnight to Eileen, then the bedroom door opened.

'Hannah, look what I've got for you.'

She squeezed her eyes shut and kept very still, pretending to be asleep.

'It's chocolate. I brought it home for you.' April knelt by the mattress and gently shook her daughter's shoulder. 'Wake up.'

Hannah rolled over, away from her mother.

'Wake up or I won't be able not to eat it.'

Hannah went stiff. She'd rather die than take that chocolate and please April, who wanted her to die. They both wished she was dead, Daddy had said so when she'd crawled under the carpet, his face white and pinched and broken-looking, and April was on his side, taking her away from Granny.

'Goodness, that child sleeps like the dead!' exclaimed April, picking up the chocolate and turning away.

Hannah looked at her betrayer in the dark, as she crept out of the bedroom.

'I hate chocolate. I don't want it.'

April turned, startled. 'You are awake. But you love chocolate.'

'I hate chocolate,' repeated Hannah.

'That's not true.'

'It is true now,' said Hannah.

Chapter One

Over the East End, one early summer day ten years later, the sun shone in a sky of the most perfect duck-egg blue. Bridie, David's mother and Hannah's grandmother, rubbed her aching finger joints, felt rain in the air and wondered, looking into the breadbin to see what was left, whether she really needed to go down the Roman Road market. She prodded the end of a loaf that lay in the brown crock and suddenly imagined the delicious, warm fragrance of freshly baked bread. Her mouth watered. She threw the crust in the bucket under the sink and lifted down the string bag that hung on a nail behind the kitchen door, still imagining butter running down chunks torn off hot milkloaf from the bakery that had once been old mother Wisniewski's eel and pie shop, when she and Lizzie had been girls.

She thought about that time, walking through Old Ford Road towards the market. Then, she'd been housemaid to Francis, who had become her first husband, and Lizzie had been a student nurse in the London Hospital. Lizzie married Johnathan, a doctor, just after Bridie's second child, a daughter, died. That had brought the past to light with a vengeance. She'd come to London at the age of sixteen, abused by her drunken father after her mother died. Francis found out and could not forgive what he saw as her deception. So she'd fled, taking her son, to fend for herself in the slums of Plaistow.

Turning a corner, into the market itself, she thought of all the times she'd walked this way with stout, good-natured Ethel who had taken her in like a daughter. Bridie had married Ethel's only son, Edward; he had died in the Arctic during the war, leaving her alone again, with her son.

David was a medical student when war broke out, so didn't fight in the forces, but Bridie suspected her son had fought his own battles, in his own ways, though she never guessed the full truth. To keep his impetuously made marriage together, he had fought demons in himself that April, his wife, knew nothing about – except for the matter of Hannah. Odd things had happened when Hannah was born, and April had complained that David was almost afraid of his small daughter and relieved when she went to spend the last years of the war in Yorkshire, evacuated with a Salvation Army family who had badly wanted to keep her. But she'd come home to the ravaged East End, and at first they'd stayed with Bridie, whose house was still standing, after a fashion. Then David and April took Hannah and moved away, first to stay in April's mother's big new house in Essex, and then to a new life of their own, in the Midlands.

There had been, thought Bridie, putting her loaf in her shopping net, too many children. David had never got on with Hannah, and things seemed more and more strained as Peter and then Jessie came along. Then, when the twins were born, Bridie saw April, once so pretty and bright and lively, become thin and worn and dull-eyed, and prayed there would be no more babies, even though as a good Catholic she knew she should have such prayers on her conscience.

'It would be wrong. Any more and she'll be . . . well, David being a doctor, he ought to know,' she'd said to Lizzie, and her friend, who'd seen more things in the London Hospital than she ever cared to talk about, nodded. Bridie sighed and said, 'Well, it isn't really the sort of thing you can say to anyone, is it?'

Lizzie kept her own counsel.

The Roman was crowded. Shoppers and idlers and children pushed and jostled and nudged and strolled their way down the long lines of stalls on either side of the road, their chatter drowned out by the hoarse shouts of stallholders and kiddies begging sweets or crying to be carried. At the near end of the long road, where trading was best and sites prime, William yelled: 'Caulis, tuppence' at the top of his voice, and Gladys Masters recoiled.

'Of course he got it,' she said, picking up their interrupted conversation when he'd stopped yelling, looking down her nose modestly in case anyone should think she was boasting. Joe, her only child and the object of her pride, shuffled round the back of the stall and wished she'd be struck mute or otherwise shut up. His hands in his pockets, he eyed the puckered piles of oranges piled carelessly next to the caulis and bent his head so his heavy dark hair fell over his face and Bill couldn't see him looking. The boy's wide, full mouth tightened and two shining brown eyes peered from beneath fine, straight brows, half amused, half alert. Bill had eyes in the back of his head, so stealing from his stall was a real challenge. Joe hunched his shoulders, blotted out his mother's voice and waited for the moment to grab.

'My word, isn't he the clever one?' answered William sarcastically, sliding his eyes suspiciously over the lanky boy, prepared to pounce at the slightest movement towards his fruit display. 'But don't get clever 'ere, son,' he snapped.

Joe shook the hair further over his eyes and made out he didn't hear.

'Caulis tuppence. Tuppence. Get yer caulis 'ere, girls,' William roared again without warning. Gladys winced and stepped outside his awning while he threw a firm, creamy cauliflower into Mrs Pickles' passing basket.

'Lovely cauliflower cheese,' he suggested, grinning. 'Only tuppence to you, duck.'

Stout Mrs Pickles squeaked to a halt, her little wheeled basket clattering down on its stand indignantly. She picked out the vegetable and turned it over.

'Mould,' she pronounced, pointing, and handed it back to William.

'Where?'

She showed him.

'Aw, that speck? They all got something, lady. What d'yer want fer tuppence? Fortnum's? Just as well they ain't all as picky as you,' he added gloomily.

'When your dad 'ad this stall you wouldn't have found no mildew. You ain't no credit to him, sellin' rubbish,' retorted Mrs Pickles calmly, her small head tilted right back to look him straight in the eye.

'Bloke 'as to make a bloody living.'

'How's he gettin' on, then?' demanded Mrs Pickles, catching sight of Gladys idly sorting leeks and Joe lurking. Gladys turned, her face alight at the prospect of a receptive audience.

William guffawed triumphantly. 'Now you gorn and done it,' he told Mrs Pickles.

Crestfallen, Gladys let her handful of leeks fall and caught her son heading away. 'Oi! I want you to carry things. You just stop right there.'

Joe stopped.

'You behave yourself,' mouthed his mother.

He kept his hands in his pockets to disguise the bulge made by an orange. Gladys picked up her leeks and stuffed them crossly into a paper bag. 'Ta,' she said shortly, handing them to William for weighing.

'Nah, come on, I don't mean it,' he said kindly. 'He's doin' ever so well. You've a right to be proud.'

'What?' asked Mrs Pickles, full of curiosity.

Mollified, Gladys turned. 'Joe's won the scholarship. For the Sixth Form.'

'I thought he already had one,' said Mrs Pickles, staring accusingly.

'He did, for up 'til now. Now he's got another one, to stay at school. And then he'll go to the university.'

Her son scowled and turned his back.

'Oh my, aren't you the clever one?' said Mrs Pickles, impressed. 'And in those funny clothes as well. Fancy.'

'Uniform,' snapped Gladys.

'Mum,' warned Joe.

'In a minute.'

'Ah.' Mrs Pickles pictured his first year's trying on of soft collars, black tie and blazer. The local paper had captioned the photograph 'Local Lad Flies High', the anguish of which had Joe burning every copy he could lay his hands on in a smoky bonfire in a corner of their tiny yard. Gladys, outraged, called him ungrateful.

'It's a privilege, a boy like you going there,' she cried,

hurt that the sacrifices might be for nothing. He tried to explain how sorely school offended and tore him in two, tried to tell her about the loneliness of it. She didn't see at all. In the end they'd lapsed into mute and miserable anger and been off with each other for days.

Surrounded by women, feeling William's gaze, Joe's mind wandered. Gladys called him sullen but she didn't know anything. She especially didn't know about Arthur.

Arthur came to the school the term after Joe, the other scholarship boy. Thinking to be kind, the Headmaster had put them in the same house.

'Plebs together,' said Arthur bitterly. He was a child who hated everything. Thin, gangly and clumsy, his arms and legs tangled themselves up in an oversized uniform bought to grow into, and big, black shoes that squeaked. Arthur's lopsided, rabbity face was made for torment and teasing. When he opened his mouth an adenoidal whine came out that stopped the conversation in one of Britain's proudest public schools dead in its tracks. As a victim, Arthur was breathtaking. He was also, said those who paid for him to be there, a genius. So far there was precious little sign of it.

'Suppose they fink we'll keep each other company,' said the weaselly child. Joe, sensing disaster, hunched his shoulders.

' 'ere,' persisted Arthur, 'smoke?'

He palmed a Woodbine skilfully and extended his hand to Joe.

'No. You'd better not let them find you with that.'

'I never wanted to come 'ere in the first place, and they ain't stoppin' me 'avin' a fag.'

'A fag is what you'll be next week.'

Arthur's cheek twitched wretchedly. 'Not me.'

'You come here, you fag. Everyone does.'

'I didn't come 'ere, I got sent.'

'So what makes you different?' demanded Joe unsympathetically.

'I keep passin' exams,' muttered Arthur gloomily, 'can't stop.'

'So do I.'

They silently contemplated their common ground without enthusiasm. Hard beds stretched to either side of them in a great, empty dormitory. A bell rang harshly.

'Nosh,' said Arthur drearily.

'If you keep talking like that, they'll think you're bolshie. Then there'll be trouble. Try not to drop all your aitches.'

'I wish they never made me come 'ere.' Arthur swung a boot against the locker by his bed. 'I told 'em I didn't want to.'

'Can't you tell your parents?'

'Ain't got none,' said Arthur briefly. 'It was me uncle said I was to come, and when they saw me school report, they took me on. I never thought they would of. Snobs.' He eased his Woodbine out of his pocket and looked at it longingly. 'I'm an experiment,' he added, kicking the locker, half laughing.

'You're not the only one,' Joe said crossly, and to his horror the skinny child opposite leaned forward and winked shiftily, fishing under his school-issue pullover. For a giddying moment Joe thought he had a shirtful of dirty pictures, then Arthur pulled out a teddy bear, flattened and worn, about twelve inches high, its eyes sewn on not quite level. He put it against his pillow and Joe, sensing a presence behind them, felt wrenching misery as he hissed, 'Put that away, for God's sake. Quick!'

'What are you doing?'

They turned slowly. Arthur held the bear by its arm, in full view.

'Oh, shit,' moaned Joe.

'What the devil's that?' cried the house prefect joyously. 'Oh, my word, look what we have here.' He yelled down an echoing corridor and footsteps came pounding at the summons, together with loud, derisive voices. Half the Lower Sixth seemed to crowd round poor Arthur's bed.

The fight that followed became a legend. After broken noses and bloodied knuckles came apocryphal tales of broken arms, broken legs, of the shortest career the school had ever known. Found by the housemaster weeping bloody tears, Arthur still held the shredded stuffing of his teddy bear and one bent Woodbine, a swelling eye squeezed tight shut against smoke and tears. Joe got a week of detentions just for being there. Arthur was spirited off, mopped, disinfected, and isolated in the sanatorium while the Headmaster made a couple of telephone calls to demand his instant removal. No one ever saw him again.

Sometimes, at first, Joe cried in secret, frightened to death he would betray himself and follow Arthur, but by the end of that term there were no more tears. He learned to be wary, closed himself off, forgot Arthur, and in very little time was thoroughly adjusted to public school life. Over the holidays he bore himself, everyone said, like a man. Gladys was as proud as Punch of her boy.

Mrs Pickles broke the silence.

'Mr Churchill went to that school, didn't he?'

'Did he? I don't think so,' said Gladys doubtfully,

wondering if she'd missed something of inestimable value, but fairly sure she hadn't.

'Just shows, don't it?' pronounced Mrs Pickles, having decided something or other to her evident satisfaction.

'I suppose it does,' agreed Gladys vaguely. 'Are you serving, William? I haven't got all day.'

'No?' he enquired rudely and went on stacking potatoes while a small queue formed.

'Here's another one,' observed Mrs Pickles, looking through a gap in the crowds to a woman in a green dress, carrying a string bag.

'Another what?' demanded Gladys, exasperated by Mrs Pickles' way of supposing one already knew what she was talking about, and the effort she was making Gladys go to, to find out.

'Mrs DuCane. She's got a clever son as well, hasn't she?' Her mouth clamped shut in a straight line in her righteous, puckered little face, as if to say "So there."

'Oh, no,' cried Gladys, looking up at the sky. Fat drops of rain splashed lazily on to the orange canvas awning. People held out their hands, looking up, beginning to run for shelter into shop doorways and under covered stalls, huddling together.

'It's going to pour,' announced Gladys. She looked round. 'Where's he gone? He'll get soaked. I don't know . . .' She appealed to Mrs Pickles who was busy beckoning towards the woman in the green dress.

'Come under here, Mrs DuCane,' she called above the noise of falling rain and squealing people caught out in it. Mud darkened on a mound of potatoes standing in a box on the kerb.

'Here!' shouted Mrs Pickles again, and Bridie came

quickly through the shower towards the canvas awning, to the shelter full of the pungent smell of wet Norfolk soil off the potato heap.

'That come on sudden,' said Mrs Pickles, 'but you ain't got too wet.'

Bridie, a bit out of breath, put down her shopping by William's scales and shook her hair.

'Proper mothers meeting, ain't it?' remarked William sarcastically, and stared dourly at the grey drops dripping steadily off the corner of his awning.

They stood in a cramped little row, leaning on the edge of William's wooden pallet, eyeing the torrent.

'Gladys's boy's got another scholarship.' Mrs Pickles nodded her head sideways at Gladys to acknowledge the proper importance of the news. Her sly black eyes watched Bridie shrewdly and although the newcomer smiled, Mrs Pickles would have sworn she was sad.

'Has he now? What is it for?'

'Sixth Form, so he can stay on until he's eighteen,' said Gladys. 'Though you ask him to do something and you might as well save your breath,' she muttered, looking out for Joe, just for show, knowing he had vanished. 'That's his fees and uniform and everything.' The rain was slackening off, splashing down in dusty puddles along the kerb. The women drew closer together, keeping their feet out of little streams running faster and faster down to the drain.

'Oh, you must be pleased!' exclaimed Bridie. 'That's very good.'

'Come and say 'ullo, will 'e then?' remarked William, listening with his arms crossed, leaning against his carrot display.

'Joe isn't no snob,' cried Gladys.

'Your boy all right, then, Mrs DuCane?' asked Mrs Pickles innocently.

'Yes,' said Bridie briefly.

'Look at 'im then. A doctor,' Mrs Pickles told them solemnly. 'Just goes to show, don't it?'

'Something or other.' Bridie glanced at her. 'This has cooled the air, hasn't it?' She rubbed her fingers gently, easing their fierce ache.

'Seen your David lately?' persisted Mrs Pickles.

'Whit weekend. He's busy, and April's got her hands full with those twins.'

'Twins!' said Gladys. 'She's lucky.'

'I'm not sure April thinks so. Lizzie Norris had some hard times with Bridget and Oliver, and April doesn't have it easy . . .'

'I always wanted twins,' said Gladys stubbornly.

'Well, I'm no help to her because I can't pick the babies up.' Bridie held out her hands and ruefully regarded her twisted fingers. 'I might drop them.'

'Uh,' said Mrs Pickles.

Sunlight broke through, gleaming brilliantly on the wet road. Bridie squinted into it. 'That's nice,' she said. 'There might be a rainbow.'

'Pots of gold,' said Gladys dreamily.

'I think you need a leprechaun first,' smiled Bridie, who originated from Ireland.

'Huh!' snorted Mrs Pickles.

'See if William will put his cap on for you.' Bridie went to take her shopping bag from its place by his scales but he reached past her, picking out a handful of tiny, early salad tomatoes and popping them into a twist of paper, then inside her bag before she could pick it up.

'Sweet as sugar,' he told her, and winked.

Mrs Pickles watched from the shadows as Bridie walked away, the washed street drying beneath her feet.

'That son of hers ain't no good, for all his education,' she sniffed spitefully.

'That's not my business and none of yours, neither,' said Gladys, refusing to be drawn.

'Sending 'em away to posh schools just makes 'em dissatisfied. You watch out for your boy, that's all, or 'e'll be off and that'll be that for your old age.' Mrs Pickles pursed her lips a final time, gathered her wheeled basket into her small hands and got ready to set off.

'That's nonsense,' said Gladys angrily.

'Oh, is it?' Mrs Pickles stood with her head on one side like an East End starling, looking just as malevolent. 'What's she makin' excuses about, then?'

Gladys went red and drew breath.

'Girls,' called William, 'give it a rest and 'op it.'

Mrs Pickles wrinkled her nose scornfully and pushed her basket out with a clatter.

'Good riddance,' muttered William, leaning very slightly on the edge of the scales as he dropped brass weights into the pan. He threw the bundle into his customer's basket and said out of the corner of his mouth to Gladys: 'Jealous.'

She caught sight of Bridie's green dress further up the market. The downpour had thinned the crowds and she watched the Irishwoman take a bunch of forced rosebuds from a pail by the flower stall.

'He isn't exactly there when I want him, is 'e? Can't exactly say he's got fancy manners from that school, can you?'

'Give 'im a chance,' growled William. 'I wouldn't like it.'

Gladys looked startled.

'Mixin with all sorts ain't easy,' said William.

'No,' said Gladys vaguely, 'but he don't complain.'

'Wouldn't dare,' William said sourly.

When he turned from serving his next customer, she was gone.

Chapter Two

April dreamed she was drowning. She sank, deeper and deeper, heavier and heavier, a shrill whistling in her ears. The sound broke into short, irregular blasts and she struggled out of the nightmare to the screams of two hungry babies. David stirred beside her and nudged her arm.

'Feed,' he muttered.

She felt him push her gently but her body was turned to lead. The twins shrieked. As one drew breath the other bellowed. In her worst moments April suspected they did it deliberately, and was afraid of them.

'You going?' David, beginning to wake, turned over and pulled the blankets up over his ears.

'You go,' she whispered desperately.

'Hmm?' He turned on his back and began to breathe heavily.

She opened her eyes and lay motionless in the half dark, listening to them, pushing away her fear. In her exhausted daydreams, half awake, half asleep, they gobbled her up, with tiny, screaming, insatiable mouths.

She looked at the clock with anger.

'It's only two hours,' she whispered. 'I fed them at two.'

David grunted in his sleep.

'Two hours.' April sank back, outraged by their neediness. They'd stopped for a minute, drawing breath, exhausted. She tensed, waiting for the next shrill, lonely cry of hunger and slid suddenly out of bed before it could start.

'Yes, all right,' she said softly, closing the door behind her so that she wouldn't disturb David. The twins lay, one each end of their big wooden cot, dishevelled and frantic. April picked up the smallest and held her, looking at Polly who was two ounces bigger and whose fuzzy head was as dark as Ingrid's was fair.

'Pigs,' she said wearily.

Ingrid snuffled against her breast and opened her mouth to howl again. April put a dummy into Polly's mouth and sat on the chair by the cot. 'Come on, then,' she said angrily to Ingrid, and the baby lunged for her breast as she opened her nightdress. April stroked the silky little head and watched milk run down the baby's busy chin.

'Ten weeks early,' she thought, trying to work out how old they really were and remembering the doctor's words. "They'll catch up, Mrs Holmes, but they'll need a lot extra to start with. But about every two hours should be enough to put some weight on them."

'How like a man,' she said to the baby, who let go of her breast and belched loudly, her eyes rolling with satisfaction, 'to say "about every two hours" as though I'm a milking machine.' Ingrid hiccoughed and Polly spat out the dummy and waved her fists threateningly.

April's stomach churned and the constant fear rose up like sickness. They asked too much. April lived in daily fear that she would fail them, that she'd begin to hate them and, overcome by the idea of the thoughts that

33

might follow and fill her head, would snatch them guiltily from their cot, smothering the tiny, bewildered bodies with kisses and hot tears of repentance.

'I could love you more,' she cried a thousand times to the babies' greedy indifference, 'if you'd let me sleep.'

Polly, painfully hungry, gave a thin cry and thrashed her legs. Hastily, April changed Ingrid.

'Come on, then,' she snapped at Polly and held her resentfully as she sucked desperately, holding April's warm skin in groping, stroking hands, transparent as fine sea shells, with tiny, pale nails that April wondered over with awe in moments of fierce, protective love.

'I don't know why I love you,' she said to them both, hearing their small, contented sounds, 'but I do.' The room, dimly lit by a faded yellow-shaded lamp, was warm and smelled of milk and Johnson's baby powder, soap, soiled nappies and soft baby skin. Polly stopped sucking and gazed intently into her mother's face with wide, serious eyes. Her mouth made tiny exploring movements, and she plucked at April, embracing her. She, heavy-eyed, gazed back exhaustedly.

'Go to sleep, Polly,' she begged, 'there's a good girl, so Mummy can go back to bed.'

As if by magic, Polly's eye lids drooped and by the time she was clean and dry again she was fast asleep.

'Thank God,' muttered April, crawling into the warm hollow by David's back, ignoring the creeping hands of the clock that in no time at all would set off the alarm and force her awake again, to the morning cries of Peter and Jessie, Ingrid and Polly, Hannah's rush to school and the whole day starting all over again, the endless round of feeding and washing and cleaning and being there. Being and being and being . . . who?

She fell instantly into a black well of sleep and fought to stay there against David's heavy arm across her belly, dragging her up again. He curled round her, waking her fully. April shrugged his arm away and turned her back. He followed her. Hopeless, she lay motionless, waiting for him to give up.

'I'm tired,' she murmured, pulling a pillow close to her, a barrier and a refuge.

David woke up properly and froze. He removed his hand and drew the covers over her shoulders.

'Yes,' he said simply and let her be. He lay listening to the ticking of the clock, checking the disappointment, the loneliness and frustration, reaching out to turn off the alarm before it went off so that she could sleep a few minutes longer, before those damned babies woke again. Children, children, everywhere. He felt the pull of a great yawing depression that sucked at him and frightened him and that he could never say anything about to April. He heard Hannah's bedroom door open and the bathroom door close. Another day. He rubbed his forehead tiredly, groped for his glasses and groaned. It was time to get up.

At two o'clock David shrugged on his white coat and pushed impatiently through the doors of Arundel Ward, scanning the windows of Sister's office in case the portly head and shoulders of Mr Spinner were already visible. The consultant liked to put one over on his team by being places when he shouldn't, popping unexpectedly out of corners and arriving at ward rounds early, enjoying his subordinates' mortification when they arrived on time only to appear to be late. The office seemed empty. Women's Medical stretched before David, immaculate. Sharp pink corners graced every freshly straightened bed, the occupant entombed within starched sheets until Spinner had been and gone, trailing his little retinue behind him. Then Sister would relax, send to the kitchen for a cup of tea and get on with things that mattered.

David grinned to himself and wandered into her cramped, untidy little cubicle. Two bouquets of flowers lay on a chair, waiting for someone to find time to put them in water, and a half eaten box of Milk Tray, fluted paper cups scattered, lay on her desk among a pile of pink folders. A nurse in Staff's uniform sat, chin cupped in her hands, studying a fluid balance chart propped on her knees.

'Morning.' said David 'Any sign of Spinner and the rest?'

The nurse looked up and shook her head. She was new on Arundel. Grey, almond-shaped eyes glanced up at him from beneath a fringe of pale, oatmeal hair that escaped from its hairpins and the stiff white cap that was meant to contain it.

'Someone phoned. He'll be a bit late.' She bent over the chart again and David saw fine greyish-blonde hair lie like down on the nape of her neck. He stood fingering the bridge of his nose, mentally running through his patients, his eyes focused unseeingly on that soft straight hair lying on porcelain skin, fingers moving unconsciously to the abrupt memory of April's sleeping body.

'You're new,' he said brusquely.

She looked up again. 'Yes.'

'You didn't train here, did you?' He was sure he hadn't seen her before, but she reminded him of someone.

'At St George's. My father's a surgeon there.'

David glanced at the nametag pinned to her dress, wondering if he knew him. His eyes narrowed. 'I've got it. I knew you reminded me . . .'

The nurse stared up at him and then it came to her too. 'You are . . . you came on Sam Saul's outing to Ipswich . . . the charabanc outing, during the Blitz.'

'David Holmes,' he said, putting out his hand. 'And you are . . . Christina. That right?'

She put her hand in his. 'We went to visit your mother,' she said. 'I remember.'

'That's it.'

'You all sang songs in the charabanc and Sam didn't know where he was going because all the signposts were down. He kept stopping and Ruthie sulked. Do you remember?'

'Sam popped a champagne cork and everyone thought the invasion had come. We were wound up like clocks, weren't we?'

'Your mother seemed very small and frail. She was badly burned, wasn't she?'

'Yes,' he said, 'and you were very, very quiet.'

'I used to be. Not now.'

He looked at her unadorned hand. 'Are you married?'

'No. I remember your wife, though.'

'April.'

'Yes.'

'She remembers you screaming.'

'I screamed?' Christina said, startled.

'Have you forgotten? You screamed, and Sam's wife had to take you out into the corridor and calm you down.'

She frowned, and the rest of her story came back to

him. He hadn't recognised Christina's voice because in those days she never spoke. The Nazis had shot her mother, and afterwards her father brought her and her sister to London. Everyone had thought Christina might remain mute with the shock. Sam Saul and his wife had taken them in until Sam's wife ran off with Christina's father. It had caused a bit of a stir.

A whirring of swing doors announced the inrush of Spinner and seven students in a flurry of white coats and swinging stethoscopes, looking round with alert, superior faces as though the entire ward ought to be holding its collective breath upon their arrival. Spinner's splendid consultant's strut leading the way, they piled to a halt outside the office door and Sister appeared from nowhere to snatch up her pink files and fall into line. David caught Spinner's eye and also leaped to attention.

'Tea after this lot?' he murmured out of the side of his mouth, bending down as if to collect something from Sister's filing cabinet. The phone rang and Christina reached for it.

'I'll ask to go at half three,' she said quickly. 'Arundel Ward, Staff Nurse speaking . . .'

She must be about twenty-five, he calculated, following Spinner round a dozen identical beds, filled with identical-looking, bovine patients. So the refugee from Warsaw had ended up at St George's, and his eldest daughter right here . . .

'Funny, that,' he said, unconsciously speaking aloud.

'Yes, Dr Holmes?' Spinner demanded, fixing his registrar with a look of sarcastic glee. David returned his stare levelly. Spinner didn't scare him.

'Nothing, sir,' he said, and all unseen by the consultant

winked at Sister, who, startled, stepped back on a student's foot.

'Yes, sir,' she said automatically and Spinner looked martyred.

'Next,' he ordered, dismissing the woman who lay at attention, quite mystified, in the bed between them. And so they moved on and the long afternoon passed by.

April threw potatoes into a pan and lit the gas. Behind her Peter looked over the side of the playpen at Jessie and reached for her hair. Jessie's howl sent her mother spinning round, catching the panhandle on her arm so that the whole lot went on the floor, potatoes and water all over the place. Peter, overjoyed, headed for the pool and Jessie screeched and rattled her bars. Upstairs Polly, or maybe Ingrid, began to cry. Peter rolled potatoes happily in the water, and April stared down at her son, at her sodden feet, at the pan upturned in the corner, and her hands still muddy from potato peelings. Peter sat down in the pool. April clutched a teatowel and wrung it viciously.

'I can't,' she said, 'take any more of this.'

Peter slid slimy potatoes across the kitchen floor and Jessie rattled to get out.

April walked out and shut the door on them, leaning on it, shaking. I can't, – she thought. I can't go on.

But she drew a deep breath and climbed the stairs to the twins, resenting the milk that stained her dress. Downstairs the gas ring burned brightly as one-and-a-half-year-old Jessie munched a gift of raw potato from her brother which later that afternoon made her violently sick.

* * *

'So,' said David, putting down two cups of coffee, 'what are you doing here?'

'I'm waiting for a place to come up in the premature baby unit. They've got a waiting list for training.'

'Don't fancy babies myself, got too many at home.'

'How many children have you?'

'Five,' he said, feeling defensive, but her expression didn't change. 'They get April down. And I don't suppose I'm much help.'

Christina sipped her coffee and hardly seemed interested. David gazed at the surname on her nametag: Nakiewicz.

'Is your father still teaching?'

'He's consulting. I suppose that's teaching.'

'And your sister? You had a little sister, didn't you?'

'She wants to be an actress, and she will be. She lives with half a dozen other would-bes in a filthy flat. She's obsessed. She'll make it because nothing else matters to her.'

'Are you alike?' asked David curiously.

'To look at? Not very. I suppose we're quite alike in other ways, though. We're both passionate.'

'Life can be distinctly short of passion,' he remarked gloomily, fiddling with his coffee spoon.

'Five babies sound like a lot of passion to me.'

His hand moved automatically to cut off the bleeper as it sounded in his pocket. 'I'll have to go.'

Christina glanced at the clock on the yellow-painted canteen wall. 'I've got two more minutes.'

'I'll see you on the ward, then.' He found himself unwilling to go. She nodded, looking up through thick, pale lashes, her gaze steady, giving him an uneasy feeling that she saw straight through him. The bleeper went off

again, sending him running to the nearest telephone then
out of the canteen without looking back.

'He's married,' said a first-year nurse at the next table,
watching her. 'Shame, really, isn't it?'

Christina took no notice. Her mouth, for no apparent
reason, was dry with terror.

Chapter Three

The summer after the affair between David and Christina began, Bridie and Lizzie sat in Bridie's garden enjoying the sun. Lizzie's faded green and red striped deckchair creaked as she sat forward, shading her face with her hand, squinting in the brilliance. At the far end of the garden the canal's gleaming water slid over the weir, a sleepy cool sound in the afternoon heat. A broad-brimmed straw hat cast Bridie's face into deep shadow and rendered her expression unreadable.

'He finally asked you, after all this time?' Lizzie squeaked.

The straw hat nodded.

'Well I never!' Lizzie sank back into the deckchair and put both hands up to shade her eyes, the better to see Bridie. 'Whatever did you say?'

The straw brim shook gently and Lizzie realised that Bridie was laughing. 'I said I thought I was too old to change my ways, and so was he.' She stirred the trug of fallen rose petals in her lap. 'This will make lovely pot pourri. But they're in a state, aren't they? I wish I could hold the clippers like I used to.'

She twisted her head round to look at the rambling roses and heavily scented honeysuckle climbing the back of her house, intertwined and flowering profusely, though the roses were well past their best.

'Stop that,' snapped Lizzie, frustrated. 'Stop teasing and tell me.'

'That's all there is to tell.'

Lizzie dropped her hands into her lap and closed her eyes against the sun's glare.

'Sam Saul asks you to marry him after – how long? How many years is it? And you turn him down and there's nothing to tell? You're incorrigible!' she cried.

'Must be – ah – fifteen? Since Ruthie went, that is.'

'We all know he's been besotted with you since the day you met,' said Lizzie. 'Fancy turning the poor man down.'

'I didn't say I said I wouldn't,' said Bridie cheerfully.

'Yes, you did.'

'I said I wouldn't change.'

'You said . . .'

Bridie swept rose petals into a heap and began to pick them over. 'He loves me, he loves me not . . .' she sang to herself, enjoying Lizzie's annoyance. 'I said,' she went on, since Lizzie refused to take the bait again, 'that I couldn't go and live in that great big house in Golders Green and I was set in my ways. He said he didn't care one way or the other, and I said in that case, perhaps I'd think it over. And we left it at that because Sam said he didn't want to rush me,' Bridie finished demurely, throwing out a handful of crumpled petals.

'Rush you?' gasped Lizzie. 'Oh, that takes the biscuit, that really does.' She wiped her eyes with the back of her hand and nearly cried with laughter, her plump round face bright pink with sun and mirth 'Oh, that's rich.'

Then Bridie's words sank home. 'You mean you're going to?' she demanded.

'I said I'd think about it.'

'You must have thought about it millions of times. All the rest of us have.'

Bridie flattened the petals and patted them gently.

'Thinking is different from doing,' she said maddeningly.

'But what will you do?' persisted Lizzie.

'I don't know yet,' answered Bridie simply.

And no amount of pressing on Lizzie's part would get any more out of her, so they went indoors to have tea and when the air began to feel damp and soft with evening dew, Lizzie went home, still none the wiser. Bridie sat watching the sun go down and swifts swooping over the canal after clouds of midges that danced in the twilight until they all disappeared with the coming of night. Bridie drew her curtains, locked up, climbed the long flights of stairs to her bedroom at the very top of the house and read for a long time, until, putting her book aside, face down on the cover, she mused over Sam Saul's proposal of marriage. Just after midnight, she fell lightly asleep.

Outside, as one o'clock struck in the distance, a small breeze picked up, rustling the chestnut trees across the park and picking softly at the stillness of the canal. There was no moon. Pitch darkness beneath the lilac hedge enclosing Bridie's front garden sheltered a furtive figure making a series of tiny clinking and scraping sounds. It kept a wary ear open for warning of a passing copper, due any moment on the graveyard shift. The sounds stopped and the figure held its breath, withdrawing silently into the lilac, waiting for footsteps to go down the road, past padlocked park gates, and on down the wide avenue towards Bethnal Green. On the night air came the sound of the policeman trying the park gates and the hoot of an owl, answered softly by its mate, hunting mice and voles on the canal bank. As the footsteps faded, the clinking started again. There was a brief splintering of wood. A moment of tense silence as the figure strained its ears, then the front window slid up and the figure was over the sill in a flash. It crouched on Bridie's floor, listening. The house settled, creaking after the heat of the day. The burglar rose, confident, sniffing the stale, lavender-scented air, warm from sunshine beating on blinds all day long. He switched on a torch.

Bridie's downstairs room was seldom used. The beam picked out highly polished wood, rows of books in mahogany cabinets, glass gleaming in picture frames: Edward in cadet uniform, Dartmouth behind him; Edward in Lieutenant's uniform, against the high side of a cruiser; Bridie and Edward on their wedding day, on the deck of the *Stalwart*, David standing shyly in front of them, holding his mother's hand. The burglar flickered his torch impatiently and jumped with fright, catching sight of himself in the mirror over the fireplace, a slight, dark boy, scowling with nerves. Cautiously opening the door to the hall, he strained his ears. In some houses he knew where people were from the snores, but this old girl was quiet as a mouse. He cursed under his breath and crept upstairs, breathing more lavender and the stale odour of good cigars. He frowned. He knew for certain she lived alone and she surely didn't smoke cigars. He sidled into the sitting room at the top of the stairs, skirting around it, sniffing at the neck of an empty bottle, picking up a crystal goblet and turning it, sparkling, in the light of the torch. What they said about her money must be true, he thought with satisfaction: it just needed finding. He searched every cupboard and drawer, working quickly and quietly, finding silver and fine glass, little trifles of odds and ends brought back by Edward from strange places, kept with love. Of money, he found not a penny.

Bridie, sleeping shallowly, half heard the gloved touch on her bedroom door. Then there was a hand over her face, a light in her eyes and someone whispering hoarsely, 'Not a sound, Grandma. Not a peep.'

She tried to sit up. A hand pushed her back roughly.

'Easy, Grandma. You goin' to be quiet?'

The smooth leather glove smelled of oil and earth. Bridie nodded. He eased his hand off her face and drew back.

'Who . . . ?' she began, outraged.

Frightened, the boy lunged, clapping his hand over her mouth. 'I said, shut it!' he hissed furiously. Nose to nose, they glared at each other in darkness. The torch beam flashed across the ceiling. 'You want to get yourself hurt?' He shook the light menacingly, his voice reproachful, as if she were a naughty child about to force him to do something unpleasant. Bridie looked from the torch, to his face, young and frightened and dangerous.

More frightened than me, she thought, lying quite still so as not to provoke him. She held his eyes, steeling herself to stay calm.

'You gonna scream or what?'

Bridie shook her head slowly, carefully.

'If you do . . .' He gestured with the torch but she held his gaze until he took his hand away.

'Sit up.'

Bridie kept her eyes on his face. Very carefully, she put her finger to her lips and whispered, 'My gown . . .'

He reached behind him to the end of her bed and handed it to her, the other hand still curled loosely round the torch. With her dressing gown on she felt braver.

'What do you want?' she asked in a muffled voice.

In the silence she realised with horror that he was convulsed with ugly, noiseless laughter.

'I come to burgle you, Grandma. What else did you think?'

He thought her absurd and she saw that he was very near an edge that filled her with terror.

'I haven't got much.'

His grin vanished in a trice and it crossed his mind for the first time that she might get stubborn.

'You can do better than that, Grandma.'

Bridie drew her gown close round her throat, trying to outguess him. 'Have you looked?'

'Downstairs and first floor.'

'Then you know there's not much.'

'You got it stashed,' he said flatly.

'No.'

'Show me,' he ordered.

Bridie sat helpless. 'There's nothing you haven't found yourself.'

He threw back the bedclothes and pushed her. 'Get out. We're going downstairs.' They both jumped and Bridie's heart beat painfully.

'Is there another one?' she cried.

'What's that?' he yelped, as a door downstairs banged against a wall in the stillness.

'Oh,' she gasped, her legs giving way.

He grabbed her arm nervously. 'You got someone here?'

'My cat. She knows how to open the larder door and then it bangs in the draught. It's windy.'

He let go of her arm.

'Haven't you looked in the kitchen?'

Hurrying furiously, he pushed her ahead of him towards the door. 'Downstairs.' He waved the torch. 'That room at the front, and no messing.'

He followed her down.

'There.' He motioned at a chair in a corner of her sitting room, right away from the window. Bridie saw in the light from the streetlight beyond the uncurtained windows that he was perhaps sixteen and very afraid. She gambled.

'Shall I make us some tea, seeing as you're stopping a bit?'

'Sit down,' he shouted, and looked over his shoulder in fright. 'You make me do that again and I'll smash your head in,' he whispered furiously.

'I'm sorry.'

Bridie sat down meekly, her hands folded in her lap to stop them trembling. 'I didn't mean to upset you.'

He shone the torch straight into her eyes. 'Where is it?'

'Where's what?'

He thrust his face in hers and she smelled his breath on her cheek. 'Shah of Persia's crown,' he spat contemptuously.

Bridie's skin crept but she didn't draw back. 'I don't know. I've told you, there's no money.'

'The safe.'

'There isn't one.'

Rage and uncertainty chased across his face.

'There was, years ago, but if someone's told you there's one here now, they've had you for a ride.'

'They said you'd got money,' he cried, younger and more petulant in a moment.

'In the bank.' She nearly added "you fool," and bit her tongue just in time.

'Nothing?' He let the torch fall, dispirited.

'Only odds and ends. You've found most of it. All easy to recognise and hard to sell, I'm afraid. Not much good in your line of business.'

He eyed her sharply but she was innocent, almost concerned.

'They said you had . . .'

'Who?'

'No one you know,' he said childishly. He turned to stare out of the window and the streetlight threw his face into bony hollows, hungry and wary, a poor tamed animal gone wild. Poverty, thought Bridie sadly. She'd seen that look a thousand times in her moneylending days. 'If you get my bag, you can take what's in it,' she offered, 'then I'll let you out by the door, since that's probably easier than how you got in, and go back to bed.'

She dropped her eyes, hiding her hope that he'd go. He picked up the crystal goblet he'd found earlier.

'Pretty, isn't it? But not worth much and too recognisable,' she said calmly.

'There's stuff downstairs, silver frames and such.'

Bridie sat up and said briskly, 'You know, you put me in mind of someone.' She frowned, thinking hard. 'Do I know your mum from somewhere? There's something about . . .'

'Pack it in,' screamed the boy, waving his torch in an arc. It flew from his fist with a thud.

'I'm sorry.'

'You're sorry!' howled the burglar. 'Bloody cups of tea and "Where's my purse?" They never said you was trouble like this.' He began mumbling to himself, searching humiliatingly for his torch behind the sofa, half tearful.

'I'll show you,' he gasped, finding his torch and snatching it up. He beat at finely leaded glass doors on a corner cupboard. Its contents spilled out on a shower of glass and splintered carving. He spat on the floor at her feet.

'You beat all, you do,' he panted. 'You ain't scared, are you?'

'I'm scared stiff,' Bridie told him truthfully.

'No, you're not,' he whined. 'I got the heebie jeebies off of you, Grandma. You ain't natural. You a witch or what?'

'Yes,' she said.

In the light from the street, he paled. 'Up,' he cried, desperate to get away. 'Get on up.'

They stumbled back, tripping in haste, up the stairs to her bedroom. 'Here,' he bleated, bundling sheets together, tying her crudely to the bedhead with her dressing gown belt in her mouth, 'that'll keep you quiet.'

Bridie gurgled through her gag.

'One sound and I'll kill you,' he yelled, beside himself.

Bridie knew that, pushed any further, he would do exactly that.

'Fucking old bag,' he told her bitterly, 'I'd be doing you a favour.' He hesitated, standing at the foot of the bed, seemingly lost in thought. He shook his head, lips working wordlessly.

'It'd be too good for you,' he quavered. 'Evil old

bitch!' Then he was gone, racing down the stairs as though the devil himself was after him.

'I hope you rot,' he screamed back up the stairwell, and was out into the dawn like a flash. Bridie, tightly bound to her bed, lay very still for what seemed a long time and then she began to shake.

Sam Saul roared through the house like a maddened bull, sweeping police, a distraught Lizzie, and several neighbours out of his way, apoplectic with rage.

'What the devil do you think you were doing?' he shouted at Bridie, who took one terrified look at him and collapsed into tears.

'It was hardly her fault,' protested Lizzie angrily from the doorway. 'Who do you think you are, coming here blaming her? Can't you stop shouting a minute and think what she's been through?'

Sam bawled.

Bridie wept.

'Just listen to us all,' cried Lizzie. 'What on earth do we think we're doing?'

'You've scared the daylights out of me,' bellowed Sam.

'*You're* scared?' sobbed Bridie.

'Stop it,' shouted Lizzie. 'She's had enough.'

'*I've* had enough,' roared Sam, 'of hanging around trying to get her to see sense.'

He and Lizzie glared at each other over Bridie's head.

'*You've* had enough?' yelled Lizzie. 'I can't believe it. You're too selfish to . . .'

'Stop,' whimpered Bridie.

They both stopped, purple with fury.

'Now then . . .' began Lizzie, trying to keep her voice down, but Sam ignored her.

'You're going to marry me, woman, whether you like it or not. Someone needs to keep a blasted eye on you. Oi yoi yoi, you're not fit to be left loose.'

Bridie's red eyes opened and out of the blue she began to giggle. 'The last time you did that was when you lent me two hundred pounds at two percent. Oh, you were cross.'

'What?'

'What you just said: oi yoi yoi.'

A policeman looked in at the doorway, bringing a doctor with him. 'Here's the victim, sir,' he said.

The puzzled doctor holding his black bag looked around their flushed faces and wondered how many patients he really had.

'I've brought a sedative . . .' he started.

'She doesn't need sedatives, she needs me!' bellowed Sam. 'I've been telling her so for twenty years, but would she listen? Well, now I'm here and I'm staying, and God help anyone who argues with me – including you!' he shouted, turning on Bridie.

'Sam, really . . .' Lizzie began again angrily, but the doctor, seeing Bridie's shocked face soften, tightened the top of the pill bottle he'd got out, and put it away.

'I'll leave a couple with you, that she can have if she needs them,' he said.

Lizzie, speechless, watched Sam sit down heavily on the bed beside Bridie and take her hand.

'We are going to get married,' he said patiently, as if speaking to a dense child, 'and I shall stay here until we are, because you can't be trusted, can you?'

'No,' said Bridie. 'Yes, Sam.'

'She doesn't need me,' the doctor told Lizzie, 'or you.' He snapped his bag shut and took a last look at his patient, clasped in Sam's arms. 'Out,' said the doctor firmly. The rest of them filed meekly down the stairs in front of him.

'Go along with you!' cried Lizzie to everyone gathered downstairs, not knowing whether she was on her head or her heels. 'She needs a bit of peace and quiet. Go home.'

Upstairs, Sam rode roughshod over his wife-to-be's shattered nerves and took a linen handkerchief to her tears.

'I'm coming home, Bridie, so don't argue.'

She remembered the last time he had dried her tears, when Edward died and he had stayed with her in the ruins of this very house, during the war. She'd asked him to stay then, and he'd lain next to her, holding her hand, all through her night of despair.

'Don't go again,' she said.

'Fool of a woman,' he snorted, 'where would I go?'

'Golders Green,' snuffled Bridie, 'I suppose.'

'I'll sell it.'

'Dear Sam,' she said. 'Dear, dear Sam.'

'Quite,' said Sam Saul gruffly, given his heart's desire at last. 'Now get some rest, woman.'

Downstairs, Lizzie shooed everyone out. She swept up the mess of glass in the sitting room and emptied the dustpan into the bin at the front.

The sound came through the open windows at the top of the house. 'She'll see to it,' said Sam 'Leave it all to us for once.'

'Yes, I will,' said Bridie.

Chapter Four

On a glorious September morning Sam went to the Town Hall to post the marriage notices. What with his being Jewish and Bridie Catholic, and neither of their sons being anything at all, it could only be a register office wedding.

'How wise,' muttered Lizzie acidly, when Bridie said it was going to be very simple.

Bridie sighed. Lizzie was jealous and made no bones about it. Two sisters could not have been closer. With both of them widowed they'd long since slipped into the gentle routine of old, old friends with shared memories and shared lives, taking so much for granted. Now Sam Saul filled Bridie's house with his presence. He interfered with the women's long established habits, spoiled their companionship and put Lizzie's nose right out of joint. Bridie could see it was serious for her friend was querulously unlike herself.

'I thought you approved,' Bridie had said in exasperation the previous day, after listening to Lizzie complain.

'You know very well,' cried Lizzie resentfully, 'that we all thought years and years ago that you and him were going to get married, and then when you never did, I thought you never would. Then you go and drop a bombshell. You can't just do that after all this time and expect a person just to say, "Oh, yes, very nice, Mrs DuCane," and not even notice that . . . that that person is upset.' Lizzie's indignation tailed off guiltily. 'Well, I hope you'll be happy,' she added, trying her best.

'Oh dear,' said Bridie, seeing there was no pleasing her. 'I think we'll all just have to get used to it.'

'That's easy to say.'

'We still miss them, don't we?' said Bridie quietly, after a very uncomfortable pause.

'I don't know what you mean,' snapped Lizzie.

'Yes, you do.'

Lizzie wrinkled her nose unhappily.

'I mean Edward and Johnathan. I was up the cemetery the other day. It's all dry and parched. I did Rosa's flowers and I thought about Edward's drowning. All that water and the graves dry as bones. And I missed him,' Bridie said simply.

'Sam . . .' Lizzie started.

'No, Sam won't change it. He was there when Edward died and he knows.'

'Oh,' said Lizzie, taken aback. 'Was he?'

Even Lizzie didn't know about the night Sam had stayed with Bridie, the night she'd thought she would die because Edward was gone, drowned in Arctic ice, taking tanks to Russia during the war. Sam had let her cry for Edward when he wanted her for himself, and that loving tenderness was still between him and her. It was his business, wanting to hide that side of himself, no one else's.

'Yes.'

'Sometimes I'm lonely,' admitted Lizzie reluctantly.

'Of course we are.'

'But now you've got Sam . . .'

Bridie looked at her quizzically so that she heaved a

deep sigh and started climbing down off her high horse. 'I miss Johnathan more than ever. Funny how it never really goes away, does it, that feeling that if you just open the door, he'll be there. Silly, really.'

'Not as silly as you and me fallin' out would be.'

'Well, you have to admit he gets in the way,' complained Lizzie. 'He's so loud.'

'Only when he's worked up about something; then he shouts. Always did.'

'You're not too old to make mistakes, you know,' Lizzie said, playing her last card.

'I'm old enough that if this *is* a mistake, it's my last one,' retorted Bridie, unrepentant.

'No fool like an old fool,' muttered Lizzie rudely.

Bridie nodded, unperturbed. 'Maybe, but who's to say? If I'm a fool, Lizzie, it's only to myself.'

'You're intractable!'

'And you always were one for the big words.' Bridie glanced at the kitchen clock and pushed back her chair. 'I'll make us some tea.'

'But it won't be the same,' cried Lizzie desperately.

'No,' snapped Bridie, losing patience, 'it won't. It'll be different. And the day nothin's ever going to change again will be the day they put you in your coffin, Lizzie Norris.'

Lizzie's mouth fell open, outraged.

'Makes you think, don't it?' suggested Bridie, struck by her own words.

'*You* certainly make me think,' said Lizzie caustically, 'and I never heard the like.' In high dudgeon she gathered her cardigan from the back of her chair, avoiding Bridie's eyes. 'I'll not stop for tea, thank you very much.'

* * *

'Daft old biddy!' pronounced Sam. 'She'll come round.'

'She's awfully offended,' protested Bridie, worried.

'Bad as each other,' growled Sam.

'I did try to be tactful.'

Sam grinned. 'You've upset your little apple cart well and truly, haven't you?'

'Oh, Sam, she's so offended.'

'She won't put thirty-odd years down the drain that easily.'

'How about you saying something to her?'

'What? And get caught between the two of you?'

'I hadn't looked at it like that,' admitted Bridie unhappily.

'Look, about the hotel,' Sam began, changing the subject to what he wanted to talk about, which was honeymoons.

'Perhaps she'll have come round by the time we get back.'

'You carry on like this and we won't,' Sam said firmly.

'Won't what? Go to Ireland?'

'Come back from Ireland,' he roared.

'Don't shout.'

'Don't go on.'

'We're quarrelling.'

'We always did,' he said smugly. 'And, anyway, you're quarrelling with everyone. Wedding nerves, my dear.'

'At my age. You wouldn't think . . . oh dear, am I really?'

'You are.' Sam's black eyes, startling beneath a shock of pure white hair, teased her. 'You are tense and squabbling and impossible. The sooner I marry you and take you off, the better.'

'Wedding nerves at my age,' repeated Bridie, flustered.

'And,' said Sam darkly, just to make her worse, 'why not?'

Bridie's faded cheeks blushed rosily. 'Go and get those tickets,' she cried.

'Yes, ma'am,' said Sam happily.

That evening David dawdled over his supper, sitting in the kitchen after the younger children had gone to bed, listening to his wife who had received a call from Bridie earlier in the day.

'She said Ruthie and Joachim Nakiewicz will go to the wedding. Anna is trying to get away from some performance she's in, and she said Christina's going, of course. She wondered if we could go down together.' April's voice was indignant. 'She doesn't seem to realise I've got five children. I can't go to London, just like that, just because your mother and Sam suddenly see fit to get married. She rings up and says, "Oh, do come," and I didn't know what to say. I always thought your mother had more sense. And what about you, can you go?'

'Probably.'

'It's time you were in bed, Hannah.'

Hannah, doing her homework at the other side of the table, stopped sucking the ends of her pigtails, looked at her father and asked, 'Can I go?'

'You've got school,' said David absently.

'You're allowed weddings and funerals. Angela's gran died and she had two days off to go to Yorkshire.'

David frowned. 'Her gran did? Good heavens.'

Hannah flushed. 'You know what I mean. If you give me a note, I'll be allowed.'

'Leave her alone,' said April. 'Hannah, if I have to tell you once more . . .'

Hannah ignored her. 'Please, Daddy. I can come with you in the car, so it wouldn't cost anything.'

Daddy planned to drive down with Christina and made up his mind in a hurry. 'You can come down with your mother by train.'

'I can't,' said April instantly. 'What about the others? You're surely not expecting me to bring them? Don't be silly, David.'

'Can't you find someone?'

'To take four children?'

'Ask Mrs Bateman,' suggested their daughter. 'She'll look after them for the day. She'll do anything for a bottle of scotch.'

'Hannah!' cried April, shocked.

'She'd stay sober for the kids,' said David.

'Batty wouldn't get drunk if she was looking after Polly and Ingrid.' Hannah tried to persuade her mother. 'Please, can I go?'

'And leave your children with an alcoholic?' April cried accusingly at David. He shrugged.

'I doubt they'll notice.'

'They aren't animals,' she snapped.

'You could fool me,' muttered Hannah.

'For heaven's sake, will you go to bed?' shrieked April. 'When will some one else have some sense of responsibility around here?'

Hannah piled her books together and stuffed her satchel full.

'Someone else pays the bills,' muttered David, opening the paper.

'Can I have a new dress?' asked Hannah.

'Ask your mother.'

April's old treddle Singer had sat in the corner of the sitting room for months, untouched.

'Bed!' screeched April.

David sighed and turned a page.

Batty was pleased. They argued for days, off and on, about whether to take the children to her place or whether she should come over to them. April, overcome one day by the smell of roasting spare ribs and whisky at Mrs Bateman's, said decisively, 'You come over to me. It'd put you out, having them over here. The twins' nappies and things are easier at home.'

Batty's watery pale eyes were sardonic. Her lugubrious beige face, flabby and plump with drink, slid into a half smile of recognition of the game they were playing.

'I'll leave you plenty to eat, and tea, and there's fresh coffee from Carwadine's . . .' April went on sturdily, refusing to be sidetracked into embarrassment. 'You're sure you don't mind?'

Batty grinned. 'I won't touch a drop. Guide's honour. I was one, once.'

April's face flamed 'I didn't . . .'

'Yes, you did. I won't. Go and enjoy yourself.'

'I don't know how to thank you,' mumbled April, beside herself.

'It'll make a nice change,' answered Batty ambiguously, and laughed aloud at April's expression. 'So you don't need to.'

They went out together, Hannah and April, and treated themselves to wedding wear.

'You should get a size bigger, leave room to grow, at

that price,' grumbled April, watching her daughter do up the buttons on a pale blue organdie dress with a sweet-heart neckline and puff sleeves.

'That's babyish, and I've finished growing.' Hannah was taller than April by a couple of inches.

'Only up. I mean out.'

'That's pretty,' said the assistant.

'I don't want pretty,' said Hannah crossly, 'I want smart.'

'There's a two-piece,' offered the assistant, her eyes sliding sidelong towards April, 'but it's a bit more.'

'What colour?' asked Hannah.

'I don't think . . .' began April.

'Cream.'

'Can I try it?'

'Hannah,' warned April, 'I can't afford . . .'

But the assistant, indifferent to their squabbles, fetched the dark cream linen suit and held it against Hannah. It was a perfect fit, which did not endear it to April.

'It won't last five minutes,' she said grimly. The assistant took a handful of tuck at the back of the jacket 'You could let it out here,' she said, 'and the skirt's got plenty of turn.'

Hannah studied her back view in the mirror and held up her hair.

'Oh, all right,' snapped April, clutching the paper bag that held her cotton print shirtwaister, 'if you have to, I suppose you can have it. But don't ask me for another thing.'

'It's lovely,' breathed Hannah, entranced by herself.

'It'll crease,' threatened April jealously under her breath.

'Thank you,' cried Hannah, delighted.

'I'll take Christina down then, since you and Hannah can't leave the babies and come overnight. She can go on to her father and I'll spend the evening at home and keep Mum happy,' said David blandly. 'I'll pick you up at the station in the morning and we'll go straight to the register office.'

'Assuming that car of yours gets there.'

He shrugged.

'What do you do if it doesn't? What will I do?'

'Call the AA. You'll have to get a bus or the underground. Don't flap, April. You know very well what to do in London.'

'It's hot,' she complained inconsequentially.

'It'll be a lovely day for the wedding.'

'David?'

'What?'

'Are you sure about leaving the children with Batty?'

'Look, please yourself. You don't have to come.'

They drove with the top down in boiling heat, sun and wind scorching their faces. Christina wound a scarf round her pale, oatmeal hair and lay back with her eyes closed, smelling hot leather, hot oil and hot tarmac, exhausted.

'. . . thought she might boil . . .' shouted David as they bowled into the outskirts of London.

'No, just me,' observed Christina, her cheeks bright red, too low for him to hear.

They roared through North London and passed the City, going East. Christina would stay with a friend.

'Sorry I've got to drop you off. We'll go and say

hello to Mum first,' said David, glancing sideways.

Christina gave a small shrug. Not far from the turning into Bridie's road, the worn gears on David's elderly car crashed and it stalled with a bone shaking jolt.

'Oh, damn!' he said loudly, wiping his face on the heel of his wrist.

Christina opened her eyes in alarm. 'What's happened?' she said, fanning her face. As soon as they stopped, the cool wind gave way to stifling heat.

Cursing, David climbed out and she watched him go scarlet with effort, turning and turning the starting handle while the engine refused to catch. She folded her hands in her lap and waited, suppressing a longing to get out and walk off as quickly as she could go, away from his sweaty, irritable face and the horrible hot day. She was thirsty. He came round and leaned on the top of her door.

'Look, why don't you get out and walk while I push this into the kerb? Mum's house is just round the corner. If I can't get the car going, I'll call the AA from her 'phone.'

'I can't go in without you.'

'She won't mind.'

'No. Not without you. It'd be awkward.'

The smell of petrol sickened her and steam rose wispily from the car's radiator, its metal too hot to touch.

'Why don't you go in the park, then?' He wiped the grease already thick on his hands. 'I'll come and find you. It'll be cooler under the trees.'

'Where?'

He pointed the way. 'If you go just inside the gates, there's the canal.'

Christina thought of delicious, cool water and swung her legs past him, out of the little car.

'All right. But don't leave me for hours.'

'As quick as I can.'

She walked away, round the corner, past his mother's house to the park gates. Just inside, there was a bridge with wrought-iron railings over a canal whose towpath was overgrown with wild flowers and long grass. The water, still and black, perfectly reflected sycamore trees and a weeping willow that touched its surface delicately, just by the side of the bridge. Christina picked her way down the bank, took off her sandals and sat with her feet in tepid water. She lay back on thick, clumpy grass and closed her eyes, seeing sunlight, blood red, through her eyelids. A skylark sang high above, hanging in brilliant, empty sky over London, a small black shape in the shimmering heat. Sitting up, she dipped her hands in the water, wishing it was drinkable, wishing once more that she hadn't had to come. The thought of seeing Bridie and Sam scared her.

'But Mum'll want to see you. She'll be pleased,' David had urged her.

'What about April?' Christina worried more, the more he denied there was any problem with his wife.

'Then don't go,' he said, meaning it.

'Don't be stupid, I *have* to go. Sam's practically like a second father to me. It's just that I hate being your secret.'

'Mistresses are secret,' he said softly.

'I don't want to be your mistress. I want to be your wife.'

'You are my mistress and I've got a wife. April doesn't know, I promise.'

'Sometimes I think I'll tell her.'

'Don't try to threaten me.'

'I'll leave you.'

'That could work both ways.'

Her eyes swam.

'But I won't leave you.' He reached out and took her hand.

'Threat or promise?' she said childishly.

'Whichever you like.'

'You don't leave April, either.'

'Nor five children.'

The children, thought Christina wearily, were the dead end every time. His excuse.

'But you can come to see my mother. You're practically one of the family, as it is. I don't know why you worry.'

'Why?' she demanded sullenly.

'Why what?'

'Do you want me to see your mother?'

David shrugged, growing bored. 'I thought you wanted to say hello to them. I'll take you straight on, if you'd rather.'

'You usually take a girl home if you're serious.'

'Ah, we're testing my nerve, are we? If I take you home, we must be serious?' He laughed unsteadily.

Christina hated him. 'You have it all ways, don't you?'

'I have you. Unfortunately, I have a wife, too. No amount of sulking will change that simple fact.'

'I'm not sulking.'

'You're getting worse than April.'

'You're such a bastard.'

David grinned. 'Aren't all men?'

'You aren't all men,' said Christina sadly. 'You're you.'

Uneasily he took the certain, the easy way out. 'I love you.'

'Of course you don't.'

'I do.'

'You don't.'

Lying under the weeping willow, dabbling her toes in the canal, Christina replayed the scene in her mind. It had ended the way they always did, in bed.

'Damn!' she said aloud, drawing her legs up and leaning her chin on her knees.

'Really?' came David's amused voice from the top of the bank. 'The car is parked outside Mum's house and she's got lemonade waiting for you in the garden. Coming?'

He reached down to pull her up the bank, holding her steady while she stood one-legged, brushing wet soil from each foot in turn.

'What do I see in you, do you think?' she asked, leaning against him.

'Something that charms you,' he joked, kissing her hair.

'A snake. Snake in the grass.'

'Do you know that snakes don't deserve their reputation? They're nice to touch.'

Christina knelt to do up her sandal, confused. 'Snake-charmer? Perhaps that's it.'

'How odd.'

'I'm dying for some lemonade,' whispered Christina. She hurried out of the shade into the glare of the sun, across parched yellow grass, wishing she hadn't said what she had. David had almost to run to catch up.

Chapter Five

In pale grey lace, Bridie looked forty-six instead of fifty-six.

'I wore grey when I married Francis,' she observed as they waited to leave for the register office. 'Do you think it matters?'

'Why should it?'

'Look how that ended up.'

Sam patted his grey-suited chest. 'We're both grey, my dear. A little more makes no odds, and you look utterly delightful. But then, you always do.'

He counted cases and checked labels for the last time as the clock in the hall struck the half-hour. He straightened up, pressing his hand to his back. 'Musn't keep them all waiting,' he said. 'Are you ready, Mrs DuCane?'

'I'm ready, thank you, Mr Saul.'

'Then let us go and be married.'

The registrar beamed and fussed and made it as much like church as he possibly could. April caught her mother's eye when Eileen pulled an envious face as Bridie said "I do" in a firm, clear voice. Hannah tried to keep her bottom tucked right in and her stomach flat, like the health and beauty ladies said, so as not to spoil the line of the suit. The effort hurt after only a few minutes and her suspenders chafed. She caught herself sagging as Sam put the ring on Gran's finger. That's three she's had, thought Hannah, and missed the rest of the simple ceremony, wondering whether Gran was immoral and if it got easier with trying, this business of being thin and pretty. She was thinking roll-ons might be the answer when Lizzie burst into tears. Hannah wished she wouldn't, pretended she hadn't, and stuck her hip bones forward like the health and beauty demonstrator had done at school. David and Christina stood at opposite sides of the flower arrangement, ignoring each other. It was Ruth they all worried about, but she listened impassively to her former husband's promise to cherish and worship the woman he'd cherished and worshipped for as long as any of them could remember.

Then they were out on grey stone steps, in front of the austere Town Hall, confetti everywhere and the photographer dancing about, pleading 'Keep still, ladies and gentlemen, please keep still.' They stood in a group; they stood separately; the groom kissed the bride; the bride kissed everyone; and the photographer clicked. Then they were piling into cars for the short trip back to the house by the canal. Sam popped very cold champagne. April drank a whole glass too quickly and went bright red. They laughed and joked and ate and drank, and through the open windows the sounds of Bridie's wedding day spilled into overheated afternoon air, tinged with sulphurous yellow. Thunderstorms growled far away.

'Better take brollies,' cried Eileen, leaning out over the sill and looking up at the sky, 'you could get caught.' In the park, leaves hung limp and motionless. A long way off, in the east, the sky flashed.

'Reminds me of the Blitz,' Bridie told Hannah, 'before you were born.'

'Aeroplanes always make me afraid, although I don't remember anything about the war,' said Hannah. 'Isn't that funny, being afraid of things you can't remember?'

'There was nothing funny about those rockets. That's what you remember when planes go over – the V2s,' said Eileen.

'Those were why we sent you away. Every time one went over, we couldn't stop you screaming,' April said.

'You've told me,' said Hannah. 'In the Blitz.'

'No, it wasn't. The Blitz was right at the beginning. What scared you was the V1s and V2s. They started when you were going on for a year or so.'

'I always thought I was born in the Blitz.'

'Oh, no. It was well after that,' said April.

Hannah thought it over, disappointed. April saw her face fall and thought tipsily, Even that, I can't do right for her. She held up her glass for more champagne.

Bridie gazed into the crystal goblet that the burglar hadn't taken, remembering her own drunken father. He'd raped her and she'd thought herself safe with Francis, until he'd found out and couldn't forgive her. She thought she would ask Sam why it was that being a victim of something violent meant you needed forgiving yourself. It was odd, but she was sure it was true and he might understand. She caught his eye and he frowned.

'What is it?' he whispered, turning his head so Hannah shouldn't hear.

'Nothing. The storm's making me nervous. I think we should go.'

'There are clouds coming up,' said Hannah.

'We must be going,' said Bridie. 'Where's your father?'

Hannah looked around the sitting room. Sam's heavy footsteps went downstairs as he took a last case out to the car.

'I shall go and powder my nose,' whispered Bridie to Hannah. 'Will you get everyone outside, so we can say goodbye?'

Hannah rose. 'Christina isn't here either.'

Her grandmother's expression was stony and she looked involuntarily at April, chatting to Ruth.

'What?' April glanced round, feeling the gaze.

'I'm going to look for Daddy,' said Hannah, and suddenly found her grandmother glaring at her. April, flushed with wine and heat, surveyed the room and understood.

'Then you'd better see if you can find Christina, too,' she said bitterly. 'I told you that suit would crease.'

They weren't in the garden. Hannah, feeling silly, even looked into Bridie's little potting shed, just to be sure. Thunder rumbled a little closer. She wandered to the edge of the canal and looked down into the water.

'Who on earth will want to marry you?' she asked dejectedly. Her reflection mouthed the question back as she spotted them.

A grove of flowering almond trees came down almost to the water's edge on the opposite bank. David and Christina leaned one on each side of a slender tree trunk, quarrelling violently. Hannah's heart beat painfully. She felt crumpled and lumpish, a fool, suffocating with dread as thunder cracked in the distance, rolling nearer. David's voice slid over the shining water like oil, curiously inviting. Christina slapped his face. Hannah winced but David shouted with laughter, caught Christina's wrist and bent her arm behind her back, hiding her. Hannah watched. The gardener had left the long grass uncut because of the drought. David's hand slid up Christina's leg, lifting her skirt. Pink silk camiknickers, Hannah kept thinking as she went back into the house, feeling frightened and guilty, pink silk camiknickers. Christina wears pink silk knickers, and Daddy . . .

'Did you find them?' demanded April, her voice as sharp as a knife.

'No,' said Hannah, scarlet with shame.

'Huh!' April stared at her. 'You're lying. But don't think I care, because I don't.'

Hannah read utter contempt in her mother's flushed face, then David came back. Everyone rushed to throw rice, cry goodbye and wave until Sam and Bridie were long gone round the corner and on their way to the coast.

'A good hotel tonight and Ireland tomorrow, Mrs Saul,' Sam announced contentedly, holding her hand. 'Happy?'

The answer was all he had ever longed for.

April went up to David and said drunkenly, 'I want to go home.'

'I'll do the clearing up, dear,' said Ruthie, seeing trouble coming across the littered room. 'You go on.'

'Now,' said April, taking no notice, 'right now.'

Hannah watched, riveted by terror in case April could see her thoughts. Evil thoughts. Pink silk knickers. She couldn't help it. Try to think about nothing, keep your face blank. Eileen wondered what Hannah was looking so guilty about and began to stack plates. Lightning flashed in the windows, and a long rolling thunderclap burst overhead. Outside the window, the tops of the lilacs rustled.

'Now!' shouted April.

Orange light from the windows played on David's glasses. His mouth set in a thin line of rage.

'Get your things, Hannah,' he said, 'and we'll take your mother home.'

No one moved.

'Now!' shouted David.

Ruthie flinched and looked round anxiously for her husband. Eileen sniffed, outraged.

'Don't you speak to my daughter . . .' she began.

'Out!' yelled David, pushing Hannah towards the door. Christina watched, white as a sheet. Lightning flashed.

She knows, thought Hannah, terrified, seeing hatred in April's yellow eyes as she was hustled by David down the stairs and into the car, with no time to say goodbye. Her mother sat in the front seat, rigid. None of them said a word on the endless drive home. April dozed and snuffled until David nudged her sharply so that she woke up and watched with an aching head as the road rolled past.

April put her key in the lock, but the front door swung wide.

'Batty?'

Peter stood in the kitchen doorway, sucking his thumb.

'Where's Batty?'

He pointed to the sitting room.

'Batty!' screamed April. 'Oh, damn the lot of you!'

David found her sobbing over Batty's lolling body, whisky tipped all over the carpet.

'There's not much left,' he said. 'You can stop wailing. Get Hannah to mop it up.'

'It's not the carpet, it's the children. I left them with her while you . . .'

'Pull yourself together,' he snapped.

'I can't. There's nothing to pull!' screeched April, falling to her knees and beating him with her fists. 'Help me, David, help me!'

He pushed her away in disgust. Hannah, burdened with terrible secrets, hid in her room and prayed for the fighting to stop.

The downpour came not fifteen minutes after they left. Christina leaned on the arm of her chair, watching rain stream down Bridie's window in heavy, blurring grey drops. Ruthie, busy offering cake, came over to her.

'Do you want some?' she asked, holding out the plate.

'No. No, thank you.'

'You're playing with fire,' said Ruthie softly, 'and you'll have only yourself to blame when it burns you. Leave him alone.'

Christina turned back to the window, leaning her feverish forehead against the cool glass.

'I've tried,' she whispered, 'and I can't. He's got to choose.'

The storm broke right overhead.

Chapter Six

David chose. Hannah came home from school and found April sitting in the rocking chair in the breakfast room, holding a letter.

'It's from Daddy. He says he's left us.'

The rocking chair creaked backwards and forwards, very gently and slowly. April stared at the letter. She had stared at it all day and still she didn't understand it.

'It's hot.' Hannah put her panama hat on the table.

'It's always hot. Look, Daddy says he's left us.' She held out the pages, pleading.

'It's to you.'

'You can read it.'

Hannah picked up a knife and began to cut a slice of bread. A wasp hovered round the top of the golden syrup tin.

'I'm starving.' She spread butter and syrup on the bread.

'You're asking for spots,' snapped April, rebuffed.

'I haven't got spots.'

'Here.' April held up the letter again.

'I don't want to,' mumbled Hannah, her mouth full.

April snatched the letter back into her lap as though she'd been stung. 'How can you?' she cried accusingly.

Hannah watched with detachment as her mother lost control.

'Don't you care?'

'I don't know what . . .'

'Then help me!' Loose sheets of paper fluttered in her mother's hands.

'I don't know how,' Hannah said helplessly.

The wooden chair rocked violently. April sank her head into her hands, crumpling her letter.

'I'm sorry, Mummy.'

April couldn't speak.

Hannah licked syrup off her fingers and eyed the back of her mother's bent head. The house was soundless around them. 'Where are the others?'

'Batty's.'

'Shall I get them?'

April's face twisted. 'At least Batty was understanding, which is more than I can say of you!'

'I'm sorry, Mummy. Shall I get them?'

A bell pealed for a moment from the church tower next door.

'You're late.'

'I stayed behind to help Miss Arnott.'

'Quite the saint at school, aren't you?'

The bell pealed again, joined by the rest.

'It's six o'clock,' said Hannah.

The bellringers practised every Monday from six to eight in the stone tower which cast long shadows over their garden.

'I know,' snapped April.

The bellringers got into their stride.

'I'll go and get them, then,' Hannah said again, seeing that April wasn't going to move.

'Say thank you to Batty,' said April, raising her voice as Hannah went out by the back door. Gemma stirred and thumped her tail, lying in her bed in the lean-to at the back. Hannah stroked her ruff and Gemma rolled soppy collie eyes adoringly.

'Gem, Daddy's gone,' whispered Hannah. 'Are you glad?'

Gemma whined softly.

'Me, too.'

Across the road, Batty's launderette was closed for the day but the door stood open to catch the breeze. The bells pealed joyously, crashing, tumbling, cascading from their tower, echoing from brick walls. The very air sang. Down the road, behind a wall, the vicarage windows stood open wide – bright white nets and tiny, early tomatoes lining window ledges; paint blistered by sun. The vicar had a fig tree that leaned over the wall, heavy with ripening fruit. Local children were not quite sure it was edible or would long since have stolen the figs. Hannah crossed melting tarmac and went into Batty's hallway, into the familiar smells of roast spare ribs and scotch.

'Mrs Bateman,' she called, waiting at the bottom of the stairs.

Batty hastily put the freshly opened bottle back inside the sink cupboard; she'd nearly given in, but April usually fetched them before this, and even if it was an emergency . . . a girl needed a little drink. Hannah knew what the scurrying sounds meant but looked up with an innocent expression as Batty's face appeared over the top of the stairs.

'Hello, dear,' she said. 'Have you come to get them?'

'Yes.' Hannah went up and stood with her hands on her hips. 'Really,' she said, nudging resignedly with her foot at the big glass bottle of fruit drops on the floor.

'To keep them happy,' breathed Batty, longing for her to go.

'They shouldn't have sweets.'

Batty dabbed at her nose with her sleeve. 'She told you what's what, over there?'

'Yes.'

'Better off without him.' Batty delivered her opinion with finality and pulled Polly to her feet. 'Time to go, dear.'

The bellringers paused and the silence was deafening. Batty watched the children cross the road's sticky surface and guzzled her first drink.

'Bloody well dry, all day,' she muttered, toasting the big square front of April's house, across the street. 'That's friendship for you. And to absent friends, because you aren't half going to need some, my darling.'

Chapter Seven

Sam and Bridie walked down a narrow Irish country lane, barely more than a farm track.

'This is it. This is where I came that morning. If you carry on, round the outskirts of the village, you come to the church.

'Bridie, if it makes you too unhappy . . .'

'No, it hardly does at all. It just seems strange, to come back after all these years. I've so often wondered what it would be like.'

They took the long way round, and found her father's grave, next to her mother's, both trimmed and neat but with no sign of flowers or anyone coming there except the gardener who cut the grass.

'There's nowhere to buy flowers.'

'Pick wild ones.'

'It's so small. I used to think the church was like a cathedral.'

'Want to go in?'

'The last time I went inside there, I had a black eye and my lip was bleeding, and I remember I was so cold. It was bright, like today, but I couldn't get warm.'

The church door was smooth under her hand as she pushed it open. 'There.' It was small, plain, and smelled of mould and aerosol polish. 'It smelled of beeswax and incense then,' she said.

'It's stuffy,' said Sam.

'The candle holder is still here. I hid in the pew, near you, and watched Father Robert stack candles. Then he saw me and called me over, and I told him.'

Sam stuck his hands in his pockets.

'In confession, of course,' she added.

He looked around for the box, and it was there, to one side.

'In that?'

'Yes.'

'Poor bastard,' he muttered.

'Father Robert?' she asked in astonishment.

'Your dad.'

Bridie sat down on a pew at the front and with her shoe touched a brass plate in the floor. 'I used to think this was pure gold. You are the first person who has ever felt sorry for him.'

'He lost the lot, didn't he?'

'Did he? It was me that lost things and had to run away. You've got a queer way of looking at it.'

'He lost you,' said Sam simply.

'Oh.' She put her hand to her mouth, like a child. 'I never saw it like that.'

'That's all I ever saw,' said Sam Saul.

'Is that it?' he asked later, as they rounded a slight bend, and there it was, a ruin with tumbled white walls overgrown with ivy and brambles, a rotting wooden gate poking up at the side of the track.

'Yes.'

The pile of stones had once been her home. They'd

asked in the village about her three sisters, Maire, MaryEllen and May. No one knew anything. People went away in the war and never came back, they'd shrugged.

'That was the fireplace. We'd cook on that, before Mam had a range. She didn't live long to use it, did she?' They sat on one of the crumbled walls, some of the stones blackened by fire. An abandoned broom lay in the deep, lush grass that covered the spot where her father had lain drunk, crying for his wife. 'There was a young man, from a farm up the way, helped me drag him in that night. We dropped him on the floor and he was dead to the world. Then . . . well, he thought I was Mam.' She shivered and drew her cardigan round her.

'Are you ready to go soon?'

Sam's watch said they had been sitting half an hour on the wall. It seemed longer.

'I feel old,' she said sadly. 'I don't know why. I'm tired.'

'Shall we go home?'

'This was home.'

'To the hotel?'

'Home is where you are.'

He broke the sentimental moment with a shout of malicious delight. 'Then I can stay in Golders Green, Mrs Saul?'

'I never meant that, you old fraud,' she cried, 'and you know it!'

'So much for promises,' he chortled, settling his long legs under the steering wheel of their car.

Bridie smiled, got in, and took out her spectacle case and the map.

'Ready to bury the past in peace?' he asked.

Bridie rustled the map innocently. 'What's the shortest way back?'

'What? Oh, boy!' cried Sam Saul, treading on the accelerator. 'Let's go, Mrs Saul.'

'As fast as you like, Mr Saul,' she said.

Chapter Eight

It was a summer of storms; the hottest in years, said the papers. Day after day, the sun rose, turning brief cool nights to high parching brilliance at noon, in a sky so fiercely blue it made Hannah giddy to look up at it. Drought-parched gardens and fields bleached the land. Sweet-smelling dust lay in drifts on pavements and under hedges, and dandelion fairies danced everywhere.

While Sam and Bridie crossed Ireland to stroll along deserted beaches on the Dingle Peninsula, April tried to hold on to what she had. The lawyers said it wasn't much, except full responsibility for her family.

'How can I look after them?' she asked in Mr Batchelor's office which was full of heavy dark wooden furniture and shelves of sagging files tied up with bits of string.

'The law is unfair to women in your position.'

'I have five children. Five!'

'I know,' said her solicitor unhappily.

'And the eldest is only just fourteen. What can I do?'

'Not a great deal, I'm afraid,' he said, 'unless you can persuade your husband to look after them. Or come back to you.'

'He won't do either.'

'Then I'm afraid he has the right to sell the house.'

'Where does he think we'll go?'

Mr Batchelor cleared his throat. 'He doesn't say.'

'Something awful is going to happen,' said April.

'I do hope not.'

The last days of term dragged. Girls dawdled and straggled in twos and threes up the long hill to the single-storey red brick grammar school at the top; fanning damp, glowing faces with panama hats; dressed in forget-me-not blue uniform dresses. Lessons crept by sluggishly in stifling classrooms, minutes marked out by the turning of pages, the strident clanging of a brass-handled handbell, and the repulsive warm milk in minia-ture bottles with short, white straws they were forced to drink at break. Teachers drew long blackout blinds, left from the war, against the harsh glare from outside. Bees and butterflies came in through open windows, and wasps lurched, dazed and drunken after gorging on fallen raspberries at the far end of the playing field. In French, Miss Walsh chased a Purple Emperor. Thirty bored, sleepy faces watched her fat ringless fingers scoop the butterfly from the blackout and shake it out of the window.

'There you are, my love, my honeybun,' she crooned fulsomely. Behind her girls sniggered cruelly, rolling their eyes. Old Walshie was a bit much, in love with the French Romantics. Lamartine made her cry. The butter-fly flew away and Hannah shivered in the heat, her head aching.

'Where were we?' asked Miss Walsh absently, picking up her book again 'Ah, yes,' she brightened, 'dear Verlaine. Who will start?'

No one offered.

'Very well,' she sighed. 'Angela, will you start? "*Je ne sais pourquoi . . .*" '

'I don't know why . . .' began Angela, sitting next to Hannah. Hannah yawned and the class drooped sleepily. Hannah yawned again, and thinking about yawning, required bigger and more contagious yawns until yawns chased each other up and down the rows of hot faces.

'Good gracious,' cried Old Walshie, 'whatever time do you go to bed?'

'It's hot,' someone said.

'Well,' continued Walshie, ignoring her, 'try going earlier and then perhaps you could all grace me with your attention. Now look what you've done!'

Miss Walsh's plump hand tried to hide a stifled yawn and the class laughed just as the bell went.

'Try and go over it again before next time,' cried the teacher, her words lost in the hubbub. Chairs scraped, desks banged, and girls poured into wide corridors, carrying books and satchels.

'Maths. Double period. What a way to end a Friday!' muttered Angela, following Hannah. 'It's sadistic.'

'My head aches,' said Hannah.

'Go and get an aspirin.'

'D'you think they'd let me sit in the sickroom?'

'You can ask.'

The sickroom was shady. The school secretary gave her two aspirins and a glass of water.

'You go back when you feel better,' she said briskly and left Hannah alone. It was very quiet. The classroom doors were closed, and she could hear only the faint pock, pock, of a tennis ball. The room was bare except for a couch and a wooden chair. Hannah climbed on to the couch, put her arm over her face and fell asleep.

Dreaming, she stood at the top of a house with big white windows and big white doors. She looked down into a bushy square garden, pathless, a place where things might hide. A boy or girl – hard to say, a creature anyway – raised a bone white face to her own, among dark green leaves. It moved, pure evil coming to find her. She ran in a frenzy, to and fro, closing doors, bolting windows, fumbling with mortal dread to keep it out. In vain. It was already inside, this monstrous thing . . .

'Come on, dear.' The secretary shook her. 'The bell's gone. Will you be all right to go home?'

Hannah woke, her headache worse than ever.

'Yes, thank you.'

'It really isn't as simple,' explained Mr Batchelor, 'as right and wrong. We'll get maintenance for you, and of course he should do the decent thing about the house, but he doesn't have to.'

'He's got it on the market already. He'll take the first buyer he can get.'

'I'm afraid that may be true.'

'He's going to sell my home, his children's home, over our heads.'

'It's up for sale, certainly.'

'You can't make him let me stay?'

'We can only appeal to his finer feelings.'

'Don't waste your time,' April said, 'he hasn't any.'

'I am sorry,' said Mr Batchelor.

'Then please do something to help me.'

'I'm doing all I can, Mrs Holmes. You'll have to trust me.'

'I don't trust anyone, Mr Batchelor, not after this.'

She had offended him by going to see another firm, lower down the High Street, but had come back, drearily apologetic.

'It seems you're right,' she had told him.

Stiff-lipped with the insult, he'd said, 'Perhaps we could get on then?' and opened her file once more.

Tossing sleeplessly in her bed, she remembered the early days. They'd been in love. Maybe there would be something to appeal to after all, if she tried, despite what she had told the lawyer. Without any explanation, April left Batty and Hannah to manage between them, and took the train to London. They sat on dried grass in April's back garden, watching Peter and Jessie and Polly and Ingrid squabble fitfully around the lean-to where Gemma lay dozing.

'I hope she knows what she's doing,' said Batty darkly.

'I bet she's gone to ask Daddy to come back.'

'Waste of time, begging your pardon, dear.'

'Don't beg my pardon. I hope he doesn't.'

'Han, darling . . .'

'Do you want me to fetch your scotch?'

Batty blinked in surprise, 'Well, yes, but I was going to say . . . did he hit her?'

'No.'

'Ah, I thought sometimes I heard . . . never mind.'

'He hit me,' said Hannah flatly. 'Where do I find your bottle?'

'In the sink cupboard,' said Mrs Bateman, more curious than ever. 'Did he really? That's shocking. Do you know whereabouts I mean?'

'Is that nice?' asked Hannah, ten minutes later.

'Not at all,' said Batty gravely. 'Don't try it.'

'Why do you like getting drunk?'

Batty glanced at her sharply. 'It's better than being sober, but you wouldn't know what I mean.'

'I think I might, actually,' said Hannah confidingly, worrying afterwards in case she'd been rude.

April arrived outside David and Christina's flat in the early afternoon. She stood on the pavement opposite for some while, gazing at the big red brick block of flats, trying to work out which windows were theirs. It was impossible. Time passed, and she didn't know what to do. Suppose she rang the bell and found Christina there? So she waited.

Christina, in dark blue Sister's uniform, came from the tube station at half-past five. She carried Waitrose carrier bags and looked tired. From a pub doorway, April watched her disappear into the flats' shabby entrance, taking a key from her bag.

That means either they are both there now, or David will come by himself, she thought.

He came out of the tube station at six and nearly walked into her as she stepped out of the doorway into his path.

'I have to talk to you,' she cried.

'I have nothing to say.' He tried to brush past her, but she ran before him and wouldn't let him pass.

'You have to,' she hissed. 'You have to speak to me. Or I'll scream, right here where you live.'

He stood before her and they waited, like two cats, for each other to make a move.

'You look down at heel. She doesn't look after you.'

'Say what you've come to say.'

'Can we go somewhere?'

'Here.'

'Where do you expect me to go with the children?'

'Let the lawyers deal with it.'

'The lawyers deal with law. I have to deal with five children. What do you expect me to do?'

'You'll manage.'

'How, with no roof over my head?'

'April, this doesn't help.'

He edged away from her, closer to the flats, and she walked quickly alongside him, blocking his way again. 'I shall have to do something. I can't just go on and on,' she cried, 'unless you come home or give up selling the house. You have to leave me something, David.'

'You'll get most of my money,' he said angrily.

'Will you come back, then? Try again.'

'No.'

'I can't go on without you.'

He turned on her furiously. 'You've been blackmailing me ever since we met. We got married because you were pregnant, remember? And then suddenly you weren't pregnant after all.'

'It wasn't like that,' she cried. 'You've twisted it.'

'And ever since then, it's been babies. Every time you got pregnant, I could have killed you.'

'You're killing me now.'

He shook his head and tried to get past her.

'I love you,' she said, her eyes filling with tears. 'I need you.'

'You don't know what love is.'

'I'm wretched, David. I can't cope on my own.'

'You're only happy when you're miserable. I want to go in. Go back home and write to my lawyer if you've got something to say.'

'Something awful will happen,' whimpered April, standing aside to let him go.

'You've threatened me once too often,' he said, swinging round. 'This time, I'm not listening.'

'You'll wish you had,' she howled at his back as he went through the doors, out of sight. 'Please, please, please . . .'

Above her head, a window banged shut.

Batty and Hannah were playing Monopoly when she got home past midnight, lying on the sitting room carpet.

'You all right?' asked Batty cheerfully, parking her glass on the side of the board.

'They're all in bed. We've had a nice time,' said Hannah. 'Did you go to see Daddy?'

April stalked into her kitchen, slammed the door on them and burst into tears. Batty emptied her glass and looked owlish, her words only slightly slurred. 'I don't think she's pleased. It's your turn.'

'Five weeks,' April said aloud into the short night; five weeks since he'd left. Letters came and went between the solicitors, bringing no comfort. Since her trip to London she had taken to leaving the house in the early evening. Hannah put the other children to bed. Or Batty. Someone did it. April wandered the fields and woods in the dark. Or the streets. She rarely knew where she was. Much of the time she talked aloud, to David or sometimes to Eileen. Once or twice she was confused and thought she was talking to George, but her father had been dead since before the end of the war. A doodlebug dropped right on top of him. When she remembered this, she hooted with laughter and then cried for a little while, bowed over by sadness. She stopped, tears on her face, and looked up at the August stars. 'I've got nothing at all,' she told them as they twinkled brightly, 'except four small children and Hannah. What does he want me to do?'

The stars shone in a sky as black as the grave.

'Is that it? Is that where he wants me to go?'

It was obvious, once she knew; it was the only way out.

Chapter Nine

Hannah watched with foreboding as April's thin face, usually pale with worry and exhaustion, took on a hectic, feverish flush. It was Saturday. The town was quiet and sleepy, everyone away on holidays. Gemma lay listlessly on the back doorstep, her nose on her paws, panting.

'Want a walk?' asked Hannah. Gemma thumped her tail and rolled up her eyes, unconvinced until Hannah got up and reached for her lead. They went to the park and sat on the swings. Hannah sat on one, Gemma sat by, her tongue lolling out of her mouth.

'Mummy's funny, Gem. Funny peculiar.'

Gemma lay down.

'Don't you miss Daddy? Gem, say something.'

The collie watched the swing go backwards and forwards, alert.

'Batty says it's things like this that turn you to drink.'

Gemma yawned.

'I hope he doesn't come back.'

Gemma got up and shook herself, retreating into the dust bowl at the roots of an oak tree. Hannah swung slowly. 'But I'll murder you if you let on I said so.'

Gemma barked, uneasy at her tone.

'He took you for walks. You're not very grateful. You must be a horrible dog, Gem.'

The whites of Gemma's eyes showed. Hannah pushed off with one foot and worked the swing up, so high it gave with a lurch at the top of the bar. 'I can touch the tree with my toe. Look! Look, Gem.'

Bored, Gemma took no notice and dozed off. They stayed in the park for hours and when they got home, April was furious.

'. . . fourteen years old and you think you can do as you please, walk over everyone, just like your father . . .' Hannah stifled a yawn as April's tirade wore itself out.

'Anyway, I've asked Milly Henderson to take Gemma.'

'Where?'

'Are you being deliberately obtuse?' snapped her mother.

Gemma's bowl was half full of tepid water. 'She needs some more.'

'Listen to me. Milly said she'd have Gemma. It's good of her, so do try to be grateful.'

'Mummy, I don't know what you mean. Why is Mrs Henderson taking Gemma anywhere?'

'Because,' said April with exaggerated patience, 'she has to go.'

Hannah sniggered. 'Mrs Henderson has to go?'

'I can't keep her!' screeched April. 'It's bad enough with you lot; I can't have the dog as well. Tomorrow, Milly will fetch her. She'll get her a basket, seeing as we haven't got one. We never do things properly, like everyone else. You can't give Milly a flea-ridden blanket.'

'I'm not giving her to Milly. She's mine,' said Hannah coldly.

'It's all arranged. Don't be difficult, Hannah.'

'She's my friend.'

'Don't be silly, she's a dog.'

'She's my friend. Which is more than you are.'

April paled with rage. 'She goes to Milly tomorrow.'

'Mummy—' began Hannah, not believing.

'I can't cope.' April began to keen, rocking herself to and fro on her heels, clasping her hands hysterically. 'If you make me cope with one more thing, I'll . . .'

'I hate you,' said Hannah, and walked out of the room.

Gemma loved to be hugged. She sagged in Hannah's arms, licking her hands. 'You don't want to go and live with Mrs Henderson, do you?'

The church bell struck six.

'I bet she's out all night, and she'll forget in the morning,' whispered Hannah. 'She forgot the dentist the other day. She keeps forgetting things. Anyway, she's gone.'

'Mummy's only gone out,' said Hannah later, catching Peter in a towel and scrubbing him dry, 'so stop making all that noise.'

He blubbered and howled.

'Sit on your bed and shut up,' she yelled.

'Perhaps he's got an earache?' suggested Jessie.

'No!' snapped Hannah.

Jessie climbed into bed, pushing back the sheet. 'It's hot.'

Hannah pulled curtains to shade the room from the evening sun. 'You can look at comics,' she said, and kissed them goodnight. Peter turned his head away. 'I want . . .' he began.

'Stop it,' cried Hannah sharply.

He turned his face to the wall, small shoulders shaking silently.

'Mummy's coming back soon. Go to sleep, like the twins, and she'll be here when you wake up,' cried Hannah helplessly.

Downstairs she cleared away their tea and sat in April's rocking chair in the stone-flagged kitchen. The clock struck the half-hour. Gemma shuffled across the flagstones and thrust her nose into Hannah's hand.

'Why do you always look guilty?' Bending to stroke her, Hannah saw April's handbag on the floor behind the rocking chair. 'I know what we'll do. I'll wash my hair and have a bath, and then I'll put the wireless on and we'll listen to it together. There's some chocolate. That do you?'

Gemma huffed and dropped on her side, stretching. April kept sachets of scented shampoo in her bag. Hannah opened it wide and began to sort through the contents.

There was a letter card, not stuck down. "When you receive this," it said, falling open of its own accord, "the children and I will be dead. I cannot leave them to suffer as I have suffered. I love David and may God forgive him for all the suffering he has caused."

Hannah crouched on the floor by the bag. On the radio someone said the Brahms Violin Concerto would be this evening's concert music, and Gemma whined, her brown eyes fixed on the radio, which she loved.

'Gem,' said Hannah, 'she's going to kill us.'

They listened to the concert huddled together in the rocking chair.

'I think I'll 'phone Granny,' said Hannah, when the

music finished. 'She might not mind it being rather late.'

They listened to Bridie's telephone ringing a long way away in London.

'She's away. I forgot.'

Hannah put the letter back carefully, so that April wouldn't know she'd read it. The announcer said good night and God bless, and the National Anthem played on the stroke of midnight. Hannah switched off the radio, took April's bottle of red sleeping pills and hid it in a kitchen cupboard. Then she went to bed. At three o'clock April shook her awake.

'What have you done with my pills?' she hissed.

Half asleep, Hannah shook her head.

April shook her harder. 'Get them.'

Hannah got out of bed, went downstairs and got them from the cupboard, handing them over silently.

'Why did you do that?'

Hannah looked away.

'Don't you dare touch them again.'

Hannah went back upstairs. There was nothing at all to be done.

Chapter Ten

Everyone said the weather must surely break soon, scanning the dazzling sky for a shred of cloud, looking hopefully for suggestions of rain. Farmers grumbled about spindly crops; people were edgy about shortages, because they remembered the war, though they didn't talk about those days very much.

Milly Henderson took Gemma, as she had promised. Hannah tried to take the dog to Milly's house, but Gemma sat down hard on the pavement and wouldn't budge.

'Pull,' ordered April.

'I am. It'll hurt her bottom because she won't get off it,' cried Hannah desperately. After half an hour of anguish, April gave in. Gemma sulked in her lean-to until Milly came at midday and put her in the car.

'I hope she bites you to death,' mumbled Hannah wretchedly, out of sight behind the upstairs curtains, watching as Milly drove off. 'May she have rabies and fleas and the plague. I hope she hates you.' But traitorous Gemma settled in well to the Henderson home.

'Rotten dog,' commented Milly. 'You could at least feel sorry.'

'Perhaps they grieve by blotting it out?' suggested her daughter. 'People sometimes do.'

'Hannah,' said Milly, to see what happened; Gemma didn't react. 'I suppose she's being very sensible in the circumstances. After all, no one asked the poor dog, did they?'

'I expect no one asked that poor child either,' said her daughter.

'It was that or else April said she'd have to have her put down. One has to feel sorry for her.'

'Why? Bloody awful woman,' said her daughter.

'Where's my twinnies?' April sang stridently, going down the big unkempt garden to where they played every day in the dry, crumbling earth. Peter and Jessie had been digging for Australia for ages. Their optimism waxed and waned, depending on whether they were squabbling or working together, leaving a wide, ragged hole in the ground. Polly and Ingrid pottered grubbily, occasionally eating unspeakable things because no one was there to stop them. April seemed excited, livelier that she'd been for weeks. Perhaps the letter was a mistake, thought Hannah, watching from her mother's bedroom window, which overlooked the far end of the garden. She squirmed with embarrassment; it would be dreadful to admit she'd read it, if her mother hadn't meant it. It was just as well Bridie hadn't been there or she might have done something awful. She ran downstairs, anxious to be helpful, to make it up to her mother.

They were all in the sitting room, April counting banknotes from one hand to another, carelessly. Hannah stopped by the door and watched.

'Let's go and spend it before he takes it. Who wants a present?' she shrilled, holding handfuls of money high over her head. Hannah tensed, thinking she was about to throw it at them, but April laughed.

'Come on, let's have a Rake's Progress.' She caught Hannah's astonished eye. 'I can read books, too,' she snapped.

Hannah flushed.

And a Rake's Progress it was. April bought her a shiny metal watch with a white leather strap. Hannah had always wanted one.

As they trailed up and down the High Street the sky steadily thickened into a greenish haze and people moved slowly, as if underwater, sweating.

'It's got to break,' said shopkeepers, feeling electricity prickle their skin. In the far distance, thunder growled. Back home, Polly threw her new doll fretfully on the floor and cried. Jessie sucked her thumb and watched April pull Peter into her lap, hugging and clinging to him, kissing his damp cheek dozens of times. Hannah turned away jealously and crept upstairs to sit on her bed. Thunder came again, but more faintly. She heard a sound and April was there, leaning on the doorjamb, her yellow eyes deeply sunk in the horrid light.

'There's *Gone With The Wind* on. I'll take you to see it,' she said abruptly.

Hannah looked at her new watch.

'Don't you like it?'

'Yes, why?'

'You seldom seem pleased with anything I do.'

'Yes, I am, Mummy.'

'We'll go to the pictures, then?'

'Can Batty babysit?'

The weather depressed Batty and made her thirsty; she hadn't been out for a day or two. Her launderette had a scrawled 'Closed' sign hanging on its door, but empties stood in a line on the upstairs windowsill, so April knew she was merely drunk.

'Batty's going to wake up with the DTs one day,' said April sourly. 'Oh, they'll be all right on their own for a couple of hours. We'll go when they're asleep.'

'Do you think . . . ?'

'Don't spoil it, Hannah.'

Her mother spoke so fiercely, Hannah's mouth fell open.

'You'll catch a fly,' remarked April meanly, going back downstairs. Hannah stared at the place where she had been, mesmerised by her own dread.

As Scarlett O'Hara, Vivien Leigh held the audience in the palm of her hand. Lights from the projector shifted and flickered through curls and clouds of cigarette smoke. Outside, leaves already yellowing ran with fat raindrops that puffed tiny clouds of dust from cracked earth. Forked lightning flashed silver in the dark sky, followed by thunder that crashed and rolled like distant gunfire.

'Eh, it's the Jerries back,' someone joked in the back row and people laughed uneasily, their eyes on the screen. April's eyes never left Scarlett. In the uncertain light her own face was fleshless, grey-lipped, her eyes dull. Thunder seemed to shake the walls.

'Let's go,' she muttered.

'It's not finished,' whispered Hannah.

April took her elbow and pulled. 'Come on.'

Rain fell in sheets beyond the cinema entrance. The whole face of the earth lit up as sheet lightning flashed continuously across the sky, a violent, eerie landscape.

April dashed out into the storm. Hannah ran after her, soaked to the skin.

The park gates were locked. April shook them, frustrated, her new dark silk dress, bought that day, shrunk to her body like some strange chameleon's skin.

'Why do you want to go to the park?' panted Hannah.

April's teeth gleamed in a grin. 'He's got her in there, hasn't he?'

'Who has?'

'He thinks I don't know.' She tugged at the wrought-iron gate, wiping rain from her eyes. 'I saw them.' Her words were lost in a thunderflash right overhead.

'Pink silk knickers,' cried Hannah into the howling wind.

April glared. 'What?'

'Come home,' shrieked Hannah.

'You can't tell me . . .'

'Daddy's there. At home,' yelled Hannah through the storm.

April's hands fell from the gate.

'He'll worry,' shouted Hannah.

April licked rain from her lips and looked towards the town.

'Mummy?'

Trees bent under the force of the wind and rain lashed as they ran down the hill, round to the back garden, through a small gate, past Gemma's empty lean-to, into the dark and silent house. The children had slept through the storm.

'He's not here.' April, standing shivering and dripping in the kitchen, turned on Hannah. 'You lied to me.'

'I only said he might be,' Hannah said hopelessly.

'Go to bed.' April's teeth chattered. Hannah got into

bed obediently and fell asleep at once. April went out into the storm and posted her letter.

Three bored faces looked up as the girl stood in the police station doorway, trying to catch her breath. One glanced at the clock. Just gone six.

'My mother has tried to kill . . .'

They swung their feet down from the table in a hurry.

'Where do you live?'

Hannah repeated her address politely. Two policemen left in a rush. The third came round the table, fastening his belt and unrolling his shirt sleeves. He took her into a small back room, shouting for tea with plenty of sugar. He pulled out a couple of chairs so they sat opposite each other across a wooden table. She folded her hands in her lap.

'Can you tell me what happened?' he said.

Chapter Eleven

'What the devil has been going on here?' David stood in the hallway and shouted up the stairs. In what had been his and April's room, at the back of the house, Hannah quailed, hearing his feet coming nearer.

'There was a policewoman here,' she said, coming across the landing.

'Police,' said David through his teeth. 'What on earth possessed you?'

'I had to.'

He threw his jacket on to the unmade double bed. 'Where are they all?'

'In the garden. I gave them two shillings out of Mummy's purse, to go and play and be good, when the police went away. Then I did the washing up and I was just going to make the beds.'

'Why didn't you telephone, instead of leaving the police to let me know?'

Hannah watched him warily. He sat down on the end of the bed and took off his glasses to rub his eyes.

'I don't know where you live.'

'Of course you do.'

'I don't. Mummy wouldn't say.'

'Mummy is mad.'

'Is she alive?' asked Hannah diffidently.

102

'Of course she's alive. It's all a monstrous bit of blackmail to get me back. It's your wretched mother's idea of vengeance.'

'Is it?'

'What else do you think?'

Hannah stood, dumb.

'I had some garbled tale,' he said, raising his eyebrows.

'Mummy had a bottle of Seconal which was full. I took it away from her but she made me give it back. She took all of that and shut all the windows and turned all the gas taps on. The police said we would have gone up like a bomb if there had been a spark.'

'Damn!'

'The gas made a noise and woke me up. I opened all the windows and pulled the others out of bed. Then I got dressed and ran to the police station. I did think about ringing someone up, but I couldn't think of anyone.'

David dropped his head in his hands and groaned.

'What are you going to do?'

'Find somewhere for you.'

Hannah's heart lurched painfully. 'Are you going to stay?'

'I can't,' he said wearily. 'I've got a job in London. I've got a home.'

'Where will we live?'

For answer, he went downstairs and lifted the phone.

The children hung back in a little row, sucking their fingers.

'The vicar over the road can take Peter and Jessie, and the Heydritches say they'll look after the twins,' said David.

'Shall I put things in a suitcase?' asked Hannah.

He shook his head. 'I'll take them over as they are.'

There were no goodbyes.

'Where shall I go?' asked Hannah in the empty house. 'When you go home?'

'You can go over to some friends on the other side of the park.'

'How long for?'

'I can't plan, for God's sake. We'll find somewhere else if we have to.'

'Can I take a case?'

'Chuck some things together quickly. I've got to get to the estate agents, and get this lot in store. And the trains don't run after midnight.'

'You wouldn't be able to get home, would you?' asked his daughter, grasping at straws. 'That's why you're going to hurry,' said David.

Hannah sat in a spare room, on the other side of the park, while David's friends locked up for the night. She gnawed her fingers, trying to cry. If someone said something, she'd cry, loosen the terrible tension. No one did. Least said, soonest mended. It was as though, in one day, six people ceased to exist. All over their house, David's friends turned out the lights and he caught the last train home.

Chapter Twelve

'It's been in *The Times*,' Lizzie told Bridie, awed, 'and in all the other papers as well.'

'Where is she?' asked Sam, wishing they'd stayed in Ireland.

'In prison.'

'Good grief!'

'I knew there was going to be trouble,' said Bridie.

Sam, incoherent with rage, had telephoned Ruthie to shout about Christina's morals until his first wife had banged down the receiver indignantly.

'That don't help,' remarked Lizzie. 'You can hardly blame her for what her step-daughter does.'

'Why not?' snarled Sam, and grumbled until Bridie lost patience.

'It'll do no good dwelling on that,' she said sharply. 'When can we go and see April?'

Lizzie pulled a martyred face and said Eileen wanted to come, too.

'She's her mother. Of course she'll want to go,' said Bridie.

'April won't want us all there at once.'

'I don't suppose they'd let us all in at once.'

'It's probably one at a time, in those places,' guessed

Lizzie. They decided that Bridie should go first, on her own.

'I wish she'd told someone and let us help. There was no need to go this far,' said Sam angrily, feeling ill used. 'Imagine thinking that killing children is any kind of way out of a mess.'

'I'll have something to say to my son,' threatened Bridie grimly. 'David'll get a piece of my mind he'll never forget.'

Lizzie, who thought hanging would be too good for him, held her tongue.

'I suppose,' said Sam, still looking out of the window, 'they'll come here?'

Lizzie looked quickly at Bridie.

'I think April and David have to decide about the children,' Bridie said.

'They aren't fit!' Sam swung round on the two women.

'Nor are we. We're too old to look after five small children. If we start meddling, we'll only make things worse, and they're bad enough already.'

'They'll put them in care,' said Lizzie.

'In care,' echoed Bridie.

'Not so long ago, it would have been the gutter or the workhouse,' Lizzie pointed out.

'Not so long ago, families stuck together,' her friend answered tartly.

Not always for the best, thought Sam.

'Go and ring the police station and find out how we visit April,' Bridie said.

'Do you want to go and see your mother?' asked Mr Batchelor. David's friend Molly nodded vigorously over Hannah's head. Mr Batchelor took no notice of her and continued to address the girl.

'I think I do,' said Hannah mechanically.

'Don't you know?' he asked seriously. 'You don't have to, you know, but I have a feeling it would put your mind at rest, make you feel better.'

I don't feel anything, she thought.

'No?' prompted Mr Batchelor.

She knew that, really, he wanted her to say yes.

'Yes,' said Hannah. 'Thank you.'

The tiny room was crowded with tall men in dark suits. A policewoman stood in a corner, hands behind her back. Someone pushed Hannah towards April who lay on a hospital bed, listening to one of the men tell her something in a low voice. He bent over to speak close to her ear and as he straightened up, she saw Hannah. White as the hospital sheet, she turned her face to the wall and silently pulled up her covers.

You really did want to die, thought Hannah, her face expressionless. You hate me for making you live.

Her mother's back was turned against her, motionless.

'Can I go now?' said Hannah.

'No!' April shouted weakly.

David thrust a bundle of papers closer to her hand on the hospital counterpane. Feebly she pushed them away.

'Sign them,' he begged. 'It'd be best for everyone.'

'I will never let you take my children.'

'You did a pretty good job of trying to take them yourself.'

She was ashen. 'You drove me to it.'

'I drove you nowhere. Will you read these and think about it?'

'Over my dead body will you get my children adopted.'

'You have a wonderful turn of expression,' he said in disgust, throwing the bundle on to the bed.

'Never!' she called as he walked away.

Two days later they transferred her to the prison hospital. Two weeks later, Bridie came up by train to visit. They faced each other across a square table in a large, green room. April was yellow, her skin tight on her bones, like parchment.

'You look ill,' whispered Bridie.

'I'm sorry,' April whispered back, placing her hands on the tabletop where the slab-faced wardress could see them.

'Is it awful in here?'

'No, they're quite nice. I am bored, though. They won't let me have knives or forks or pens or pencils. Nothing I could do myself a mischief with. So I have nothing to do except think.'

'What are they going to charge you with?'

'Mr Batchelor thinks they'll drop attempted murder.'

'What might they drop it for?'

'Exposing the children to gas, or something.'

'That doesn't sound as bad.'

David's name hung between them. They picked their way with terrible delicacy around it.

'I suppose it doesn't,' April said.

'There's others to blame for this,' said Bridie stoutly.

'What has he done with the children?'

'They're wherever he put them.'

'I can't keep up,' April said dully, 'and they make me take pills so I can't think.'

'I thought you looked sleepy.'

'He wants to have the children adopted.'

The wardress said, 'Five more minutes,' and stared at the back of Bridie's head. April's hand shot out and clutched Bridie's like a claw.

'I can't let him,' she cried. 'You tell him, will you?'

Bridie covered the claw with her own scarred fingers and said nothing.

'I love him,' whispered April urgently. 'Tell him if he comes back, we can start again. Tell him I forgive him.'

Bridie took her hand from April's fingers and sat back.

'Time,' said the wardress.

'Well, you might, but I don't think I do,' said Bridie.

'Come along,' said the wardress.

'My daughter-in-law is upset, she's not a common criminal,' Bridie said stiffly.

'If you'll pardon me, that's just what she is,' said the wardress impassively.

'You see?' said April.

'I can't say that I do,' retorted Bridie. 'I can't see why you'd want him back, and he's my son. That's what I came to tell you.'

April's gaze sharpened. 'You think he's in the wrong?'

'I think he's done wrong.'

'Even his own mother doesn't take his side,' April told the wardress, perking up.

'You've got to go back,' the woman said. 'This time, I mean it.'

'I never said I'm taking sides,' said Bridie as April stood to go.

'You said he'd done wrong.'

'He has. So have you.'

'I'm innocent,' hissed April.

Bridie nearly laughed in her face, only it would have been cruel and was not at all a laughing matter.

'You're either for her or against her,' reported Bridie. 'She can't see her part in it at all.'

'You'll never know the truth of it, I daresay,' said Sam, 'but I'm sorry for her.'

'I could bang both their heads together, only it wouldn't do no good.'

'Not the slightest,' said Sam brusquely. 'I can't see much good coming out of any of it, can you?'

Chapter Thirteen

'I invite you to decide that this is a case where an unfortunate woman truly merits kindness.' April's barrister pulled at the sleeves of his gown, appealed to the Bench and hoped fervently that she would not have a last minute outburst; she'd been very unstable all day. Bridie, Sam and Lizzie had been banned. April said she couldn't bear them to watch and Mr Batchelor wrote to say that if that was how she felt, then they'd probably do more harm than good by coming.

'Anyway,' he explained on the telephone, 'we've got the attempted murder charge dropped, and since there's no possible doubt that she's guilty of attempted suicide and filling the house with gas, it's not a matter of affixing guilt, but of deciding what is to happen next.'

'They'll never send her to prison, will they?'

'It's a criminal offence,' said Mr Batchelor, pursing his lips (cases that hit headlines in the national press didn't come more than once in a lifetime), 'but I'm hoping they'll be lenient, given the circumstances.'

Bridie's expression set hard at the oblique reference to David.

'Ask him if she'd want to come to us for a bit,' Sam put in, 'if they don't put her away.'

Mr Batchelor said he thought not. 'She wants to go straight to her mother's.'

'She's cutting herself off,' said Bridie. 'It's a terrible shame. There's no need.'

'I suppose you are the other side, in a way.'

'She's embarrassed.'

'I believe she is,' said Mr Batchelor.

'It's understandable. We're his side, Eileen's hers.'

'I'd rather have our side, any day,' muttered Sam, listening to her end of the conversation.

'That's just the sort of remark she's afraid of,' snapped his wife. 'Don't you see?'

They did see, and sympathised, but April still wouldn't have them in Court. She wrote a letter on yellow prison notepaper, asking them please not to come.

'She'd rather I wasn't there and there's an end of it,' said Bridie.

Sam looked at her under his heavy brows and asked if she might not want to be there with David.

'It would do no good.'

He didn't pursue the matter.

On the day of the trial Eileen, a small, grey, upright figure, sat alone at the back of the public benches, never taking her eyes from her daughter, ignoring David, who was sitting with his solicitor to one side. Her gaze wavered only when, at the end of the proceedings, someone brought in the children. But that was at the every end, when April's vastly expensive barrister had finished pleading her cause.

'I ask for kindness for this woman, who has already, God knows, been punished enough for a crime any one of us, given such circumstances, might unwittingly commit – the crime of despair,' he concluded.

'Yes!' cried a woman's voice.

The Clerk of the Court looked round. The members of the Bench leaned forward.

'What would be your client's intentions, were she free?' asked the chairman, a local headmaster. April cowered.

'She would like to live with her mother. Although she has not been in employment for some years, she intends to apply to become a nurse, Your Worship.'

April crouched lower, a picture of contrition. The headmaster turned to stare at David; he and his solicitor had said little beyond the brief acknowledgement of facts not in dispute.

'No chance of a reconciliation, I suppose?' he inquired.

Good grief, thought Mr Batchelor.

'I thought not. Has your client expressed any wish about his children?'

'His situation does not allow him to take care of them himself, Your Worship.'

'Is that so?' The magistrate lowered his spectacles to the tip of his nose and poked his head forward, appearing to examine David with interest. He reminded himself that it was Mrs Holmes on trial, not her husband, and sat back. He turned to his colleagues.

'Neither of 'em's fit,' wheezed the short stout man on his right. The third magistrate nodded. 'We make them wards of court,' whispered the chairman. 'Do we agree?' Reporters, roosting in a row, pencils poised, watched the three grey heads turning, one to the other, conferring in whispers. David sat staring fixedly, his mouth a thin, angry line.

'If only half the things we have heard in this room today are true,' began the chairman of the bench, 'we deplore the fact that a man could be so callous. Our sympathy,' he said to the reporters firmly, 'goes out to this poor lady, whom we place on probation for three years.' He looked at April. 'A condition of your probation is that you do not seek the return of your children before that period is over.'

Mr Batchelor heaved a sigh of relief and the reporters' pens raced. 'We do not regard you, Mrs Holmes, nor you, Dr Holmes, as fit persons to have custody of your children. We therefore make them wards of court and the County Council will look after them.'

The clerk beckoned the Child Care Officer, sitting previously unnoticed, a short plump woman with curly brown hair. She rose, dipping and swaying on a withered leg. She handed a sheaf of papers up to the bench.

'Will you bring them in?' asked the chairman.

April turned to stare unwinkingly at the door at the back of the court. Reporters chattered and fidgeted. Eileen sat on the hard bench, ramrod straight. The children came in.

They'd sat still for what seemed like hours and hours, not daring to move because just outside was a man in a long black cloak, and several policemen. They sat where the limping lady told them to wait, bare legs sticking painfully to shiny brown leather seats. The tiny, narrow room, lit at midday by brown-shaded lights that barely lit the brown walls and brown ceiling, was just like a railway carriage.

'Why have we got to stay here?' whispered Jessie, who had sat still so long her bottom hurt.

'Shut up,' hissed Peter.

'Why?' she hissed back.

'Because.'

'Where's that lady with the leg gone?' Peter shrugged.

Polly unstuck her own legs. 'It stings.'

'It's a train,' said Jessie after a long silence. They all considered this piece of wisdom.

'Don't be silly,' Hannah said from the corner and closed her eyes again, drifting in and out of what was happening. When she opened her eyes there seemed to be, as it were, a pane of glass in the way. Nothing was real. This preoccupied and frightened her much more than the evasive words of the leg lady.

'It's a funny station,' remarked Peter.

'How many stations have you been in?' demanded Jessie.

He looked uncertain.

'Well, then. We just haven't gone anywhere yet,' she said bravely.

'I want to go,' cried Ingrid.

Jessie looked at her sternly. 'Don't be silly. Oh, that. You'll have to wait.'

'I can't.'

'You can if you want to,' Hannah said from her corner.

Ingrid wriggled threateningly on the shiny seat.

'There's lavatories in stations, stupid,' said Peter, showing off.

Jessie peered out of the narrow window. 'There are policemen out here, and there's a bat.'

'Where?' Peter asked, interested at last. 'Look.' Jessie pointed, her breath misting the glass. A lawyer stood, his head bowed over some papers, his gown billowing in the draught.

'Ooooh.' Polly went bright red, trying her best not to cry.

'I want to go,' moaned Ingrid, crossing and uncrossing her small legs.

'She'll come back in a minute and you can ask,' Hannah said disinterestedly.

'Oh.' Ingrid sound surprised and rather pleased.

Hannah squinted down and closed her eyes again. 'They'll just have to mop it up. Don't start grizzling.'

'That lady said we'd see Mummy.' said Polly in her clear, determined way. 'Perhaps this train goes to where Mummy is.'

Ingrid's puddle spread and she sighed with pleasure.

'Oh!' cried Polly, edging out of the way.

'Here she is,' said Hannah.

'Oh, dear,' cried Miss Worthington, wrinkling her nose. 'Couldn't you have waited?'

'No,' said Ingrid haughtily.

'I suppose it can't be helped. Do you remember I told you you might have to go into Court?' They stared back at her blankly. 'Oh, never mind, follow me.' She swivelled on her good leg, callipers creaking rapidly ahead of them.

'I think she needs oiling,' said Peter kindly. Their reluctant Pied Piper led them into a big hall. There were no trains.

'It was Euston,' declared Jessie afterwards.

'I wonder why her leg got shrunk,' observed Peter thoughtfully.

Inside the Court the man from the *News Chronicle* nudged the chap from the *Daily Mirror*.

'Nothing to follow up on the kids, I suppose?'

The *Mirror* drew doodles on his shorthand notebook and shrugged.

'Bad, losing both your parents like this.'

'Those two? Better off without 'em.'

'You don't feel sorry for her?'

The *Mirror* yawned and capped his pen. 'For my money, you can put the two of 'em somewhere nice and safe and throw away the key.'

'He drove her to it,' protested the *News Chronicle*, caught the *Mirror's* contemptuous eye and added quickly, 'but I see what you mean.'

'Do you, now?' inquired the *Mirror* sarcastically.

'Pocket handkerchief time,' murmured *The Times*, august in a row of his own. 'Dash a tear from your eye, chaps.' He drew a thick line under the end of his copy.

The leg lady shepherded the children down. They didn't look in April's direction. The magistrate leaned over the bench and everyone strained to hear.

'When did you last see your father?' murmured the *Mirror* cynically. 'And not a dry eye in the house.'

'Shut up,' hissed the *Chronicle*.

The *Mirror* winked and wiped away a mock tear. 'An editor's dream.'

'Silence!' shouted the Clerk, and Ingrid burst into tears. The Clerk dropped his gavel noisily and blushed crimson with guilt. The headmaster beckoned them forwards and Miss Worthington's clumsy leather boot creaked as she fussed anxiously, gathering them into a tight little knot.

'Ingrid smells,' complained Polly.

'You are,' said the man looming over them, 'Hannah, Peter, Jessie, Ingrid and Polly Holmes?'

'Yes, Your Worship,' said Miss Worthington triumphantly.

'No, you're not. I'm asking them,' said the magistrate testily.

'Yes,' said Jessie, and went scarlet. The Court sighed gustily.

'I'm sorry you had to come here, but it was important for me to see you before I sign some papers. They can go.' He nodded dismissively at the leg lady. She dipped and swayed up the aisle, dragging Ingrid fiercely behind her, the others trailing behind.

'That's that, then,' remarked the *Mirror*. 'Simple really, isn't it?'

'What?' The *Chronicle* took the bait resignedly.

'Getting rid of kids. Where's the best pub, then?'

'Pig and 'tater,' called a very young man with pimples, from the local paper, starry-eyed among the Fleet Street hacks.

'The Court will rise.' said the Clerk modestly, having recovered his gavel.

'Well done,' said the barrister, gathering his papers from a table.

'Where have they taken my children?' asked April weakly.

'They'll arrange foster homes. We've been over that, several times, Mrs Holmes,' he said. 'I should go and find your mother.'

David spoke in low, rapid tones to his solicitor, who nodded now and then, his eyes fixed on the floor. April looked across.

'Now then,' warned Mr Batchelor, following her gaze.

'He gets off with nothing, and I'm put in prison, put on probation and have my children taken away . . .' she began bitterly.

'He's not getting off with anything. He hasn't been charged.'

'If there was any justice, he should be.'

'Some might share your opinion, but that won't help now.'

'They do realise, don't they, that my husband is a doctor, that he wants to become a psychiatrist?'

'April,' said Mr Batchelor in a tired voice, 'we all know your husband is a doctor. We have used that fact to argue the culpability of his behaviour, its utterly inexcusable nature, even more than for an ordinary person who is not a doctor.'

'But . . .'

'. . . and,' went on Mr Batchelor determinedly in the empty courtroom, 'on that basis we got the consideration for you, and the verdict for you, that we'd hoped for.'

And, he thought crossly, you could show a bit of appreciation! He put his hand under her elbow and pushed her firmly towards the exit. David and his solicitor had left rapidly, banging through the doors, and stood just beyond them, the solicitor writing something in what looked like a diary. Mr Batchelor tightened his grip and steered April past quickly.

'Don't,' he said sharply, and she averted her head, letting him hurry her on.

'Only one side has been told. There's another side to all this, April, and it hasn't been told here today.' David's cry rang behind her as they burst through the outer doors on to some steps. Clouds scurried across a dull, dirty sky.

'I thought I'd better wait for you here,' said Eileen, 'and keep out of the way of that lot.'

'All the dailies were here,' said Mr Batchelor, 'but it'll be a nine days wonder. Next week it'll be someone else. Take no notice.'

'Get your things, April, we've got connections to catch.'

'Can I see my children?'

'You'll have to apply to the Court for access,' Mr Batchelor said levelly. 'We've been over that several times, as well.'

'I expect it's hard for her to take it in.' Eileen tucked her handbag under her arm. 'She can think about it on the train.'

'Of course she can.' Mr Batchelor had the odd sensation of gratitude to a woman he intensely disliked. She would take her daughter away. April looked as though a breeze would blow her over.

'You'll hear from me,' said Mr Batchelor cheerily. 'Congratulations again, and all the best.'

'Come along,' snapped Eileen, losing patience, 'or we'll miss that train.'

April followed her mother down the short flight of steps.

'It could have been Holloway, you know,' Mr Batchelor muttered.

From a window above, Hannah watched her mother and grandmother running away. Behind her the leg lady poured tepid milk into thick white cups and opened a packet of biscuits "while we wait".

Are we waiting for something? thought Hannah, seeing her mother and her grandmother scurry round the corner, out of sight. She felt a great dull pain, a frightful tension. She tried and tried to feel something real, except the tension. All there was, was sham.

'Here you are.' Miss Worthington was brightly holding out a cup and a ginger biscuit, to cheer her up.

'No, thank you,' said Hannah, politely.

'Stephenson was the same,' April cried to her mother, who almost ran along in front of her. 'Lawyers are all bastards.'

'Really, April!' Eileen was shocked. 'I thought he was quite good to you. You'd better start looking forward, now, dear, not back. Put it all behind you.'

April shifted her small case to her other hand and tried to catch Eileen up, refusing to run.

'I hope he rots,' she said savagely.

'Poor Mr Batchelor,' Eileen panted.

'I don't mean him, I mean David,' gasped April, breaking into a trot. 'I wish you'd slow down.'

'We're going to get that train.'

And they did. Just.

'Oh, goodness me! Look at that,' Gladys spread the *Mirror* open on her scullery table and gaped. April and David had a full centre spread. She read it carefully. 'Good heavens,' she gasped, and shot into the front room for her cardigan where the thought of Joe gave her serious pause.

She stood with her cardigan in her hands, considering. David had made good and now just look at this. No, thought Gladys, you never could tell; it just went to show. With that cautionary thought, she set off briskly, all agog to see what the rest of the East End had to say.

Chapter Fourteen

April was on nights when the telephone rang. 'Yes?' she said, bored, watching Nurse Edwards, a self-willed first year, carry a bedpan into the gloom at the far end of the ward on silent, crepe-soled feet.

'It's me,' said Eileen.

'It's just as well it's me, then,' answered April. 'I wish you wouldn't do this, Mum.'

Eileen sniffed. 'I thought you ought to know.'

April waited as Edwards pulled curtains round someone's bed with a muted clatter of brass rings. She gave in.

'Know what, at three in the morning? What on earth are you doing up, anyway?'

'I'm just back from Rachael's,' said Eileen, and her voice sounded muffled, as though she was crying. 'She's gone.'

April listened to the woman in the nearest bed groan in her sleep and turn over painfully. She glanced at the clock; the patient's painkillers would be wearing off.

'April?'

Rachael had had painkillers, too. April had often given them to her towards the end, angrily and helplessly watching the growths eat her up. There was so much pain. Sitting alone in the little lighted office, surrounded by restless darkness, she said: 'I wish you'd waited and told me later.'

Edwards emerged with the bedpan.

'I thought you'd want to know.'

A detached part of April's mind asked how one could possibly want to know that someone dearly loved, though old and sick and riddled with cancer, who had always been there and now never would be again – was dead. Did one *want* to know such a thing?

'What a funny question,' she murmured.

'What?' asked Eileen. 'I'm sorry if I've done the wrong thing. At least she's out of pain.'

She's lucky, thought April. There was a tense silence over the telephone. 'Will you be all right until I get home?' she asked, accepting that Eileen couldn't help the call.

'She went just after two.'

April sighed. Edwards came out of the sluice and stuck her head round the door, raising her eyebrows, her hand to her mouth.

'Please,' mouthed April.

Eileen snuffled, blowing her nose. Weak, aching anger passed like a pain through her and April heard her own involuntary sharpness. 'Look, we really are busy. I'll get home as quick as I can.'

Rachael gone. She felt giddy.

'You all right?' Edwards brought in two cups of slopped tea, a packet of biscuits under one arm.

'Someone I know just died.'

Edwards stirred her tea, embarrassed; April was old enough to be her mother and she didn't know what to say. No one she knew had died except patients, which was different.

'I'm sorry,' she said, and edged a teacup nearer to April's hand. 'Shall I put sugar in it?'

'What for?'

Edwards was aggrieved, her sympathy rejected. April understood the look exactly. 'Go and turn Mrs Jones when you've finished that,' she snapped, 'and then you can lay the trolleys for breakfast – we're late already.'

She's only a third year, Edwards thought sulkily, rinsing her cup. Bossy old bag.

'If you carry on like this, you'll make yourself ill,' Eileen told her. 'Why don't you ask for leave?'

The funeral over, Rachael's children and grandchildren went home, taking her husband Gordon to live with his eldest son, leaving the house shut up, perhaps for good. April moped, putting Eileen's nose out of joint. Rachael had been her friend. April's mourning diminished her own.

'I'm not due any.'

'You're peaky.'

'You don't get time off nursing for being peaky. And I'm studying.'

'They ought to give you compassionate time off.'

'No.'

Matron knew all about April and her probation. They'd had a heart-to-heart about it and Matron had been so painfully kind, April had to chew her lip not to spill everything, the whole awful story of George and the first April, and how a kitten had died in freezing rain on the Wanstead Flats, and Rachael had taken her in. Matron had seen a sad, tense little girl, anxious to please, in the thin, lonely woman before her. After that interview, they avoided each other; Matron from tact, April from fear.

'I can't ask,' she told Eileen. But Sister, seeing her listless, dragged the story out of her and sent her to Matron without a choice in the matter.

'Take a week off. Don't dwell on it, my dear,' she was told.

April's sallow cheeks flushed. 'I'd like to go and see my children.'

'D'you still need permission?' Matron pushed the telephone across her desk and stood up briskly. 'I've got to pop into School. You can use that.'

April's eyes filled.

'Don't start bawling,' hooted Matron kindly, 'just get on with it, Holmes, do.'

April picked up the telephone and rang Mr Batchelor.

'I should think you can visit. I'll call you back,' he said.

'Yes,' said Miss Worthington, who had had the Holmes children on her case load for not far short of three years now, 'of course she can.'

Visiting her children, April knew, was in some ways truly a cross to be borne; vicars, and church, and Christian gratitude expected from her who didn't believe in it. Peter and Jessie strained the patience of a vicar and his wife, in the Malvern Hills, while the twins were the charges of another philanthropic clergyman and his wife. Mrs Heydritch kept count of the Reverend Heydritch's ex cons, and her own accumulation of children. Hannah, for a short time in a household full of large dogs, was said to have behaved badly. The leg lady had taken her to a Home, from which there was silence. No one asked what Hannah thought, and Hannah didn't tell.

*　　*　　*

'I don't know how you stand it,' April rubbed her knees crossly, 'it's a bit much, having to do all the services; all that kneeling. I never know where I am in that book.' She felt eyes on her back as she thumbed wafery pages, trying to match the words with the vicar's sing-song chanting, always a bit behind. Jessie giggled and told tales, whispering in her mother's ear.

'Mrs Wilks made him eat five choc ices.'

Peter scowled.

'Good heavens,' April whispered back. 'Why?'

'Because,' started Jessie gleefully, 'at choir practice someone heard him tell Mr Harrow – that's our choir teacher – we never have ice creams because the Wilkses are too mean.'

Peter aimed a kick at her ankle and missed. Jessie smiled angelically. 'So Mrs Wilks marched straight out and got him five choc ices and he had to eat them all, didn't you?'

'I'll have a word with that woman.'

'He was telling fibs.'

April pulled Peter on to her lap. He wriggled off at once.

'He wasn't sick or anything. Greedy pig.'

'Don't you miss me?' asked April miserably.

They swung their legs, brown from country living, belonging there. 'When are you going, Mummy?' asked Jessie, helpfully, anxious to please.

'None too soon, evidently.'

'Ass,' observed Peter coolly.

'I didn't mean it like that . . .' cried Jessie.

But the damage was done and April left a day earlier than she'd planned, to Mrs Wilks's undisguised relief.

'They've been a handful since she came,' said the

Reverend Wilks. 'I almost wish she wouldn't visit.'

'She's their mother, dear.'

'Hmm,' snorted the vicar uncharitably.

After April left, Jessie taunted Peter, 'Crybaby, cry-baby' until she saw real tears in his eyes. Then she shut up because she wanted to cry herself.

Reverend Heydritch was tall, thin and preoccupied with his soul. He had a tubby, resigned, shortsighted wife, preoccupied with making ends meet. She tried to do so largely by being the worst cook in the world.

'Who?' he demanded, when Mrs Heydritch said April was coming to stay.

'Their mother.'

Reverend Heydritch chewed steadily on pumper-nickel, because it was good for the bowels, and tried to work out how many people lived in his household just at that time. His bowels were the profane side of his worries in life. He sighed, inhaled a crumb and coughed.

'Someone rang about a black prisoner,' she said when he'd dislodged the crumb.

'Oh, dear.'

'There's space in the shed,' said Mrs Heydritch imper-turbably. 'I can't have any more in this house.'

'It's warm at night, I suppose.'

'It'll do, until he gets back inside.'

'Recidivism is our fault . . .'

'Not personally, dear. April's coming for two days.' Elsa Heydritch, blinking rapidly, pushed the butter within his reach. 'And Ingrid screamed for weeks last time.'

'I expect we'll cope.'

'*I'll* cope, you mean.'

'I've got parents coming to arrange a christening.'

She gathered crumbs into a neat little pile on the tablecloth. 'Have you, now? I suppose I'll have to deal with it.'

'Fourteen, if you count the dog and cat. They eat, don't they?'

'Fourteen what?'

'People. I think they should see their mother, you know.' Seeing his wife's expression, he fled.

Rain spattered at the big, shabby old house and a bantam hen wandered in from outside, clucked, settled its feathers and put its head on one side, eyeing her.

'They say God doesn't send us more than we can bear,' Elsa told the bird, 'but when it comes to the Holmeses, I have doubts.'

The chicken fluffed itself and pecked the kitchen floor. Pigs, chickens, cons and blasted Christian charity . . .

'Out!' she shouted, starting up from her chair to make the hen run squawking into the garden. She wandered myopically after it to check for eggs; they were often off by the time she discovered them. The eggs were bad and the sky opened over her grey plaited head. She gathered her skirts and ran back into her comfortless kitchen.

If the howling and kicking and screaming afterwards were anything to go by, Polly and Ingrid enjoyed their mother's visit immensely.

'I'm sorry about Rachael,' said Hannah, trying to change the subject.

'You've only got yourself to blame if you don't like it here,' snapped April. 'Those people did try, Hannah.'

'Dog people.'

'They had a lot of dogs, but that was no excuse for behaving the way you did.'

'They hated me.'

'I'm sure that's not true.'

'All right, I hated them.'

That satisfied her mother; it had been so evidently and embarrassingly true.

Hannah hadn't been with the Jameses long before things came to a head. Miss Worthington said it was quite a coup, to find a foster family willing to take a much older child. She took Hannah there in late October, after April's trial in September.

'Do try, won't you?' begged Miss Worthington. 'They are nice people.'

'Yes,' said Hannah politely.

'Try and sort of . . . be a bit livelier, do you think?'

'Livelier?'

'No good moping, you see.'

'I don't feel anything at all,' said Hannah, trying to reassure her, and got out of the car.

Christmas came, bright and dry and cold. The Jameses' cottage smelled of damp ivy, coke fires in the Aga, and pine needles. And dogs. The television was constantly on, its black and white screen blaring in the low, beamed room. In front of the fire five labradors jockeyed and scuffled to get close to the heat.

'Have one,' said Mr James, offering chocolates and cartons of chocolate ginger. He worked in the Cadbury's factory and always had chocolate for free.

No wonder they're all so fat, Hannah said to herself. She talked a lot to herself, or the dogs, which was very slightly less lonely. Even the dogs were podgy and one was gross, with goodness knew how many puppies. Their milling and smelling and shedding of hair in the tiny cottage made her feel sick.

'Want one?'

Mrs James's son didn't belong to Mr James. She had been married before, and divorced. Which, said Miss Worthington to her colleagues, made them ideal. Barclay was twenty-four, stout, and shorter than Hannah, with orange-coloured hair. She shook her head.

'Please yourself.' He popped a chocolate into his mouth and turned back to the television. 'Like your soap on a rope, did you?' he asked, chewing noisily.

Ever since she had unwrapped his present, Hannah had wanted to ask why it had a rope, but didn't dare.

'Yes, thank you.'

'I'll come in tonight and wash your back.' He giggled, looking her up and down. 'All right?'

The pregnant bitch snored and twitched in her sleep. Mrs James put out a stout leg and nudged her. Hannah stuck her nose in the air and left the room.

'Hmmm, nice,' murmured Barclay, eyeing her sideways.

'What have you said to her, now?' asked his mother idly, throwing a log on the fire.

'Who? Me?' He looked at Hannah's empty chair, wide-eyed. 'Nothing.'

'She's over sensitive,' said Mr James, looking at the Milk Tray menu. 'Who ate all the coffee creams?'

'There's one left underneath,' said his wife.

He teased it out from its crackly brown wrapping. 'Anyone else want it?' He ate it himself, since nobody did.

Upstairs in the cottage, floors and ceilings sloped all over the place. A heavy mahogany bed and wardrobe took up almost all Hannah's small room under the eaves. She had a table and chair, for doing homework. There was a mirror fixed to the wall opposite the window, where it reflected the light. She pulled up her jumper and looked at herself, then pulled it down angrily. He was right.

It was too cold to sit and do nothing. The television blared downstairs. She scratched itchy chilblains and stared at herself in the mirror. Long, mousey hair, long face and a long expression. And breasts, for that creature downstairs to stare at. Soap on a rope. That was it. He was going to get her.

Hannah leaped to her feet, grabbed the end of her bed and heaved. With a screech it slid across, blocking the doorway. She jammed it fast with the wardrobe. Downstairs they looked up at the ceiling.

'What on earth's she doing?' asked Mr James.

'Moving furniture,' said Barclay.

'On Christmas Day?' said Mrs James. 'Thoughtless little hound.'

Barclay grinned. 'Shall I go and see?'

There was no sound from above.

'Tell her to come straight down and stop fiddling,' said his mother.

Barclay went up. Hannah looked out of the window, but it was too high to jump.

'Come on, darling.'

Hannah stared at the turning doorknob.

'Locked yourself in?' He sounded amused.

Mrs James came halfway up the stairs and shrugged. 'She'll come out when she's ready. The dogs need walking.'

Barclay rattled the door. 'Silly bitch, grow up.'

He aimed a half-hearted kick at the door. She listened to him lumber back down the narrow stairs and shut the door at the bottom, then got into bed in her clothes and pulled thick grey blankets over her head. The television went on and on, the dogs went out, came back, doors banged and Mr James called up to her to stop being so silly and come down for Christmas cake and mince pies. They called and knocked and tried the door at midnight. She was asleep. The house stilled and when the fire died, it was freezing.

Shortly after three o'clock on Boxing Day morning Hannah woke, shivering from nightmares, wishing with such desolate passion that she were dead, her own warm body was yet another betrayal. There was nothing to keep her alive, but she lived, and knew it, because it was agony. She crept out of bed, edged the furniture away enough to slide through the crack of the door, and went downstairs on bare feet. The kitchen was warmed by the Aga. Close to it the pregnant bitch sprawled in her basket, soon to give birth. Hannah spread her paws wide and the dog shifted back in the basket, making room for her to creep in.

'Cuddle me,' she whispered. She lay down between the animal's paws, awkwardly, and went back to sleep.

Mr James found them at six o'clock, when he came down first, to put on his porridge. By lunchtime Miss Worthington was outside in her little blue car and by teatime Hannah was in The Chestnuts.

'Good grief,' spittle flew from Mr James's lips, 'she's unnatural! I know that girl's been through a lot, and I can tell you now, it's affected her.'

'She isn't half touchy.' Barclay sauntered out to look

at the modifications made to the car, to accommodate the officer's callipers. He leaned on the door, interested. Hannah came out carrying two cases.

'We're sorry to call you out on a holiday, but it all got too much,' said Mrs James.

'Say goodbye and thank you at least,' hissed Miss Worthington. 'They'll never take another child and we're so short . . .'

Hannah looked straight ahead and Miss Worthington pulled an apologetic face.

'Upset.' She raised her hands, helpless.

'You can only do your best.' Mrs James smarted under the insult.

'I'll talk to her. I expect she'll write . . .' Miss Worthington lifted her leg into the car, watched by Barclay. He liked plump women. She knew he was staring and threw him the starting handle. 'Would you . . . ?'

The car started and Barclay threw the handle into the back. 'Cheerio,' he called, bending down and waving to Hannah, sitting stonily indifferent in the passenger seat.

'I only hope you like where you're going, young lady. I'd hoped to keep you out of The Chestnuts,' the welfare officer said.

'Why do you care? I don't,' said Hannah in a very clear, cold voice.

Miss Worthington negotiated a corner, slowed down and looked at her. 'I do care, but I haven't got anywhere else to take you.'

'I don't mind where you take me. I am perfectly all right.'

Miss Worthington glanced sideways at her white-faced, frigid passenger and doubted that very much indeed.

'Fancy putting an adolescent girl in a bedroom next to a single man,' April had said to Mr Batchelor when she heard about it. 'Don't these social workers have any sense?' By then, though, the damage was done. Hannah stayed at The Chestnuts.

'It's not all that bad, is it?' remarked April, trying to make the best of it, walking down the very long drive that hid The Chestnuts from all but the determined visitor. This is like one of the old isolation hospitals, she thought; send them where no one can see them. 'Your father could send you to boarding school, you know. You don't have to stay here.'

'I don't want to go.'

'Why not?'

'Just don't.'

'You like it here?'

'I don't not like it.'

'There's no pleasing you, is there?'

'I don't feel anything to be pleased about.'

'Just like your father,' said April.

Chapter Fifteen

Life in The Chestnuts wasn't exactly living, but it had its moments and Wendy Dawn's nits were one of them. Everyone was impressed because Wendy Dawn Hobbs had the biggest, fattest, blackest, fastest lice they had ever seen. The Chestnuts was full of experts; most children had shaved heads and woolly hats when they first came in. Wendy Dawn was amazing. She sat in bed, because she had tonsilitis, and scratched until Hannah noticed and told Mum, a martyred, colourless-looking Welsh woman who ran Reception's twenty-five disturbed children with her sing-song voice and a rod of iron. When they'd adjusted and were no longer disruptive, they went to the cottages further down the drive. Two for boys and two for girls. They were nearly always full. Mum had a civilising influence on her charges.

She bustled along with a folded old sheet and a tooth-comb and out fell Wendy Dawn's lice, wriggling across the bed so fast they nearly got away.

'Do they jump?' asked Hannah, who had the next bed. 'I never had them.'

'Me dad had crabs,' remarked Wendy Dawn pertly, and Mum dragged the comb through her hair with a sudden jerk that made Wendy Dawn squawk.

'Crabs?'

135

Hannah considered crabs. Surely they'd be much too big, and anyway they lived in water.

'Down there, by his, you know.' Wendy Dawn pointed with one bitten finger nail and Mum chased a fugitive louse furiously. 'We don't want . . .' she started.

Hannah's eyes were speculative. 'How do you know?' she demanded, and Mum was lost.

'Dad used to . . .'

'Wendy!' thundered Mum.

'. . . you know, so I got them, too. If you itch down there, you should look and see,' finished Wendy with relish, running her fingers through her hair and bending forwards over the sheet on her lap to see if any stray ones fell out.

'Bath,' muttered Mum ominously, 'right away. Never mind the tonsilitis. And you,' she rounded on Hannah, 'you get in there with her. Be on the safe side.'

'Why?'

'Just get in that bathroom and do as you're told,' cried Mum, sweeping up the sheet with its horrible contents. 'There's shampoo on the side.'

'In the middle of the day?'

' 'cos they do jump. And crabs catch,' said Wendy Dawn wisely.

'Ah.' Hannah decided to look as closely as she dared at Wendy Dawn in the bathroom. The bathroom with its two baths, side by side in the cramped space, made no allowances for modesty and the two girls stood back to back, keeping their knickers on to the last minute. Try as she would, Hannah couldn't see anything out of the ordinary about Wendy Dawn. They lay back in green chemical shampoo that killed everything and was much loved by Mum, and contemplated the taps.

'Wendy,' said Hannah, unable to bear it any longer, 'what's crabs?'

Wendy Dawn told her. Hannah didn't believe a word of it.

'You're making that up to get attention,' she said severely, using one of Mum's favourite expressions.

'I'm not. That's why they put me in this place,' said Wendy Dawn stoutly. She licked her finger and pulled a face. 'Cross my heart and hope to die in a cellar full of rats.' Then she sank back into the hot water and looked rather as though it had shrunk her. 'He did it all the time until my aunty told the police. They put me in here.'

There was a long silence.

'All right, I believe you.'

Wendy Dawn said she really wasn't bothered.

Appearances, Hannah discovered, could be deceptive. Wendy Dawn had a pudding face and limp dull hair the colour of dead leaves, but she went to grammar school and was clever. Gradually it emerged that she wasn't merely clever – she was smart. Her two shallow drawers in their shared plywood dressing table were stuffed with embroidered hankies and miniature bottles of "Evening in Paris" from Woolworths. She had at least twenty pairs of stockings that she couldn't wear and a manicure set in a pink plastic case with glass diamonds stuck on it that they shared, sitting with their backs to the door, ready to shove it under the pillow if anyone came in.

'I steal them, of course.'

'Aren't you scared?'

Wendy Dawn grinned knowingly. 'That's the fun.'

'I don't have fun.'

'Why are you in here?' Wendy Dawn showed a rare interest.

'My mother tried to kill us and my father went to live with someone else. He didn't want to be bothered.'

'Go on, tell.'

Hannah told, and Wendy Dawn looked sceptical. 'Is that true?' she demanded. 'You're not making it up?'

'Cross my heart. There are some newspaper cuttings in my locker, that I saved.'

They got them out and pored over them.

'Where's the rest of you?' demanded Wendy Dawn.

'I'm not really sure where Jessie and Peter are. Polly and Ingrid live with some people near our old house. They've got a funny kind of church in their garden.'

'Don't you ever go and see them? I've never seen you have visitors that come here.'

'I don't see anyone. I don't think they want to see me. My mother used to come sometimes, but not for ages.'

'Your parents are pigs,' pronounced Wendy Dawn definitively.

It was a whole new perspective on the matter.

One March weekend they were bored. Wendy Dawn helped herself to a home perm from the beauty counter in Woolworths. They spent a long time rolling her shoulder-length hair round thin plastic curlers and dousing it in evil-smelling liquid. The instructions said you had to wait and neither of them were good at that.

'You're going to have golliwog curls,' said Hannah doubtfully. 'They're ever so tight.'

'Corkscrew,' corrected Wendy Dawn, studying the label on a bottle of hydrogen peroxide. 'Do you think this will go with the perm stuff?'

'I think all your hair will fall out and you'll look so awful you won't be able to go to school, and Mum'll shave your head and put you in a nit hat.'

'Let's try it, then.'

'Not both at once.'

'After the neutraliser, silly.'

Hannah cupped her chin in her hands and leaned on the narrow window sill, looking out over the sloping field that isolated them from the nearest road.

'Lonely, here, isn't it?'

Wendy Dawn prodded her forest of curlers, trying to see the back of her head in their dressing-table mirror.

'I'm nearly cooked. Then let's go somewhere.'

'Like where?'

Wendy Dawn rolled her spaniel eyes and sought inspiration. 'Picadilly Circus.'

'That's stupid. We haven't got any money.'

'You hitch,' said Wendy Dawn, knowing everything. 'Pour the neutraliser over for me.'

They went down to the bathroom and Hannah dabbed the curlers with wet cottonwool.

'Ta,' said Wendy.

'What would we do?'

Wendy Dawn dripped neutraliser into Mum's well scoured basin. 'You know,' she said offhandedly, 'have a good time.'

'What sort of a good time?'

'Oh, Lord!'

'What?'

'You know – men.'

Hannah started undoing her curlers. 'There was this man at my foster home called Barclay and he . . .'

Wendy Dawn screeched with laughter when Hannah

finished. 'Now who's telling stories?' she cried derisively.

Hannah flushed scarlet. 'I'm not,' she said sulkily.

'You are.'

Stung, Hannah glared back at her. 'I'm not.'

Wendy Dawn pulled out her curlers. 'Let's leave the bleach.'

'No.' Hannah fetched the peroxide. 'You do it for me.'

Wendy Dawn took the bottle. 'Might as well go the whole hog, if we're going out,' she cried, and began to dab at Hannah's hair with a flannel soaked in bleach. 'How blonde do you want to be?'

'Ash.'

When they'd finished, they were a picture. It was three o'clock by the time they'd done, a cold, wet, windless day.

'Hadn't we better wait until tomorrow?' asked Hannah. 'It's pouring.'

'Tomorrow's Sunday.'

'So?'

'Sunday's no good.'

'It's an awfully long way.'

There was a knock on their door. Guiltily, they jumped. Jenny Heydritch, the only outsider ever to set foot in their room, came in and stopped in her tracks.

'Oh, wow.' She walked round them, impressed.

'Do you want to come?' asked Hannah, grasping at straws.

'Where?'

'Picadilly Circus.'

'That's in London.'

'We're going to hitch,' said Wendy Dawn boldly.

'Come with us,' begged Hannah.

'My mother'd murder me.'

'Your hair's nearly dry.' Wendy Dawn grabbed Hannah's yellow head and felt it, 'It'll do.'

'You'll get into the most awful trouble.'

'Coming?' demanded Wendy Dawn.

Jenny shook her head.

Hannah took her coat out of the cupboard and looked out of the window. There was a steady downpour. 'We'll nick Mum's umbrella,' she said.

'You're mad,' said Jenny, astonished.

They waited five minutes on the main road to Birmingham, then got lifts with three lorries that each went a bit of the way to west London. It was already dark. 'I'm hungry,' complained Hannah.

A posh car stopped.

'Hey, look at this one,' hissed Wendy Dawn, running after it. They peered through the window at the driver.

'We want to go to Piccadilly,' said Wendy Dawn. 'Are you going that way?'

'I could do,' said the driver.

They got in.

The police picked them up near Watford, sitting at the side of the A1, underneath a streetlamp. They had bruises and scratches.

'But he's got more than that,' said Wendy Dawn viciously. 'I got him.'

Hannah shivered and couldn't stop.

'Can you describe him?' asked a policewoman later.

Hannah still shivered and when she started thinking about his red, angry face and his big yellow teeth bared in a kind of horrible, hurried smile, her teeth chattered.

'No,' said Wendy Dawn, 'we can't.'

'You're asking for everything you get,' the

policewoman told her in a very unfriendly tone of voice. 'Where did you think you were going?'

'On the streets,' said Wendy Dawn savagely.

'You're going straight back home,' snapped the woman.

Wendy Dawn laughed sourly, right in her face. 'Where's that, then?' she sneered. 'Where's home for her and me?'

The policewoman closed her little notebook with a snap and tucked it into her breast pocket.

'Wherever you came from,' she said with disgust.

Wendy Dawn's curls straggled, limp with damp and cold. 'We don't come from nowhere, so there!' she snarled, dragging Hannah towards a bench. 'You can bloody find out for yourselves,' she shouted at the police, and pulled the two of them down on the wooden seat.

'They were nice when my mother did . . . you know,' whispered Hannah, pulling her arm away. 'Why are you being so awful?'

'I hate them,' Wendy Dawn hissed bitterly.

'Why?' whispered Hannah.

'They dragged me out when my dad . . .' said Wendy Dawn through her teeth. Her face flamed and she couldn't go on. Hannah put an arm round her shoulders and hugged her close. Wendy Dawn cried secretly, into her coat collar, so no one would see. Hannah sat until she got cramp, hugging her and getting damp, until someone came and took them into an office where they took a telephone call from Miss Worthington.

'Oh dear, you wretched girl!' cried the leg lady. 'You've caused endless trouble and worry, and now I've got to drive all the way down and fetch the pair of you.

Everyone's cross with you, and serve you right.'

'It wasn't just me,' muttered Hannah.

'You should know better,' snapped the social worker.

Looking at Wendy Dawn's blotchy face and torn jumper, the unreality torturing Hannah faded for a moment, letting in the fierce pain of love. 'I'm sorry, Wendy,' she cried.

'I should think so,' said Miss Worthington.

'Not you,' said Hannah drearily.

'Oh, screw 'em,' muttered Wendy Dawn.

'She'd better come to us,' said Elsa Heydritch resignedly. Jenny begged and pleaded, Miss Worthington negotiated, and Mum had watched with narrow, furious eyes, scared they'd hop it again and it'd be her responsibility next time. She'd said to Matron more than once that she couldn't be expected to take responsibility and Matron, it seemed, had listened.

'What's one more?' remarked Mr Heydritch. 'The twins have gone home and replacing two Holmses with one is at least working in the right direction.'

'She's got two more years at school. And it's seven more,' snapped Mrs Heydritch pedantically. 'The cat's had her kittens.'

'She can share my room,' cried Jenny.

'She had the kittens on your bed.'

'Hannah *must* come.'

Elsa Heydritch sighed resignedly; Jenny would get what she wanted. She generally did.

'I've been dying for you to come.'

Hannah took her head out of her suitcase and looked at Jenny coldly. 'Someone could try inviting me for once,' she muttered bleakly and slammed the case down,

143

depressed and angry and sad. They'd taken Wendy
Dawn to a hospital because she'd started screaming and
crying. Matron said she didn't think she would be coming
back.

'Pigs!'

'Pardon?' said Jenny.

'Nothing.' There was never any point in trying to
explain. Wendy Dawn had at least taught her that.

Chapter Sixteen

Sometimes, very rarely, David visited the Heydritches.

'You are actually rather pretty,' he said, walking rapidly round the edge of the park where April had clung to the railings nearly four years earlier. Hannah dragged her feet behind him.

'I'm not. I'm fat and spotty. Mrs Heydritch says I look as if I'm in a bad mood all the time.'

'Mrs Heydritch is so short-sighted I doubt she sees anything much.'

'I would give anything to be pretty. You and Mum used to say I never would be.'

'Your mother and I said a lot of things we didn't mean. You shouldn't take any notice.'

'*You* always take notice.'

'When do you go off to university?' He changed the subject.

'First week in October.'

'You must come and see us. We're so close, you could walk from the college.'

It meant nothing. April had made it painfully clear that visiting David and Christina's flat would be to draw battle lines. David said, 'Never mind your mother, do what you want.'

'How do I know what I want?' she muttered, trailing after him.

Her father turned, green, unreadable eyes like a snake's masked as usual by his glasses. 'It's a privilege,' he was saying pompously.

'What is?'

'University.'

'Why?' She really did want to know , but he turned away instead of explaining. Psychiatrists, she thought, were supposed to understand people. Perhaps he was right, and his impatience was all her fault. They had chicken and chips together at a cafe.

'Chicken's not fattening,' she said desperately.

'People have been known to starve on a diet of chicken.' The sarcasm brought tears to her eyes.

'I'm going to diet tomorrow.'

'Of course you are.'

She hated him.

'Pinching an inch?' inquired Jenny that evening, blonde, grey-eyed and slim as a reed.

'No,' snapped Hannah.

'It's Mum's awful cooking. You'll lose it like anything when you go,' said Jenny, meaning to comfort. 'You're not half as fat as you think.'

You're skinny and you belong. I'm fat and I don't. 'Do you think so?' Hannah said aloud.

'Positive,' said Jenny.

'You could at least try to be grateful,' David had said, irritated by the way she pushed food around on her plate when he'd paid for it. 'Everyone does their best. God knows, it's difficult.'

'I do try,' said Hannah.

'Do you?'

'I can't please anyone.'

'Can't, or won't?'

Hannah lifted her fists and uncurled fingers, one at a time, her voice flat. 'Mr Heydritch says I have an angry purity. Then he sends me away from his study and won't explain, because he wants to read the Bible. Mrs Heydritch says why don't I just cheer up and go for a ride on my bike? Jenny keeps saying I'll get skinny when I go away. You say I don't look too bad really and to take no notice of Mum.'

David listened with a face like stone.

'Where was I?'

'You needn't go on.'

'Yes, I should. Mum says, don't speak to you because that is letting her down. You say, come and visit us. But you won't listen if I tell you that, if I do, no one else in the family will speak to me. Not that anyone does. I haven't seen them for years, not since the twins went back to live with Mum, because you and Mum don't want us talking in case we find out things you don't want us to know. No one ever speaks Christina's name in case Mum drops dead, and you say it's up to me to try harder to know what I want.'

Hannah stopped, struck dumb by her outburst.

David's personal feelings and his psychiatrist's expertise fought each other plainly across his face. The psychiatrist won. 'You are bound to be angry . . .' he started, and all Hannah's fiery temper died, leaving her cold and dreary as a dawn grate '. . . and you owe me no filial debt.'

Hannah, beyond surprise, wondered what he thought he meant. Wendy Dawn Hobbs would have stuck two fingers up at him, but she was too much of a coward. She turned away, defeated.

'Of course I do,' she said.

"You make it very hard for me if you spend time over there. But please don't let me prevent you if that is what you want to do." wrote April. "And, remember, Sam Saul is very close to Christina, so your grandmother probably is, too."

In other words, thought Hannah, don't go near Sam and Bridie.They are not among the Allies. She tore the letter into tiny pieces and threw them down the lavatory. 'Is there anyone left I can talk to?' she cried, knowing everyone was out. 'Oh, damn you and damn you and damn you to hell!' She banged the seat down and pulled the chain, then sat dry-eyed and trembling on her bed with a half-packed suitcase at her feet. It would pass; it always did.

When the time came, she thanked the Heydritches politely for having her for two years.

'You're lucky. Another year of school! I don't know how I'm going to stand it,' Jenny complained.

Mrs Heydritch handed her a tiny velvet box and said, 'I had these made for you, so you can wear them and think of us. The stones are from an old brooch I had and they've set them nicely.' Hannah opened the box and found two little turquoise earrings pinned to green velvet. She tried to put them on but Mrs Heydritch in her short-sightedness hadn't noticed that her ears weren't pierced. The earrings were no use at all.

Going to university was farewell to all that. The college lay back from the Finchley Road, behind sloping green lawns edged with daisies, an easy walk from Hampstead Heath. It was a sprawling cluster of white columns, red brick walls, pretty arched passageways hung with wistaria leading to cobbled quadrangles. The English Department was a rambling house on the main road. On the first day of lectures Hannah climbed wide oak stairs to a room at the top, full of scarred desks. An elderly woman wrapped in a faded black gown sat waiting, reading, making notes in a margin, books and papers piled before her. Bent over her books, she had the look of a puffin with bright, close-set eyes and a great beak of a nose over a fine, sensitive mouth. She had interviewed Hannah and taken her in on the spot, despite the Head of Department's doubts about the history they'd had from her school.

'Come on in, child. Don't stand and dither.' Hannah stood in the doorway, hearing footsteps coming up the stairs behind her. 'You're in the right place,' said Miss Sheaffer kindly. The lecture room was otherwise empty, smelling of chalk and dust and ink and stale sweet scent. Miss Holmes was a challenge Miss Sheaffer was prepared to relish.

'Anglo-Saxon. Ever heard it?'

'It's dead,' said Hannah, taken aback. 'No one speaks it.'

'They still recite it,' Miss Sheaffer said haughtily. 'I have a tape I shall play, assuming some of you have chosen to listen.'

Girls in gowns settled into two short rows.

'All of you here?' demanded the lecturer, looking at a register. 'Should be twelve of you. Are there?'

'Yes,' said someone from the second row.

'Anyone read *Beowulf*?' she inquired hopefully.

No one had. They all opened their texts at the first page.

Emily Ryder watched Hannah's pencil move steadily down the text, following Miss Sheaffer's translations and interpretations with evident ease. Emily doodled idly on the corner of a page, a snaffle and bit on a Thurber horse; she came from a racing family in Newmarket who sent her to boarding school the moment she was out of nappies. Her mother, heaving a sigh of relief, climbed back on her racers and galloped, rejoicing, over the low Newmarket hills, out, to all intents and purposes, of Emily's life. Except for how much money it had cost, Hannah and Emily had a surprising amount in common.

Emily was a dainty, doe-eyed, black-haired, flawlessly pink-cheeked child in slacks, tweeds, and cashmere twin sets. She had a wholly superfluous and most prestigious college bursary. Hannah's county scholarship was worth more financially than Emily's, with none of its prestige. Miss Sheaffer was slyly pleased to see them sitting together, finding it suitable. Rivals and sisters under the skin, they took to each other instantly, and by the end of the first week were the firmest of friends.

Chapter Seventeen

'Pete Seeger was so romantic,' said Emily, wriggling her toes in front of Hannah's tiny gas fire, sighing blissfully. 'By the time he was half way through, he was holding my hand.'

'Pete Seeger was?' demanded Hannah sarcastically, though envious.

'Ken,' said Emily patiently. 'We were right up at the top, where you have to stand, and it was packed – absolutely packed – and you could hear a pin drop, and he started to sing and people joined in and were crying and Ken said in the interval he was a political refugee from South Africa, then he put his hand over mine on the railing, and it just sort of happened.'

'There are too many "he's". What just sort of happened?'

'Ken just sort of happened.'

'Oh. Do you mean . . . ?'

'He's got a flat in Swiss Cottage.'

Hannah felt cold.

'Your father's a doctor, isn't he?'

'Why?'

'I don't want to get pregnant.'

'He's not that kind of doctor, it's no use asking me.'

Worldly wise, a boarding school lass, Emily stared at

151

the little blue flames in the gas fire. 'He'd know, though, wouldn't he? Family planning clinics won't look at you unless you're married.'

'Won't they?'

'No. But there are places.'

The answer was obvious: Christina. It wasn't a train of thought Hannah was keen to follow.

'Go on,' wheedled Emily, 'you'll want to know for yourself anyway, won't you?'

'I definitely will not,' snapped Hannah.

'Your daughter is wanting contraceptives,' announced Christina several days later, 'so I sent her to Stockwell. I hope you don't object? She said it was for a friend. I don't know why she couldn't just ask.'

'Don't you?' said David.

Hannah lay on her back in bed, listening to morning sounds outside: girls' voices on their way to the dining hall, birds singing, and the occasional car accelerating up the slight hill. She tried to drift back into the dream but it was gone. Christina had written the address on a bit of paper, with a telephone number, and Emily had screwed up her courage and made an appointment. For today, thought Hannah, and longed to go back to sleep.

"Twinset and Pearls," they screeched afterwards, holding their sides and staggering down the Stockwell Road. It had been a revelation.

Mrs Twinset and Pearls, an elegant middle-aged woman, was breathtakingly out of place in a large, clean consulting room warmed by a hissing gas fire, over a shop that sold rubber appliances and surgical trusses.

She was kind and brisk and matter-of-fact. The room was cluttered with framed portraits of bald babies and adorable blonde toddlers.

'My grandchildren,' she boasted, bringing out a fourth rubber cap and stretching it gently between her fingers. 'This one might suit you. I'll show you how to try it.'

Mrs Twinset and Pearls was everything a mother ought to be and wasn't. She bowled them over. An hour later Emily chose a slimline model, having tried the lot.

'You keep it inside for eight hours afterwards,' Hannah heard Mrs Twinset and Pearls explaining through the half open door to the little cupboard of a trying-on room where she had ushered Emily.

'Yuk,' thought Hannah, crushing unspeakable jealousy.

Loneliness ached within her, a physical pain. Emily saw Ken every weekend, coming back radiant with love on Sunday evenings.

'You ought to get out. Join something.'

'You sound like an agony aunt,' Hannah snarled, as solitude closed in like a vice. 'Leave me alone.'

'You don't try,' answered Emily. 'It's your own fault. The world won't come knocking at your door, you know, and if you avoid people, they'll avoid you. You can't treat people like they've got the plague and expect to have friends.'

Bugger off, thought Hannah wretchedly.

Emily scolded and cajoled, invited her over, lent her her radio and her weekend rations.

'I'm fat,' said Hannah.

'You are,' agreed Emily cruelly, 'and if you got out

and ate less you'd lose it instead of just fussing about it. You get awfully boring, you know.'

Many months after the trip to Twinset and Pearls, Miss Sheaffer looked over the top of *Beowulf* at her Friday afternoon class, dozing in weak wintry light, stupefied by boredom and overheated radiators. She wondered who felt worse about Anglo-Saxon being timetabled for late Friday afternoon.

'You're all asleep,' she accused, 'and so am I. Go away, and come back next week prepared to stay awake.'

The class woke up, stunned.

'What brought that on?' whispered Emily, shutting her books with a bang. Hannah contemplated the weekend prematurely stretching away, empty.

'Miss Holmes, a word if you please.'

'What have you done?' asked Emily.

'I don't know.' Hannah went back into the empty lecture room.

'Can I help?' said Miss Sheaffer, without any pretence whatsoever. 'Is there anything at all I can do?'

'Is my work that bad?'

'Your work is excellent.'

'Then . . .'

'You don't look well. You look strained and tired. If you want to come and talk to me, my door is open to you.'

Hannah panicked. Miss Sheaffer never made overtures. A demanding, reclusive woman, rumour had it she'd once seen a unicorn. Her tenderness was terrifying.

'No, oh no, there's nothing . . .'

'Stay awake next week, then.'

Hannah ran.

'Miss Holmes?'

Anxiety knifed Hannah's chest.

'I've been looking over your work.'

'Yes?'

Miss Sheaffer gathered her gown and climbed off her stool. 'Go and write.'

Hannah looked hastily round. The room was empty. Miss Sheaffer had said what every one of them longed to hear; they all wanted to write, secretly not daring to try.

'I can't.'

'Yes, you can,' the lecturer said harshly. 'Go and write, Miss Holmes. Whatever it is, for goodness' sake go and write about it and get it off your chest.'

Emily hung over the bannisters. Her room was on the landing above Hannah's. 'What did she want? D'you want the radio?'

'Nothing. No,' cried Hannah, then her door banged shut with a crash.

'She doesn't exactly help herself, does she?'

Emily flounced back to her room. Hannah sat on her bed, shaking.

'Miss Holmes is unhappy,' observed Miss Sheaffer to the Principal in the Senior Common Room after dinner.

'Miss Holmes is a very vulnerable young woman.'

'Can we do anything?'

'I doubt it. I doubt she'd let us interfere. We can only keep an eye open.'

'She runs away.'

'Bright girl. It's a shame.'

'Should get a First. Won't,' said Miss Sheaffer sadly.

The Principal sipped her coffee and Miss Sheaffer kept her fears to herself.

*   *   *

Hannah lay as darkness fell, without a light. Across the road, college buzzed with Friday night life. Beyond the sloping gardens behind Hannah's house, the Finchley Road roared, clogged as cars headed out of Town for country weekends or into Town for theatres and restaurants, headlights shining. Hannah got to her feet like a sleepwalker, opened her cupboard door and took out the one bright dress inside, of crimson crepe. She twisted her long hair into a pile on the top of her head, drew black lines round her eyes, spat in the little box of black mascara, ladled it on and stood back to review the result. It would have to do.

Outside, a freezing January night watered her eyes into dark pools of mascara and she blew her nose. Traffic thinned out, the rush over. A kerb crawler slowed hopefully, peering up, his face a pasty blur under the streetlamps. Hannah caught a bus that passed the end of a street where there had been a party announced on a poster inside the college entrance. It was unlikely anyone she knew well would be there.

The smell of beer and smoke poured steamily from the basement door. The room rattled to the fast beat of a song on the record player. Hannah picked her way down the steps, over a mess of discarded bottles, into the roaring jam of bodies.

'Coat in the back room, darling. Just chuck it in,' someone yelled. 'Booze in the kitchen.'

Disordered heaps of coats and scarves in university and vet college colours warmed couples burrowed into the beds beneath. Hannah threw her own on top of them and followed the corridor to a kitchen covered in bottles. A very thin young man with dark hair and hairy wrists held one up to the light and squinted at it. 'Want some?' he asked, seeing a red dress in the doorway and someone with smudgy black eyes staring at him. He poured whisky into a used teacup and offered it.

'Glasses all gone. Sorry.'

Hannah took the cup, drank what was in it and shuddered.

The skinny vet filled his own mug from the bottle and waved it at her. 'other one?'

Hannah held out her cup.

'I'm Donald Ross,' he said gravely, pouring whisky until the cup was nearly full.

'I'm Hannah Holmes.'

'Dance?' He waved vaguely at the passage, full of people standing, sitting, lying, sliding half way between the two.

'Queue,' he observed owlishly, 'for the bog. End of corridor, brown door with hole in it.'

'A hole?'

'Fight. Someone's foot,' he explained. 'Don't know what for.'

Hannah swirled the whisky in her cup, detesting the smell of it. A girl with black hair down to her waist pushed past and picked up bottles quickly, shaking them. 'Bloody run out,' she said. 'Someone'll have to go out.'

'Keg's still going,' the thin student said cheerfully.

'I hate beer. Who'll go before they shut?'

He shrugged. 'Hannah won't, will you, Hannah. Just got here.'

The girl looked at the crowded stairs. 'I suppose I'll have to,' she said, sounding cross.

'Someone'll bring some,' offered the vet. Hannah

edged towards the door, hoping the bad-tempered girl would think she had tea in her cup.

'You go,' demanded the girl. They seemed to know each other well.

Hannah slid round the door and squeezed into the crowd, tripping over legs. Lonnie Donnegan sang of seven golden daffodils and someone threw up at the far end of the passage, to shouts and banging on the broken door.

'Lost you. Julia's gone to get some wine.'

Hannah felt his hands on her waist and his breath on her neck as he reached round and put the whisky bottle on the mantelpiece over a big unlit gasfire. Her head swam as his arms slid round her, and they began to sway gently backwards and forwards in time to the music.

'You from down the road?' he breathed into her ear.

'Women's college.'

'Thought so.'

'Why?' His hands fumbled at her red dress, running up and down her back. He laughed 'Oh, ladylike,' he mumbled, making fun of her. Hannah reached past and found her teacup empty. 'Knock it back,' he remarked, pouring. He tipped the bottle to his mouth. Hannah giggled, her head floating. People came and went in a curious sort of way and she clung to Donald Ross who pulled her close and began removing her hairpins, scattering them on the floor. Her hair tumbled free.

'Lovely,' he murmured.

'Booze,' hissed Julia. 'Don't tell them or they won't leave any. It's in the pantry.'

'Oh,' moaned Hannah a little later.

'Shit!' muttered Donald, pulling her towards the door, battling the dead weight of clinging, dancing, lurching bodies who didn't care and wouldn't get out of the way. Hannah turned towards the front door.

'Fresh air'll make it worse.' He dragged her by the hand, up the stairs. 'Lie down's best.' The walls spun and so did her stomach as she fell into a warm heap of blankets.

'You OK?' Donald swayed over her, his shadow long and spidery on the ceiling. 'Get out,' he shouted, and the door, which had inched open, closed again hurriedly.

'This is my room,' he confided drowsily, collapsing on to his knees on the bed and snuggling up beside her. Hannah felt him gradually undo the long zip of her dress, and his exploring hands. 'That's like stroking a cat,' she heard herself say, 'it's nice.'

'Scared, kitten?'

'Not scared,' denied Hannah.

'I feel like death,' she muttered feebly the next morning.

'You don't look so good either,' remarked Donald, keeping his own head very still.

'I've never got drunk before. It's horrible.'

'I thought it was pretty nice, myself. Didn't you?' He forgot his agony and half sat up to look at her.

'I'll never drink again.'

'Not the whisky.' He grinned and pulled her dress from the floor under the bed. She was conscious of the rough blanket against her skin and flushed scarlet.

'You don't remember, do you?'

She shook her head and cried, 'Ouch!'

'You are sweet.'

Hannah's mouth was dry. His dark, curly hair fell in his eyes. 'Oh, Lord, and I thought you were kidding.'

'Why would I lie about that?'

'Women sometimes do. I'm sorry.' He had very composed, self-possessed hazel eyes, a very direct look. He was quite nice-looking, really.

'I don't tell lies.'

'I've said I'm sorry. We were both drunk.' They lay side by side on the narrow bed. Mid-morning light crept round the edge of the curtains.

'It's what I wanted. It wasn't your fault.'

'Did you?'

'Yes.'

She edged away from him and he turned on his side. 'Would you like,' he asked gently, 'an aspirin, a mug of coffee, a bath and a walk on Hampstead Heath?'

'I've got no clothes and it's freezing.'

'Julia'll lend you some, and I've got a parka you can borrow.' He lay back on the pillow, his profile beautiful in the shady light. 'Go on, you can't just get up and disappear.' She thought about Emily and Ken; this is how it was, then.

'Julia is my sister,' he said, misinterpreting her silence.

'I suppose I'd better go and see Mrs Twinset and Pearls,' she said faintly, half amused, half desperate with disappointment.

'What?'

'Twinset and Pearls. A joke. Where's your aspirin?'

'In the bathroom.'

'With the broken door.'

'I'll stand guard.'

'It's only ten minutes by bus. I could go back.'

'I'll take you later.' Donald threw back the blankets and shivered, naked. He lit a gas fire and the flames spluttered and hissed until the fire glowed red. Hannah felt the heat on her face and watched his strange, loose, bony body wrap itself in a thick, dark blue dressing gown. 'We're quite civilised, really, once the peasants have gone.'

'I've never seen a man with no clothes on.'

'You have now, darling.' He did up his belt and brought her some aspirin.

Bathed, breakfasted and huddled in his parka and college scarf, she walked the Heath with him under a faint, cold sun that went down by three o'clock, leaving last night's frost still crisp under their feet. He talked and she listened, breath pluming on the bitter air. They marched briskly, clapping their hands to keep warm under leafless trees hanging still as stone. There was thick ice on the Ponds.

'I'll drop your things back,' she said at the turning that led up to her house. 'Tell Julia I said thank you for lending them.'

'Can I see you again?' With her cheeks bright with cold, the clown's make-up washed off and shining hair in a pony tail, wrapped in his scarf, she wasn't half bad-looking. She looked down at her feet and didn't answer, then up at him again.

'You've got the saddest eyes I've ever seen,' said Donald, taking both her gloved hands in his, 'a bit like a cow in labour.'

'Thanks!'

'I like cows.'

Hannah felt his hands tighten on her own, and fear wormed its treacherous way around her heart.

'Stupid cow, you mean,' she said. 'But all right.'

'Thanks.'

She saw she had provoked him. 'I didn't mean . . .' She never knew how to put things right.

'Look, I've liked being with you and I'd like to see you again. But you don't have to.'

'Twinset and Pearls time,' said Hannah bleakly, 'and if you would like to come up, I'm in that one.' She pointed down the slope of the road to her house. 'In the room straight ahead of you at the top of the stairs.'

Donald let go of her hands, puzzled.

'If you're sure, I'll be round.'

'Will you fetch the clothes you've lent me? Or shall I bring them?'

'It'll be an excuse to see you.'

Hannah beat her hands together in the bitter half dark as he hurried away. She shivered in her unheated room, dark and cold as a tomb. With numb fingers she put a shilling in the gas meter and lit the fire.

Emily came home with a packet of crumpets, a half pound of butter and some strawberry jam. When she looked in her cupboard and saw nothing touched, and her radio where she had left it, she ran down to Hannah's room where a bar of light was showing under the door.

'Toast, with Ken's sister-in-law's strawberry jam,' she cried, bursting in. 'Have you been out?'

'It's fattening. But bring it in, anyway.'

They sat on the floor, eating the crumpets. Hannah fitted the last one on the toasting fork, her hands red in the fireglow.

'I'd better go and see Mrs Twinset and Pearls,' she said blandly.

Emily stopped in mid-mouthful. 'Good gracious! I thought you were waiting for wedding bells. Anyone I know?'

'More a case of someone I don't know,' said Hannah.

Chapter Eighteen

'If you ask me,' observed Emily, filling the coffee percolator from the bathtap, raising her voice for the entire house to hear, 'what you'll end up with is a dose of something very unpleasant.'

'At least we know where the special clinic is,' said Hannah nastily, 'after your little escapade in the summer.'

'That was only a fling.' Emily held the coffee pot in front of her defensively as if to ward off the words.

Hannah giggled. 'All round the Mediterranean with a belly-dancing troupe! You could have got a lot worse than the . . .'

'. . . and you,' interrupted Emily angrily, 'are making a habit of it, and it's stupid.' Her engagement ring caught the light as she waved the coffee pot, spilling water, and Hannah's heart went out of the row. Emily had Ken to come back to. That was the difference.

'What do you suggest, then?' she asked listlessly.

'I don't think you should be . . .' Emily hesitated.

'Cheap?'

Emily shrugged unhappily and balanced the percolator on the little gas ring above Hannah's fire. 'You said it.'

'Maybe I'm a pearl without price.'

'It's the price I'm worried about, even if you aren't. I'm concerned for you.'

'I haven't caught anything.'

'I don't mean just that. I mean at what you're doing to yourself.'

Hannah tried to laugh. 'I counted up the other day,' she said, 'and twenty-two men have asked me to marry them. I've slept with nearly all of them and turned them all down. What do you want me to do? Marry someone I don't like?'

'You could stop sleeping with people you don't like.'

'Is that what I'm doing? I thought I did like them, only not enough to marry them.'

'Get your head examined,' snapped Emily.

Hannah stared at her oddly. 'That's exactly what my father would say.'

'Perhaps he's right.'

'He's always right, haven't I told you?'

'You've told me. It's nearly ready.' Emily lifted the lid of the percolator and a tiny jet of coffee flew out. 'Not quite.'

'It used to be, "Oh, do get out and stop moping," and now it's, "Oh, do stay in and stop gadding." Make your mind up!'

'I don't think I use people.'

'Meaning I do?'

'Sometimes. You do use men, Hannah, and you go around absolutely asking them to use you. And I don't think you should do that.'

Hannah went very white.

'I'm sorry,' said Emily.

The smell of roasted coffee filled the bedsit. Hannah looked vaguely at her desk in the corner, piled with papers, revision not done, Finals only weeks away. Miss Sheaffer had sent a card, saying, "Keep up the good work" and it lay face down, burdening Hannah with her tutor's affection.

'I only say it because I like you. People do care about you, you know.'

'I can't think why.'

'You are full of self-pity.'

'Not self-pity.'

'It comes over like that.'

'Self-loathing.'

'Well, you hide it well, then, because to the rest of us it feels like it's us you're rejecting, and we don't know what we've done.' Emily poured coffee into two mugs.

'You haven't done anything.'

'I sometimes wonder if that's the trouble.'

'What on earth do you mean?' Hannah asked after an embarrassed pause.

'Someone ought to look after you, because you don't do it for yourself.'

'Who took you and me to Twinset and Pearls?' cried Hannah indignantly.

'Oh, Hannah,' yelled Emily, at her wits' end, 'there's more to life than that.'

Hannah thrust her face very close to Emily's. 'Is there? Well, I haven't found it yet, and I only know one way to look, so you go and have your nice wedding and buy your nice house and have some nice children and leave me alone.'

'We don't want to leave you alone . . .' began Emily.

'We? Who's we? Who else is in this?'

'It's not a conspiracy.'

'It sounds amazingly like one.'

Emily put her mug in the hearth. 'A lot of people care about you, but you use them, Hannah. If you go on the way you are, don't come to me looking for help, that's all, because one day you're going to need it.'

'I think you'd better get out.'

The coffee boiled dry on the ring and later, girls' voices drifted past below the window, signalling supper time. Where do I go so wrong? Hannah asked herself, over and over again, until her head ached. Emily didn't come back, and anyway Hannah couldn't ask her. In the end she shelved the question, as she always did, too worn out to find the answer.

Chapter Nineteen

The Easter vacation before Finals brought, as always, the problem of where to stay while college was closed. On the last day of term Hannah piled untouched revision into a suitcase on top of some clothes and sat on the lid to force it shut. Then she opened it again and rummaged for a scrap of paper with an address on it.

'Where's Maida Vale?'

Emily knew and could even tell her the number of the bus.

'Whose room are you borrowing?'

'One of last year's lot. She's going somewhere or other for her job for a couple of weeks and she said she wouldn't mind the rent. So I said I'd have it. It'll tide me over.'

'I could kill your parents, not making sure you've got somewhere to go. You'd think your dad would, living so near.'

'It's partly my fault. Sometimes I wish I did like that woman, just to spite my mother.'

'Everything in your family comes with a price tag, doesn't it?'

'At least there's one person who doesn't think I make it all up.'

'Make them up?' cried Emily. 'You'd do better to

write a novel, only no one would believe them.'

'They are unbelievable, aren't they?' said Hannah, depressed, but Emily began to giggle.

David and Christina had given a Christmas party the previous December and sent an invitation. Hannah, born at Christmas, invited Emily. 'Come and help me make those rotters sing "Happy Birthday".'

'Are you sure?'

Brittle and adamant, Hannah had insisted, so they went dressed to kill and fortified by sips of Emily's sherry, left over from a summer trip to Spain.

'We look brilliant,' cried Emily, vamping down the stairs. 'Look at you. Mud in his eye.' She offered Hannah the bottle over the bannisters, down from her little landing.

'Do you think we've overdone it?'

'Definitely,' Emily said gleefully.

They looked like a couple of hopefuls from the Kings Road, all peacock blue, crimson and false feathers, Elizabeth Taylor eyes blacked solid with spit and cake mascara. They swayed on winkle-pickered feet into David's tiny, crowded flat, past an elderly surgeon who was charged with answering the door. He ushered them in, astonished, and took their coats as Christina came through the crush from her kitchen, carrying a candle for the sitting-room coffee table, to gleam among crystal glasses and flatter the complexions of doctor's wives, who chattered and smiled and sipped in the best of all possible taste. Shielding it with her hand, her face lit softly, she bent seriously over the flame, a calm and lovely madonna.

'Oi.'

Beyond the candlelight, Christina saw nightmare visions in her hall.

'We're here,' cried Hannah. 'Where's Dad?'

Christina stood, her fingers curled around the heavy glass base of her candlestick, and curbed an urge to throw it.

'Your father's in the lounge.' Christina sounded grim.

'This is Emily,' Hannah announced.

'Through there.' Christina waved with her guttering candle. 'You'd better go and find him.'

'My friend from college.'

'And get yourself a drink.'

'I think we are persona non grata,' murmured Emily, stifling hysteria.

'Hello, Emily.' Christina caught the eye of the surgeon and recovered herself. 'Do go along through.'

Their heels left pock marks in the cheap carpet and people asked each other, with amusement, 'Who . . . ?' Seeing them, David froze in mid- sentence. 'Excuse me,' he said to his consultant, looking round for Christina, hoping she would head them off.

'Daddy!' cried Hannah, and every head in the room turned. The murmur died.

'I didn't know you had . . .' The consultant looked Hannah up and down appreciatively. 'Is the other one yours as well?'

'No,' said David, 'this is my daughter.'

The buzz of voices swelled again with fresh enthusiasm. David grabbed Hannah smartly by the elbow. 'In my study.'

She turned to Emily. 'And this is my . . .'

'How nice to meet you. My wife will look after you.'

'Wife?' Hannah stiffened. David hustled her through

the crush away from Emily, into his study off the hall with its creaky wooden floor, leaning on the door when he'd closed it. 'What on earth do you think you're doing?'

'Coming to your party. Wife?'

'I thought I could trust you.'

Hannah lowered her eyes deliberately and stared at the carpet.

'What do you think you look like?'

She picked at her backcombing. 'Much the same as practically everyone else.'

He stared at her shoes.

'Everyone wears them.'

'After all the effort we made to buy decent shoes.'

'At least they'll be my bunions, not yours.'

'It's not just how you look. Those people are my colleagues, and it's taken me years to pick up my career after your mother . . . she wanted to destroy me and she very nearly did.'

'It's my birthday.'

'Yes.'

'You haven't said anything.'

'Happy birthday.'

'Not so far. No one has sent a card. Why do you suddenly care what I look like?'

He drummed his fingers on the door behind him.

'You look vulgar. So does the girl you've brought.'

'You can go anywhere in London and see people like us. It's fashionable. What's it to you?'

'You embarrass me.'

'I embarrass everyone.'

'Hannah, please will you be discreet at least?'

'What about?'

'Christina.'

'You've never gone and got married?' Bigamy? Was that what the fuss was about? She brightened.

'Look, people think we're married. To get a registrar's post . . . oh, you wouldn't know about all that. Would you say Christina's your stepmother, and can you get your friend to be discreet? I wish you hadn't brought her without asking.'

'You want me to pretend I haven't got a mother, and she's her?'

David winced. 'I thought you were reading English.'

'Is that it?'

'Yes.'

'What is supposed to have happened to my real mother?'

'No job, no maintenance, Hannah. When you see April, you could try pointing out that if she didn't expect so much, I could . . .'

'Don't try and make me your go-between,' Hannah said bitterly. 'I've had enough of that. You know perfectly well I'm a pariah because you both want everyone on your own rotten side and I don't knuckle under. You both use me.'

David was deaf. 'I wish you didn't dislike Christina. She's in a very difficult position.'

'What kind of position do you think I'm in? Look how you ignore what I say.'

'I keep meaning to talk to you, but you appear out of the blue and then you disappear again. It's you, too, you know. You make it very hard.'

'Talk.' Snorted Hannah. 'When I want a psychiatrist, I'll get one for myself.'

'I think . . .' began David furiously.

'Do you say she's dead?'

'What?'

'Do you tell people she's dead?'

'She won't divorce me. I have begged and grovelled. What can I do?'

'*She* begged and grovelled when you had what she wanted. You're evens.'

'You haven't the faintest idea.'

'How would you know if I had?'

'This is hardly appropriate just now.'

'Was I ever appropriate?'

'Come back and we'll talk when I'm not in the middle of a party.'

'I'm very inappropriate, aren't I?'

'I don't think it helps . . .'

'Of course not. Fancy your daughter being a highly educated tart. Most inappropriate.'

He paled. Hannah examined her fingernails.

'I think . . .'

'No,' she said tightly, 'I wouldn't want to embarrass you and my poor wicked stepmother any more than I already have, and Emily's much too nice to want to upset anyone, so we'll just get our coats.'

'There's no need for neurotic . . .'

'I would hate to embarrass you,' she hissed viciously, 'by standing up and saying, "Listen, everyone, what we have here is the real whore, with a curtain ring on her finger . . ."'

She bit off her words as he smacked her face.

'Get out!' He pushed her violently towards the door and she twisted free, throwing his hand off savagely.

'You think I'd stay?'

Hannah took Emily by the hand. 'Come along,' she said in a little girl voice, 'we have to go.' Emily held her glass up to the candlelight. 'I've met this really nice doctor,' she protested.

'We have to go.'

'Oh.' Emily put down her glass and smiled at the man beside her. 'We have to go. Sorry.'

'What the hell . . . ?' she demanded outside in the damp and dark, pulling her coat around her.

Hannah told her.

'Bloody hell,' said Emily, shaken, 'what a pig. We did have to go.'

'Oink, oink,' shrieked Hannah. Emily put an arm round her shoulders, hugging her close, trying to warm both of them. 'They aren't all like that. Try and forget it.'

'Do you know what?'

'Go on.'

Hannah hesitated. 'The only time I forget to hurt is when I'm asleep or with a man.'

'I don't know what to say.'

'But do you see?' she said bleakly. 'Every time you go on at me . . .'

Emily, at last, did. 'I'm sorry,' she said.

'I hurt all the time like I did in there just now.'

'Have you thought about seeing a doctor?'

'I have. He told me to go to parties and get out, have fun. So I did.'

'That's why you suddenly upped and offed.'

'And he gave me sleeping pills like my mother's.'

Emily shivered. Darkness lay behind the bright lights of Hampstead. 'Chips,' she cried, 'let's get a huge bag of chips and stuff ourselves. And tea. Come on.'

'Fattening.'

'Don't be a drag, tinribs,' yelled Emily, dancing on

the kerb for warmth. Somewhere further up the road lights changed and the traffic stopped, headlamps dulled and diffused by drizzle. Emily shot across the road, dragging Hannah after her.

Inside the fish and chip shop was warm and steamy and bright with bluish neon light. Salt and vinegar stood in big brown shakers on top of a pile of cut newspaper. They gobbled hot chips before the vinegar soaked away.

'Better?' Emily asked, licking her fingers.

'Yes, much.'

They went back to the counter for seconds, and the chippy grinned and gave them generous scoops, a big wink over the greasy counter top, and a saveloy slipped in for free.

'Thinking about it, you're better off in Maida Vale. Can you stay there the whole vac?' asked Emily.

'Yes.'

'It's funny, you know,' she said, helping shut the case.

'What is?'

'When we're here, day in, day out, you can get on my nerves something rotten, but when I'm at home, I miss you.'

'Don't talk as though it's already over.'

'Only one more term. Won't you be lonely, all by yourself in some room? Why don't you come home with me?'

'Thanks, but I can't.'

'Yes, you can. I'm asking you.'

'I can't.'

'Please yourself.'

'I'm sorry.'

They parted stiffly, half resentful, Emily rejected, Hannah too frightened to go with her. Newmarket was full of fresh-faced, jolly people in outdoor clothes. Emily's mother ran her household like one universal horsebox and had hardly noticed Hannah the summer she had gone to stay, filling her with agonising anxiety. Why am I so bloody scared that I can't go? she wondered wretchedly, knowing that one day Emily would give up on her. One more term and it would be over. They'd go their separate ways.

'Where will I go?' she asked the empty room.

Maida Vale, for now. She picked up her case.

The bus was nearly empty. Hannah climbed upstairs and sat in the front, to look out at trees newly mantled with bright leaves and heavy pink blossom. People hurried in a chilly spring wind full of petals.

'Will you tell me my stop?'

The conductor nodded dourly, bored. 'Supposed to leave that case downstairs.'

'I don't want it nicked.'

'. . . keep an eye . . .' he mumbled, lurching as the driver changed gear jerkily for lights.

'I'll give you a hand getting off.'

Hannah and the conductor turned. A dark-haired man, probably in his thirties, sat four rows back behind Hannah. They were the only people on the top deck. The conductor shuffled back towards the stairs, whistling between his teeth, indifferent.

'Shall I come down?'

'If you like.'

He sat beside her and she saw out of the corner of her eye that he was long and lean and had an air of being alert and relaxed all at once. His hands lay on his knees – fine, strong, bony fingers with very short, clean nails, quite calloused.

'We're getting off at the same stop.'

'Oh.'

'D'you live round here?'

'Hampstead.'

'Lovely day.'

'Yes, isn't it. Sort of.'

She was proving hard work, but he studied the delightful curve of her high cheeks, russet skin and wide, wary eyes, and persevered.

'I'm on my way to work,' he said, flexing his fingers.

'What do you do?'

'First violin. BBC Symphony Orchestra.'

Hannah looked at his beautiful fingers and imagined them dancing and flying over the strings. He slid his hand into his breast pocket and brought out a scrap of paper.

'It's our stop in a minute,' he said. 'I don't know whether you've got anything on this evening, but if you haven't, you might like this.' He put it into the warm palm of her hand and curled her fingers around it before she could look. 'Take it,' he said, and hefted her case, ready to get off.

He left her standing by the side of the road. Hannah sighed, picked up the heavy caseful of books and set off.

The room was claustrophobic and fusty. She sat on the single bed and gazed out of a greasy grey window on to a bit of next door's roof and guttering. There was an elaborate television aerial tied to a chimney. She stared at it for a long time, then sat and contemplated possibilities. There was nowhere to cook or eat, nothing to do, and she had hardly any money. Kicking her case idly with one foot, she leaned back against the wall and sat perfectly still while loneliness wormed through her, so wretchedly familiar it was almost a comfort.

Early evening traffic and hunger woke her up. Going through her purse to count what little was in there, she found the violinist's ticket to that evening's performance in the BBC studios.

The spring vacation was short, barely four weeks. They spent every day together when he wasn't rehearsing, and she went to all his concerts. Half way through the second week, she said he could stay. Sebastian brought his violin back to the tiny room and stood in the doorway. 'We can't have a honeymoon here,' he said decidedly. 'I'll find somewhere else.'

'You have to be married to have a honeymoon,' snapped Hannah, rebuffed.

'I am,' he said calmly.

'What the hell are you doing standing in my bedroom, then?'

'Hoping to make love to you, but maybe you'll mind too much, and we won't.'

Hannah put her hands on her hips, outraged. 'Do you always tell a girl you're married just before you ask her to go to bed with you?'

'I don't often ask girls to go to bed with me,' he said evenly. 'But I'm asking you and it bothers me that I don't quite know why. The minute I saw you . . . I don't know, I can't explain it and I can't justify it. You're special,' he ended lamely, completely sincere.

'I'm special, all right,' she muttered bitterly. 'I should go, if I was you.'

'I can't make love to you for the first time in a hole like this. I'll take you somewhere I know. It's private.'

'What about your wife?'

'What about my wife?'

'Won't she wonder where you are?'

'Yes, but she's used to it. Sometimes I'm away for months, if we do a big tour.'

'But you're not on tour.'

'I love you.' He hadn't put down his violin. 'Shall we go? Or shall I go away and not come back?'

'I'm not used to choices,' she said.

The hotel stood back from a lane, enclosed on three sides by tall poplars. Beyond the trees was absolute darkness, unseen countryside, no light except stars.

'Where are we?'

'You'll see.'

She followed him speechlessly, clutching her things in a carrier bag. 'I can't go in there,' she hissed, ashamed. 'However much does this cost?'

The bellboy's mouth twitched and she crimsoned.

'Couldn't you leave your violin in the car?' she snapped, to cover her shame.

'No.'

'Stupid, taking it everywhere.'

'No, not at all stupid. It's precious.'

They came to the top of the stairs and her legs turned to lead at his words. She was lost and homesick for a home she didn't have and wanting, after so many years, to cry and cry and cry. She stood, stuck and desperate, looking back down the dimly lit stairwell.

'Darling?' He came back and put the violin case down at his feet.

Hannah's eyes swam. 'I can't,' she whispered, frantic with shame, hiding from the bellboy's impassive back. Sebastian put his arms around her and said in her ear, 'Then don't, my love.'

'I want to be precious,' she wept.

'But you are, I mean it,' he said. 'You're safe.'

'Ah! Norfolk, I love it,' he said, breathing deeply. They walked in flat fields, an Easter sun on their faces, breathing sweet cold air from the fens. 'The sea isn't far. Would you like to drive over?'

She shook her head.

'You want to go back, don't you?'

'I'm terribly, terribly sorry.'

'Stop that.'

'What?'

'Apologising.'

'Sebastian?'

He walked on beside her.

'Why do you love me?'

'I fell in love with you on the bus.'

'Why?'

'You had the saddest eyes I'd ever seen.'

'People keep telling me that. You like sad eyes?'

'I'm a sucker for beautiful, broken things. I have a basement full of violins I mend when I've got time. There's something about making them sing again . . . I thought I might make you smile.'

'You made me cry. I wanted to cry.'

'I know. I couldn't keep on doing that.'

They drove back to London. He stopped the car at the corner of the road and she could see the house with her bleak little room. She needed to explain.

'No,' he said sharply, 'I told you not to do that. I'll think of you and I'll play for you, and I'll never see you again because otherwise we'll go on hurting each other, and my wife, and there would be no end to it.'

'I wish my parents could do that.'

'Someone else will love you.'

She shook her head and he drove away.

'You what?' squeaked Emily. 'You're making it up. Those things don't happen.'

'They do, and I met a decent man. What's so odd about that?'

'Given your track record,' answered Emily unkindly, 'quite a lot. Let's hope it lasts.'

Hannah dreamed often about Sebastian, whose hands flew over violin strings like moth's wings and had touched her with love. In May, Finals came and passed in a fever, then suddenly it was over. Summer loomed, long and empty and purposeless, with no new term at the end of it.

'What are you going to do, Miss Holmes?' inquired Miss Sheaffer in the last week but one, when there was nothing to do but sit on the lawns and stare at the tops of the trees.

'I don't know.'

'You could try elsewhere for research.'

Hannah had been avoiding the subject, knowing the Professor had put his foot down. She'd assumed he didn't like her, which hurt after three years.

'She's not doing research in my department, I won't have her,' Professor Twentyman said, and he stuck by it, despite all Miss Sheaffer and her supporters could do.

'I'll supervise her,' she had offered, 'and Dr Williams would be her director of studies if we asked her nicely, I know she would.'

'All that Anglo-Saxon doom and gloom would finally push her over whatever edge it is she's been hanging on all this time, can't you see that?' said Professor Twenty-man irritably, thinking that Miss Sheaffer might try climbing out of Grendel's mother's pit occasionally and facing up to the realities of life. 'Stick that child in some library all day with the *Dream of the Rood* and you'll have a neurotic on your hands, and nowhere to put her. She's unstable enough without us helping her along. She needs a proper job and the discipline of everyday life. In any case, she'd drive me potty,' he added for good measure.

Miss Sheaffer thought it over and admitted he was right. But she couldn't resist one last effort, standing over Hannah, throwing her into shadow on the daisy strewn grass.

'I don't think for one moment I'll get a First,' Hannah said, looking up and shading her eyes, 'and I don't think I'd get a grant without one.'

Miss Sheaffer bit back the 'Nonsense'' that rose to her lips and let the lame excuse lie.

'I'll miss you,' she said abruptly. 'You have your moments, but you've been a joy to teach. You should have done research. Go and grow up, and then write when you're older.' She stomped away up the slope, a crusty old woman with what some called vision.

Miss Sheaffer didn't know the half of it, thought Hannah dismally. She had nowhere to live, no job, no plans, nothing. Something heavy weighed her down every time she tried to get going, and with every day that came and went, the weight got heavier and her purpose weaker. For her, there was neither Professor Twenty-man's discipline nor his ordinary life; she seemed unable to make them happen, she had no experience of such things. It looked very much to Hannah as if she had no future at all.

Chapter Twenty

Emily got married in a froth of white lace and orange blossom, followed by a rowdy reception and staggering quantities of champagne. The sun shone upon her and the gods smiled over the flat brown curves of Newmarket hills. She seemed truly blessed. Among the untidy heaps of present wrappings and tissue paper, discarded stockings and silken underwear, lay the self-addressed envelope posted by Professor Twentyman when the Finals results came through.

'An Upper Second? That's splendid, darling. Pink or pale pink varnish?' Her mother examined the tiny bottles, more used to polishing horses' hooves, then looked out of the window at caterers carrying silver dishes into the marquee. 'I hope they're careful with that cake.'

Emily sighed and cupped her chin in her hands, staring at her own perfect reflection. 'It's bloody brilliant. It's mean of her not to come. Everyone else has.'

'Who, dear?' cried her mother, triumphantly pouncing on a tiny bottle of lollipop pink.

'Hannah.'

'Oh, yes. Shame. What sort of degree did she get?'

'I don't know.'

'Well, you've done awfully well, darling. Now, hold still,' said her mother.

Emily held still.

'What a shame, but you never could really stick at things, could you?' said David, reading Hannah's note from Professor Twentyman. 'You should have got a First. A Lower Second won't get you far in the academic world, I'm afraid, so what will you do?'

Thick white coffee cups lay before them, white scum congealing on their cold contents. Lyons Café clattered and chattered around them on the corner of Marble Arch, and beyond the windows traffic crawled past.

'I've got the same room I had at Easter.'

'I meant, what will you do about a job?'

Listlessly she pushed grains of sugar around on the formica top. 'I know someone whose uncle works in the BBC. I thought I'd ask about that.'

David's expression relaxed. 'Ah, now then,' he said with a rare show of enthusiasm, 'if you can get into the BBC you'd be doing very well indeed.'

She wouldn't give him the satisfaction of knowing it was a low grade, temporary clerical post, which was just as well because it was a disaster. She couldn't concentrate. Every time the phone went, her mouth dried up and her hands shook and the simplest things became intractable muddles. 'She's a graduate,' someone said, 'makes you wonder, doesn't it?' The next day, she couldn't get up and missed work. The following week she missed twice.

'I don't really think this suits you, does it?' said the supervisor.

'I haven't been well, I get pains,' Hannah protested, desperate to stay.

The woman looked doubtful. 'You'd better get a

doctor's note. You can't just take time off without a reason.'

'Pain is a reason, isn't it?'

'Depends what's causing them. You'll have to get a note.'

She went back to her job, sorting piles of application forms to join the BBC Club, to process and file them and send out coloured cards for different types of membership. 'You'd have thought,' she said frantically to herself, hiding in the lavatory, 'that a person with an English degree could manage this.' But at the end of the week they suggested, quite nicely, that she would do better to leave. The next day she couldn't get up again, for pain, and after that she never went back.

The rent needed paying, though she could do without food. She took the supervisor's advice. In the doctor's waiting room she looked at magazines without seeing them. Patients sat meekly on wooden chairs around the wall, neatly arranged, trying to cough quietly. The clock on the wall ticked louder and louder. She began to sweat, feeling every eye on her, the magazine slipping from damp hands, skin prickling as if her hair were standing on end. The receptionist glanced up at the bang of the door. 'Well, some people!' she said.

In her coffinlike room she lay face down on the crumpled magazine until, after a while, the panic passed. Open on her pillow, the situations vacant page had a long list of vacancies for nannies. First on the list was in Switzerland, near the Italian border. Three children, good rates, generous time off, holidays St Moritz and the Riviera, live as family. Hannah stared at the words. Live as family. She posted an application an hour later.

Someone who called herself Hannah Holmes, and

who looked just like her, went to an interview in Cadogan Square, produced references as to character from impeccable sources and was offered the job. It all happened quickly. The day the first-class tickets arrived to take her by train to Lugano, she had no money left at all, not even enough for a stamp to let Emily know she was going. It no longer seemed to matter.

By the end of her first month Hannah mentally rechristened Mrs Twitchett, Mrs Twerp. The Twerps lived rich, spoiled, bored lives in a marble-floored mansion overlooking Lake Como. They had three beautiful rich, spoiled, bored children, though Hannah thought if they'd been less rich and allowed to go and play with others, they'd be very pleasant children. Hannah, surrounded by wealth, was bored almost to death. Listening in for the children while the Twerps went out, even though she was supposed to be off duty, she faced the fact that she bored herself. Pain became leaden boredom, constant, to be lived with like a gross deformity that no one could see. The setting sun flushed the Swiss sky blood red, turning the lake to bronze, fading colours into nightfall over trees shedding the last leaves of autumn.

She wondered in terror if there were such things as the living dead and if perhaps one night her eyes would turn yellow and her teeth grow and Mrs Twerp would fall down dead of fright at finding a vampire in Nanny's room. Hannah felt her teeth furtively; it was silly, mere fantasy. But some unknown something inside her breathed shallowly into life and said in a strong whisper that such things might be so and walk upon the Earth. Hannah leapt up from the dark place on the verandah where she was sitting, dashed inside and switched on all the lights.

'Don't be so bloody stupid,' she hissed at herself in the silent house, remembering that even the servants were out, 'or you'll make yourself go mad thinking about going mad. Stop it.' When the Twerps got home at midnight, she was watching Swiss television.

'I didn't think you spoke German, dear,' commented Mrs Twerp, who had once been a hairdresser with classic bone structure that had for a brief while caught Mr Twerp's eye, which everyone knew was presently focused elsewhere. She clacked across the marble floor, shedding bits of fur and chiffon between the front door and the drinks tray.

'I got O-level.'

Mrs Twerp, momentarily touching base on reality, eyed her nanny over the rim of a glass. 'What's a clever girl like you doing this for?'

Hannah rummaged in her memory for the excuse she'd invented for her interview.

'I got tired of life,' she said.

The glaze settling over Mrs Twerp's eyes cracked for a second.

'Academic life, I mean,' said Hannah.

Chapter Twenty-One

Guilio's was busy. The end of a mild March found almost all the snow gone from the top of the mountains and Hannah and Sasha, a Dutch au pair, in the nightclub, both with the weekend off.

'*Tu sei romantica . . .*' crooned the brilliantined little singer in his shiny black trousers and a splendid, velvet-collared DJ. His voice drifted with the cigarette smoke over noisy customers, shrill-voiced with excitement, having a good time. Giulio packed them round tables like sardines; predatory men whose liquid eyes darted and slithered caressingly over lithe, bronze-haired women, tanned from skiing. It was like watching a Fellini picture, all the characters on the prowl for each other. Hannah caught the gaze of a man sitting half-hidden by his wife's black silk bulges. Dense smoke diffused light from candles in chianti bottles and a pinkish bulb glowed weakly up on the ceiling.

'*Grazie, grazie,*' cried the crooner, to the desultory clapping, and raised the microphone again to his full lips, licking them determinedly. He took a deep breath and burst into full-throated song, rich and deep and ecstatic.

'He thinks he's Caruso,' observed Sasha acidly.

'They all think they're God's gift . . . pardon?'

Hannah jumped at an unexpected touch on her shoulder.

'*Sind sie Deutsch*?'

'No, English.' She turned back to Sasha, pulling away.

'Ah,' the man bent towards her apologetically, 'You look German.'

'I'm not,' she said ungraciously.

'You like to dance?'

Couples shuffled on the spot on a barely discernible space between tables; it was an excuse to fumble.

'No, thank you.'

Sasha kicked her ankle, grinning, squinting against a curl of cigarette smoke. 'Go on.'

The crooner howled throatily while two sweating waiters carried trays of drinks above their heads, squeezing and twirling between chairs and people like hissing Houdinis "Si, si, si." Sasha waved for fresh drinks and smiled at the hovering German. 'She would like to dance really, she's been complaining how bored she is.' Hannah scraped back her chair, bumped the waiter, who was scribbling orders on a pad and scowled rudely, letting Fritz edge her into the dance floor and put his arms around her waist, pulling her close.

'I was watching you,' he murmured into her ear.

Hannah concentrated on his hands, promising herself that the second they began to slide, she'd . . .

'And I think, such a beautiful girl, and so sad.'

Hannah ignored him, pulling away, but was promptly pushed hard against him by the press of the crowd.

'Why?' he asked.

'Why what?'

'Are you sad?'

'I'm not.'

'Oh, you . . .'

'I'm not,' she insisted crossly, trapped into an idiotic conversation by the dense throng of people swaying around them.

'OK.' He pulled her closer and pushed his hips against hers, 'So we have at nice time, *ja*?'

Sasha had gone. Hannah glimpsed her across a sea of bobbing shoulders, glued to an Italian whose wife watched from the side of the room, glowering. He was her lover. They met this way every Saturday, under his wife's nose, teasing her. Sasha said the rows were spectacular. All the men did it.

'Are you on holiday?' asked the German, his tongue tickling her ear.

'No.' She turned her head in disgust. 'Don't do that.'

'You live here?'

'I work near here. As a nanny. I hate it.'

'You should do something you like. Like this.' He aimed his lips at hers but she dodged. They shuffled to and fro, barely moving. Sweat trickled between her shoulder blades where his hand rested on her skin.

'I don't like anything.'

He tightened his arms, squashing her nose against his jacket, smiling triumphantly.

'I have a flat in Milan. I show you something you like.'

'You live in Milan?' she mumbled into the jacket.

'Dusseldorf. The flat is business.'

'I bet I know *what* business. *Und ihre Frau ist auch in Dusseldorf*?'

'*Ach, du spricht Deutsch*,' he cried happily.

'Not really, only O-level.'

'My wife is in Dusseldorf also,' he said blandly.

'What are you doing here, then?' asked Hannah, to keep him at bay.

'Travelling. I sell.'

'What do you sell?' she asked, picking his hand off her bottom and planting it angrily back on her waist. He grinned.

'Rubber.'

'Rubber?' exclaimed Hannah, thinking of rubber trees and erasers. It wasn't something you came across often. 'Who on earth do you sell rubber to round here?'

He roared with laughter. 'Everyone wants rubber goods.'

'What kind of rubber goods?' she demanded, hitching his hand up again.

'Oh, darling, I show you, if you come to my flat.'

The crooner bit off the end of his song and swallowed it with a sentimental gulp, reduced to tears.

'You come?' persisted the German, refusing to let her go, in the midst of a press of couples going back to their tables. Sasha passed and winked, nodding her head at the wife who was leaning with her bosom splayed on the table, shouting in wailing Italian at her husband who listened with a fat smile and half closed, dishonest eyes. Hannah felt tired and sick with the terrible longing for love that shamed and tormented her. Sebastian had seen how easy it would be to destroy her. This man would see nothing, she knew.

'All right,' she said, tugging his arm, 'let's go to Milan. It can't be worse than this.'

'*Bitte*?'

'I said, all right,' she snapped. As they went out, she wondered if, in some appalling way, they each got what they deserved, and what he had done to deserve her. Then they were in his big black Mercedes, speeding across to Milan, half an hour away, and his anonymous travelling-salesman flat, somewhere to take girls when away from home and complacent, fat Teutonic wives.

'Oh, damn, damn, damn!' cried Hannah, pounding his back with her fists as he lay on top of her, his trousers round his ankles in his haste, the wretched business over.

'It was not good?' he asked, surprised, rolling off her. Behind him, spread open on a night table, lay his case of samples with its neat rows and packets and boxes and piles of condoms, all colours, he said proudly, all textures and thicknesses and some with these little bumps that . . . Hannah burst into tears.

'Oh,' said her German, put out at the slur on his performance, 'so it was bad?'

'You didn't use one!' she screamed, 'You never bloody used one. You used me, but you didn't . . .' She threw herself back on the bed, writhing and howling and screaming.

'You are mad?' He backed off, really scared, pulling up his trousers, quickly, catching the zip like a little boy, looking round for something to quiet her before a neighbour . . .

'Will you be quiet, please, *ja*?' he begged, and swore lengthily in German when she wouldn't. 'Please?'

Hannah shot upright. 'You,' she panted, 'you . . . oooooh!' and lunged for the samples case, her black dress caught round her hips, pelting him furiously with hundreds of tiny sealed foil packets. When they were all gone, she hurled the case itself, wild-eyed with rage in a litter of rubbers that rolled and dropped like obscene confetti on to the floor around the stunned German.

'So bad?' he repeated, gaping.

Hannah took a step towards him.

'No, please . . .'

'Do you know the worst thing?' she shrieked.

'You stop shouting?' he asked hopefully.

'I don't even know your bloody name,' she yelled.

He stood up very straight, bowed from the waist and smacked his socks together. 'Wolf,' he said formally.

Her mouth dropped open. 'Is the whole German nation called Wolf? I'm Hannah.'

'Hannah, I will take you home, *ja*? Don't worry.'

She stood in the litter of rubbers. 'Sure, that's nice of you after this. I'm sorry.'

He dropped her off outside the Twerps at half past three in the morning and screeched off down the drive in relief. Mrs Twerp woke up and nudged her husband.

'You'll have to tell Nanny not to stay out 'til all hours,' she mumbled 'she can't possibly look after the children properly if she goes out so late. You'll have to tell her.'

Mr Twerp turned over in his sleep, leaving his wife to fret. Hannah saved him the trouble by handing in her notice that morning. 'What is this?' demanded Mrs Twerp, nocturnal disturbances forgotten. 'I can't find someone else at such short notice. What do you expect me to do? Really, you have an obligation, you know . . .'

'Look after your own spoiled brats.'

'How dare you?'

'Because I don't give a damn. Not one single damn.'

'Are you mad?' Mrs Twerp asked coldly.

'Probably,' said Hannah indifferently, 'and possibly pregnant as well.'

It was time, no matter what, to go back.

'Going home?' chatted the English guard, checking her through ticket.

'In a manner of speaking,' answered Hannah.

The guard looked at her steadily, swaying gently on his feet as beyond the window yellow-green spring country-side sped past.

'You say something's going home when it's had it, don't you? When it's all worn out and no use any more. I'm going home.'

The guard handed her back her ticket. 'Then good luck to you, young lady,' he said kindly.

'I've a feeling I'm a bit short on luck.'

'Goes for us all, love,' he said, 'goes for us all.'

He went out of the compartment, pulling the door closed, and Hannah shut her eyes, listening to the wheels clattering over the rails. One time, I've only risked one time, she thought; my luck can't be that bad, surely. Please, God, give me just one break. Don't make me be pregnant.

Chapter Twenty-Two

'I thought you were in Switzerland!' cried Jenny Heydritch.

Hannah stood in the boarding house doorway, holding a case, her mouth set in a straight line of bravado. 'I was.'

'Why do you look so awful?'

'I just came back.'

'Here?'

'I don't mean to put you out.'

'You're not. I'm just surprised. Come in.'

'No, I'm putting you out.'

'Don't be daft.'

'I'll manage.'

'Oh, for goodness' sake, you're as irritating as ever,' said Jenny, losing patience. 'Go on, straight ahead, upstairs. Right at the top.'

They climbed narrow, thinly carpeted stairs to an attic floor where two girls sat cross-legged on a crumpled pink candlewick bedspread, books scattered on the bed between them, coffee mugs balanced on a couple of textbooks with well-thumbed pages.

'My foster sister, Hannah,' said Jenny, dumping the case on a second unmade bed, stuffing underwear under a pillow in one grey bundle. ' 'scuse us.'

The girls looked up. 'Want us to go?'

Jenny nodded.

Hannah half sat, half leaned on the bed, next to her case. 'I'm sorry,' she repeated as the bedroom door closed. 'I'm putting you out.'

'Their room's next door.'

'I mean you.'

'I don't mind. What's happened?'

Hannah stared at her hands expressionlessly.

'D'you want a coffee?'

'I got to the station, in London,' blurted Hannah, 'and I stood on the platform and I'd come all the way back from Italy and I'd never thought until then where I was going. You think, "Oh, I'll go home," and all the way back you think you're going home, don't you? And then at the station I just stood there, like an idiot, and I thought, "Where is home?" How do you go home when you haven't got one?'

'Oh,' said Jenny. 'Yes.'

'So I came here. I'm sorry.'

'Do stop saying you're sorry.'

'The thing is, you see,' Hannah hurried on, 'I never thought, I just got on the train. So I walked around and then I asked a policeman. They used to say ask a policeman, didn't they? And he said, try the YWCA. I stayed the night in a dormitory, but I can't stay there. I'm terribly sorry.'

'Look,' Jenny spread her hands at the cluttered, chaotic little room, 'you're welcome to sleep on the floor if you want.'

'I don't . . .' began Hannah.

'For God's sake stop apologising and let me get a word in! I can't put you up for long because the landlord rents the whole boarding house out to the university during term time, and we have to stick to his rules. One of them is no visitors to stay.'

'Then . . .'

'But a few nights, and no one's going to notice.'

Hannah sat down on the bed heavily. 'I'm in a mess, I think. It's why I came back.'

'What sort of mess?'

Hannah pulled a face.

'Oh, no,' said Jenny.

'I haven't had a test.'

'Shit. How long?'

'About a month.'

'Seen a doctor?'

'I haven't got one.'

'You'd better find one, quick.'

'But I don't live anywhere. I think you have to live somewhere to have a doctor.'

'You go temporarily. There's one at the university.'

The same thought struck them both. Jenny shrugged. 'He might,' she said, 'though I don't suppose he's supposed to. But he's a really nice man. It's worth a try.'

'I need a really nice man.'

'I'll take you up tomorrow,' promised Jenny.

Later they ate fish and chips, leaning on the railings near the Palace Pier, looking out over the sea.

'You know what,' remarked Jenny thoughtfully, peeling batter off her fish distastefully, 'This is disgusting.'

'What?' Hannah asked, watching the heaving sea pound on the pebbles, sucking them down, rolling and rattling into the edge of the waves.

'You could try gin. It might work since you're so early.'

'Gin and hot baths?' Hannah half laughed, a chip held in her fingers. 'Do you know, I always eat fish and chips in a crisis.'

'Might work.'

Hannah put the chip back in its newspaper. 'I only ever once got really and truly drunk.'

Jenny stayed silent, staring out to sea.

'What do you know about it?' asked Hannah, frightened.

Jenny watched the horizen, bright with reflections from the dying sun. 'It's probably better than the other way. A scrape.'

'What sort of scrape?'

'Hannah,' cried Jenny, 'you can be so annoying. You really are ignorant. You aren't the only person who ever got pregnant, you know.'

'I know I'm not,' said Hannah, confused. 'Why do you think I think I am?'

Jenny's profile, dark against the sunset, hardened.

'You? I don't believe it.'

Jenny rounded on her angrily. 'Well, you'd better, and it costs a fortune, so have you got some money?'

'Gin doesn't cost that much.'

'You are so bloody obtuse. Not for gin, you ass, for a scrape.'

'I didn't know. I'm not trying to be obtuse.'

A ship crossed the shining grey water quickly, moving from end to end of the horizon with surprising speed.

'Loads of people have them.'

'They're all right, then?'

'I bled like a pig afterwards and it hurts,' said Jenny shortly.

'Shall we try gin, then?' suggested Hannah diffidently. 'Would that be best, do you think?'

'You might get an abortion on the National Health. You've got so many problems, I think they'll do them these days, for people like you.'

'Well, that's charming!'

'But while you're waiting to see, we could give it a go, if you like.'

'Let's buy some some, then.' She hung on the railing, avoiding Jenny's eye.

'I should think you have to drink a lot, though. D'you like gin?'

'I never tried it. It's been mostly wine or beer.'

'I think you might have to have about a bottle or something.'

'Unless I have it, and not an abortion.'

'Don't be ridiculous.'

'I'm not being.'

'A baby?'

'The pox,' snapped Hannah, hurt.

'You're kidding.'

'It's my baby.'

'It isn't anything yet.'

Hannah felt the warm metal of the railing between her hands and knew her baby was real.

'You couldn't look after a baby; you haven't even got anywhere to live, don't be stupid.'

'It'd be someone to love, though,' murmured Hannah, smoothing the metal, thinking how soft a baby's skin was, how tender the touch.

'What?' demanded Jenny.

'I said,' replied Hannah, letting go of the railings, 'where's the off-licence?'

Their backs to the sea, they crossed past the pier and uphill towards the station.

'We'll get a whole bottle, I think,' said Jenny.

'And do you know—' she demanded crossly, two days later, 'I had to wash your hair, because you were out cold and sick everywhere. You try washing someone's hair when they're unconscious and throwing up.' She rolled the whites of her eyes. 'I could have strangled you.'

Hannah put her head down on her arms again and moaned. The hangover was appalling. 'Don't keep on . . .'

'You were totally shitty,' snapped Jenny, unforgiving.

'I was drunk, and we did agree to do it. I don't remember a thing.'

'Count yourself lucky,' snarled Jenny as Hannah shot to her feet. 'Oh, not again.'

Coming out of the lavatories in a miasma of gin fumes, Hannah caught sight of herself over the basins, grey and drawn with bloodshot eyes, bringing back memories of Mrs Twerp and lonely evenings on the veranda.

'You'll turn into a vampire yet,' she muttered, and the red-eyed thing in the mirror said back, 'With a clutch of devil's eggs on the hatch. Bah.'

Unmoved by its dose of gin, Hannah's baby hung on.

'He'll do,' said Jenny suddenly, looking to the far end of the students' union where they'd been sitting all morning.

'Do what?' asked Hannah, startled out of her stupor.

'Joe Masters. He's got a flat and he doesn't give a toss about anything. He'll put you up.'

'Hey!' cried Hannah, but Jenny was half way towards him. A pair of brown eyes glanced briefly at Hannah with utter indifference. He had heavy, long dark hair that flopped over his face. He turned back to Jenny.

He's saying no, thought Hannah, humiliated, seeing him say a couple of words then turn back to the girl beside him, unsmiling.

'That's that, then. We've got somewhere for you to stay,' announced Jenny, looking pleased. 'Says you're welcome to his bed and he'll sleep on the couch.'

'But he . . . ?' Hannah said, open-mouthed.

'Why not?' demanded Jenny impatiently. 'He doesn't care.'

'I haven't even spoken . . .'

'I'll take you over later on,' said Jenny, dismissing her. 'I just said you were looking for somewhere to doss.'

'Does he know . . . ?'

'Just dossing, I said.'

Hannah looked over at Joe furtively, afraid he'd be staring back. He was talking earnestly to a curly-haired girl as though he and she were the only two people on earth.

'Is he nice?' she asked nervously.

'Bit of a loner, but he's all right. He's an English postgrad. I don't know him all that well.'

'But you just asked him for his bed.'

'That's how things are around here. You'd better get used to it if you're going to hang around, it's no big deal.'

'I'll try,' said Hannah, out of her depth.

'He gave me a key.'

'Where does he live?'

'Right down by the sea.'

Hannah remembered the swelling waves, the wet,

glistening grey pebbles and the warmth of the railings under her hand . . . and the clear green glass of the gin bottle. She bolted for the lavatory.

Hannah wondered afterwards whether her ferocious morning sickness was the consequence of gin, neurosis or just plain worry got out of hand. Joe, for *his* part, claimed morning sickness started the day he fell in love with her, but no one ever quite believed him.

Chapter Twenty-Three

Outside Dr Ashley's consulting-room window seagulls swooped, wheeling and calling excitedly as bulldozers turned up and down, criss-crossing green Sussex fields with great brown scars, throwing fat worms to the surface.

'They're building halls of residence,' said the doctor, leaning on his third-floor windowsill, looking down. A gull hung close by, dirty white against grey sky that looked like rain. It screamed hoarsely.

'I wish I could do that,' said Hannah.

'What? Fly?'

She shook her head nervously. 'Scream.'

'Yes, I'd imagine so,' he said dryly.

'And not care if anyone heard.'

'But you do care.'

'Yes.'

'Have you never told anyone this story before?' He turned from her, seemingly intent on the bulldozers.

'It's embarrassing.'

He glanced at her quickly. 'You're embarrassed, eh?'

'Terribly. I am a disaster.'

'I should have thought the disaster lay elsewhere.'

He looked lost in thought. Hannah tried to unclench her fingers and relax as he had told her to but the effort made her sick. 'I embarrass myself,' she went on, since he made no effort to speak, 'because I do things I don't really want to do, and I don't know why. I make it worse. I feel part of a picture, somehow, but because I'm inside it I can't see it, and unless I can see what the picture is, I can't . . . stop myself.'

'What is it you feel? Do you want to stop?' He spoke without turning round, sounding sad.

'That's part of the picture I can't see. I don't know.'

'There's a song,' he said, 'some pop thing I've heard. About being a rock, an island, and feeling no pain. Something like that.'

Hannah could see the drab sky, now empty of birds, outlining his head. 'It's more like walls.'

'I thought it might be something like that.'

'As though I'm inside great walls and nothing can get in, only I can't get out either. So I'm stuck. I build them higher, or they build themselves . . . oh, I don't know.'

'You are stuck.'

'I never cry. I wish I could. I'd give anything to cry.' It wasn't entirely true, she thought, remembering Sebastian, but the memory was gone again in a flash. 'But when you've been in a Home and not really belonged anywhere, I suppose you end up like me. You're bound to. I think Wendy Dawn did. You end up in a kind of prison. I think I might make the prison myself, but I don't know how. Thinking is no use; thinking makes me run into walls. I want to do something better than what I do do, but . . . I'm not making sense, am I?' she said, running into the very wall she was describing, bruising herself once more, blindly.

'We'll do a test,' decided Dr Ashley, turning his back on the gulls, 'and see. If you aren't pregnant, we'll see if we can do something about the walls. If you are, then we need to do something about that, first. I can send you to someone in London. He'll see you and arrange for a termination.'

'You mean, in hospital?'

Jenny had said 'for people like you'.

'In hospital. You seem surprised.'

Hannah looked down, refusing to meet his eyes, hiding the enormity of her guilt, terrified because she saw it all perfectly clearly. He had swallowed her tale and thought her worthwhile. If he knew how bad she was, how hopelessly promiscuous, how lost a soul he had before him, he wouldn't help. Hannah became wary; if he really knew, he'd know she didn't deserve it. The whole thing was not to let on, or they'd send her away again as a cheat.

'We'll take a specimen, and if you want to wait here for the result, you can. The rabbits take a couple of hours.'

'I'd like to stay here.'

'I'll get someone to make you coffee.'

'Thank you,' Hannah whispered, embarking on a perilous fraud of innocence. Dr Ashley sent in his nurse and went to lunch, leaving the suite of Health Centre rooms silent and empty. She sat in the waiting room, staring at nothing.

Tom Ashley pushed his half-full plate away and looked at his watch. 'The trouble with abused children,' he said crossly, 'is that they fight you. They never believe they deserve anything decent. They end up shifty as hell, trying to pull wool over your eyes without there being the slightest need for it, and thinking you don't see what they're doing . . . and I shouldn't by rights be seeing her at all. She's not a student here and strictly speaking she's none of my business.'

'She?' someone asked.

'This girl wandered in off the street. You can't say get lost to someone who's lost already, can you?' he appealed across the table to a corduroy-clad professor with tired grey eyes above a thin beard.

'I haven't the faintest idea what you're talking about,' he answered, pushing his chair back.

'I'm not sure that I have,' muttered Tom, 'but someone's got to do something, haven't they? Someone has to deal with the damage.'

'Try the mind-numbing effect of a dozen first-years on the subject of Milton's Free Will,' suggested the scrawny professor mildly, 'then you'd know what brain damage was.'

'Shit,' muttered Tom Ashley ambiguously and went to fetch more coffee from the counter, to cheer himself up.

'It's positive, I'm afraid,' he told Hannah an hour later.

'I knew it would be.'

'We'll do a second, to be on the safe side.'

'There's really no need. I'm pregnant.'

'What do you want to do?'

Choices again. It was too difficult to explain that if none of the choices on offer was what you actually wanted, how did it make sense for someone to ask what you wanted? Hannah had the familiar feeling of running round a maze that had exits only others could see.

'You said you could send me to London.'

'I'll give you a letter. They'll send you an appointment. Do we know where you're staying?' Dr Ashley shuffled some papers, looking. Hannah gave him Joe's address.

'Is there someone to look after you?' he asked vaguely, thinking he wanted to offer to see her again, keep an eye on her, but she was impossibly touchy and the whole thing most irregular.

'I don't really know,' answered Hannah.

'I feel guilty about your sleeping there,' she told Joe two weeks later, holding out hot coffee and watching him roll over on the floor in a sleeping bag.

'Why?' he asked, yawning, not really wanting to know.

'Taking your bed and your room.'

'Bed is best, but this'll do. I sleep all right,' he said. 'You're welcome.'

'Why are you doing it?'

Joe breathed in steam from the coffee and started to wake up. 'Dunno. What's the hassle?'

Hannah wasn't used to these students' kind of talk, their casualness; it made Hampstead seem like a prissy finishing school.

'Well, it's awfully kind of you,' she said lamely.

'It is,' he agreed, reaching for his coffee, 'and if you go on about it enough, I might wonder why I'm doing it, too.'

'I'm sorry.'

'I can't stand sorry women.'

'I . . .' She saw the look on his face and fled.

'There's a party,' he told her several days later, watching her go to the doormat, looking for letters. 'Are you waiting for something? You go scuttling out there every morning.'

'Yes. What party?'

'Devil's Dyke. Want to go?'

'I don't know.' The dull nausea that threatened all day and all night sharpened and Joe saw her go pale.

'Are you ill or something?'

'Must have eaten something.'

'Bloody well must eat a lot of it, then,' observed Joe sarcastically, hearing the bathroom door bang, 'because you've been up to that game ever since you've been here.'

'I think I picked up a bug abroad,' said Hannah, coming back.

'You don't get bugs in Switzerland, it's the cleanest fucking place in the whole world.'

'Superbugs,' she said, grasping at straws.

Joe studied her for a moment. 'Why are you telling fibs, sweetheart?'

'I'm not,' she protested, flushing.

'Sure you're not.'

She bolted. Joe got to his feet lazily and followed her as far as the kitchen doorway. Hannah fumbled with the kettle, spilling water.

'Now then, fibbing to me in my own house,' he remarked dryly.

'I'm not fibbing. That's a childish word, anyway.'

'Childish is a good word for it,' answered Joe equably.

Hannah turned her back.

'So is flouncing a good word. I like English words; they're nice.'

'Stop it.'

'You stop it, and tell me why.'

'What's it to you?' she said sullenly.

His room was strewn with books and bits of clothing, his sleeping bag thrown over the end of an aged sofa covered in scratchy, threadbare stuff. Bix Beiderbecke played, turned down low on the record player on the floor in the corner. Orange boxes stacked two high held his collection of seventy eights; hundreds of them. It was home and she wanted to stay.

'I'll tidy up.'

'Well, that's a question, isn't it, what is it to me? Don't bother, I hate being tidied up.'

'I haven't the vaguest idea,' she snapped.

'Now there's gratitude,' said Joe, refusing to get angry.

'I offered to clean up.'

'Just telling the truth would do.'

'I hate charity,' said Hannah sullenly.

'That's really nasty.' He sounded surprised. 'I didn't have you down as nasty.'

She went scarlet. 'I've got to go over to Jenny's.'

'When you're ready, sweetheart.'

'I am ready.'

'To tell me,' said Joe.

They glared at each other in the tiny room, then grinned uneasily.

'The funny thing is that ever since you arrived I've been feeling a bit off-colour myself.'

'That's impossible,' cried Hannah, startled.

'There's nothing wrong with you. My point exactly,' said Joe.

On Friday he had a session with his supervisor who picked up a wad of sheets covered in Joe's bold handwriting and held it out, grinning.

'Serious this time, is it?' he asked, shaking the papers gently so that the hairpins holding them together fell out in a shower.

'Oh, shit.' Joe picked them up, holding them in the palm of his hand.

'Judging by the unaccustomed output, she must be good for you, whoever she is.'

Good for me, thought Joe, there's an intriguing thought. 'Maybe she is, what a gas.'

The senior lecturer, a pedantic man, looked pained. 'There are some points I've noted further on,' he went on, 'that you should go over again, and you need to check some phrases in Act Two . . .' and was distracted by Joe's counting of hairpins.

'She loves me, she loves me not . . . she loves me, so there you go. The pins have it.'

'I've had it,' said his supervisor, throwing papers together in a pile. 'Fancy a pint?'

'Super idea,' drawled Joe, pocketing the pins, and they went to prop up the bar until late. He didn't see Hannah until the next afternoon which was the day of the Devil's Dyke party.

Chapter Twenty-Four

'What on earth are you doing?' demanded Joe, finding Hannah in the kitchen, balanced on a stool, leaning backwards at a dangerous angle to see herself in a tiny mirror nailed to the wall.

She wiggled inside the skintight black lace dress she was wearing and said crossly, as if it were obvious, 'Seeing if I look too fat in this. What do you think?'

He stood back and considered. 'You don't want to know what I think, sweetheart.'

She straightened up and the black lace looked even more full of holes in the direct light from the window. 'Why not?'

Joe sighed. 'Do you ever think about anyone else's feelings?' he asked dispassionately, avoiding looking at the holes. 'I take it you're going to wear something underneath that?'

'I haven't got anything black.' She leaned back again, sucking in her stomach. 'It's not too bad if I stand carefully.'

She was perched squinting into the bit of glass when Joe kicked the stool from under her and caught her in his arms.

'What did you do that for?' she shouted, scared.

'Go and get dressed.'

'I am!' yelled Hannah. 'For the party. I've sewn it up, look. Jenny said it was all right.'

Joe bent down and glared. 'You enjoy the world looking straight up your crotch, sweetheart?'

Hannah tugged at the hem and a safety pin caught the light. 'It isn't that bad.'

'You aren't going anywhere in that.'

'I am.'

'You're not.'

'I'll go where I like.'

'Who with?'

'Jenny, Tim, Paul, Jill – they're all going from there.'

'Don't expect me to bring you back,' he said furiously. 'I'll take you, but don't think I'm going to hang around, and don't expect bringing back because I've got other things to do.'

'I don't!' shouted Hannah.

'And I won't.'

They stopped quarrelling, out of breath.

'Are you just naive or what?' he bawled finally.

She rubbed her foot on the back of her leg like a stubborn little girl. 'No.'

'You're not going looking like that with anyone—'

'I am.'

'—except me.'

'How shall we get there?'

'I've got a lift. But don't think I'm hanging around you when we get there.'

'I never thought you would,' said Hannah, backing into his bedroom that he hadn't been in for weeks, 'so why are you shouting?' She banged the door before he could answer.

He flung himself into his armchair and let out a yell. 'And mind your fucking hairpins!' he roared at the closed door.

It seemed like hours later she came out.

'I thought you hadn't got anything black.'

'Ink,' explained Hannah offhandedly. 'Took ages to dry.'

Joe looked closely.

'Not me, stupid, I dyed a bra and knickers. Want to see?' she asked sarcastically. She'd put up her hair, too, and put black rings round her eyes and stuff on her lashes, and got high heels on the end of legs you could run your hand down like . . .

'Jesus wept – black tights,' he groaned.

'So?' said Hannah, standing straight for inspection.

'You look like an absolutely fabulous . . .'

Hannah waited.

'. . . tart,' finished Joe, handing her her coat.

They had a lift in someone's car, and sat in stiff and stubborn silence all the way up on to the highest part of the Downs.

'All right, I've said I'm sorry.'

Hannah sniffed.

'But you do,' he said, grinning.

She sulked and went inside the house. A harrassed woman in floaty Indian cotton kissed Joe and took Hannah's coat, waving them to drinks at the far end of a beautiful, well-polished room with wide windows opening on to a stone terrace. The friend with the car who'd brought them went outside and stood looking at the garden and a pale, pocked moon floating like gossamer high in the sky. 'Look, you're the first to arrive,' the hostess

213

said. 'Can you manage for a bit? I'm popping back up stairs for a minute.'

'Of course we can,' said Hannah, sitting on a blue sofa for two. Joe fetched two glasses of red wine and sat down beside her. Other people came. The room filled with talk and smoke and laughter. Someone sat on the arm of the sofa and slid her arm along Joe's shoulder, peering at Hannah over the top of his head, whispering in his ear.

'I don't expect you to stay with me,' Hannah hissed at him from her side, her lips touching his ear. Joe shivered in the heat. The other girl said something and laughed and Joe shook his head.

'Go on.' Hannah nudged him, putting her hand on his as it lay on the blue fabric between them.

'This is Suzanne,' he said.

'Hi,' said Suzanne.

'Go with Suzanne.'

'Outside.' Abruptly pulling her to her feet, spilling wine, he dragged her through the dense press of people, pinioning her arms fiercely.

'What are you doing? Now what have I done?'

Stars shone over the hills; the moon, now brilliant, rode high. The garden sloped upwards, lawn upon lawn, laced all about with grave lights in glass saucers that twinkled in a rockery, necklaced white stone steps, and skirted recently mown grass. People lounged, glasses clinked, cigarettes glowed and gave off the cloying smell of hashish on the fragrant night air. Voices rose and fell in intimate, delicious whispering in the dark. A man laughed softly. His shadow lengthened for an instant close by them, then disappeared.

'Find somewhere to sit,' ordered Joe, 'and I'll get a drink.'

He turned back into the crowd and the light. Hannah went up into the garden, and felt something tug at her ankle.

'Sit by me.' The grave lights burned with steady flames, just lighting a doll-like Chinese face, eyes thin black crevices above high cheekbones. 'Please,' he begged. He moved to make room for her and Hannah sat down by a low wall.

'Do you know me?'

He talked rather fast, monotonously, in a thready voice. After a little while Hannah saw that he was quite, quite drunk. He told her a long, long story that had got lost in its own words by the time Joe came back with two wine glasses and took her away, leading her round a bed sprinkled with night stocks and tobacco plants, to where no one else sat.

'He's an alcoholic. I've never spent enough time with him to find out why. He'll die soon.'

'Oh,' said Hannah.

They sat and watched the dancing inside the French windows; someone turned the music up and it spilled to the end of the garden.

'Do you want to dance?'

She rubbed her bare arms. 'It's chilly out here. Shall we go back?'

'No wonder you're freezing in that stupid get-up.'

'Don't start again.'

'If you're cold we'll go down.'

'Why do you keep doing that? Up and down, up and down. Can't we sit still for five minutes,' she complained.

He left the wine on the grass and dragged her down into the crush, into his arms.

'Oh, shit.'

'Now what?' The crowd pushed them together, she felt his arms tighten.

'Because you are silly and impossible and a liar and the most beautiful woman in this room.'

'None of that is true . . .' Hannah began indignantly, willing to argue, but he kissed her instead, and they danced until the moon was long gone and the sky paling in the east, the room nearly empty, the candles gone out.

'I love you,' said Joe.

She thought tipsily of a small basement flat full of music, a white bedroom with a fan heater to ward off damp and mildew from the piles of records and books. The early morning sun touched the whitewashed wall of the courtyard each day and a strutting thrush broke snails on a stone in the weeds. Most mornings Joe made coffee, brought it in to her and turned on the jazz very low. Then they'd talk for hours. Just talk and talk. For the first time in her life, she wasn't afraid.

'I love you,' she said.

'Let's go home, sweetheart.'

The taxi drove through a wet sea fret that made haloes around the street lamps on the front. The flat was chilly. Joe fetched the fan heater and they sat on the floor before it, their backs to the sofa, warming their fingers round hot coffee mugs as the sun came up and warmed the whitewashed walls of the courtyard outside the kitchen window.

'It's tomorrow,' said Joe. 'Sleeping bag time.'

'You should have your room back.'

'I ain't bothered.'

'I am.'

'Don't think,' said Joe carefully, 'that I want you out

of my room.' Hannah pondered the many meanings of that and was silent. 'It's more a case of wanting you in it.'

'I know.'

'There's a lot of buts, the way you said that.'

'Some.'

'I sleep beautifully out here. No sweat.'

'You should have your bed back. I could stay here.'

'You can't have my sitting room as well. You're enough of a nuisance in there,' he said indignantly.

'I can leave, if you don't want me.'

He leaned back and touched her neck where the long hair was still held up by a little row of pins. 'Oh, I want you, sweetheart.'

She froze.

'I'd invite you into my sleeping bag, if you want to be proper about it. It just seems like passing up a good thing to leave my bed empty when it's definitely best in bed . . . Hannah?'

The bedroom door slammed shut and only the dawn chorus, going full blast outside, broke the silence.

'Shit,' cried Joe, astounded, 'now what have I done?'

He leaned over and switched the record player on. Muddy Waters, where he had been before they went out, now seemed out of place. Joe threw the seventy-eight on to a pile, settled Bojangles back where he belonged, closing his eyes, listening to the silence beyond the jazz, attuned to something else. In the end, as the sun shone full on the wall, throwing the near half of the small courtyard into deep shade, he turned the music off and went to his bedroom door. 'Hannah?'

There was a faint scuffling and a click.

'Hannah,' roared Joe, losing patience, 'what the fuck

is this—?' He stormed into an empty room, and was brought up short. The window was shut, and there was no other way out. 'Where are you?' he demanded wearily. There was nowhere to hide.

'I'm stuck,' came a muffled, panicky voice.

Joe went over and sat down deliberately on top of his trunk, a battered, brass-cornered leftover from public school days.

'Why are you in my trunk, Hannah?'

There was a sob, then some thrashing around.

'Claustrophobia . . .' Her wailing was muted by old clothes he couldn't be bothered to throw away and some pairs of battered boots.

'Well, no one put you in there.'

'Open . . .'

'Can't hear.'

'Please . . .' she howled, banging on the lid underneath him.

'When you tell me.'

Silence.

'OK. Call me when you're ready.' He slid off, treading heavily.

'I promise.' The trunk rattled desperately and Joe unclasped the catch. Two red eyes, swimming in tears, looked out. He leaned over her and asked, 'What are you doing in there, Hannah?' as though if he were reasonable about it, she might turn out to make sense, but she clutched the lid next to his fingers, pulling it almost shut again.

'I can't tell you.'

'You promised,' he said severely, relinquishing the heavy lid to her clutching hands. He sat down on the floor, on her level. 'You're a coward, you know. If you really did love me, you could tell me anything.'

The lid wavered.

'I'm waiting.'

'Do you?'

'What?'

Silence came heavily from the trunk.

'Oh,' said Joe, as if suddenly enlightened, 'do I love you? When you're sitting in my trunk, for God's sake? At seven o'clock in the fucking morning? In my bedroom, that you've taken over without a by your leave, and after what I thought I was telling you all night, and you want to know . . . Christ Almighty, Hannah!'

The trunk held its breath, then muttered something inaudible.

'Yes, I do love you. I haven't figured out why and frankly it's a bit of a strain, but I love you. What I've done to deserve it, I don't know.'

'Oh.'

'So why don't you come out?' The lid lifted several inches. 'I'm fat,' she said through the gap.

'You managed to get in. Presumably you can get out again.'

'. . . because . . .' she said, pushing the lid up against the wall, hectic with nerves and carbon dioxide.

'You are certainly an unusual sight,' he remarked.

Hannah sat up straight, with dignity. '. . . I'm pregnant.' She sat in his travelling box and stared at him over the side. 'So now you know.'

He rubbed his eyes exhaustedly. 'So that's it. I thought you weren't too concerned about getting your life going.'

'Oh.'

'If getting in boxes is a habit, it's tiresome, Hannah. I'd rather you just said.'

'Shall I go now?' she asked in a very small voice. She watched Joe turn away, saw his hooked nose and amused mouth, heavy dark brows pulled all together in a frown that became a thunderous scowl.

'Yes,' he snarled, out of patience, 'you'll go now, out of that ludicrous dress, into the bathroom to do your teeth, like a good little girl, and then you will go to bed and stay there. And so will I.'

'Us?' hiccoughed Hannah, looking up out of the box.

'Us,' yelped Joe.

She climbed out. 'But I'm pregnant, don't you mind?'

He pinched the bridge of his nose to dispel the feeling of disbelief. 'It simply doesn't make any difference,' he said. 'Don't ask me why.'

'Oh.'

'Cheap on the contraceptives.' He wondered if he should try to joke it away. 'I don't mind shop soiled.'

He saw she was appalled. 'I didn't mean that. I'm trying to say, I don't care. I only care about you.'

'I wish . . .' said Hannah, sitting down on his bed, her head in her hands.

'Go to bed,' he said.

'He was a salesman,' said Hannah.

'A salesman.'

'Yes.'

'Is that all?'

'All what?'

'It's a funny way to describe someone you're having a baby with.'

'It's not *with* anyone. I didn't know him.'

'One night stand?'

She swallowed hard. 'More a pick-up.'

'Like that.'

'Yes.'

'You must have been desperate.'

'I was.'

'Desperate how?'

'Lonely,' she whispered.

'Go to bed,' he said again. 'It doesn't matter.'

'It does to me.'

'Of course it matters to you.'

She pulled the bed's light cover back and touched his hand.

'Are you sure?'

'I'm not sure about anything in the whole wide world, except I don't want to be without you.'

Joe pulled off his shirt.

Hannah unpinned her dress and it fell to the floor. She lay down.

'And the rest,' he said, sitting beside her. She curled up, shivering. He took the fan heater from the sitting room and put it beside the bed and switched it on. It hummed loudly and the sun shone round the edges of the faded curtains.

'So you won't be cold,' he said.

She took off the rest and lay back, her head on his pillow, her eyes shut, embarrassed. She folded her hands over her belly but he took them with tenderness, laying them palms up on the sheet at her side.

'No, let me see.'

'Please,' she whispered.

'My God, you are lovely.'

He let her pull up the sheet, over both of them, and its frayed edges moved slowly in the air from the fan.

Chapter Twenty-Five

'Let your knees flop,' said the obstetrician.

Hannah lay on the high, narrow couch, trying to make out this wasn't happening, listening instead to the clink and chink of shiny stainless steel trays on steel trolleys and the swish, swish of nurses' black shoes on tiled floors. Curtain rings rattled down the line of cubicles, as someone new came in and stood on a pair of scales, with the nurse making a note of the reading. She did as she was told, looking to one side at the beige folder that held the letters and referrals and assessments that flew back and forth in slow motion. They had all agreed that it would be best to kill the baby.

'We'll let you know,' said the consultant, refusing to look her in the face.

'I'm still terribly sick all the time.' Hannah had mustered the courage to ask him how long she would have to wait.

'There are a good many young women in your unfortunate position, and we have people with cancer. They must come first. When we have a bed for you, we shall let you know at once.'

'I'm sick,' cried Hannah despairingly, 'all the time. I can't eat at all and my stomach feels sort of raw.'

'Then you'd better see your GP,' snapped the white coat, turning its back.

'I'm sorry,' Hannah said to the nurse, who smiled thinly.

Everyone wanted to help, everyone did help. They were kind. But everyone seemed to Hannah to disapprove of her. It was an administrative cat's cradle that Dr Ashley and Dr Tate spun between them, spinning her backwards and forwards, in the Brighton Belle, to and fro, Sussex to London, London to Sussex and back again, through warm, rainy summer days. Joe wrote his thesis, page by laborious, annotated page, and loved her. The baby grew, apparently unperturbed by their monstrous plans for it. Joe's morning sickness made him queasy and irritable, then he'd say it must be because they were so close, laugh, and turn up the jazz. Hannah knew there would come an end to all this. She hoped, when it came, that she'd turn to a pillar of salt like Lot's wife. Or stone. Who then would care about the details?

She tried to be stoical about the interview with Dr Tate, only it hadn't worked out.

'He's the kindest man in the world,' said Dr Ashley.

The kindest man in the world worked in dusty rooms in a white house that didn't look like part of a great London hospital at all. He told someone in a white coat, with a stethoscope round his neck, to interview her. It was like taking a suitability test for a position she didn't want, but had to have. She sat in the waiting room under a flickering fluorescent light, terrified.

'Are you Dr Tate?' she asked timidly, sitting on a wooden chair opposite a young man who said he was not. Hannah waited, but without saying who he was, he uncapped a pen, cleared his throat, and began to ask questions.

'Take seven away from a hundred and keep going,' said Anonymous when he'd written down her name and her age and all the other details that they had already written in their folder a dozen times.

Her mind instantly went blank. He looked up for the first time, expectant.

'I'm no good at maths,' she muttered.

'Ninety-three,' he urged.

'I can't,' mumbled Hannah.

David had hated her stupidity at maths. Tense with frustration that she couldn't do it, he had tried until he was beside himself to make her calculate. In the end, she could calculate nothing at all.

Anonymous wrote something down and cleared his throat again. 'Were you, er, virgo intacta?'

'Pardon?' said Hannah.

'When, er, you became pregnant, were you?'

'I don't know.'

He met her eyes at last. 'You don't know?' he said in astonishment.

'What that means. Intact . . . oh, yes. No, I wasn't.'

His pen hovered. 'Is that yes or no?' he asked doubtfully.

'It's no,' said Hannah, firmly, overcoming an urgent longing to lie, in case the truth prejudiced them against her. Even Joe didn't know how much she feared they would judge her and find her despicable.

'Not virgo intacta,' she added loudly, just to be on the safe side.

'Thank you,' said the young man and wrote it down.

'Have you discussed termination with your baby's father?'

Hannah's jaw dropped. 'No,' she said, and it came out as a squeak. She coughed. 'No, I haven't.'

His face was no longer impassive; he looked human and young, vulnerable himself. 'Don't you think he'd want to know?' he asked earnestly.

'It never crossed my mind,' said Hannah truthfully, 'He doesn't even know I'm pregnant. It wasn't that kind of relationship.'

'You do know who . . . ?'

Hannah flushed. 'Yes.'

'Will you tell me?'

Her face burned like fire. 'We met in a nightclub,' she muttered.

He wrote busily. 'Go on.'

'Nothing to tell. We went back to his flat. That's all.'

'You didn't see him again?'

Hannah shook her head. Insanely, her mouth began to quiver and all her pent-up nerves spilled over in a great gale of giggling that grew into humiliating laughter that she couldn't stop until she was crying and crying and crying.

'He was a contraceptives salesman,' she shrieked, as the demon shook her to pieces before the medical student's open-mouthed gaze, 'isn't that funny?'

He watched as her tears flooded over.

'Not very,' he said sadly, and put the top on his pen.

'Will they do it?' Hannah asked, terrified, blowing her nose. 'I'm sorry.'

'I'm quite sure they will,' he said, putting his papers together. 'I'll recommend it.'

'Who . . . ?' she said, as he got up to let her out into the flickering light again.

He leant towards her. 'Sorry?'

'Who are you, if you don't mind my asking?'

He gave a half-smile. 'Me? I'm a medical student.'

'My father was a student in this hospital,' said Hannah without intending to, 'isn't that strange?'

He eyed her oddly. 'From what you've told us, profoundly disturbing.'

Hannah longed to ask what he meant.

She waited and waited.

'Why don't you go out and get some fresh air, dear?' asked a woman in a pink twinset. 'They won't be ready for you until after lunch. You can get coffee and something to eat at the corner.'

She did, chewing dry tasteless sandwiches then rushing back in a panic, fearing they'd find her gone and think she didn't want . . . but the white house seemed empty as ever; even the pink twinset had gone.

'Miss Holmes?'

In the doorway stood the tallest man she had ever seen. He held out his hand, reminding her instantly of Sebastian.

'I am Dr Tate.' His hand was warm and dry, wrapped right around her own. 'Will you come with me, please?'

They went down several corridors, up stairs, past rows of windows with sills white with pigeon droppings. Somewhere a typewriter clacked busily and a telephone rang and stopped quickly, but there was no sign of people.

'Here we are. Will you go in?'

Dr Tate opened a door and held it, stepping back so

that she could go first, and she went in, past his arm, past a screen, into a vast room full of rows and rows of people who all stopped chattering as she walked forwards, into such a silence as you could hear a pin drop.

'Please sit down,' he said, indicating a chair facing the audience.

She sat down. 'Could you tell us something about yourself?' asked Dr Tate. Hundreds of eyes watched intently. There were not, Hannah saw, enough chairs for the show; people were standing at the sides and round the back.

'Have you noticed anything different about yourself since you've been pregnant?' he prompted quietly.

'I've got fatter,' gasped Hannah, her cheeks on fire.

'Anything else?' he murmured.

Hannah burst into tears, hiding her face in her hands, frantic. Dr Tate took her arm and led her out of the auditorium into a small office. He took out a vast, white linen handkerchief and gave it to her.

'I'm sorry,' Hannah knew she'd spoiled everything now, 'I didn't mean to. I didn't expect all those people.'

'Keep the hanky, I've lots.'

She blew her nose.

'I thought you did rather well.'

Hannah raised her streaming face, astounded at the smile in his voice.

'Yes, I thought you did very well indeed. We'll let you know as soon as we have a bed for you. Don't worry about the hanky. Really, you can keep it.'

'Thank you,' she whispered, stunned.

Joe found her sobbing over the kitchen sink next day instead of cooking spaghetti. 'I dreamed about the baby last night,' she said. 'I dreamed it was a very, very ancient old man, who was being reborn as my baby. He knew everything there is to know. He was a wise, wise old man-baby and he knew I'm going to kill him. He was at one end of a square room, and I was at the other. A kind of balloon kept us right apart, squashed against opposite walls, and I kept saying, "I'm sorry, I'm sorry, so terribly, terribly sorry," and he told me, only without speaking – I just sort of knew what he was saying – that he knew, and he understood everything, and he would go back this time. He understood everything and he was infinitely sad. But he forgave me, even though I haven't done it yet. He forgives me.'

'It's more than you do for yourself. You'll tear yourself to pieces, going on like this.'

'I can't do it,' cried Hannah desperately. 'I'll have it.'

'Sweetheart,' said Joe, 'you can't have a baby. Not now. Not this baby.'

'Why? Why can't I ever do it right?'

'You do do it right, but not babies right now. One day you'll have a love child, and then it'll be right. This isn't right.'

She splashed cold water on her face. 'Always howling. I'm hideous.'

'Only to you. Forget the spaghetti.'

They went down to the beach and lay on warm brown pebbles. Hannah thought about what Joe had said, wondering if the love child would be his. Listening to the moving sea grinding stones ceaselessly with small summer waves, grinding and grinding exceeding small, she knew that it would not.

Chapter Twenty-Six

Hannah's grief for her baby became a deep and constant mourning, a subterranean river of unshed tears. Those students of their crowd who didn't go away for the summer worked in pubs and bars, sat on the beach, swam, sunbathed and played lazily through the long days. One brilliant afternoon, with a brisk wind disguising the heat of the sun, they all went to the top of the cliffs to play miniature golf. They went round in two big groups, holding everyone up, clowning and laughing and playing the ass. Hannah looked out over the silvery sea below and imagined that she was one of them, one who belonged. She pretended the baby was Joe's baby, wanted. How envious everyone else would be if she were as happy as that. It was a glorious day but that night he could see she'd been crying.

This thing will spend itself and she'll get back on her feet, he thought, and couldn't imagine otherwise. She was sensitive and when she wasn't moping, he loved her the more for it.

Jenny was exasperated.

'You get your teeth into something and you never let go, do you?' she cried. 'You're the original British bulldog. For God's sake, we've all been through it. Stop making such a meal of it.'

Hannah tried to stop making a meal of it, and failed. She struggled and struggled to put something into words for Joe, sitting on the beach one overcast afternoon, the sea a dirty green sludge.

'It's as if my feelings have me when it should be the other way round. The dog wags the tail. Jenny says I'm selfish and self-indulgent, and I think I am, and she says to get my finger out, but I can't. My will isn't strong enough, however hard I try. It's a terrible thing, because it makes me false. Even to you.'

'Are you false to me?'

'In the way I mean, I might be.'

'I don't like that, it sounds like a kind of possession.' He was running pebbles over and over in the palm of his hand, leaning on his elbow.

'That's just what it feels like. Possessed and empty at the same time. Full of emptiness – there's a conundrum for you.'

Joe threw pebbles into the advancing sea. 'The tide's coming in.'

'And they are going to empty me of the baby.'

'I hadn't seen it like that.'

'I am so scared of what that will feel like.'

'Is this why you cry so much?'

'Yes. Though I know I couldn't look after a baby and it's not the answer. I know it doesn't make sense.'

'You sound all bloated out like someone who stuffs themselves on rubbish all the time and then feels sick. You need some decent food.'

'What a horrid idea. Anyway, stopping eating doesn't work since I throw up all the time, anyway. I'm thinner now than I was in Switzerland.'

Joe was stumped; he hadn't meant it literally.

*   *   *

They talked constantly, walking hand in hand along the sea front, down the cliff walk to Rottingdean, dodging great gouts of spray over the rocks. In the flat, Joe played jazz endlessly, the black discs spinning around and around and around like Hannah's thoughts, lying warm skin on warm skin in bed.

'What about your Mum?'

'I'm damned if I'm on her side, damned if I'm not.'

'Dad?'

'Doesn't care whose side I'm on since he doesn't know there's another point of view than his.'

'He's not the only one like that.'

'He ran off with, let me get it right, my step-grandfather's Polish foster daughter. How's that for a muddle? Mum would like to murder both of them. She's into murder.'

'I think I'll avoid them.'

'I've got three sisters and a brother but she keeps us apart. I miss them. We were too young really to know each other when we split up, but I think I'd like them. I'd love more than anything to have a family.'

'Not much good, then.'

'Emily used to say, "What pigs." No, not much good.'

'Got grandparents?'

'Mum lives with her mother in Ilford and I haven't seen either of them in years. Mum's dad died in the war; a bomb fell right on top of him. Dad's mother has been married three times and is still around, so far as I know. She's not all that old because she had Dad when she was a teenager, or something. She left her first husband and earned a fortune going round the East End lending people sixpences. Dad's such a snob, he hates to be reminded. They must have been very poor once, but I think she's quite well off now. I used to know her when I was a kid, but we moved away.'

'Where in the East End?'

'Plaster or something.'

'Plaistow.'

'That's it.'

'That used to be slums. Most of it went in the war.'

'She was living in Hackney when I was born. She's still there, in the same house.'

'My mother still lives in East Ham, that's not far away. I got out when I went to to school.'

'Did you like boarding school?'

'Some of the time. Some things I hated.'

'What?'

'Bullying, snobbery. No privacy. A lot of the time it was lonely and you had to make places that were yours, or you'd have gone crazy.'

'Sounds a bit like The Chestnuts.'

'Let's go home.'

'We are home.'

'To see my mother.'

Hannah was amazed. 'Your mother? You want me to meet your mother?'

'She'll read things into any girl I take home,' said Joe gloomily. 'And you'll go down like a lead balloon.'

'Why take me, then?'

'She might as well know the worst.'

'What is the worst? Me?'

'When this hospital thing is over.'

'Perhaps the letter won't come. Do you think they've changed their minds and aren't letting me know?'

'Oh Lord,' groaned Joe, 'don't start on that again.'

'All right. What was your dad like, then?'

'He died when I was a little kid and I don't remember. They doted on each other.'

'There you are, people do.'

'I'd go in and she'd be sitting there, chatting to him.'

'I thought you said you didn't remember.'

'After he was dead.'

'After?'

'She said, they loved each other so much, he'd come back to see she was getting along without him. She says she'd see him, clear as you or me, standing at the end of the bed. They used to gossip,' Joe finished, shaking his head.

'That's a hard act to follow.'

'You reckon?' He disappeared to rinse mugs, clattering them in the sink.

'I reckon,' echoed Hannah under her breath, 'you'll leave me one day. I'll make you leave me, I know I will.' She wondered how it would happen, and had an eerie feeling that maybe it already had, that she was looking back with hindsight from the edge of some future moment on what was yet to come. For one instant, time broke its bounds, slid around itself, mocked all human laws, a living nightmare. The moment passed, leaving its chill.

'Put some sugar in mine, please,' she called.

On the beach Joe skimmed stones over the flat sea, ducks and drakes. She counted the bounces and wished she could make them spin like he did.

'What you said the other day – do you feel that about me?'

'What?'

'About things being too strong, not having a choice how you feel?'

Hannah stared at the horizon until her eyes ached, putting off answering. Joe skimmed several more stones.

'I think I probably do,' she said, when the silence wouldn't stretch any further. 'I love you too much.'

'Can you love me too much?' He tried to make his voice light.

'I do.'

He tried to see some meaning in what she had said, but it eluded him. He sat down beside her and a thin mist drifted over the sea, clouds blotting out an angry, yellowish sun, foretelling change.

'It's the best I can do,' said Hannah. 'I'm sorry. I do do my very, very best.'

Joe hurled a stone at a gull, riding the greasy swell indifferently. 'Shut up.'

She buried her fingers in pebbles, biting her lip.

'You are the greatest person I ever met and if I don't marry you, I'll marry what I can find of you in another person,' he said hurriedly.

She held her breath and let it out when she was sure she wouldn't cry. 'Me, too.'

The gull flew up, out of the sea, screaming. The tide crept in over the groynes, its currents sucking and sliding over the stones, burying all manner of things, while two old men lingered at the top, leaning on green railings, looking out to the horizon over the sloping beach, thinking it empty and a storm coming up.

'It's a deal, sweetheart.'

'It's a deal, my love.'

Chapter Twenty-Seven

Hannah counted the weeks on the calendar, bleary-eyed, and put it back down on the floor by the bed with limp fingers.

'It's nearly twenty-three weeks,' she said, her voice slurred. Dr Ashley's phenobarbitone calmed her down and made her feel drunk, but only partially stopped the restless terrors that drove her hither and thither, vomiting blood. She lay back, exhausted, longing to sleep.

It's not really that long, is it? I feel, she thought exhaustedly, as if I've travelled a million miles, all uphill, and yet only half an inch. Why do I feel that? She turned fretfully to Joe but he wasn't there.

He was in the library, surrounded by quiet, ordinary things. Ordinary order that she'd die to have for herself and never could. Everyday things, beyond her reach, stacks and shelves and tables full of books; people who knew what they were about. Calm, orderly people, solid people, sure they existed, taking if for granted . . . holding admission tickets to reality. Hannah shot up in bed, sweating. The pills brought stupefying, waking dreams. She put her face to the edge of the bed, staring at the rows of books laid out on the floor, marching in neat procession, marked in dozens of places by bits of paper; his filing system, Joe called it. He'd be a doctor soon. Not the medical sort. Clever Joe, with bright brown eyes, who could roll cigarettes with his toes and do all manner of things that Hannah couldn't, like living . . . her breath came quicker and quicker as jealousy ballooned, a vicious aching longing for so much out of reach; for comfort.

'Millstone,' she cried aloud, feeling the dead weight of herself. She closed her eyes, feeling herself a great crude burden hung around his chest, knowing it would be too much and that he would cast it off.

When Joe got home, she was asleep and he tip-toed out of the room, holding the brown envelope with the hospital stamp at the top, that had come at last.

Chapter Twenty-Eight

They did not put her in a maternity ward. There were no mothers, no babies; only side wards full of silent, motionless elderly women with neurological illnesses of a seemingly terminal sort. Hannah, in a single room opposite the nursing office, broke the hush by shrieking twice, at the end, and then they quickly took the baby away in a silver bowl with a lid; they were very discreet. Their kindness distressed her terribly. It made it seem inconsiderate to ask was it a boy? A girl? Her labour and the stillbirth lasted two days and two nights and afterwards they washed her face and hands, patting her dry with small dabs of scratchy, overlaundered hospital towels. Well done, dear, they said.

'It's conclusive,' said Joe owlishly, coming in with an unwieldy bunch of chrysanthemums.

'That's a nice turn of phrase,' answered Hannah sarcastically.

'I haven't felt queasy since you came in here. That's the first time for ages.'

'I feel hollow,' said Hannah.

'I feel better.'

'I'm glad you feel better.'

'The hollow will go.'

'I hope so.'

'Cheer up. It's over.'

Hannah turned away and looked out of the sooty window, across the roofs to St Pancras station, invisible behind high brick walls. A certainty that had budded while she lay in labour now blossomed into full flower.

'I think it might only have started. I can't feel anything, you see.'

'Hey, come on, it's the blues.'

'Except scared – I can't feel anything. I've been sitting here, trying to find words for it. I feel I'm a fraud. I'm not real.'

'Bullshit.'

'No. I've been lying here wondering who I am and if I exist. When you look at me, do you see anything? I don't think I'm there.' Her voice was rising. 'If I walk into a crowd, I see people get out of something's way and I don't know whose. I try to feel myself being myself, and I can't. I'm scared to look in a mirror in case there's nothing there.'

Pigeons sat outside the grimy window, scuffling long scaly toes on the worn stone sill. Joe watched them, his mind blank, cupping his chin in his hand, feeling yesterday's stubble. They avoided each other's eyes, both aware of the pit at their feet.

'You see? I'll tell you something. Can I?'

'Of course,' he said unhappily.

'I couldn't sleep last night. I was hot, and it's stuffy in here, and I got hotter and hotter and thought I'd burn up, all dry and bloody, like I'd been flayed. That little red light was on and it kept me awake. I kept having the idea it was burning me. I told myself not to be stupid but it kept on. And I wanted to cry, for the baby, but it wasn't real, and

I'd have given anything to feel it was real, and I bit my fingers, to try and make myself real, but I got tenser and tenser, really frantic, so in the end, I rang for the nurse, and I did my usual stupid act, apologising and taking five minutes to say please could I have a cup of tea, because I couldn't get it out straight.'

Joe drew breath but she rounded on him violently. 'No, wait. She brought me the tea, and a sleeping pill. Another one. And she stood just there, by your feet, and she talked. She told me about how she's taking her finals this year, and I said – my big mouth ran away on its own – I said, isn't that interesting and why do you like it and why do you take in people like me . . . ?'

She paused, twisting the faded coverlet in her fingers.

'And she said,' Hannah went on recklessly, 'that nursing people like me was interesting. Interesting? I said. Yes, she said, and then she realised and got a bit shifty like she was embarrassed, but I wouldn't let her stop. Interesting? I said. How? And she said – oh God, she said disturbed people were interesting. And then she went and took the cup out to wash it up and I realised she meant me.'

Hannah looked at Joe. All eyes, he thought wretchedly. She wants me to say no, say she's got it all wrong. Please.

'I'm crazy, is what she meant.'

'You are not,' he said stubbornly.

'Think about it.'

He turned yellow chrysanthemum petals in his fingers, crushing weak earthy scent out of them.

'You have done some funny things,' he said slowly. 'But then, we all do. With your family and everything, I'd say you were doing fucking brilliantly.'

'I'm not doing brilliantly, Joe. Remember the deal?'

He nodded.

'It's on.'

'What is?'

'I don't know the words for it,' she said patiently.

'I don't know what you're on about.'

'Nor do I. That's the trouble.'

'Aren't you coming home, then?'

'Home?'

'Back with me.'

'And do what? Drive both of us out of our heads?'

'Don't be stupid,' he said angrily.

'I'm not stupid. I'm trying to tell you how it is – hopeless.'

'You might be . . .' Joe started, but she cut him short.

'I am hopeless.'

'But I love you, and you said you loved me.'

'I don't love anything. I can't,' said Hannah.

'Then what was all that about?' yelled Joe.

'The more I love you,' she went on as though he hadn't interrupted, 'the more I hurt. Love is a great big pain just here,' she touched her ribs, 'and the more I want you, the further I have to run away. And I get worn out by it, so I make you run away instead. I can never, ever be still. Or peaceful. Perhaps I'm wicked. Anyway, it isn't you, it's me. I do love you, and I always will, more than anything I ever imagined, more than fairytales, and it scares me to death.'

'And what about me?' he demanded resentfully.

'We can keep the deal.'

'Fuck the deal.'

'I haven't got anything else. The baby's gone. I've only got me and that's nothing. Now there's only the deal to go on for.'

'Jesus, this is heavy.'

'I am heavy, I told you, I'm a millstone.'

He leaned forwards, grabbing her shoulders angrily, putting his face to hers. 'You aren't going anywhere, you hear me?'

Hannah, feeling his heart beating, stared over his shoulder at the spectre of his going away, looked her worst dread in its face and bowed to it unresistingly. 'I don't know where I'm going, and that's the truth,' she said calmly.

Joe laid his face in her neck. 'You know something,' he said against her hot, dry skin and felt her shake her head, 'when I took LSD I realised the whole world is inside my head. Or the whole world *is* my fucking head, I never figured which.'

'What's LSD?'

'An hallucinogen.'

Hannah nodded vacantly.

'Perhaps it's all in your head. You might not have to go any further than that. And that ain't far.' The joke failed miserably.

'I don't know. I don't know anything at all.'

'Straws in the wind.' He lifted his head. 'You never know.'

'That's too deep for me. I'm floating over it all. Thistledown.'

'I thought you said you were heavy,' he said, sensing a return to normality. 'Make your mind up.'

Then she spoiled it again. 'I haven't got one,' she said bleakly, 'that's the point. When I have, I'll tell you.'

'Oh, fuck,' said Joe, tears in his eyes.

Awkwardly, half embarrassed, he let go of her, and wretchedly they moved apart.

Chapter Twenty-Nine

Miss Michael, social worker to the psychiatric department, stood at the end of Hannah's bed, a bosomful of beige card files between herself and a caseload full of needy people, whose neediness she strove daily, without much success, to staunch. Eavesdropping professionally on Hannah's unsatisfactory performance upon being told she could go home, Miss Michael sighed. NALGO was always complaining that huge caseloads meant low standards, but what could you do? She shuffled the top folder open and waited.

'We're happy for you to go as soon as you're ready. You've got a follow-up appointment in six weeks, haven't you?' Dr Tate sounded distanced, as if she had already gone. She knew he meant today or tomorrow.

'We need the bed,' Sister had said, meaning, another girl, another abortion. Dr Tate stood up.

'Please,' said Hannah.

He stooped to listen.

'I've still got your hanky.'

He began to straighten up. 'Keep it.'

'I thought you'd want me to bring it back. Ironed.'

'No need.'

'I think,' said Hannah at the same time, and they both waited. He leaned closer.

'I think,' she whispered, 'I'm going to do something silly.'

Dr Tate frowned and sat back on the side of the bed. 'Why?'

Hannah shook her head which was spinning in terror.

'What do you think you might do?'

'I don't know.'

He turned, caught Miss Michael's eye and looked back at Hannah.

'Could you give me some idea?' he suggested.

'Something embarrassing.'

He looked at her white knuckles and waited.

'I'm not sure whether I can control it.'

'What can't you control?'

'I don't know. It might be some sort of . . . making a fool of myself.'

Miss Michael shifted her considerable weight to her other foot and put her folders on to the bed table discreetly.

'What if we send you home?' prompted Dr Tate.

'I think, I'm afraid, I'll disgrace myself.'

There are no beds anywhere, thought Miss Michael, feeling persecuted, foreseeing she'd be expected to find one. Dr Tate was asking questions, sharply interested for the first time. 'I'm terribly sorry, we hadn't realised,' Miss Michael heard him say. 'If we arranged some convalescence, would that help, do you think?' Hannah saw her last chance disappearing. She was about to say yes, and heard herself say no.

'What would?' asked Dr Tate as though, at last, he really wanted to know.

Hannah spilled it out before fear made it impossible to say anything. 'Somewhere safe. Please.'

'Safe. Miss Michael, can you find somewhere safe?'

'I should think so.'

'We'll try to find somewhere.'

'Can I stay here?'

Dr Tate grinned. 'Sister won't be too pleased, but I expect she'll put up with you for another day. Miss Michael will probably have something tomorrow.'

Oh, yes indeed, right out of a hat, thought Miss Michael grimly, as if placing young, depressed, neurotic postnatal women was as easy as scattering sand on the shore. 'I expect we'll find something.' She tried not to let martyrdom creep into her voice.

'I'm terribly sorry to be a nuisance. I'm sorry, I'm sorry, I'm sorry.'

'Classic depressive syndrome,' said Dr Tate to Miss Michael, going through the swing doors. Syndrome. Hannah was the one with an English degree and she didn't know what it meant; when Miss Michael arrived with only one file, the next morning, she didn't ask. She was too frightened of the answer.

'I've got your train ticket,' said Miss Michael, opening her folder to take out an envelope. Hannah sat fully dressed on a chair by her bed, astonished that such things could be done, thinking you could only buy tickets at stations.

'Where am I going?'

'Sussex.'

'I mean, what kind of place?'

'Somewhere where people will understand,' said Dr Tate, pushing open a swing door, popping his head in and standing there, half in and half out, 'about feeling silly.'

'Oh, yes,' said Miss Michael, 'indeed.'

'Will they?' asked Hannah, looking back and forth at the two of them, full of doubt and hope.

'There are people there who will help,' said Dr Tate gently. 'I came to say goodbye. I'll have to leave you in Miss Michael's capable hands because I'm afraid I've a few other people to see.'

'He's always going somewhere,' observed Miss Michael, powder blue bosom heaving in sympathy as the doors swung shut behind him. 'He's the most frightfully busy man,' she added proudly.

'Dr Ashley said he was the kindest man in the world.'

'Oh, he is,' cried the social worker. 'Who said that? Oh, yes, Dr Ashley, of course. You came from . . . didn't you.'

I don't like you, thought Hannah, you are slithery. Like Miss Worthington, you don't tell the truth.

'Can't I wait until Joe comes, and travel with him?'

Miss Michael's mouth pursed. 'No, dear. You'll be met at the station. They send a car.'

'I'd very much rather go with Joe, if you don't mind. It's in Sussex, too. Brighton, I mean. That's where he comes up from and we could go back together . . .' She faltered at the black look on Miss Michael's well-powdered face.

'Do you want to keep this place or not? You said you wanted someone who'd understand,' the social worker sniffed accusingly.

'Yes, but . . .'

'That's what you want?'

'Yes, but . . .'

'That's what you told Dr Tate. You can't chop and change, you know.'

'I . . .'

'If you don't, you'd better say. They're under terrible

pressure for beds. They're doing me a bit of a favour because I thought it was urgent.'

'Are they?'

'Yes. You can get to Victoria?'

'Yes,' said Hannah sullenly.

'Then I'll leave your tickets with Sister. She'll know.'

Know what? Hannah felt another stab of pure fear, so ignorant of what she was doing, she didn't know what questions to ask when Sister put the train ticket in her hand and gave her a little hug of encouragement, saying, 'You take care now, and good luck.' Her silver nurse's badge dug into Hannah's chest.

Why do I need so much good luck? she wondered.

When Joe, on the telephone, had demanded to know all the details, she had to admit she didn't know any.

'Where the hell are they sending you?' he asked.

She was sure it would sound terribly ungrateful to ask.

There were four of them at the station, standing diffidently in the leafy car park, cases at their feet, avoiding each other's gaze and longing to say something.

'I expect it's Daniel,' offered a scrawny woman in a faded green duster coat.

They scuffed their feet in the dry black dirt and said nothing.

'Daniel's the handyman. He gets sent when no-one else fancies the trip, and he's always late.'

'You going to Ridley Manor?' remarked one of the two men offhandedly.

'I'm a readmission,' said the thin woman eagerly. 'I only managed a month this time.' Her mouth smiled, her eyes pleading and anxious.

They pondered the significance of this, standing in

dappled sunlight beneath sycamore trees, dazzling reflections bouncing off windscreens and polished chrome. An old black car rounded the corner with a squeal of tyres and drew up with a jolt in a cloud of dark dust. The driver leaned on the steering wheel, peering up at them. Then he got out, saluted sardonically, stuffed all their suitcases into a cavernous boot. They all climbed in and sat hunched in the back, except for the readmission who sat in the front, next to Daniel, studiously taking no notice of her at all. They shrank away, trying not to lean on each other and touch as he whirled down country lanes, much too fast, the hedges and ditches a gorgeously lush green after London's wilted summer parks. Daniel's window was open and air flew in, blowing back Hannah's long hair, cooling her face.

'Here you are.' They swung in through open iron gates. A sprawling house stood at the end of a drive, its uncurtained windows like empty eyes. On a low wall, to one side, a crowd waited, watching the car expectantly. 'Reception committee's out,' said Daniel derisively, and skidded the car to a halt.

A woman came and opened the door on Hannah's side. She could have been a secretary, in her neat grey skirt and handknitted cardigan. Her manner was bossy. She's like a head nurse out of uniform, Hannah thought, so that is what she must be.

She climbed out, putting down her bag uncertainly. 'Welcome to Ridley Manor,' the woman said and spied the readmission in the front of the car. 'Oh, it's you back, is it?'

'It's me.'

'I won't welcome you, then.'

Why? wondered Hannah.

The crowd began to break up into ones and twos, drifting away.

'They're supposed to help,' said the bossy woman crossly. 'Oh, well, come on in and I'll show you.'

The scrawny woman skipped like a goat up the steps, seeming eager to get inside. 'No need to show me,' she called over her shoulder but the other woman called her back sternly. 'You don't know where they've put you. You'll have to go through, same as everyone else.'

They turned down a corridor into what had once been a fine drawing room, great windows overlooking lawns that sloped to an orchard. The room was spotless. Every inch of carved woodwork shone.

'There you are. Sit yourselves down and I'll get you to sign in.' She picked up a sheaf of papers from a side table and, watched by some of the crowd, who had come silently in, laid them in four small piles. 'One each, there you go,' she cried, pushing cases into a corner with her foot and pulling out chairs. The readmission looked round for a pen.

'Here you are.' The woman offered Hannah a biro. 'These are for reading later, rules and stuff, and this is for you to sign now.' Hannah read a short paragraph typed on a sheet, then read it again.

'All right?' said the woman, thrusting the pen before her.

'I can't sign this.'

'Why not?'

'It says, I have to accept any treatment I'm offered. What treatment?'

The woman waved her hands, shrugging.

'What treatment?' cried Hannah again, panicking. 'Is this a hotel or what?'

The small crowd stared knowingly down the long, shiny conference table. The scrawny woman held out her hand for the biro, her mouth hanging open.

'Hotel?' shouted someone, and burst out laughing. 'That's a good one. Who have you been talking to, darling?'

Hannah flushed deeply and looked to the grey-skirted woman for help. 'What is this place?'

The woman grinned pityingly. 'A mental hospital for people with high IQs,' she said, 'boarding school for the batty. In a word, a bin. What did you think it was?'

Somewhere they'd understand about feeling silly.

The words of the kindest man in the world ringing in her ears, deadly pain swept over Hannah. In the high-ceilinged, airy room her fellow inmates looked on as she signed the piece of paper.

'That's a good girl; sensible. We all do it,' said the woman, giving the biro over. 'Here you are, Alice.'

'You?' said Hannah, the world turning inside out.

'We're all patients. You haven't met any staff yet.'

Hannah looked round the circle; it moved closer, hemming her in, blocking the doorway. Her case had been moved, to the other side, beyond reach. And they'd driven miles through empty countryside from the station.

'You'd better stay,' encouraged her fellow patient understandingly.

'I had no idea,' whispered Hannah.

'Sometimes it's better, not knowing. It can be better that way,' said the woman.

Chapter Thirty

Dr Dickens, also known as Tricky Dicky, peered over half-moon glasses at his new patient and wondered when she'd stop bawling. 'Why are you crying?' he inquired, when she showed no sign of obliging him.

Hannah lay, naked to the waist, on a couch, a rug over her.

'I want to examine you, but it's very difficult when you will keep on blubbering.'

'I've had an abortion; I was examined the day before yesterday,' sobbed Hannah.

'Yes, I expect you were. But, you see, I have to do it again. Just heart and lungs and that kind of thing. We have to keep our own records.'

He pulled down the blanket, warming his stethoscope in his hand, his fingers brushing her breasts.

'Milk?' he asked, as if very surprised.

'I just had an . . .' cried Hannah, trying to find the edge of the blanket, to pull it up.

'No, no,' he murmured, as if to a stubborn child, and his fingers probed and drummed on her skin, lingering softly.

'You are perfectly healthy, so would you care to get up and stop snivelling?'

Hannah closed eyes swimming in tears. 'I can't stop.'

'Oh, yes, I think you can,' he said, turning away.

She pulled up the blanket, turned her back and cried until his cushions were sodden with tears.

'Oh dear, oh dear,' sighed Dr Dickens reproachfully, pressing a bell. 'You really can't keep on like that.'

'I want to go.'

'You only just came. Are you always impatient?'

'I want to see Joe.'

He shook his head. 'It's unsettling to have visitors the first week or two. You'll settle down.'

There was a soft knock on his door and a nurse came in with a tiny dish containing two blue pills.

'Put her in the single,' ordered Dr Dickens without preamble.

'Come along,' said the nurse, giving Hannah her clothes from the back of a chair, taking her along a wooden-floored corridor to a tiny room under some eaves, with nothing in it but a bed and a big mirror on the wall. 'Here, take these. He's given you them every three hours.' She fetched a glass of water. Hannah, swollen-faced and worn out from crying, swallowed them down and five minutes later was fast asleep.

The crying was Fat Ginger's fault. She'd had the bed next to Hannah's in the long dormitory on the first floor and had insisted on talking while watching Hannah unpack.

'What are you here for?' she kept saying.

'I don't know.'

'I don't usually go to tea but I will if you want to,' she offered generously, ignoring the ringing of a bell from below and Hannah's silent back.

'I've had an operation,' Hannah mumbled in the end, to shut her up.

'What kind?' demanded Fat Ginger, screwing up round blue eyes suspiciously. 'I bet you've had what I had. I thought, as soon as I saw you . . .'

Hannah put things one by one into a locker, for something to do, to avoid conversation.

'I had a baby,' announced Fat Ginger, getting no satisfaction from her probing. 'I bet that's what you've had. Mine's been adopted. Has yours?'

'It's dead.'

'It died?' Fat Ginger sounded awed.

'I killed it.'

'Oh, you had an abortion,' Fat Ginger said offhandedly. 'They said I could, but I didn't want to.'

Hannah burst into tears of fury and guilt, a neverending flood; the tears that wouldn't come in the hospital ward, that she'd bitten her fingers to bring. Too many, Dr Dickens said impatiently, and demanded they stop. A nurse who woke her with a poke in the back brought tiny blue pills every three hours that kept her asleep for three days and three nights. When they let her wake up, the crying was over, leaving her as dry and as tearless as ever.

Chapter Thirty-One

While her eldest daughter learned to live tidily with all her wordly belongings on the single shelf of a locker, April's flat in the top half of her mother's big house looked as though a bomb had hit it. Eileen clucked and sniffed with disapproval, thinking that David had his faults, but at least when he and April had lived there, it had been tidy. Now his children ran riot, thought Eileen, pausing on the stairs with half a dozen empty milk bottles in a wooden crate. She'd got tired, she reflected, looking into the bottles before putting them out to make sure they were washed, of telling April she should get out, remarry, find someone to be a father to those children.

April agreed, nodded, made jokes about the surgeons she worked with, but they were nearly all married, while year in, year out, she herself stayed stubbornly married to David.

'Why don't you divorce him and good riddance?' demanded Eileen when April got the last of her children, except Hannah, from the Court. 'You've got everything you want except a proper husband. Why hang on to that good-for-nothing?'

'I love him.' April ran the Singer along the seam of a dress; she made all their clothes.

Eileen gave a short laugh. 'Love?'

April turned the seam and began double stitching.

'Haven't learned, have you? I gave the best years of my life to your father and look where that got me. And now look at you, throwing your life away on a man who doesn't even want you. Same old story, isn't it?'

'He'll get tired of her.'

'Huh,' sniffed her mother, giving up, 'more like the other way round. You should have more pride.'

'I can't afford pride. I can't afford anything now I've paid for Polly and Ingrid's school uniforms.'

'They need a proper father, not a maintenance cheque three months late, or whenever his lordship deigns to remember,' snapped Eileen.

'Don't go on and on, Mum. Pass me the scissors.'

Eileen passed the shears and settled her glasses firmly underneath her hairnet; they tended to catch on the white nylon strands that matched her hair. 'And you don't eat. You've shrunk.'

'So have you. It's age,' retorted April.

'Not with you, it isn't. What it is with you, isn't age, my lady, it's rage. You used to do it as a child; you'd go and be sick and you didn't think I knew what you were up to, but I did.'

April glanced at her mother unmoved, her mouth full of pins.

'You see, I know you,' cried Eileen, 'you'd starve rather than give him the last word. Years, you'll keep it up, while he doesn't even notice. That Christina isn't thin. It's not attractive, you know, looking like a chicken leg.'

April spat pins into a little tin. 'You're a wicked old woman,' she said bitterly. 'If I had somewhere else to go, I'd . . .'

Eileen cackled. 'You haven't. You'll have to wait, dear, 'til I'm gone.' April felt the house as a tangible presence around her, malignant, as she gathered fabric together for tacking.

'I've spent all my life trying to get out of here,' she said wearily, 'isn't it odd? I hate it, but it's always turned out to be the only safe place – for me, then me and David, and now me and my children. And I'll be alone in it, I suppose, when you've gone and they go. It's as if I've never got away, just rattled my chains every now and then but only as a gesture.'

'I don't know about that, I'm sure. But you could speak to Polly. That Welfare woman was round from the school again the other day, saying she hasn't been for . . . oh, ages. You should take some notice, you know. It's not for me to say anything to the Welfare, is it?'

'All that uniform money down the drain. I'll wring her neck,' muttered April.

'It's not the money, you know. If she had a father,' began Eileen again with enjoyment, 'she'd have some discipline.'

'Not necessarily. David pontificates and rants and raves but I wouldn't call it discipline. Look at Hannah.'

'I haven't looked at Hannah in a long time. Where is she?'

'She doesn't bother letting me know.'

'You're her mother, you ought to know. Does David?'

'Hannah turned her back on us a long time ago.'

Eileen poked at the fire, forcing feeble yellow flames to burn half- heartedly.

'I've enough trouble as it is. They squabble because we live in each other's pockets. You can't blame them.'

April looked round her mother's ample rooms and sighed with frustration.

'You'll have to wait for when I'm gone.'

'Don't talk like that, Mum.'

'Granny!' cried Jessie nine weeks later. Eileen lay in the hallway and Jessie stumbled over her as she let herself in from school early. She dialled 999 and whispered, 'Hurry up, hurry up,' as the bell rang, terrified Eileen would die right there in front of her. On the second ring someone said, 'Which service?'

'Quick,' cried Jessie, 'Granny's ill.'

The woman on the other end had to be very patient and ask for the address several times. Eileen twitched and moaned, so she couldn't be dead. With great presence of mind, Jessie dragged the eiderdown off Eileen's bed in the front room downstairs and put it over her, not daring to move her. She stood indecisively with a pillow in her hands, wanting to put Eileen's thin white hair on to something soft. The ambulance came, racing down the road ringing its bell, so the neighbours tweaked their curtains and looked out to see. When Peter and Polly and Ingrid came home, one after another, dragging schoolbags and feet, they found crumpled bedding in the hall and no lights on. Jessie had left a note in the kitchen upstairs that they all had to get their own tea.

In the same hospital to which they took Eileen, April answered her telephone in the operating theatre suite.

'Can you come down, Sister?' someone said in casualty, their voice neutral.

April looked at the clock. 'Won't Staff do?'

'Mr Hurst told me to ask you to pop down,' said the voice.

'Ten minutes?'

'I'd come at once, if I were you,' said the voice sympathetically, and the phone was put down.

April told Staff to take over and, once she was out of sight in the long green corridors, broke a cardinal hospital rule and ran.

'A bleed from the aorta,' said Mr Hurst cheerily. 'But we can patch her up.'

'Oh.'

Her mother lay quite still under the flourescent lights of the casualty department. They made her look green.

'We'll need your signature,' he said, 'here, and here.'

April signed.

'Age?' he demanded.

'Seventy-one.'

Mr Hurst swung his stethoscope and said he thought she could withstand the anaesthetic. April leaned on the end of the trolley, her legs gone weak.

'X-ray,' Mr Hurst told a nurse, handing her a small sheaf of papers.

'I'll go,' said April.

'No, you won't,' said Mr Hurst. 'You will go and sit in the office and have a strong cup of tea. And while we're waiting for the X-rays we'll go over what we can do. She's fit as a flea and if we give her a spot of non-stick in the aorta she'll be back on her pins in no time.'

'Non-stick?' said April stupidly, 'She's not a frying pan.'

'We'll mend her like one. Teflon graft. Works wonders.'

'Of course.' She knew they did, but with her own mother it was a shocking idea.

'Ring your husband,' ordered Mr Hurst. 'Get a bit of support, you know.'

'I haven't . . .' April opened her mouth to set him straight, half grateful, half detesting him for not knowing and not understanding, until it dawned upon her that he was right.

'I'll use the phone in the office,' she said.

David didn't sound pleased. He said he was in the middle of dinner and they had people with them, but he'd be there later. April let him ring off without arguing. Neither of them mentioned Christina.

'She's not family,' said Jessie. 'She won't come here.' They all sat in the nurses' canteen, bored and scared and wishing the hands on the clock would move forward, but they dragged more slowly than ever.

'I wouldn't put it past him to bring her.'

Polly said, 'Oh, not again, Mum . . .'

April heard the warning and drank weak tea from a machine. 'And you shouldn't do that, 'specially in here,' she said, when Polly pulled out a packet of cigarettes.

'Why not?'

'They give you cancer and it's a bad example.'

'Who to?' demanded Polly, looking at the empty place behind the serving counter with its wiped shiny display shelves, all empty. A lethargic black woman dusted chairs with a grimy yellow cloth, swiping at the tops of tables, flicking her wrist contemptuously. 'I'll go in the bog, if you'd rather.'

'No, and I wish you wouldn't talk like that. They open up again when the night staff come for their dinner.'

'I couldn't eat my dinner at two in the morning,' said Polly cheerily and lit up.

'Those smell like cigars.' Ingrid had a sudden fit of coughing and Jessie looked up from her book. Polly was holding her breath.

'Ass. Not here,' hissed Jessie.

'Mum and Dad together?' Polly let the smoke out in a trickle.

'I know what you mean.' Jessie went back to her book.

'I don't want to stay if he's coming,' said Peter.

'Yes, you do. You'll all behave decently,' snapped April.

'Huh,' said her son, relapsing into indifference.

'Don't make scenes.'

'*I* won't make scenes, Mum,' he said, turning his back, watching the door across the half-lit room for his father to come in. After a while, he dozed.

'Is she still upstairs?' David asked, looming over the back of April's chair, giving her a fright. 'You all ought to go home, you know, there's no point in waiting around.'

Five faces turned towards him.

'You'd be better off getting some sleep.'

'I couldn't possibly leave her,' said April sharply. 'Trust you to suggest it.' The hospital hummed around them and over the tannoy someone called a name and then cut off with a resonant click.

'Are you all right?' he asked, looking from one to the other. His children's eyes shifted away, hiding their thoughts. 'What do they say?'

'They're trying to give her a graft,' said April fretfully.

'Mr Hurst says, don't worry, but of course I do.'

Polly looked him full in the face, boldly. 'Hello, Dad. Fancy seeing you. How are you?'

'I'm very well, thank you, Polly,' David said stiffly. 'I'm sorry about your grandmother.'

Polly flicked a spent match at an ashtray and missed. 'Is she going to die? You're the doctor.'

April looked outraged.

'I haven't spoken to her surgeon. I came straight down here,' answered David evenly.

'Stop that,' cried April, feeling battle lines being drawn already, over her head.

Ingrid stared at the back of his head, where he was going bald, and tried to remember how long it was since she'd seen him. He sat down by her mother and they spoke tensely, leaning towards each other but not touching. Peter slid down in his low chair, facing the other way, not looking around at his father. The clock ticked and Polly fingered the envelope of hash in her pocket, wondering if lighting up again would be worth the row. Thinking about it, she brightened up and was pulling the bundle out when the door swung open and Mr Hurst looked round, his little green cap still on his head.

'Oh,' breathed April, ready for the worst, grabbing David's arm.

'Fine, fine, fine,' bellowed the surgeon, coming into the canteen. 'She'll do fine.'

David prised April's fingers off his sleeve and went to shake hands.

'She's doing well, we had no trouble and I think it would be best if you all went home,' said Mr Hurst. 'Come back in the morning when she'll have woken up, though she'll be a bit sleepy for a while.'

'Can I go in and see her first?' asked April, gathering courage to argue, but he merely said yes, of course, and the others could all take a quick peep if they wanted to.

They marched in loose, reluctant file through the hospital, Peter slouching angrily, not keeping up, out of the canteen, through corridors, up in a lift and into a side room where a nurse was flicking a drip with her finger, counting drops under her breath. She went on with her work as they crowded in the door.

'Why is she so white?' whispered Ingrid. 'Is she all right?'

'Yes,' said April, her heart in her mouth at the sight of Eileen lying so pale and so still. A blood pressure gauge was wrapped around her arm and the nurse began to pump it up, watching the mercury in the tube, then she stopped and they all listened to the hiss of air as she let it out. 'She's doing nicely.' The nurse's voice startled them.

'There's no need to stay, you know. She'll sleep until morning and she won't remember anything,' David said.

'She looks as though she's dead, doesn't she?' Ingrid whispered, desperately wishing Granny would open her eyes and prove she wasn't.

'It's only the anaesthetic,' said David.

They waited in the doorway for someone to say what they should do next.

'Can we go now?' muttered Polly.

'Really,' said April under her breath.

'She's scared,' mumbled Jessie, feeling miserable herself.

Something in the corner went beep, beep, beeep and the nurse turned to look but David saw it first and pushed back into the room suddenly, shouldering them aside. 'Where's Hurst?' he shouted.

'Gone,' said April, turning to look.

'Call him. Fast,' David said, and the nurse went to a telephone and began to dial.

April came to life. 'Go and sit in the corridor or find the waiting room,' she ordered, pushing them out, very quickly, very strongly, once more in control.

They sat in a dejected row outside.

'I'd bloody well hate to be a nurse in Mum's theatres. I bet she's awful to work for,' said Polly, lighting a cigarette.

'You're asking for it,' said Ingrid.

'It's an ordinary one. I'm not stupid.'

'Could have fooled me.'

There was no heart left in them and in the end, the crisis turned out to be a false alarm. David drove them home at four in the morning and said he'd come back the next evening. He dropped them off outside Eileen's house and left, driving off with a roar.

'What a berk,' said Peter, unutterably depressed, careful not to let his mother hear. They went indoors and to bed, except for April who sat up in Eileen's kitchen, making tea and mourning everything and everyone, until it was breakfast time.

Eileen seemed to get better. David rang up and said since she was on the mend, he wouldn't come again, only in emergencies and he didn't feel he'd done much good anyway, despite his midnight dash across London. April didn't argue with him, just looked haggard.

'What did you expect?' asked Polly.

'I don't know. I thought he might have cared a bit.'

'You like banging your head on brick walls,' Polly told her bluntly, hitching her skirt exactly level with her knickers.

'That's a nasty thing to say,' snapped April. 'You can't come to the hospital looking like that.'

'It's cool,' said Polly sweetly, pulling on a black leather jacket. 'And it doesn't ride up on the back of a bike.'

'If it rode up any further you'd show your all,' said April sourly. 'But I take it we'll see you this evening?'

'Fred'll bring me.'

'Must you come on that bike?'

'Don't be draggy, Mum.' Polly gave her a kiss. 'I'm late.'

'Be careful on that bike.'

'You're just jealous.'

April rubbed her eyes wearily and went to get ready for work herself. Polly was right, she was jealous of their freedom and their future, when she had none.

'The children will come in this evening,' she told Eileen later, sitting leaning her elbows on the carefully tucked green bed cover, her chin in her fists, exhausted. She undid her dark belt with its wrought silver buckle, that she'd been so proud to get, and slumped. 'How am I going to look after you, when you come home?' she asked.

Eileen lay asleep, her skin's soft folds loose and pallid, like spilled wax, her mouth half open. 'I can't do any more, Mum. They'll have to send someone in because I can't take the time.' Eileen's eyelids flickered. 'Don't go, Mum, don't go and leave me.' April longed for her to wake, sit up and make some mean, malicious comment, so that they could all heave a sigh of relief that things were back to normal.

'What?' April's head jolted forwards and she woke from a doze with a start.

Eileen's breath gurgled.

April lunged for the bell at the head of the bed as a gout of blood shot from Eileen's mouth to the ceiling, soaking everything bright red as the carefully stitched repair in her artery burst. People came running, prised her hand off the bell and took her away, mopping and saying, 'Let's take your dress off, Sister, you're drenched.' They gave her an injection of something and made her lie down.

'Is there someone we can call?' they asked.

'I don't want anyone.'

'Try and rest, then,' they said. She dozed, then woke, fretful and terrified. 'Is my mother dead?' she cried, like a child.

'Yes,' they said. 'Who shall we call? Your daughter? Peter?'

'My daughter?' said April, pushing her hair from her forehead, confused and disjointed. 'My daughter has gone.'

They looked surprised. 'Sister, your daughters are at home. We rang them. They want to know if they should come and fetch you.'

'She's in York. Look.' They saw tiny scars on the palms of her hands, like stigmata. 'I had to leave her.'

'Keep her in,' said Mr Hurst.

Jessie took the telephone call.

'They say she's wandering and talking rubbish because she's shocked.'

'She's not the only one,' muttered Ingrid.

'You'd better ring Dad,' said Polly to Jessie, as she stood with the 'phone in her hand.

'I won't. You can, if you want.'

'I'll do it, give it here.'

David answered after a lot of rings, sounding very soft and polite until Polly said it was her.

'You'd better go and see Mum. She's in hospital.'

'What?'

'Granny's dead and Fred never turned up and Mum's had such a terrible shock she's in hospital. You ought to go and see her,' snapped Polly 'So there.'

'You shouldn't have done that,' remarked Jessie.

'He's in no position to tell me what to do.'

'*I'll* tell you what not to do – don't come to the funeral on Fred's bike.'

'Why not?'

'You'd embarrass Mum to death.'

'Really?' Polly cheered up after that.

The funeral parlour had tidied Eileen up nicely, so they could all look in the coffin and take a quick glance at death. Fred leaned on the seat of his bike, refusing to come in, his inside pocket padded with grass as a sincere gesture of sympathy for Polly later. April, thought David, sitting alone at the back of the crematorium chapel, looked more like a starveling than ever.

'They fought like cats,' he'd said to Christina, 'but in their own way, they were devoted. I wonder how she'll manage.'

'She'll have the house, I suppose.'

'Almost certainly.'

Christina snorted, looking round their tiny, rented flat.

'I know,' said David tiredly, 'don't let's go into it again.'

'I hate second-hand,' she muttered.

'Then you must hate me,' answered David, trying to make light of it, pulling his black tie straight, 'because I'm second-hand.

Christina put her hand up and ran her finger right round his face and over his lips, lifting up his glasses to study his eyes. 'Do you love me?' she asked.

'What's love?'

'Passion?'

'We are well suited, then.'

She brushed his dark jacket, turning him round with her hand. 'Maybe.'

'Your father might be at the funeral. Will you really not come?'

Christina tightened the belt of her robe and put the clothes brush back in its drawer. 'You know nothing at all, do you?' she said.

Surrounded by her family, April listened to the creaking mechanism that drew Eileen's earthly remains into the fire. Dark blue velvet curtains swung shut, their corners not quite touching, a hint of something moving behind. April felt sick. Then it was everyone crowding round, Sam and Bridie each holding one of her elbows, making their way out past a little crowd of mourners waiting to come in, and it was over.

They drove back to what was now April's house, for small helpings of brandy and weak, tasteless tea. Peter put his arm around her and said, 'Send them all home, you're whacked,' but she smiled a hollow smile and said, 'I can't,' so he went away angrily and didn't come back.

Jessie started a new book, Ingrid boiled kettles in Eileen's old-fashioned kitchen and looked into the old copper to see what was there. Polly sat in Fred's lap and cried, well out of sight of the rest, furiously and quietly, holding the packet of grass squeezed in her fist. David sat holding a cup of colourless tea in Eileen's best china, listening to Bridie ask April about the house, and what she'd do with the extra room.

'It doesn't take long, does it?' he muttered to Sam. 'Old girl's only been gone five minutes and it's already, you could do this and you could do that, with what she's left.'

'I didn't think you saw eye to eye, you and her.'

'We didn't,' said David gloomily, 'but that's not the point, is it?'

'Well, if I go before Bridie, I hope she enjoys herself and makes the most of what's left,' replied Sam briskly, dispelling gloom. 'There's no point having it in the first place if you can't enjoy it.'

The silence got awkward.

'No, I suppose not. Look here,' David said in an undertone, 'I've been wanting to come over to see you, but what with one thing and another . . .'

'You'd better tell your mother that.'

'No, I mean you. Not just her.'

'Then you'd better keep your mouth shut about it altogether,' said Sam acidly.

'Christina . . .' David went on, disregarding the interruption.

'Sore point,' said Sam sotto voce. 'Very sore point. All round. Best left alone, I'd say; in present company 'specially.'

'She's terribly homesick,' said David, 'and I wondered if you couldn't ask her family to visit. Would there be any chance of a reconciliation there, do you think?'

'They've come down hard on her, that's true.'

'People who live in glass houses,' muttered David.

'Perhaps that's why they're so hard on her. Blasted righteous people! Just because my wife ran off with a man who was my guest, doesn't mean she's going to be gracious about Christina running off with you. I'd have thought you'd have known that, being a psychiatrist. Haven't you got it all worked out?'

'All what?' asked April across the room, catching Sam's raised voice.

'What we're going to do,' answered David baldly.

The women's faces froze and in the scullery Ingrid turned the tap on hard and kicked the door shut with her foot.

'I'm asking you in front of everyone. Please, April, will you divorce me?'

April held her cup steady in the air, half way to her lips, then very slowly put it down, into the saucer on the arm of her chair.

'This would be a good time to end it,' David went on, his voice falling into the stillness like a knife. 'You're secure now, and the children are nearly old enough to fend for themselves, and I'd like to marry Christina. I want to marry her. I owe it to her.'

April smiled. 'Owe it? What do you know about owing things? If you knew what your debts were, David, you wouldn't have left me, and you wouldn't have the gall to talk about this while my mother's hardly cold in her grave.'

'Pot,' murmured Polly, listening red-eyed from outside the back door. 'They put her in a pot.'

'Urn,' called Fred in a low voice. 'Pot's the other.'

'Give it a rest.' She turned back to listen to the words coming through the door.

'We can't drift on forever.'

'I don't drift,' said April very sharply. 'And what you do with . . . her . . . is up to you. Only you would bring that up now, of all times.'

Ingrid's kettle whistled and she didn't take it off the gas, glad of the noise. David looked at Sam, who looked back, noncommital.

'I want a photograph,' said April, gathering herself up deliberately, ignoring the atmosphere. 'All of us outside, by Mum's pear tree, to remember her by.'

'It's too cold,' said Jessie.

'Coats on,' called April. She gathered them together, protesting and shivering, under the old tree where she'd sat with Sam Saul more than twenty years earlier, while Hannah ate jelly babies in his lap. She opened her camera while they bunched together, to fit in the frame. Fred stood on the end, half in, half out, and April waved at him to move closer.

'We're all here. There we are.' She clicked the shutter. 'That's it. The whole family together.'

Polly coughed loudly and Jessie frowned and said something.

'Yes,' said Sam, 'I was wondering.'

'What?' asked April, preparing to take another snap, looking up at the sky. 'Do you think there's enough light for them to come out?'

'I said, you'd better put a different label on that one,' said Jessie, 'when it comes out.'

'This isn't the whole family,' said Polly.

'Where's Hannah?' asked Bridie.

April looked at David who looked at his feet.

'Hannah doesn't keep in touch,' said April defiantly.

Bridie looked at David expectantly; he shook his head. Jessie and Polly and Ingrid shook their heads. Peter pretended he wasn't listening, then unwillingly shook his head.

'Doesn't anyone know where Hannah is?' demanded Bridie. 'I thought it was just us you cut off, because of Christina. But you've turned the whole family against each other. You'd let your children go missing without even bothering. What in heaven's name do you think you're doing?'

'I tried,' said David stiffly. 'She doesn't want to talk to me.'

'Talk!' cried his mother angrily. 'That's about all you do. And what about you?' She rounded on April, who drew herself up.

'It's the same.'

'Well, a fine bunch you are. Hannah doesn't want you, eh? I never heard of a child that didn't want its parents, but I'm beginning to realise that there are parents who don't want their children, and blame the victims for that.' She moved close to Sam and took his arm. 'I'm sorry for the lot of you, and the way you two go on is wicked. Come along.' She marched the length of Eileen's garden, holding Sam's arm, her back like a ramrod.

'I'm glad someone's said it,' cried Polly shrilly, but Fred jerked her arm and said, 'Shhhh.'

'It's not Mum's fault,' said Peter.

'Bloody mother's boy,' muttered David and Peter flushed with rage.

'She said what people think,' said Jessie in a chilly, grown-up kind of voice.

Left beneath the pear tree, David and April stood angry and embarrassed.

'I will not divorce you, David,' she said finally, 'and

the children are right, we should stop arguing about it.'

He stared after her as she went indoors.

'That's not what was meant,' he shouted furiously, 'if you hadn't bloody well manipulated it to have the last word.'

April left him alone in the garden.

'Checkmate,' mumbled Sam, thinking about it in the car going home.

'What?'

'She's not going to let him marry Christina. She'll drag it out for the rest of her life, if she can.'

'I don't know how they can do it.'

'Oh, I think I do. They enjoy it.'

'What are we going to do?' demanded his wife.

'Nothing at all. There's nothing we can do. You did all anyone could by saying what you did.'

'Hannah?'

'If she comes, we're here.'

'That's all?'

'I doubt she'd thank us for meddling in that nest of vipers.'

'I hope you're right,' said Bridie.

Chapter Thirty-Two

It was nearly Christmas. It's the same old story every time, Joe thought drunkenly, the girl's face pressed into his shoulder. They shuffled, old friends contentedly propping each other up, to the beat of the music. The only light came from a small table lamp that lay on its side on the floor in a corner, casting shadows up the wall. Tight as ticks, life and soul of the university's research endeavours, the post grads were enjoying themselves. Someone gave a relaxed and resonant belch.

'Gross,' sighed Suzanne.

Beside them another girl spat on her finger and began to draw in a puddle of wine spilled on a table top '. . . I said, if you take vector A as smaller than vector B, see, you change . . .' she explained to several people sprawled in low chairs, taking no notice.

'Did it work?' said one, gazing at the wine drawing with boredom.

'Reaction times,' a mousey man with a beard said loudly, 'she's got perfect recall, and I only found out afterwards. You try finding subjects when it takes an hour or more,' he continued, swiping his arm sideways with a laugh, jolting someone else's beer. 'They don't want to know. Sorry.'

'That's me,' said Suzanne.

'What is?'

'I'm the one with perfect recall. I've fucked up his statistics because I remember everything.'

'Keep knocking that stuff back and you won't have a problem much longer,' said Joe, looking for where he'd left his glass. 'You could try remembering my beer.'

'How many brain cells does one glass kill, d'you think?' she said, sitting down on a big cushion, cupping her wine glass in her hands.

'Ask the psychologists.' Joe focused on his beer glass in the near darkness and reached for it. 'Death by drowning.'

'I heard,' she said, turning on her back and putting her head in his lap, 'that you'd got a pale and interesting-looking woman.'

'You're dark,' said Joe, grinning, drawing up his legs so that he cradled her close.

'Have you?'

He yawned. 'Kind of.'

'Not here, though.'

Joe put his head back against the arm of a sofa and closed his eyes, feeling the weight of her, hearing the ceaseless talk, talk, talk of this world of ideas; he thought of ear-numbing silences in libraries and laboratories, their efforts to express ideas picked clean of subjective, feeling bias; the doubtful search for pure intellect.

'No wonder we get pissed out of our heads. She doesn't belong here,' he said, stretching his legs, letting Suzanne fall gently.

'Bring her.'

'This is like family and she wouldn't fit in.'

'What does she do?'

He yawned again, his mind wandering. 'Not a lot.'

She reached up casually and pulled his head down, grasping soft, thick hair in both hands.

'Come back with me?' suggested Joe later.

'Brewer's droop?' Suzanne asked kindly, lying back, squiffily content to go to sleep.

'Looks like it. Sorry,' he said, angrily aware he was lying.

'Maybe in the morning,' she said drowsily, snuggling down, dark hair catching his mouth. Joe caught himself staring at his travelling box, closed and piled high with clothes for the launderette.

'What a gas,' he said furiously, sitting up in bed, neither properly drunk nor properly sober, frustratingly in between. She tried to curl up.

'These days,' he said tipsily, 'I have to make love to girls in boxes. Why aren't you in a box?'

'That's a perversion,' she said, opening one eye, 'and it sounds uncomfortable.'

'It's fucking uncomfortable,' he said, caught short by the shocking fact that he cared this much.

'And boring.' She gave up trying to go to sleep and sat up, pushing her hair back, looking at her watch. 'Which you never were before.'

'Half-hearted,' he muttered. 'I can't believe it.'

She shrugged. 'What's it between friends?'

He turned and ran his hands over her breasts. 'You're beautiful and available and I can't be bothered and I don't believe it.'

'No.' She pulled the sheet up to her chin. 'I'm not available, and I'm tired and fed up and insulted, and if you won't shut up, I'll go home.'

Joe got out of bed and pulled on his jeans. 'I'll take you.'

'You're joking.'

'I'm not.'

She sat on the edge of his rumpled bed, staring up at him, turning her dress the right way out.

'I'm sorry,' he said.

'I'll live.'

'I didn't mean the way it sounded.'

'It sounded awful.'

'I never had this before.'

'Bad beer I can handle,' she said, dispelling their embarrassment with a long giggle, 'but wanting it in boxes isn't my style.'

'Not sex in boxes – we just met in one.'

She pulled her dress over her head. 'You are being a pig. Do my buttons, will you?' She stood in front of him, part angry, part rejected, part motherly.

He did up her buttons. 'I'm sorry.'

'I'll expect I'll forgive you. What's this paragon's name?'

Joe picked a sweater out of the pile on the trunk and opened the door, rubbing his eyes wearily. 'Hannah. She ain't no paragon.'

When he got home he put on the fan heater, found some notepaper and wrote to Gladys, who wasn't on the telephone, that he would be coming home. He went round to the postbox in a pearly dawn and posted the letter, then went back and fell asleep to the scratchy music of an over-used Bojangles seventy-eight, which turned and turned and turned with its needle stuck, as he slept until mid-afternoon.

Chapter Thirty-Three

Gladys knew she was fussing, but couldn't help it. Peering from behind net curtains for a first glimpse of Joe, she made out she was looking for rain. The curtains were snowy and each time she looked up and down the road, she rearranged them with meticulous care. The gasfire hissed and glowed. Feeling hot, she turned it off, then turned it back on again in case Joe thought she couldn't afford it. Then she straightened the cushions on the sofa again. At about the time he said he'd arrive, he did.

Gladys scurried into her kitchen and snatched up the peeler. For all Joe knew, when he found the door on the latch and Gladys bent over the sink, she'd been busy and hardly remembered he was coming.

'You've come, then,' she said, holding a potato under the tap and her cheek up for a kiss.

'Hullo, Mum.'

She turned off the tap and thrust a colander at him. 'You can make yourself useful, now you're here, and slice those up for me. Chips. While I put the kettle on.'

Joe slung his bag round the doorhandle and sat down at his mother's blue formica table with the dripping potatoes.

'I expect you'll want to go round the corner, after your tea.'

Joe wiped his wet fingers and picked up the knife while she got out cups and saucers. 'If you come.'

'You'll want to see everyone,' she said, pleased, 'while you're here.'

'I came to see you.'

'Aren't you stopping?'

'I've got to go back tomorrow.'

She looked so disappointed. Guilt dragged at him, just as it always did at the beginning and end of term, when he left her alone, knowing she was crying and defying him to comment on it. She poured boiling water into the pot, stirring the brown leaves noisily with a teaspoon so that he would know she was angry.

'I'm writing up,' he explained. 'It's not easy to put down and pick up. You lose your train of thought. And my grant runs out in June. I'd never have the discipline to write up after I've left, so it's now or never.'

'You could surely give it a day or two?'

'Sorry, Mum.' Joe blew on his tea and she thought, There are some things no amount of schooling knocks out of them.

'What are you going to do when you leave the university?'

He sliced potato into thick, even-sized chips.

'I want to go back to America.'

'What for?'

'I'm in love with San Francisco.'

'Why can't you stop in one place for five minutes?'

'I have, for more than five years.'

He picked up the last potato.

'It's an awful long way away. I thought you might want to settle down after all this studying.'

'I'll settle in San Francisco.'

'It's that school. I knew I should have kept you at home and not let you go off at that age.'

'People get married at sixteen,' said Joe 'And I did an exchange visit to America and I want to go back. I always meant to, it's nothing new.'

Gladys remembered the postcards. 'It's pretty, I suppose.'

'A bit more than pretty. It's fabulously beautiful.'

'I suppose you'd come back again,' she said bravely.

He sliced the last chip and pushed the colander towards her. 'You make the best chips in London.'

'But you can't wait to leave,' she snapped, getting up to put the fat on to heat. 'How many sausages?'

'You got four?'

Gladys sniffed and told him to get the Daddies out of the cupboard, piercing pink pork skins with a blunt fork.

'Have you ever thought of getting married again?' he asked casually, getting the sauce bottle out of a cupboard.

Gladys speared a sausage. It hung on the fork. 'Why?' she said, turning round. The fat began to smoke.

'I just wondered.'

'You did not,' said Gladys. 'You've got a reason.'

'Just curiosity.'

'It has crossed my mind once or twice,' she said, 'if you must know, but I never met anyone who could hold a candle to your dad.'

'Does he still put in his appearances?'

'He hasn't been back in a good while, no,' said Gladys, as though he'd been abroad for a long stay instead of being dead.

'His ghost coming along on your honeymoon would put a dampener on things, wouldn't it?'

Gladys pulled the fat off the gas quickly and looked at him narrowly. 'What's put all this in your head? You got someone giving you ideas about honeymoons?'

Joe scraped sauce off the side of the Daddies bottle and licked his finger. 'She isn't giving me ideas about honeymoons. But she's called Hannah.'

Gladys pushed sausages around and thought furiously. 'You're too young to get married.'

Joe laughed. 'I'm twenty-four.'

'Hannah. It's a fancy name.' She shovelled sausages on to a plate under the grill, to keep warm. The chips sizzled and rose to the top of the churning fat.

'She's not fancy.'

'What does she do? I suppose she does something.'

'She's done a degree, same as me,' he said, and fleetingly despised himself for being too cowardly to tell her the truth.

The chips turned golden.

'Why haven't you brought her home?'

'I will.'

'Don't go getting married,' said Gladys, grabbing the chip basket, fat flying everywhere but past caring.

'She's been living in my flat.'

'I don't approve.'

'I didn't ask you to.'

Gladys shoved his tea in front of him. 'Does that mean you are going to marry her?'

Joe shook the Daddies and a blob fell on to his plate. 'One day I will.'

Gladys left her food untouched and Joe realised how much the truth would hurt her. He glanced around, half expecting his father's ghost to appear on the spot, pointing an outraged ectoplasmic finger.

'I might ask her to come to America with me.'

'Oh, yes?'

'I don't know we'll actually get married.'

'She don't know you're off?'

'I've told you first.'

Gladys ignored the sop and started to clear their plates, putting his on top of her own, squashing the uneaten chips. 'You can do the washing up, later.'

'It's not opening time, I'll do it now.' He pushed back his sleeves and ran scalding water from a gas heater over the sink.

'What are you going to do in San Francisco? Be a flower power child?' demanded his mother sarcastically.

'I'll only be a part-time flower power child. The rest of the time, I'll earn money.'

'Doing what?'

He rinsed plates under the cold tap. 'Anything that comes. Organising things, theatre, concerts . . . whatever there is. I've had enough of books.'

'What a waste.'

'It's not a waste. I want enough time to do my own thing.'

'What might your own thing be?' she asked sarcastically.

'Writing plays.' He waited for her to laugh but she didn't.

'Plays.'

'Theatrical plays.'

'I didn't know you did that.'

'It's a secret.'

'Does anyone see them?'

'There's not much to see. I work hard and produce little. But every time I decide to give up because I'm no good, I can't. It's like going back on the bottle.'

'Can't you write plays in England?'

'There's no money in it here. It'll be easier to earn enough to patronise myself, if you see what I mean, in America.'

'I'm not sure I see at all,' she said, and for a horrible moment, he thought she was going to cry. 'But I'm proud of you, and so would your dad have been.'

'It's no big deal,' he muttered, ashamed at all the things he wouldn't tell her.

It was cold and the Roman Road market was busy. Joe followed Gladys from stall to stall, hands in his pockets, recognising fewer people than he had last time he'd been down, depressed by the way things changed and people moved on.

'Only the women seem to stay,' he said.

'Not like they used to before the war. Now her son went away like you and a fat lot of good it did.' Gladys pointed to a bric-a-brac stall. 'Mrs Saul as now is.'

Bridie turned, hearing her name.

'I was just telling my son people don't stop in one place like they used to,' said Gladys. 'This is Joe. Mrs Saul used to be Mrs DuCane. Remember Ethel?'

Joe shook his head.

'He wouldn't. You went away to school,' said Bridie, looking up at him. 'I remember you in that uniform, in the paper.'

'He's going to America,' announced Gladys.

Bridie looked impressed. 'What will you do there?'

'Get a job,' Joe said, 'nothing's fixed. Mum's jumping the gun a bit.'

'Talking of shotguns,' Gladys said, 'he's got a girl.'

'Are you engaged?' asked Bridie.

Gladys frowned.

'No,' he said.

'They live together,' hissed Gladys. 'I tell him straight, I don't approve, but will he listen?'

Bridie's smile was genuine, thought Joe.

'I don't suppose so,' she said to his mother. 'Did we ever listen?'

Gladys shook her head and they both laughed.

'Then don't be going on at him,' said Bridie.

Joe smiled and liked her a lot.

Chapter Thirty-Four

'This place,' said Hannah at lunch one day, 'is a hope factory.'

'You what?' said Linda, giving herself a fourth helping of buttered potatoes. The food was quite good.

'Never mind.' She had begun to perceive that they all passed their time there willingly, on account of a misplaced hope that something would happen to make them get better. Looking at all the people who came back again and again, she suspected that it was a hope seldom fulfilled. It sprang eternal, nonetheless. The staff's job was to nourish it. They fed it with a diet of pills to relieve symptoms, regular meals, somewhere to sleep, daily callisthenics and a regular avalanche of mosaic ashtrays and vases out of the occupational therapy hut. The monotony of it did nothing, thought Hannah, to dull her pain. It did contain it, though, after a fashion.

Every now and again, someone broke the unwritten rule about going on hoping and then there was a catastrophe, but mostly they all plodded on. The nub of the matter was seeing the doctors, who tacked up their lists each day on a notice board by the pill hatch. Dr Dickens's lists very often held empty promises and being on them was no guarantee that a person would ever see him, but three weeks after Joe went home to see Gladys,

Hannah spent a whole afternoon in his consulting room.

'Wow,' cried Fat Ginger, 'he must fancy you like mad.'

'Don't be stupid. He's a gnome.'

Fat Ginger sniggered. 'He needs a little woolly hat and then you could put him out in the garden. But some people stay here until they go home again and they never even see him once. You're favoured.'

'That's rubbish.'

Fat Ginger looked superior and pursed up her cupid's bow of a mouth. 'You'll find out. You can be on that list every day at the top and if he doesn't feel like seeing you, he won't get round to you.'

'Why do people let him do that?'

Fat Ginger shrugged.

Hannah remembered his soft touch on her breast and how she had bared her soul to him by crying that morning. 'There's got to be some point to it,' she said defensively.

'Look at me,' said Fat Ginger simply, 'what's doing me any good?'

'Perhaps that's your fault,' said Hannah.

'You're a fast learner,' observed Fat Ginger bitterly.

'What do you mean?'

'That's always their excuse. Whose side do you think you're on?'

'Mine.'

'You'll be lucky,' said the freckled girl. 'I don't think you've learned anything after all.'

'I'm not like you,' snapped Hannah but Fat Ginger burst out laughing.

'And I thought you were smart.'

'I'm seeing him tomorrow.' Hannah played her trump card and Ginger stopped laughing.

'You don't know what you're in for.'

'Then I'll find out,' retorted Hannah and stalked away.

'Silly cow,' muttered Fat Ginger. She sat staring out of the big landing window, listening to the nurses gossiping in the cubby hole behind the pill hatch, until a door from the kitchens below opened and a man carrying a cardboard box went towards the walled-off dustbins.

She got up off the bench and went, unnoticed, downstairs to a side entrance, murmuring. "This little piggy went to market" in a singsong whisper, wondering whether one day it wouldn't simply be easier to slit her own throat and let the whole terrible mess pour out that way.

'Then they'd have to see,' she mumbled, the words lost in the metallic clink as she lifted the lid off the freshly filled bin. First Ginger always had a good rummage, then this little piggy began to eat.

'I missed supper,' she said virtuously in the dormitory several hours later. 'I'm dieting.'

The dormitory ignored her. Iron bedsteads marched the length of the long room, its uncurtained windows flooding the pale cream walls with evening light. Several women of various ages sat or lay on their beds. A girl with a curtain of long, chestnut hair was writing on some bits of card.

'What's that?' asked Hannah, standing over her and looking.

'This,' said Helen, holding up two sheets stuck together with sellotape, 'and I'm going to stick it up here.' She knelt on her pillow and began to tape the message to the wall.

'Thou shalt not covet thy neighbour's chocs,' read Old

Mary from opposite, seeing the coloured letters easily with longsighted eyes 'Oh, really, Ginger, have you been taking things again?'

'If anyone,' threatened Helen, still kneeling facing the wall, 'steals anything out of my locker again, I'll . . .'

'I didn't!' cried Fat Ginger.

No one argued.

'Just don't do it again.' Helen threw herself flat on her covers.

Old Mary opened her handbag secretively behind her locker door. 'Here,' she said, hobbling over.

Helen looked at the half-crown and shook her head.

'Go on, you get yourself some more.'

Helen folded the old woman's knobbled fingers gently around the coin. 'No thanks, I couldn't.'

Old Mary shuffled back to her own bed and put the half-crown back in her purse.

'Jim'll bring some sweets in,' said a reedy little voice in the corner.

Hannah sat on her own bed, by the door, and wondered how such a small voice could come out of such a huge woman. Linda was married. Her husband worked on the railways and was away a lot. Her lover was her milkman. They both worshipped her, taking unacknowledged turns to visit. They vied with each other to buy Linda and make her love them. When the dormitory had ordered cream in the strawberry season, Linda's locker had had to be scrubbed because pints and pints of it went off in the heat. Her milkman brought her her favourite butter toffees in five-pound tins and the occasional bag of potatoes off his float which Linda didn't know what to do with. Her husband brought Roses chocolates in big jars and spent his visits sorting the purple ones into a separate pile for her. He never sank to potatoes. Linda seldom knew what to do with anything, including her husband, lover, five children and eighteen stones of herself. That was her trouble. So she simply ate and ate and waited for someone to tell her. No one did and it had mortally depressed her for years.

'I don't like toffees,' said Helen from her prone position.

'That's not very nice,' said Margaret, coming out of the washroom at the far end of the dormitory. 'Why do you always say no when people want to be nice to you?'

Helen raised her head and stared at her neighbour. 'Why do you have to wash your hands until your nails fall off?'

Margaret's pale, puckered hands fussed at the coarse towel over the rail of her locker.

'Well, there you are,' said Helen, getting no answer, lying back.

'That's mean,' said Hannah.

'Why are you so bloody miserable, too?' snapped Helen.

Linda stopped on her way to the bath, looking over Helen's feet at her angry face. 'Some people just like being miserable.'

'Some people screw the milkman for Dairy Box. All I'm saying is, God help anyone I find in my Dairy Box, darling.'

Fat Ginger's mouth watered nervously. 'When you've all quite finished, I wouldn't mind some toffees.' Her frizzy orange hair was all up on end.

'I thought you were dieting,' said Hannah, sitting cross-legged. Fat Ginger scowled. Old Mary began putting metal curlers into her sparse grey hair, taking them one at a time from two carefully arranged equal rows on her counterpane. 'Suffering is an addiction. It's the hardest one to break because it comes from right inside you and stopping it feels like dying.'

'That's deep,' observed Helen with interest. 'What are you really here for?'

Old Mary took a curler from one row and began to wind her hair, looking into a little pocket mirror on top of her locker, 'Me?'

'You. You've been in here loads and loads of times, haven't you?'

'I suppose,' said Mary, spearing a curler with a pin, 'they don't know where else to put me.'

'Why do you need putting somewhere?' asked Hannah.

'I couldn't really say,' answered the old woman, fishing her stick from behind her locker, ready to go and wash. 'No one's ever said. Why are you here? Lovely young women with good jobs and everything.'

'I wish that were true,' mumbled Hannah.

Helen grinned nastily and said she'd been sent.

'Why?' Mary leaned on her stick with her towel over one arm. Helen lay back on her bed. 'I'm a Section. They didn't like my trying to die in their stinking hospital, so they sent me to someone else's stinking hospital to get rid of the mess.'

'And you a nurse,' said Mary reproachfully. 'What a waste.'

'Are you a nurse?' cried Hannah, remembering the nurse in the night and how she had envied her.

Helen rolled over on her side and fixed Hannah with a glare. 'So?'

'I think you're lucky.'

'And I'd rather be dead.'

'Sometimes I would, too,' said Hannah boldly.

All down the row of beds faces turned blank. Suddenly everyone had something to do.

'You see,' Helen sneered, 'you musn't say it. It upsets people.'

'Not the doctors.' Hannah slid off her bed and came nearer.

Helen croaked with laughter, lying on her side, hair hanging nearly to the floor. 'They're the worst of the bloody lot.'

Hannah stopped right at her side and knelt down. 'Do you tell them?'

Helen grinned and looked ghastly. 'All the time.'

'Don't they help?' Hannah crouched closer.

Helen seemed to consider.

'Do they?' urged Hannah, terrified.

'They make it easier to do.'

'Ring me back,' babbled Hannah, pressing the button when Joe answered, standing in darkness by the coin box in the hall. She was shaking from head to foot.

'Hey, calm down,' he said when he got back to her.

'Joe?'

'Sweetheart?'

'Joe, this place is driving me mad.'

'Then why are you there? Why don't you come home?'

'I can't.'

'You can.'

'Listen, people want to kill themselves here.'

He let the line hum.

'I feel like that, too.'

'That is the most horrible thing you ever said.'

'Am I mad?' she cried, as if he hadn't spoken.

'What you just said is.'

She froze.

'Maybe I love a crazy person. If I do, I'll have to think hard about whether it matters. But you haven't proved to me yet that I love a crazy person, though you seem to be trying hard. Until you do, I haven't got a problem.'

'I *have* got a problem,' she shrieked, and dropped the receiver.

'Maybe I have too,' muttered Joe, replacing the telephone, rubbing his ringing ear. Hannah stood in the dark hall, her hands held tightly over her mouth to stop her voice coming out of its own accord.

Everyone was waiting on the landing in a long queue for sleeping pills and hot water bottles. Old Mary had kept her a place, her night hairnet tied under her chin.

'I wish Helen hadn't said what she did.'

The old woman raised watery eyes. 'Is it catching?'

'I'm scared.'

They moved along the line until they were nearly at the pill hatch. A white-jacketed male nurse handed out little saucers, watching intently, making sure everyone swallowed the contents.

'Don't get involved.'

'How can you not?' demanded Hannah nervously.

'Keep yourself to yourself.'

'Doing that gets you in here.'

The nurse checked a card and handed Hannah her own saucer.

'Sleeping pills, antidepressants and something for anxiety.' She stirred the small, multi-coloured heap with the tip of her finger. 'And Joe tries to make out there's nothing the matter.'

Mary leaned both hands on her stick while the queue shuffled and grumbled its way behind them.

'Take them here,' ordered the nurse impatiently.

'He must love you.'

Hannah blushed to the roots of her hair. 'I can't see why he should.' She swallowed her pills.

'Then I'm sorry,' answered the old woman.

'And I'm afraid that he'll be sorry. I can't live up to being loved.'

'Everyone's sorry in here,' said Old Mary sadly.

Early in February the days were short and it rained most of the time. Hannah spent most of them, sulking and bored, in the occupational therapy room, listlessly sticking little blue tiles on to a jam jar, pretending to turn it into a vase. The open window let in little gusts of cold, wet wind and the grunting of men doing exercises in the yard outside.

The Keep Fit woman was a German Mick Jagger fan with splendid teutonic muscles. She told them daily that a healthy mind needed a healthy body as they slouched unwillingly into the bracing winter air. Only if it really poured or snowed were they allowed indoors. Fat Ginger and Linda muttered about writing to their MPs because it was worse than prison but their threats fell on indifferent ears. Outside, Mick Jagger howled that he couldn't get no satisfaction and shrill cries of "Bend und thrust, bend und thrust" made Linda go pink and feel in her pocket for sweeties. Through the window, Hannah watched the odd assortment of men jump and sway and puff to the music, following the neat movements of their teacher.

'*Nein, nein, nein*, you do not try.' A faint memory of nine nine nine drifted through Hannah's sleepy head. Mustn't mustn't dial nine, nine, nine . . .

'If you co-operated, Miss Holmes,' whined the benign and disorganised woman who ruled the ceramic tile table, 'you might get that done by the end of the week.'

Hannah banged down the jam jar irritably. 'What use is sitting making these stupid things? I don't want them.'

Mick Jagger was stopped in mid-yell and then started again from the beginning.

'Joe plays jazz all the time,' Hannah said to Mary, who sat each day with the rest of them, dozing, too arthritic to pick up tiles or a needle. 'Twenties and thirties. I'd rather have seven golden daffodils and skiffle.'

'Jazz,' said Mary, 'that was in my day.'

Hannah remembered April telling her it was rude to imply people were old.

'I'm nearly seventy.'

'Oh, I'm sorry.'

'Why are you sorry?'

'I can't imagine living that long.'

'You will,' answered Mary, and dozed off again.

The heroin addicts were out of seclusion, fretful and itching and cocky, full of bluster and bad intentions about how fast they'd score once they got out, disrupting the lunchtime queue for more pills.

'Pick me up, put me down. I'm a chemical yo-yo,' muttered Hannah, swallowing chalky blue pills for depression. Tricky Dicky, in her two-hourly sessions each day, talked of Electra, told her she was set like an insect in amber in her need for Daddy. Hannah blushed with shame, as confused as ever.

'What's an Electra?' asked Fat Ginger with scepticism.

'I don't know.'

'How can pills get rid of an Electra?'

'I don't know.'

'You don't know nuffink, do you?'

'I don't know nuffink,' said Hannah.

'Perhaps,' said Hannah, when Joe kept asking if she'd come home.

'I'm coming to see you then.'

'I'd rather you didn't. Not here.'

'Why?'

'I'm embarrassed.'

'I miss you.'

'I miss you, too,' she said shyly.

'When I miss you badly, I go and sit on my trunk,' he said. 'What an idiot.'

'What are you doing?'

'Working. Celibacy is good for me; I've never worked so hard in my life.'

'I'm sorry. I'm making you celibate.'

'Sex isn't important.'

'It seems to be to everyone else.'

'Only with the right person. No good without,' he said feelingly. It had taken days to patch things up with Suzanne.

'I don't think I'm the right person for anyone,' said Hannah.

'You certainly try hard to persuade me of that.'

'Joe?'

'What?'

'Who is Electra?'

'Was. A Greek bird who fell in love with her father. Why?'

'Nothing.'

Tricky Dicky was talking out of the back of his neck; she hated David. 'Back to square one then,' she said. At that moment, her shilling ran out and for once he didn't ring back.

The next day, with the bitter taste of the pills on her tongue, Hannah went to wash her hands for lunch. Taking her towel from her locker, she heard a faint moaning from the washroom.

'Margaret's at it again,' she said to Ginger, who came and planted herself moodily on her bed.

'I can't face lunch. No more food.'

'You been in the bins again? I wish Margaret would shut up.'

'No,' snapped Fat Ginger in the voice that meant she'd not only been in the bins but also in the lavatory, alternately chewing laxatives and throwing up.

'I don't know how you can do it,' said Hannah.

'Then don't try,' snarled Ginger wretchedly, 'and for God's sake, tell her to stop.'

'She can't stop any more than you can.'

Fat Ginger bounded off her bed. 'Then I'll stop her bloody racket.' She marched into the washroom and straight back out again, her freckles standing out against ashy pallor. Hannah stared at the bright red sticky footmarks left as she backed steadily down the dormitory, her fist pressed to her mouth.

'What . . . ?' demanded Hannah, watching the footprints get fainter.

Fat Ginger stared at the washroom door, saucer-eyed, moaning quietly.

Hannah went to see. Margaret wailed aloud in the white-tiled bathroom, taps full on, drains gurgling. She shuffled jerkily, like a puppet on strings, from basin to basin, catching a piece of green soap that slithered and slipped from her poor sodden fingers, washing herself away.

'Stop me, stop me.'

They all knew better than to try. Water ran over the basin sides, slopping down white walls, into a crimson pool. Margaret, chasing her soap, knocked another milk bottle over, spilling an exact pint of Helen's blood. Four full bottles stood in a row. Rolled to and fro by the water, a syringe lay on the tiles.

'I couldn't stop her,' cried Margaret.

'She syringed her own blood out? You saw her?' Hannah felt faint.

Margaret touched the milk bottles with white fingers. 'It's still warm.'

Helen's body lay like a foetus, bloodless. Hannah was sick in a basin as the nurses arrived.

'Look at that,' breathed someone. 'Good God.'

"Goodbye Helen" was written on the wall with a finger dipped in her own blood.

'Stop her screaming,' said Hannah to the nurse, meaning Margaret.

'It's you,' answered the nurse, picking her up and carrying her down the dormitory, through the landing, into a treatment room. 'I'm going to give you an injection.'

'You see,' Hannah said as the drug took effect, 'I know how she felt. That's what I'd do, if I had enough courage.'

'Don't talk such nonsense,' said the nurse.

* * *

Next day Tricky Dicky's mouth was a thin line beneath his half-moon glasses, his wrinkled face furious.

'Unfortunate,' he said, his mouth opening and closing like a tortoise's. 'I'm sorry you've had such a dreadful shock. That unhappy young woman has caused terrible trouble.'

Hannah felt as empty as the wind that blew rotting leaves across thin winter grass in the orchard.

'We were going to offer you treatment,' he continued, tapping her file on his desk.

'What treatment?' she asked dully.

He came to life, softly tapping his thumbs together. 'The unlocking of the unconscious. It takes years and years in analysis, but we can do in weeks what analysis does in a decade. Go straight in.'

'Pardon?' said Hannah.

'You must have heard?'

She shook her head. 'Heard what?'

He gave a little sigh of satisfaction. 'They are discreet, then. That's good.'

'Do you mean I'm to go down the tunnel?'

Tricky Dicky's face darkened with annoyance. 'I'd prefer it if you wouldn't use that kind of terminology. Treatment suite.'

'Everyone calls it the tunnel. The nurses do.'

'Do you know what it is?'

Hannah stirred the sluggish morass of her mind. 'It's that red-carpeted corridor that no one's allowed down.'

He clicked his tongue irritably. 'Do you know what I mean by treatment?'

'No.'

He gave her a sudden, sunny smile. 'Lysergic Acid Dyethalymide.'

'What's that?'

'A hallucinogen.'

'LSD.'

'Yes.' Tricky Dicky sounded delighted, as if she'd made astonishing, irreversible progress towards some marvellous goal.

'My boyfriend has had that.'

'Illegal.' He scowled at her over his half-moons, as if it was her fault.

'It's legal here?'

'Of course. We've been using it for some time. That's why you signed a consent form when you first came.'

Puzzling things began to fall into place.

'We offer it to a tiny minority of patients.'

'Why are you offering it to me?'

'You are suitable.'

She wanted to ask what suitable meant, but didn't dare. 'What happens?' she asked instead.

'You will have a pilot dose, and if that is satisfactory, we give you slightly larger doses each time, and discuss the results.'

'What kind of results?'

'I can't predict.'

'What do I look for?'

'You'll have no trouble seeing. It presents itself.'

'Do I have hallucinations?'

'Images from the unconscious.'

'I'm not sure I want to know what's is my unconscious. I don't think it's a very nice place.'

'It will help you get free.'

'Of the depression and panic?'

'Neurosis. Yes.'

'I'll do it.' She had an odd sense that she was able now to please or disappoint him in a way neither of them controlled.

'We will start on Monday,' he said.

'If I'm going to have the treatment,' she said, meeting his eyes boldly, 'I'd like to go home first and stay with my boyfriend.'

She stared him down. Dr Dickens shrugged.

'You can go any time.'

'I can't afford to go any time, I haven't got enough money. I'll have to hitch hike. And I haven't got a coat. I've been borrowing Ginger's when she doesn't need it and she wears it to go in the bins. It's disgusting.' Hannah knew that, briefly, they were equals. He wanted her to accept the treatment.

'Tell them what you need in the office and they'll give you some money,' he said abruptly.

They got money out of a safe in the corner. 'We'll need a receipt for the coat,' said the secretary.

Hannah ran down the front steps and down a side path to occupational therapy, wanting to tell Old Mary she was going to see Joe. Half way along she nearly fell over Fat Ginger's bottom, sticking out of a carelessly parked bin, steaming with scraps from teatime. Ginger straightened up and belched furiously, caught in the act.

'How can you?' shrieked Hannah. 'How can you do this?'

Ginger licked the open palm of her hand. 'I hate it,' she said clearly. 'I hate it totally and I have to do it. It's just not a secret, like whatever you do is.'

'What do you mean, whatever I do?' yelled Hannah,

squeezing the coins in her pocket, hanging on to what was outside, beyond the walls of the madhouse.

'I don't mean. I eat. Then I throw up. Bugger off,' said Ginger grimly, turning back to the bin, 'and leave me alone. Go away, Miss High and Mighty, and think about what made you come here.'

'I'm not high and mighty.'

'You reckon?' said Ginger bitterly.

Old Mary touched her arm diffidently 'You listen to that jazz,' she whispered, 'and you listen to your young man. Don't go listening to people who just want to hurt you.' Hannah leaned down quickly, kissing the old woman's cheek. A childlike smile of pure pleasure lit Old Mary's glum features.

'I'll try, I promise,' said Hannah.

Chapter Thirty-Five

Hannah sat rocking.

'Stop that,' said Tricky Dicky. 'I thought you were going out for the weekend.'

'I put it off. I keep thinking I see Helen. Dr Dickens?'

The half-moons gleamed.

'Do you really think the treatment will help? I feel so tight, like there's a piano wire inside me that wants and wants to go snap, but it never will, so I can't stand it, but I can't let go of it, either. It gets tauter and tauter but it never breaks and it never stretches.'

'You have a neurosis. We've been over and over it. All men are not like your father.'

'Those are words,' cried Hannah, 'and I can't feel them. They don't ease me.'

'Take this to the office.' He handed her the prescription card.

'Will LSD snap the wire?' Hannah begged, starting to rock again.

'They'll give you something,' he said.

'Will it?' she persisted, seeing herself try his patience and having to go on.

He steepled his fingers. 'I wouldn't give you a treatment unless I thought it was going to do some good, would I?'

A part of Hannah said that he might give her a treatment because it was interesting, but she heard her own voice say meekly, 'No.'

'Try and enjoy yourself,' said Dr Dickens cheerfully. 'Cheer up, for goodness' sake. You are always so miserable.'

'I try to cheer up and I can't. I'm a depressive,' she snapped.

He sighed, watching her twisting her hands.

'I feel dead inside but I hurt. It doesn't make sense. If I'm dead, I shouldn't feel anything. Why do I panic?'

'I don't know, why do you panic? You'll have to tell me, it's not my job to tell you.'

'I can't,' she whimpered.

'Monday morning at nine o'clock,' said Dr Dickens.

'And being with Joe makes me go deader and then I'm more scared than ever. I don't want to go and see him, but I will anyway. Dr Dickens . . . ?'

'Monday.'

'Yes. Thank you,' said Hannah.

Outside she bumped into Henry fumbling his way along the wall towards the treatment hatch.

'Watch where you're going,' snapped Hannah, feeling his sharp elbows dig into her.

'I can't watch,' said Henry reproachfully. 'I'm blind.'

Hannah watched his big, glassy eyes turn in all directions. 'You aren't really blind. They tested you, and it's hysterical. Everyone knows that.'

'And you are an unfeeling young woman.'

Hannah began to laugh mirthlessly. 'How do you know I'm young? You're blind as a bat. Look at you. And I'm dead but I can feel. What does that make us?'

'Zombies, I think,' he said, twitching his long, bone-white nose, considering the matter seriously.

Mrs Twerp's balcony had hung above the lake, the mountain opposite strung with its necklace of lights, twinkling jewels in velvet darkness.

'I once felt my teeth,' she shouted at him. 'We're vampires.'

Henry shrugged 'Vampires. Zombies. Living dead. We're all the same in here.'

'You don't mean it.'

His sightless eyes stared over her. 'Oh, but I do.'

'It can't be true.'

'Every day,' said Henry.

She went to give her prescription chart to the nurse in the hatch. 'Do you do crucifixes?' she asked.

The nurse was near the end of her shift and humoured her. 'Not on National Health, dear.'

'You ought to,' muttered Hannah.

On Saturday morning she got the earliest train she could and surprised Joe by arriving for breakfast. The warm smell of his room comforted her instantly. After Ridley Manor's high ceilings, long corridors, great carved staircase and mysterious forbidden tunnel, the walls of Joe's flat closed in like a welcoming hug.

'You're here,' he cried, leaping up and sweeping her into his arms. 'I was going to walk up and meet you.'

They had lunch and tea and supper, all rolled into one, whenever they felt hungry, in bed. The white walls of the courtyard dripped with dense fog from the sea and Hannah saw her reflection in the dark uncurtained window. It would soon be March.

'Is your thesis nearly finished?' she asked, seeing

almost all the filing system was gone. The stack of card indexes higher than it had been.

'Yes.' Joe knew the question had to come and let her figure it out for herself, waiting.

'What will you do next?' She laid her head on his arm and touched his warm skin with her lips, tasting the dark hair on it.

'I was talking to my mum about that when I went home after Christmas.'

'Yes?'

'I've applied to go back to the States.'

She put her head back wordlessly.

'I want to talk to you about it.'

She kept very still.

'What do you think?'

'I don't. I don't think at all.'

'Hannah, don't sulk.'

'I'm not sulking. That's just what my father always said if I didn't react the way he wanted.'

'You could come with me.'

'No.'

'Why not?'

She beat at the blankets with her hand. 'You know I can't. It's obvious. You're cruel to ask.'

'I don't see everything the same way as you.'

She slipped out of bed and pulled his shirt around her.

'Come back and talk about it.'

She felt around in the bottom of her duffle bag. 'Look at this.' She held out her cupped hands and he counted seven small brown bottles of pills.

'You need that many?'

'Just to get through the day. There's a big bottle of black and green things somewhere, for night.'

'Even here?'

'I haven't tried, but I expect so.'

'Even with me?'

She nodded, her eyes on the bottles. 'How,' she asked bleakly, 'could a person like me go to America? They probably wouldn't even let me in. They don't like cripples, inadequates and vampires, do they?'

'You're losing me, sweetheart.'

'It's me who's lost.'

'You don't want to come?'

'Don't pretend I have choices I haven't got,' she said wearily.

'You always have choices.'

'Not people like me. The people at Ridley Manor understand that. They don't understand much, but they do know about being stuck with no choices. They're the people I have to stay with. Crazy people, like me.'

'I know there's an awful history, but . . .'

'It's more than history. I go over and over the history with Dr Dickens, but it doesn't make me better. I can repeat it by rote, and it always comes out like it all happened to someone else; like I read it in the paper. Tricky Dicky says that's what the LSD is for. To make sense of how I am and how I fit in the history.'

'You see the whole world in a ginger biscuit, kind of thing. Not just your own history.'

'How do you know?'

'I had some in San Francisco.'

'Isn't there anything I can do that you haven't done first?'

'You've got a fistful of firsts, sweetheart.'

'Not the way other people have. I can't come with you. You'll have to stay here,' she said, terrified.

'I'll come back and marry you, then.'

He was going. Contempt broke free and rose, proud and strong, an invincible barrier against pain.

'You'll forget you ever knew me, in no time at all. Don't worry about me,' she said, an empty smile on her face.

'Don't do this, Hannah.'

'Do what? You're going away. I can't possibly come with you, so that's it, isn't it? Thank you; it was nice while it lasted. Wham, bam, thank you, ma'am.'

'I can't believe you mean this.'

'I mean it.'

'You're hurting me. I want you to know this hurts.'

'It has always hurt. I tried to explain,' she said exhaustedly.

'This isn't the way.'

She unscrewed the top of one of the little bottles and tipped a small pile of blue tablets into her hand. 'No, this is.'

'I think you should get out of that place. I think you should let someone else help.'

'Who? LSD will help. He's practically promised.'

'You reckon?' He looked into her face. 'What will it do? It paints pictures inside your head, but you've got so many pictures inside yours already, I don't think any more will be good for you.'

'Pretty pictures?'

'Not always pretty.'

'Mine won't be pretty. There's nothing pretty inside me.'

'Yes, there fucking well is!' shouted Joe furiously.

'What?'

'Everything. It's your fucking parents, Hannah. Get them off your back and you'll be fine.'

'I live with a whole houseful of people who could tell you it isn't that easy.'

'And me? What about me?' he asked.

'You don't have to go, no one's making you. Don't ask me for sympathy.'

'And don't try and make me feel like a murderer just because I want to live my own life.'

'You're killing us.'

'You just tried to tell me "us" doesn't exist.'

'I'm sorry.'

'I'll come back. In two years. I'll come back and marry you.'

'I bet you do.'

'I love you.'

'And I love you.' But her words twisted like a knife.

They got dressed in miserable silence and went to the pub and played shove ha'penny, but their hearts weren't in it and it wasn't fun. Joe sat gloomily drinking beer and Hannah fingered the bottles in her bag, in a wilderness world. She closed her hand secretly on the bottles, warming them.

'Let's get something to take back,' she said, when closing time came.

'With all those pills?'

'I'm all right.'

Joe scanned her face and doubted it, but he went anyway and bought cider at the bar with the money he had left. They walked home hand in hand, distant in a way they hadn't been before, speechlessly wretched with each other.

Joe held her tightly, pinning her arms around him as he fell asleep. She was careful not to wake him, slipping free. She hated cider. She put the empty bottles in a row on the draining board, so that Joe would not have to wonder about anything. Then she lay down on the sofa where he'd slept when she first came, and closed her eyes.

It hurt to swallow. She could hear a roaring in her ears, and through it, the sound of someone talking, very angry. Fast, loud words, words spitting and slashing. Joe swearing beneath squares of bright light.

'You're in fucking intensive care,' he hissed, seeing her eyes open, 'before you ask.'

Her throat was too dry to speak.

'A whole week. They put a bloody tube down and pumped you out, and you've been out cold a whole fucking week.'

She closed her eyes, exhausted.

'Oh, no, you don't,' roared Joe, and two nurses came squeaking in on black shoes, to stand between him and her bed, saying he must be calm or go. Kind voices, firm and sure. Protection. Hannah turned her face away.

'OK, OK,' said Joe.

They retreated, unsure of him, keeping an eye open, watching other beds in case their critically sick occupants were disturbed.

'Why?' he demanded, leaning on her pillow, forcing her awake. 'Why?'

'I'm tired.'

'If you don't answer me, I'll shake it out of you.'

Hannah turned her face to his. 'I'm tired. Too tired to go on alone, and you are going away. That's all.'

'And you thought doing this would make me stay? Is that it?'

Hannah made an effort to think if that really was it.

'No. I have to have a point. There wasn't one without you. I'd lost it.' Her throat burned painfully.

'I asked you to come,' he said.

'And you knew I couldn't. You didn't mean . . . it wasn't real. You were lying, and you never did before.'

Joe felt the nurses' eyes on him and covered his face with his hand. 'I said I'd come back for you.'

'You wouldn't, and I can't wait. I'm too empty, Joe. I can't bear myself.'

Every word took them further away from each other.

'Nothing's real for you, is it? The more I try, the less you seem to be there for me. And now fucking blackmail, sweetheart, like I don't believe.'

'That's it,' she whispered weakly, 'I haven't been real for years and years. And nor has anything else. I go around quacking like a ventriloquist's dummy, that's all.'

He was baffled.

Her sore throat rasped. 'Go away. Go to America and leave me alone.'

'Do you mean that?'

'I mean it.'

'I finish in June . . . there's time.'

'Go away.'

'What will you do?'

She turned away in the hospital bed and a drip line snaked, colourless, over her arm. When the nurses looked over, he'd gone and Hannah lay motionless.

'She can go up to the ward,' said Staff. 'She'll be fine.'

'I'll ring up and see if they can take her tonight.'

'What makes them do it?' wondered Staff aloud, watching someone putting morphine through a canula for a young man nearly dead after a motorbike crash.

'Boyfriend trouble,' said the other nurse. 'Attention getting, I suppose.'

'He cared an awful lot, I thought,' said Staff. 'Oh, well, we'll never know, will we?' And she busied herself with other, more important, things.

'Well, well,' cried Suzanne, bumping into Joe by the fountain in front of the university's main entrance. 'Back in circulation, I hear.'

'I don't give a fuck what you hear,' said Joe, making to get past her.

'I only asked. Don't take it out on me.'

He stopped and looked at the water playing on the surface of the pond, falling and falling. 'There's a party down in one of the boats,' he said.

'Cad's houseboat.'

'It's a converted torpedo boat; huge. Made completely of steel. Or iron, or something. Amazing it floats.'

'I know,' she said. 'Cad's got more than a pound of hash.'

'You going?'

She nodded and her dark hair caught droplets drifting from the fountain, beading the crown of her head with tiny grey pearls. 'Are you?'

He watched the water waver in the breeze, early darkness closing in. 'Yeah, why not? It'll be a gas.'

Suzanne sighed; he was more hurt than he realised.

'OK,' she said, and they went in to sit side by side in the silent library.

Chapter Thirty-Six

'Is it true,' Hannah asked, curiosity getting the better of caution, 'that you've taken it yourself and smashed the place to pieces?'

'Is that what they say?'

'Yes.'

'It's only a small dose the first time,' said Dr Dickens, avoiding her question.

'What happens?' asked Hannah.

'Not much. It's a tolerance test, to make sure we can give it to you safely.'

'How long does it last?'

'A few hours. It varies.'

'What time do I go down the tunnel?'

'Treatment suite. Nine o'clock.'

'And do I see you? Will you be there?'

'Someone will stay with you, if you wish. There's always someone on call.'

'But you?'

'Afterwards,' he said vaguely.

Hannah was terrified of afterwards and equally terrified to press him about it, in case he changed his mind and withheld the magic cure. He repeated that they would go straight into the unconscious and save years and years of costly analysis.

'I don't know that I want to go straight into my unconscious,' Hannah confided to Old Mary. 'I've a feeling it's a nasty place. What if I don't come back? I bet you can get stuck.'

'People go berserk,' said Fat Ginger enviously. 'You watch it.'

'You couldn't be nasty,' Old Mary tried to comfort.

'Wanna bet?' said Ginger sarcastically. 'She just sent her boyfriend a Dear John and got shipped into casualty on six bottles of pills.'

Old Mary seemed to shrink, turning wooden as her walking stick. 'I didn't know about that,' she said, and wandered off.

'She ought to be in a geriatric place,' said Ginger spitefully.

Hannah nursed her anxiety in secret, away from speculative eyes. Very few went down the tunnel, and what happened down there had an arcane and bloody reputation. Stories went around. Patients had run amok, maddened, with the strength of ten; people had died. Hannah swallowed her sleeping pills with relief that night and within minutes dissolved into shallow, nightmare-ridden sleep. A mad butcher chased her down alleyways running with blood and she fled in mounting terror down streets closed in by high stone houses, furnished with stone. She climbed into a stone tomb, her heart pounding with terror, buried alive, scarcely breathing in case he sensed her presence and came roaring in for the kill. The butcher rampaged until morning and she woke thready with nerves. At nine o'clock precisely she opened the door of the tunnel and looked into its red-carpeted length. It was still and silent as her stone dream tomb.

'Come in,' said Leila from an open door. The nurse had raven hair, black gypsy eyes and a heart warm enough to melt the North Pole.

'I'm glad it's you.'

Leila turned back into the room. 'Here we are.'

The hypodermic lay in a silver dish, ready.

The first time she itched and giggled and was bored. By mid-afternoon Leila had given her an injection to stop the drug working. Frustrated and disappointed, she went skulking down to find Old Mary and found her dozing by a radiator.

'My unconscious is itchy,' pronounced Hannah, half relieved, half annoyed by the damp squib of a treatment. Mary mumbled her false teeth and wasn't interested, her bones aching from the winter winds that swept inland from the sea thirty miles away. Howling over the beach, whipping the sea, they made Joe's basement damp so that he fed the meter constantly, leaving the fan heater on all day. Letters came from sunny California; he needed this permission and that reference, but he would be able to go. His thesis was nearly done. Fifty thousand words, sixty thousand, and he sent it for indexing. The binders sent quotes by the same post as a note from his supervisor saying the external examiner could come in May.

Leila pulled the curtains across and asked where Hannah was going for the weekend, holding the syringe loosely in her hand. Hannah turned over and pulled up her night-dress, tensing against the quick sting of the needle.

'Nowhere.'

Leila clucked disapprovingly and threw the needle like a little vicious arrow.

'What about that boyfriend of yours?'

'It's over.'

'Shame.'

'Not particularly.'

'Comfortable?'

'Thank you. It is a shame, you're right.'

'You might make up.'

'No. He asked me to do something I couldn't, and he knew I couldn't.'

'That's a bit black and white. Can't you talk it over?'

'There's nothing to talk about. It's over.'

'Would you like some coffee?'

'Coffee? Is this room service?'

'You can have anything you want, within reason. We don't run to caviar and champagne.'

'What kind of things?'

'Coffee, tea, hot water bottles, baths, fresh clothes, someone to talk to, hold your hand, sandwiches . . . anything, practically.'

'No wonder everyone wants to get down here. I'd like coffee, please.'

'Huh,' said Leila, knowing it all, looking to see if Hannah's bell was on her bed. 'I'm around. I'll come at once if you press the bell.'

'Nothing happens.'

Leila smiled and went away and as the door closed behind her, the coffee crawled out of its cup. Hannah watched it with detached interest. It hovered indeterminately and subsided and became ordinary coffee again.

'Coffee can't crawl, she thought. But it had. Joe's words appeared on the surface of the air, drawn in long sloping black letters. All the world in a ginger biscuit.

313

'Joe?'

His name reverberated in her ears, as if her ear drums themselves were speaking and the teardrops that oozed and ran from the green walls were crystal, turning to blood as they dripped and ran, clear to pink to the deep crimson flood of Helen's death. Hannah rang her bell.

She rang it again and again as the weeks passed, and Leila always came quickly.

'Tell me,' she said, every time, and Hannah described the visions, the heaven and hell. They flowed from the walls, hanging like ripples in jelly, in thick, solidified air.

'Look,' said Hannah, drawing shadow pictures on the air, like black chalk-lines on an invisible blackboard. She told her mind to rub them out, and they went, obedient.

'What are you drawing?'

'Dear Daddy,' said little Hannah, whose fingers made clumsy scribbles, who could not yet write. 'I love Daddy.'

Leila sighed and brought fresh coffee. The walls wept bloody tears and would not heal; they dripped upon the faded old rug on the floor and did not stain it. Then it shone with living colour, pools of incandescent radiance.

'Oh!' she said, staring at heaven.

'What do you see?' asked Leila, again and again, and Hannah told her.

'Do you tell Dr Dickens?'

Leila's face was inscrutable.

'Will he come? Will he tell me what it means? Why do I see so much blood and tears?'

'He's interested. Shall I bring you some coffee?'

'I don't want you to go away.'

'Then I'll stay.'

'No, go.'

Leila went. She never argued or reasoned, just gave a bigger dose each time Hannah went down the tunnel on Monday mornings.

Weeks went by and sometimes hell no longer went back where it belonged, despite injections and pills to send it away. The visions lingered more and more. Hannah never went out. She sat huddled next to radiators or waiting in the treatment landing, hunched in the duffel coat she'd bought with Tricky Dicky's money. Hardly anyone spoke to her any more.

'Being crazy is lonely,' she told Leila. 'It's the loneliest thing in the world.'

'Are you crazy?'

'I'm a princess in cuckooland, one of the chosen few. Isn't that being crazy?'

'Not necessarily.'

'Leila?'

'Yes.'

'The genie doesn't get back in the bottle, you know. I see things.'

'Do you?'

'I do.'

'I'll tell him.'

But the doses got bigger each week.

Linda and Margaret and Old Mary went home in April. Blind Henry had gone because someone suggested an operation might do him some good, so someone else said, let's give it a try. Fat Ginger cut her wrists with a razor one night and emerged, bandaged by a very cross nurse, shouting, 'If she can stay, so can I.'

'You're being manipulative,' came an angry shout.

'That's their favourite word. You do anything they don't like, and you're manipulative. Why should you get special treatment?' she cried.

Hannah sat on her bed in the dormitory and took no notice. Every day Fat Ginger sent her own doctor notes – she wanted LSD. But no one answered.

The dormitory was full of new faces. Hannah and Ginger became old lags, like persistent offenders. A freezing spell brought snow, a blinding white shroud for the face of the countryside. Wet boots lined the hall downstairs after the illegal runs to the pub in the evening, giving the game away to nurses who turned a blind eye. Already, they were talking of Easter.

'I keep seeing things.'

'What sort of things?'

'It's not exactly seeing. It's feeling there's something I can't quite see, on the corner of my eye.'

Leila squirted her hypodermic, making sure the liquid contained no air.

'One thing I never see is Dr Dickens. I haven't seen him, not once, since this started.'

'Are you angry?'

'No. I just wish he would tell me what it means.'

'You should be. I am,' said Leila.

Hannah pulled up her dressing gown. 'You're angry?'

'I'm angry. There you go. Let's hope that's the last.'

'What happens then?'

'I don't know,' said Leila.

Hannah rode a roller coaster, a psychic riot. Walls burst their arteries in fountains of blood. Gelled air clogged her lungs, yet she breathed, fish-like, through gills. Fantastic colours streamed, like life itself, through the universe. It came to an abrupt stop, as though the drug had died.

They chatted and ate ham sandwiches.

'It's over for today. That's strange,' said Hannah.

Leila took away the plate, to wherever she went, and Hannah lay on her back. Light crept into the room like a brilliant sunrise and the ceiling dissolved into fathomless blue sky. A golden midday sun shone above orange desert sand. Hannah began to sweat. Her mouth shrivelled. Figures moved far, far away, busily doing something under the hot copper glare from the sky. Sandhills undulated, shimmering, beyond the horizon. She moved over the burning sand like a ghost and came to the figures. Two skeletons dug in the slithering sand, a grave to bury themselves.

'How can you bury yourselves? You are one skeleton, yet you are two. You are one skeleton burying itself,' she said.

They went on working, taking no notice of the fact that she stood watching. The sun beat down.

'You are one, and two. You are burying yourself,' said Hannah sternly. 'Don't think I can't see.'

It was putting one of itself in the shallow grave. Sand kept falling in and filling the hole, so it had to work fast. One of it got in and lay down and a stench filled the room.

'I'm rotting,' shrieked Hannah as mouldering flesh crept back from her bones, gnawed white by maggots.

Leila flew into the room.

'I'm dead. Look.'

Leila stood still.

317

'I stink. Oh, God, I smell the stench of myself.'

'Why do you smell?'

'Dead. I'm rotting.

'Tell me.'

Hannah told about the skeletons, who had faded away.

'Burying itself. One made two, burying itself. I stink.'

Leila stood with her hand on the bed.

'Can I wash it off?'

'We can try. You want a bath?'

'A very hot bath.'

Holding her nose, Hannah sat in a deep, hot tub and let Leila wash away the shame of the stench.

'There,' she said. 'That better?'

Hannah sniffed. 'I can still smell it, but it's not so strong, and I look alive again.' She opened the wrinkled palm of her hand. 'See? It's stopped rotting.'

'I see,' said Leila sadly.

'What does it mean?'

'It means you've had enough. It's pointless going on, because no one does anything with it.'

'I'm going mad.'

'You have never seemed, to me, to be the slightest bit mad.'

'What do you think it means, if I'm not mad?'

'I think it means that you have buried a part of yourself, and it is sending out these awful signals. It isn't dead and is troublesome. The dead don't bury the dead. Only the living bury the dead. You are alive, but part of you is rotting because you try to make out it is dead.'

'Then what should I do?'

'I think you should go away and stop this, before it gets out of hand.'

'There's nowhere to go,' said Hannah, putting on a fresh nightdress.

'Who sent you here?'

Hannah's eyes opened like saucers. 'Can I write to him? Do you think anyone would mind?'

'They might,' said Leila grimly, 'but I think you ought to do it anyway.'

'I will,' said Hannah.

A brown envelope, two sheets of Ridley Manor paper and a stamp lay on the end of the bed when she woke. Fairy Godmother, thought Hannah, writing that day to the kindest man in the world, asking if she could come back. Leila left without saying goodbye. Someone said she resigned. The day an answer came, giving her a time and a place to see him, Hannah put all her belongings into a carrier bag, and ran away. On the way to the station, the German exercise teacher got on to the bus.

Don't send me back, prayed Hannah, planning to fight.

The teacher looked straight through her and no one tried to stop her arriving at the white house near Marylebone High Street.

'Come on in,' said the kindest man in the world, coming to meet her. 'I'm really very, very sorry about this. I had no idea.'

Hannah knew the rest of her life hung upon his decision. So she told her story again, repeating the facts outlined in her letter. He listened carefully, saying little.

'We have made a mistake,' he said sadly. 'We were so overstretched, we didn't realise how badly you needed to stay with us. We should have done. I'm sorry we sent you away. Would you like to come back, if I can find you a bed?'

'Now?'

'Now. Let's try to give you some of the care that has been so woefully lacking.'

'If you can find a bed.'

That night she looked out across the pigeon-stained roof towards St Pancras station and wondered about Joe and about how far they both had travelled since they last met in the same little room. She had come back and Joe was at the other side of the world. Slowly she unpacked, feeling the great weight of her sadness.

Chapter Thirty-Seven

For six months, Hannah stayed in the room above the rooftops and talked. Where Tricky Dicky tacked up lists, Dr Tate came, punctual to the minute, and listened, really listened, to her trying to put into words things that had never been said before. Kindness made her depressed. For weeks on end she lay motionless, curled like a foetus on top of her bed. No occupational therapy, no ash trays, no vases, no physical jerks. The nurses were kindly, left her alone to do what she had to: survive.

'I wish I could see you more often,' she said, roused from a stupor that constantly threatened to send her back among the buried skeletons.

'That would be quite hard to arrange, because of my outpatients. I have a lot of people who feel like you do.'

'I don't care about them.'

'I must. I tell you what, why don't you draw it, or write it? Put it down for me when I'm not here. Sister can get you some pencils or maybe even some paints, if we ask her nicely.'

'I'd rather write it.'

'Then write.'

'That's what my tutor used to say – "Go and write, Miss Holmes." I feel shy, putting it down.'

'You don't have to show me.'

'I want to.'

She wrote it down for him, her feelings, her confusion, her terrible fears. She painted a picture of a Disneyworld cat staring with narrow green eyes at a tiny bird. The cat's paw was stretched out to go pat, pat, pat.

'That is a classic,' said Dr Tate.

'That's just how they made me feel.'

'Your parents?'

'Yes.'

'I think we're getting somewhere,' he said cheerfully.

But she lapsed again into hopelessness, doing nothing.

'It's no good,' she cried, when he came in to see her. 'You'll send me away. If I don't get better, you'll send me away, won't you?'

'That seems back to front, to me. I usually send people home because they are better.'

'The drugs don't work.'

'They might keep it at bay.'

'You mean I could be worse?'

'Oh, much. Do some more writing,' he said.

Winter crept into London, bringing dirty grey skies and cold, constant rain. Jenny, with a degree in her pocket, came to town to look for a job. She did a secretarial course instead. Just before Christmas, when the lights were on in Oxford Street, she was idling along, window shopping outside Selfridges, when a reflection appeared beside hers in the big window. She turned.

'I thought it was you,' said Hannah.

'Fancy bumping into you. I wouldn't have recognised you.'

'I permed my hair.'

'There's something else different.'

'I'm trying to find a job.'

'So am I.'

'No luck so far.' Said Hannah gloomily.

'Let's go somewhere and have coffee.'

'I've no money.'

'I'll pay.' Said Jenny.

'Why won't anyone give you a job?' asked Jenny as they queued in the Wimpy Bar.

'They want to know what I've been doing.'

'What have you been doing?'

'I'm in hospital.'

'Looking for a job in hospital? You're still in hospital?'

'Yes. They said I could work and stay on there.'

'How odd.'

'Everything I do is odd.'

'I've got a flatshare.'

'What do you do?'

'Secretarial course. I finish at Easter and then I'll go for PA jobs. The money's quite good.'

Hannah sighed enviously. They collected their coffees.

'Do you ever hear from Joe?' asked Jenny, hanging her coat over the back of a chair.

'No.'

'He went to America.'

'He said he would.'

'Back in June. He got his PhD, you know.'

'No, I didn't. But I knew he would.'

'Dr Masters,' said Jenny cheerfully. 'You were an ass to let him go.'

'He wanted to.'

'That's not what he said.'

'Where's your flat?'

'Pimlico. Why don't you come over?'

Panic made Hannah's hands damp as Jenny chattered about work, her home, her friends, her men.

'I can't do any of those things. It's different for me.'

'Well, then, I'll come and see you.'

'I don't think . . .' but Jenny ignored her, pushing a paper napkin across the table.

'Write down the address,' she said.

Hannah told Dr Tate about the meeting. 'I don't know that I want them to come here, I get panicky.'

'We can tell Sister not to let them in.'

'That's not very fair, they're kind to come. I have to start somewhere, don't I?'

'You have seemed better, certainly.'

'But I can't cope on my own.'

'We could try to get you a job in the hospital. Live in and work on the premises, as it were.'

'Why do you bother so much?'

'Someone should have done it long ago. We can only try to make up.'

'At Ridley Manor they didn't think that.'

'I had your parents in mind. We're very much the next best thing.'

'You won't send me away?'

He gathered his long frame, ready to go. 'I'm rather hoping you'll want to go one day.'

'For the sake of the NHS budget?'

'The NHS would be pleased, I'm sure. But I had in mind, for your own sake.'

'I can want all I like, but it doesn't make me able to do it.'

'The bed is yours until you want to leave it.'

I ought to leave, she thought, watching him go.

'Oh dear, oh dear, she will misunderstand,' said Dr Tate when Sister said Hannah got into a dreadful state after he left and they'd sedated her.

'There are others could do with that bed,' said Sister. 'She's been here a very long time.'

'We can try to do the job properly with a few, or get nowhere with all of them.'

Sister nodded, having her doubts; if everyone thought like he did, things would grind to a halt, unless people went private. 'She's a fixture. Look what we've tried: ECT, pentothal, keeping her asleep for days on end, never mind the drugs bill.'

'There is a lot of improvement.'

'I suppose we might get somewhere in the end,' she said doubtfully.

'We keep on giving her what she needs, and hope it's enough. Twenty years of neglect – you can't make it up in a day.'

'And when she goes, you'll send me another one.'

'There's no shortage. Unfortunately the world is full of them.'

'This is Rodney. He was at school and university with Joe,' said Jenny, perching on an orange plastic chair by Hannah's window. 'Do you know each other?'

'Do we?' Hannah asked Rodney.

'I saw you in the students union when you used to come in with Joe.'

'Oh,' said Hannah vaguely. She sat on the edge of her bed, looking from one to the other. 'Nice to see you.'

'You broke up with Joe before he went to the States, didn't you?'

'Yes.'

'Why are you in hospital?' he asked, curious.

'Her head's in a mess, isn't it?' said Jenny. 'You ought to get out. What's sitting in here doing for you?'

'I can't explain.'

'We're having a party.'

'Are you?' said Hannah nervously, wishing they'd go away.

'You're allowed to go to parties from hospital?' said Rodney. 'How peculiar.'

'I expect so.'

'I never heard of that before. Tell you what, I could come and get you. You're not ill or anything, are you?' cried Rodney. 'Shall I pick you up?'

'I'll ask.'

'Can I go?' asked Hannah, hoping Dr Tate would say she couldn't.

'By all means,' he said. 'Enjoy yourself.'

That'll be the day, she thought angrily, and smiled.

Rodney drove over and fetched her and they stopped off at a pub by Pimlico tube and bought beers.

'I'm in computers,' he said, putting two glasses down, mopping up froth with his finger. 'What do you do when you're better?'

'What is being in computers?'

'Banking. I work in the City.'

'I've never used one. I don't know anything about computers.'

'They're taking off like you wouldn't believe. Day will

326

come when we've all got one at home to do our shopping and . . . well, everything.'

'I like doing my own shopping.'

'It'll make everything accessible.'

'That's no use if you haven't got any money. Poor people won't want computers.'

'Computers will make us more profitable. Fewer poor people.'

'I don't believe in a computer Utopia.'

Rodney swallowed his beer.

'Do you live round here?' she asked, to change the subject.

'Canonbury. It's not far.'

'Oh, I'm on your way.'

'Not exactly.'

'What time should we get there?'

'I used to see you around, with Joe,' said Rodney.

'Did you?' said Hannah dully.

'I used to envy him. I was at a party on the Downs and you were there. You wouldn't remember.'

'I do.'

'You and Joe danced all night, I'll never forget watching you from outside the French windows.'

'We did,' she said.

'I watched you from outside in the dark, and I thought, if ever I get the chance, that's the girl I'm going to marry.'

Hannah stared into her beer glass. 'I think we should go.'

'Will you marry me?'

She raised her eyes in the smoky pub and looked at him in amazement. 'You don't know me.'

'I know I want to marry you.'

'Why?'

'That time, you were magic. I never got you out of my head. I never felt like that about anyone else. Will you?'

She sat back on the hard wooden bench and considered the future. "You may want to go of your own accord, for your own sake." It was a way out, before the kindest man in the world had to send her away.

'I don't love you, I don't even know you. You must be joking.'

'I'm not joking.'

'You can hardly be serious.'

'Love at first sight.'

'Love?' She pushed the beer over to him. 'I take pills and I shouldn't drink.'

'Jenny said you hadn't been well.'

'I'm a depressive. I'm sick.'

'Jenny said you'd had a hard time.'

'That's why. It makes me impossible to live with.'

His wavy brown hair stood on end as he ran his fingers through it earnestly. 'But I want to try.'

Joe was gone.

'All right,' she said. 'But don't say I didn't warn you.'

'You'll marry me?' he whooped, stunned. People at the next table looked over. The barman dried glasses, unmoved.

'I'll marry you,' said Hannah bleakly.

They arrived at Jenny's flat and he shouted it out. Jenny, carrying a wine bottle, tripped over someone's outstretched legs in shock. Hannah bent down and picked up the bottle.

'You're going to marry him?' Jenny cried, horrified.

'Why not? I've nowhere else to go. Who cares who I marry, since the person I should have married has gone and will never come back?'

'You're mad,' squeaked Jenny, getting up off the floor, 'both of you.'

'Madly in love,' shouted Rodney, grabbing his betrothed.

Jenny pulled at Hannah's other arm. 'What are you doing?' she hissed.

'Getting out of hospital,' Hannah hissed back.

'You can't do this,' whispered Jenny desperately.

'I've told him. He's too stupid to care.'

'Too stupid to care!' Jenny's whisper ended in a scandalised squawk. 'What kind of marriage is that?'

'My kind,' said Hannah, pushing the bottle into Jenny's arms. 'What else do you expect?'

Jenny went into her kitchen and fished a full bottle of vodka from its hiding place under the sink. 'I'm going to get drunk,' she announced, taking it through into the sitting room, crammed with people. Hannah and Rodney danced, clutching each other, in a crush of bodies.

'That can never work, not in a million years,' said Jenny to her flatmate, and slopped vodka into a paper cup. 'Never. It ought to be illegal so that someone could stop them.'

'Are you quite sure?' asked Dr Tate.

'He's got a flat and a good job and he can afford me better than the NHS.'

'That isn't usually how one starts out on marriage.'

'I don't expect a relationship.'

'It doesn't seem as though he's too realistic on that score, either, but you may find you've got one, whether you expect it or not. Just being together will make some sort of relationship.'

'I expect nothing.'

'Then I fear you may be disappointed.'

'How can I be, if I don't want anything?'

'You want something, but you may not like what you want. Will you come back as an outpatient?'

'If you'll let me.'

'I think we've lost this round,' he said to Sister.

'You can't do it for her,' she said.

'Of course not.' But he was disappointed, all the same.

Chapter Thirty-Eight

Rodney and Hannah's daughter was born just over a year later.

'Postnatal depression,' said Dr Tate, looking at Hannah lying comatose in a cubicle. 'I'm afraid it was to be expected. We'll keep her asleep for a couple of days, see if that helps.'

'What are they doing with the baby?' asked Sister.

'I think it's gone to a neighbour. The husband couldn't cope and called the Child Care people in.'

Sister pursed her lips. 'She should have known better.'

'You can't blame her for wanting a baby.'

'I can, and I do. She should have known she couldn't handle a baby, not with her problems. Look at all the time you've spent.'

'It will never be enough. She needs a psychoanalyst,' he said sadly, signing a prescription form for seconal and antidepressants, 'but we'll have make do with these instead.'

The morning post arrived early in Hackney. Sam and Bridie read their letters over breakfast.

'David's heard from Mrs Heydritch that Hannah's had a daughter.' Bridie held the sheets of letter paper out of the marmalade, her spectacles on the end of her nose.

'It's a fine thing when you hear about your own great-granddaughter through someone else, isn't it?'

'Hmm,' muttered Sam, non-committally, thinking back to the day when he and April had sat in the garden under the old pear tree, before Eileen's house had been flattened by one of Hitler's rockets at the end of the war. Hannah had sat in his lap, finding jelly babies in his pockets, a baby herself. Now she had a baby. He sighed.

'I'm going to get their address and ask to see them.'

He lowered his paper. 'Do you think that's a good idea?'

'Why not? I want to see my great-granddaughter and if I leave it to them to arrange, I never shall,' Bridie observed crossly. 'It isn't right. Blow the lot of them.'

Sam grinned. 'Sparks might fly if you put that lot in a room together. They've been avoiding each other for I don't know how long.'

'Then it's time I banged their heads together. I want to see Hannah and that baby.'

'Hold your hats,' muttered Sam.

'And you can stop that.'

'What?'

'You've gone along with their nonsense quite long enough, Samuel Saul. Now it's time for us to put our foot down.'

Sam shook his paper. 'I like a quiet life, at my age,' he complained, to egg her on. 'We're getting too old, Bridie.'

'That's just what I mean. I want to see that baby before I die.'

'Not thinking of that just yet, are you?'

'I'm sixty-five years old,' she snapped, 'and you're nearer seventy-five. We could go any time.'

'You don't have to be quite so . . .'

'I've a right to see that baby.'

Sam watched her start to clear the table and brushed toast crumbs off his waistcoat. He finished reading the letter and shook with silent laughter.

'What now?' demanded his wife.

'Did you get this far? They've called her Georgina.'

'What's wrong with that?'

'It's a Freudian slip.'

Bridie stared at him suspiciously over the top of her spectacles. He read books that were too much for her and they filled his head with ideas.

'George. April's father and this baby's grandfather.'

'So? What's that slip you said?'

Sam refused to be pushed. 'David, with all his psychiatry, will probably pull a long face,' he said, amused.

Bridie clattered dishes, so he knew she was annoyed.

'I'll explain another time,' he told her, and went to fetch his stick from its stand by the kitchen door, to go and bring in the milk.

'Explaining does no good. You have to get them together and make them sort it out between them and face up to each other. None of this avoiding and keeping out of each other's way. It's gone on too long.'

'There you are.' Sam put down the milkbottle.

'I think if April is going to go on the way she is, she should give David a divorce, so he can marry Christina and make things regular.'

'He'll listen, I'm sure, seeing as you wouldn't marry his father. He'll reckon you're well placed to give advice.'

Bridie's faded cheeks flushed.

'I don't think we should meddle,' he said, as they were on to one of their favourite hobby horses again. 'It doesn't do to meddle.'

Bridie sat down again at the half cleared table. 'I don't mean to meddle.'

'Then don't. It's a failing in women.'

This time she wouldn't rise to the bait. 'I'm going to have a party,' she said slowly, 'for my sixty-fifth birthday, and I'm going to invite them all. They won't dare not come and it will be the first time this family has all been together since April and David fell out. If there's going to be divorces and weddings and babies, we should do them together. What's family for if we can't even fight our battles together?'

'Internecine warfare is very nasty,' observed Sam.

'I don't know about inter whatevers, but I do know about babies,' said Bridie firmly. 'And that baby is coming here, and we're all going to welcome her properly.'

'What a prospect! Good thing she can't understand things yet or we'd have to keep her ears covered,' said Sam with relish, 'because the air will be blue. Civil war all around her, poor little perisher.'

'And I want you sticking up for me!' cried his wife.

'Yes, ma'am,' agreed Sam, grinning from ear to ear. 'This might be fun.'

'I'll give you fun,' she warned.

'You always have,' he answered, and meant it.

Chapter Thirty-Nine

Rodney and Hannah had been married for three years and things were not going well.

'She's only a good lay,' yelled Rodney one evening, standing in the thickly carpeted hallway of their smart Canonbury flat.

'How many times have you slept with her?' Hannah shouted back. Behind her, in their bedroom, Georgina began to cry.

'I haven't exactly notched my belt.'

The anger drained out of Hannah; he was pathetic. 'Does that mean you don't know?'

'You're being stupid.'

'How long?'

'What's the point?'

'How long?'

He shrugged. 'I don't know. I met her about two years ago, but I've only ever seen her when she comes up for meetings.'

'When I was pregnant,' she said flatly.

'A lot of men play around,' Rodney began to gather his defences, 'when their wives are pregnant. It doesn't mean anything.'

'Why do it in the first place, then, if it's meaningless?'

'This whole argument is a cliché.'

'Why do you want meaningless sex?' persisted Hannah.

'I didn't say I did.'

'Is it meaningless with me?'

He went into the bedroom and picked up the screaming baby. 'Here, take her.'

Hannah didn't hold out her arms. 'Is it meaningless then, with me?'

'No, for God's sake! There just isn't enough of it.'

'What does it mean, with me?'

He stared at her. 'You're my wife.'

'What does that mean?'

He held Georgina clumsily across his chest and the baby stopped crying and stared up at his face with intense concentration. 'I don't know what you want me to say. I love you, I suppose.'

'Do you?'

'Of course I do.'

Hannah reached over and took Georgina from him, back into their bedroom, to change her. 'I shouldn't have thought there was any "of course" about it.'

'I hope you're not going to make a bad atmosphere,' said Rodney.

'I can only just breathe this bloody atmosphere,' whispered Hannah to the baby, digging a nappy pin into terry towelling viciously. 'Next time this will be him.'

'Oh lord, more bloody tantrums,' said Rodney, and went to open a bottle of beer.

It was ten o'clock in the morning in San Francisco. On Haight Ashbury the sun streamed through slatted wooden blinds, touching a sleeping face with a single brilliant ray. The face puckered, groaned, and a very

British voice swore as Joe woke to a thundering hangover and the alarm clock. The Chinese girl next to him rolled on her side and went on sleeping. The littered room bore disordered witness to the evening's highs; they had swung on a star, he remembered, and at some point, fallen . . . the stardust had turned very tinselly and booze had failed to polish it up. He felt the stubble on his face and tried to convince himself that he'd never do it again. But the sugar bowl wasn't empty yet and the only way to pay for more, when it was, was to get up and go to work.

'Work hard, play harder,' he muttered, spooning coffee into a mug, chewing aspirins. The girl didn't move as he left half an hour later to supervise cables and gantries, microphones and speakers. Joe ran a high technology, high pressure, high profit specialist company providing sound systems to pop concerts. There was a lot of call for his services and it more than paid for the sugar bowl. The Family Dog auditorium would be crawling with workmen setting up the systems for a huge open air concert that evening where a hundred thousand swaying rock devotees would caper together, dancing topless, stoned out of their skulls, mixing drugs like paints on a palette.

Morning sun burned off the last of the sea fog and hurt his eyes. Last night's palette had been blinding. He put on sunglasses and sprinted for the cable car, to work to have fun again, to shake the psychic kaleidoscope, paint another palette. Living was hectic. Very occasionally he got out a pile of shabby notebooks and sat looking through them, a pen in his hand. It was a long time since he'd added to them. They contained three plays, all consisting of a first act. They were good beginnings, very good beginnings. The rigours of Haight Ashbury life left little time for middles and endings; living for the moment was much more exciting.

It was ten o'clock in the evening in London. Bridie put down her pen and said, 'Make a cup of tea, Sam.'

'All done? It would have been easier to ring.' He woke up from his snooze and looked at the pile of letters stacked on the table in front of her.

'If I ring them all up, they'll argue and ask questions and find reasons not to come. They're too lazy to answer letters,' she said cheerfully, tidying the pile of envelopes, 'so they'll not bother until the last moment, and then they'll either have to make up excuses, or come.'

Sam leaned over her and looked at the envelopes. There was one for everyone on her side of the family.

'You're not asking Ruthie?'

'Too complicated. This is my family's affair and I don't think she'd want to come. Poor Ruth doesn't want to cope with David and April and Christina under the same roof.'

'Are you quite sure you know what you're doing?'

Bridie chuckled. 'I don't know what will happen, if that's what you mean.'

Sam frowned. 'It could get very unpleasant.'

'Then it's time,' she said decidedly, 'that we had the unpleasantness out in the open. I don't like all this secretiveness and people not speaking, and sending each other to Coventry. I'd rather have one good row and get it over with.'

Sam wondered uneasily if her view of human nature wasn't a touch simplistic. 'I think they'll know you're up to something. Do you really think they'll come?'

She laughed. 'Poor April can't stand her own curiosity

and can't bear to be left out of anything, so she'll come. David worries about my will and doesn't want to offend me. And he's dreadfully embarrassed about it all, so he'll bring Christina so he doesn't have to talk to you and me, because she'll do it for him. One thing Christina has got is manners. April's children will come because she will bribe them or make them feel guilty if they don't. And they are curious, too, because she's told them so many fibs and they know it and they're interested in finding out the truth. Hannah, I think, will come because she needs to find her way back to us, and coming to my birthday gives her a chance. She'll bring her baby and, I suppose, her husband with her. And then we'll have to see how they all get on, won't we?'

Bridie took a book of stamps from her purse and began sticking them on to her letters. 'The Honourable Rodney Hitherington Mathers,' she read aloud. 'Fancy marrying a name like that. Some people don't know when enough's enough, do they?'

Sam knew when there was no point in arguing. 'You know them inside out, don't you? I'll get the tea.'

'Hallucinogens,' cried Joe, making to take something from the Chinese girl's hand. She pushed them underneath papers on a clipboard, following him as he checked and rechecked some wiring. As London slept through the early hours of the morning, on the other side of the world the sun began to go down over the Pacific. Behind him, the beat started up and loudspeakers blared into life, bringing a stir to the thousands sitting on the grass, waiting.

'Come on,' said Joe, laughing. 'Give.'

The Chinese girl slapped his wrist softly and snatched the tiny plastic envelope away.

'Not now,' she said. 'I don't want you falling.'

Joe looked up at the giant gantry, black against the sky. 'I might fly,' he grinned.

She scowled. 'You might just try. You could kill yourself.'

'Later, then.'

'You take too many.'

'See you, sweetheart.'

She put the envelope in her pocket and he went back to his work.

Chapter Forty

'Hide it,' whispered Lizzie, giving Sam a big square tin with faded roses on the lid, 'and keep it upright or you'll spoil the icing. Did you get enough candles?'

'Half a dozen packets. I don't know how you're going to get them all on.'

'Six rows of ten and a five will fit if we put the holders very close together.'

'She'll burn her fingers.'

'Not if you light them for her.'

Sam tapped his pockets. 'Matches,' he said, and went off to find some, carrying Bridie's birthday cake.

'Fireworks, more like,' murmured Lizzie, watching the old man go to their basement kitchen. 'Light the family touch-paper and stand clear.'

Bridie had invited everyone for three o'clock. Lizzie looked at her watch; it was just after two. The house was primed, smelling of lavender-scented beeswax polish from the hall stand and gleaming banisters. A brief shower rattled against the coloured glass in Sam and Bridie's front door then died away. Lizzie stood at the foot of the stairs, thinking how little the passing years had changed this house, and that places changed less than the people who live in them. She sighed and went upstairs. Bridie looked all violets and old lace, sitting at her dressing table patting on rouge from a miniature cardboard box.

'Can I come in? Happy birthday,' said Lizzie, kissing her and putting a little oblong packet into her lap.

'Oh, this is lovely, Lizzie,' cried Bridie, opening the present.

'It's for a picture of the baby.'

Bridie held the worked silver frame away from her longsightedly, head on one side.

'Do you like it?'

'Very much. I was just wondering whether I've gone too far and if I'll ever get a picture to put in it.'

'I thought you heard from Hannah, that they'll come.'

'I did. I don't know for sure that she'll turn up, though, until she comes through the door.'

I'll go over to Canonbury and drag that wretched girl here by the hair of her head, baby and all, if she doesn't turn up, thought Lizzie. Fancy putting people to all this worry and trouble.

'Sam's put a new film in the camera.'

'I'm sure they'll all come,' said Lizzie, meaning to comfort, but Bridie smiled slyly and said, 'That's rather what I'm afraid of.'

'Well, it's too late for that,' said her friend.

April arrived with Ingrid and Peter and Jessie, in a nervous, excitable state. She gave Bridie a pot of exquisite china flowers, ignoring the thanks, criticising her children. 'I take it David is coming?' she said. 'Do sit down, Jessie, and stop fidgeting.'

Peter sat in Sam's armchair by the window and pointedly kept to himself, wanting no part in family games, finding his mother's agitation disheartening.

'Would you like a cup of tea?' Bridie asked him, leaning over the back of the chair to look down the road.

'I don't drink it,' he said rudely.

Bridie caught Lizzie's critical expression and they sat making awkward, desultory conversation, all ill at ease with each other.

'This is a birthday party?' Jessie complained to her mother, and April gave a shrug that told her to be quiet. A motorbike rounded the end of the street and roared up to Bridie's gate with a tremendous revving of its engine and screeching of brakes.

'Fred,' said April.

'And Polly,' said Jessie.

April sighed. 'You know they got married?'

'No one told me,' said Bridie.

'Went off one day to the register office, came back and she was wearing a ring. I wanted to cry.'

'I don't know why. Fred's all right,' remarked Jessie. 'Polly's lucky she's found a decent bloke.'

'A decent man wouldn't marry her behind everyone's back,' said April.

'It's not very good manners,' observed Lizzie, 'but a lot of people can't afford big weddings, can they?'

'Here we are,' cried Polly, let in by Sam, who followed her upstairs with great enjoyment.

'Black leather skirt. Good Lord. Or is it a large belt?' On the pretext of working it out, he followed her every move, enjoying himself hugely, in happy contrast to everyone else in the room.

'When's Dad coming, then?' demanded Polly, bending over to park her crimson helmet on the floor and to give Bridie's old man a proper eyeful and maybe a heart attack. 'Here you are, Granny.'

Well, someone's remembered nicely, thought Lizzie.

Polly put a tightly wrapped slip of a parcel into Bridie's hand, a kiss on her cheek. 'Happy birthday from Fred and me.'

A generous one. Just goes to show they're not all bad, doesn't it, thought Sam, liking her enormously. The parcel held three squares of damask, each closely embroidered with a nosegay of spring flowers.

'Dressing table set. I hope you're into that kind of thing,' said Polly. 'Mum said you would be.'

The doorbell rang. April paled and clutched her saucer.

'You can all breathe again,' Peter told them in his most bored voice, 'it's Hannah and her bloke and a baby.'

April looked at Bridie accusingly.

'I asked all of you.'

'I wish you'd warned me.'

Sam went down again, to let them in. When Hannah came round the door with Georgina, they were all sitting as though waiting for the Last Trump. Hannah stood awkwardly, trying to hide behind her baby, but Bridie got up and gave them both a hug, and the moment passed.

'Look at this baby,' she cried, turning to April. 'Isn't this the most gorgeous baby you ever saw?'

Hannah saw hostility in her mother's face and clutched Georgina closer.

'And this is your husband?' said Bridie.

'Rodney, this is my grandmother, my mother, my sister Jessie . . .' Hannah nodded at them one by one.

Sam cleared his throat loudly and said he could do with a hand downstairs. Fred took the hint and nudged Peter, who shambled unwillingly to his feet.

'My eye,' said Fred, seeing him standing for the first time since he'd come in, 'wherever did you get that?'

Peter brushed the crumpled pile of his dark green velvet smoking jacket and affected not to hear. Fred, about to make a remark about nancy boys, jumped when Polly kicked his ankle viciously and jerked her head at the door.

'Well, he is,' said Fred, and ambled off.

Georgina gazed around from her mother's arms.

'Well, don't just stand there holding her,' said Jessie, moving up the sofa to make room. 'How old is she?'

'Two.'

'Funny to be an aunty all of a sudden. You're a dark horse, aren't you? If Mrs Heydritch hadn't written to Dad, we'd never have known.'

'No.' Hannah let Georgina slide off her lap on to the carpet.

'Come and see your granny,' said Ingrid, going to pick her up and take her across to April.

'Here's Dad and Christina,' called Peter from downstairs. 'Shall I pour boiling oil over them from the landing window?'

'You haven't,' wailed April.

'I told you I invited everyone,' Bridie said more calmly than she felt. 'It's time we got this sorted out. They can't eat you, and you can't go on and on stopping everyone speaking to everyone else. It's no good to anyone. And that baby don't deserve to be done out of her family just because of pride and bitterness. We've got to stop it.'

'You've got a nerve,' said April angrily.

'If you like.'

David and Christina came in.

'Happy birthday,' he said to Bridie, and surveyed the room sharply, 'though I should have thought you'd have avoided this.'

'You're the one for avoiding,' said his mother. 'Come and have some tea.'

'Where's Sam?'

'Downstairs with Fred and Peter, putting candles on my surprise cake.'

Christina put her hand on David's arm. 'You have forgotten something. We've brought a present, if he can find it. David?'

'Happy birthday.' He gave Bridie a heavy gift wrapped in thick, silvery paper. She took the cut glass vase from its wrapping and it flashed in the light from the window.

'It's lovely. I'll put it on Polly's covers, on my dressing table, with my picture of the baby beside it. It's as though you all got together to plan it, everything goes together so nicely.'

'That'll be the day,' said Fred cheerfully, carrying in a plate of cheese straws. 'Where shall I put these?'

No one took any notice, so he sat on the floor at Polly's feet and started to eat them, caught Rodney looking and offered the plate. 'Want one, mate?'

Rodney squatted down and took a straw. 'You family?' he asked under his breath.

'In-law,' said Fred, offering his hand. 'Welcome to the snake pit.'

'Tense, aren't they?'

'This is our best behaviour, mate.'

'Sam seems OK.'

'The old ones are. You need to tiptoe round her, though,' he warned, indicating April, his mouth full of cheese straws.

'Difficult?'

Fred took another straw. 'And then some.'

'Pigs,' said Polly, leaning down to rescue the plate. 'Want some, Hannah, before they scoff the lot? Shall I give one to George?'

'Georgina,' said Hannah.

'Georgina. She's sweet. You could have been more careful, though. She'll get called Georgy Porgy at school. How would you have liked it?'

'And now,' cried Sam, coming in with bottles under his arm, 'the toasts.'

'You and your champagne,' said Lizzie, bringing up a white cake smothered in candles, on a big silver board. 'I always think of you when anyone mentions champagne. All through the war, Sam had champagne. We were starving but he acted as if it came out of a tap.'

'Do you remember the day we all came to see you in the hospital in Ipswich?' Christina asked Bridie. 'He had champagne then, and when the corks popped everyone thought the Germans had come. We were so edgy, weren't we?'

April's face hardened.

One of the present corks popped and flew against the windowpane.

Edgy then is nothing compared to edgy now, darling, thought Sam. For heaven's sake be careful what you say.

Christina smiled brightly at April and got a blank stare in return. She sighed and April's fists tightened in her lap.

'Lizzie makes wonderful cake,' cried Bridie.

Sam counted the candles aloud, holding a new box of matches.

'There should be sixty-five,' Hannah told Georgina, pulling her on to her lap. 'You only have two, don't you?'

Georgina wriggled, wanting to get off.

'Let her come,' said April. 'I'll see she doesn't touch.'

Hannah's expression was stony. 'Go on, then,' she said reluctantly, and gave Georgina a little push.

'Come and see your granny,' said April to the child. Georgina toddled across.

'What about Grandpa? You going to see your grandpa?' she asked, making deliberate mischief. 'Our granddaughter, isn't she lovely?'

'Yes.'

'Well, let's hope you do better with her than you did with us,' remarked Polly sotto voce.

April was waxen with tension. Sam struck a match and threw the box to Lizzie. 'You start the other side, or they'll burn down before I've lit them all.'

Bridie put a glass into David's hand and said, 'Let her be.'

'You can't be doing this expecting no bad feelings?'

'I was hoping you might all have grown up enough to forgive and forget.'

His jaw set angrily.

'Here, take your drink,' she said.

'No,' he said furiously, 'have it your way. April, there's something I want to talk to you about, and since my mother insists on interfering we'll discuss it now.'

'Stop at once,' cried Sam, shaking a match that had burned his fingers. 'First you sing, then you squabble. This is your mother's birthday.'

'April,' called David, very red in the face.

'Afterwards,' roared Sam, sucking his fingers.

'I told her,' Lizzie muttered reproachfully.

Ingrid wanted them to stop. 'Happy birthday to you
. . .' she sang desperately, and shamed them all into
joining in, ragged at first, then bellowing the last words
out when Sam kissed Bridie and Polly called 'Wish,
wish.'

'There's no secret about my wish,' said Bridie. 'I
wish for a real family. I wish we could make up this
terrible business so that we can look each other in the
face again. I wish we could forgive each other, even if
some things can't be undone. That's my wish. But to
see the way you carry on, it doesn't look like coming
true.'

Sam tried to break the mood of embarrassment. 'To
the family,' he said, raising his glass. And it would have
worked, perhaps, if David hadn't yelled that he wasn't
going to be conned again, and began to shout at April
that they had to settle things once and for all.

'Here we go.' Fred nudged Rodney with relish. 'Two
cats in a bag.'

Hannah grabbed Georgina. 'I'm going,' she said, but
David's shouting drowned her out.

'I want a divorce. I've been begging and pleading for
years, April. Now I'm telling you . . . I won't wait any
more.'

'I will never divorce you.'

He lunged, trapping her in her armchair, one hand on
either arm. 'Now!'

'That'll do!' shouted Sam.

Bridie watched her son in dismay.

He used to be a child she adored, thought Lizzie

unhappily. What is wrong with him? And her. We loved her, too.

April numbly shook her head.

'David, please,' said Christina. He ignored her.

'You disgust me,' she said icily. 'I'm going outside.'

'Enough!' thundered Sam, pulling him away from April. 'You'll behave in my house.'

David swiped viciously and caught the bridge of his nose. Blood streamed down and Sam wiped it away with his fingers, looking completely amazed.

'It is my mother's house,' yelled David, 'get out of my way.'

'You won't—' raged Sam.

'Won't what?' David raised his fist.

'Stop it,' yelled Hannah, snatching the long sharp knife Bridie was going to use to cut the cake and slicing it clean through David's arm. 'Don't you touch him or I'll kill you.'

He stood quite still, watching his own blood running on to the carpet. 'Good God,' he said, sober with shock. Hannah had the bloody knife in her hand when Christina came silently into the room.

'Oh, what have you done?' she said, as though making polite conversation, then she began talking in a high, little girl voice.

'She's talking Polish,' said Sam. 'Why's she doing that?'

'Nazis,' said Christina clearly. 'You are Nazis.'

'They killed her mother and her grandmother,' said Sam, understanding.

'You.'

April brayed with nervous laughter. 'What is she talking about? We fought the Nazis.'

'You,' said Christina, pointing at David, 'are like him. The one who killed my mother.'

'Oh God,' cried April hysterically, 'she thinks you did it.'

'She thinks I am like him,' muttered David, clutching his arm. 'Can someone find something to soak this up and take me to get it stitched?'

'You're just like her bloody Nazi,' said Hannah, still holding the knife. Georgina cried and clung round Rodney's neck.

'That'll do,' said Bridie.

'Perhaps that's what you find attractive about him?' said April. 'It happens, that kind of thing.'

'You should know,' snapped David.

'I do,' she answered sadly. 'Don't sneer at me for telling the truth.'

Jessie took Hannah's knife away. 'Can someone get bandages or something?'

Lizzie said, 'I'm a nurse,' at the same moment that April said it, too. David clutched his arm and swayed and Christina knelt down and began to cry, crouched like a child.

'Oh, God, the stage is littered with corpses,' muttered Peter.

'Will one of you open the window?' ordered Lizzie.

'You'll need that stitched,' said April.

'Will someone for heaven's sake do something?' he said weakly. ' I feel queer.'

Bridie's legs let her down all of a sudden, and she sat on the edge of a chair, shaking.

'Sweet tea,' announced Lizzie, 'and you call an ambulance, Sam.'

'I'll take him,' said Fred. 'Where's his car?'

'I can't,' mumbled David.

'Why?' asked Fred. 'You just said, would someone take you. I'm offering.'

'I . . . I . . . I'm a doctor . . .' stammered David.

Lizzie snorted with laughter as she went to put the kettle on for urgent cups of tea.

'I'll bandage you up so you don't die of blood loss before you get there,' said April sarcastically, touching his arm. David winced. Sam squeezed Christina's limp hand. 'I'm sorry it turned out like this. It's a mess,' he said.

She was mesmerised. 'He is so like,' she murmured, tears filling her eyes. 'Sam, he is so like.'

'He's really like the man who killed your mother?'

'The Nazi had little gold glasses and fair hair and he was short, just like David, and he had the same anger in his face, and blood on his hands. My mother's blood.'

'And when I found you in Soho, you were mute. This is the first time you have talked about it?'

She cried and cried.

'Shhh,' said Sam, tears coming to his own eyes. 'Let it come.'

'We haven't got any morphine, don't be absurd,' snapped April, giving David two aspirins and a cup of tea. 'And I suppose I have to hold it for you, as well?'

'I'll die of blood loss if you don't hurry.'

'It's a flesh wound,' she snapped.

'I meant it, you know,' he said drearily.

'What, the divorce?'

'Yes.'

'I thought if I kept saying no, you'd come back one day,' she admitted.

'It's gone too far for that.'

'Not for me.'

'She needs me.'

'Does she? Don't you think I needed you?'

He shook his head. 'Not any more, not in any way that would do either of us any good. You need something, April, but it isn't me.'

'I'll divorce you. I never thought I'd hear myself say those words.'

'Don't!' sobbed Christina through her tears. 'I'm not coming back.'

'Bravo. One for good sense,' murmured Sam.

'Don't everyone leave me,' wailed David.

'Oh, really,' muttered Lizzie.

Fred tossed the car keys in his fist. 'I've got it round the front, waiting, when you can manage to get down.'

'What are you going to say in casualty, when they ask you what happened?' asked April.

Everyone turned to looked at where Hannah had been sitting, Rodney with his mouth open, ready to argue, but she wasn't there.

'This is impossible,' muttered Bridie.

'I'd better go after her,' said Rodney. 'But now you've seen for yourselves what she can be like, don't blame me for whatever else she does.'

'What an absolute creep,' said Polly.

'Go and find her, and try to bring her back,' said Bridie.

'Why on earth would she want to come back?' asked Sam.

'Will you come to the hospital with me, April?'

April caught Bridie's eye and her mother-in-law gave a decided shake of the head. 'I'd leave each other well alone, if I was you. I was wrong, there's nothing to be

353

gained. Get divorced, April, and leave each other in peace.'

'Logic, yet,' muttered Sam.

'I probably will divorce you, but I'll take you to the hospital first,' said April.

'Come on,' urged Fred, and they all helped David out to the car.

'Aren't women fools?' remarked Sam after they'd gone.

'Aren't women wonderful?' snapped his wife angrily.

'It depends how you look at it,' said Sam agreeably.

'Women are always left with the mess, aren't they?' said Jessie, sweeping broken cake icing into a dustpan.

'Always,' snorted Bridie.

'Well, there's one thing,' Sam pointed out, in his tolerant voice, 'you got you own way, and, since your family has thrown my champagne all over my drawing room carpet, I'm going to have a brandy.' He opened the cabinet where he kept his bottles and pulled out his favourite.

'Granny got her own way?' said Ingrid, surveying the debris of Bridie's birthday.

'She wanted you lot back together again, and your parents speaking to each other, and poor Christina sorted out. And that, like it or lump it, is what she's got.'

He retired into his favourite armchair, nursing the brandy bottle and looking offended.

Jessie said, 'I'm not surprised you're cross. We've made an awful mess. I'm sorry.'

Sam held a glass out towards Christina and poured a large brandy into it for her. 'Here, this'll bring some colour back. I'm cross you've been so hurt, you didn't deserve it.'

'You'll never persuade Mum that,' said Jessie.

'You're the original scarlet woman as far as she's concerned.'

'I shall go to my father,' said Christina, reclaiming her dignity.

'Tomorrow. You'll stay with us tonight,' Sam said firmly. 'You aren't in a state to go anywhere.'

Bridie picked at the ruined icing on her birthday cake. 'Hannah and the baby,' she said unhappily. 'What do we do?'

'We do nothing,' snapped Sam, 'there's been too blasted much done already. David will never bring an assault charge against her, there's no need to do anything.'

'She seems terribly tense and unhappy,' said Jessie.

'That young man doesn't seem to have the wit to take care of her,' said Sam.

'It's my fault,' moped Bridie, 'I started all this.'

'No, you didn't. They've all been at it for years and years,' said Ingrid.

Her grandmother cheered up. 'In that case, put the kettle on and make some fresh tea and we'll salvage Lizzie's lovely cake and wait and see what happens. April will bring David back, and I hope Rodney will have the sense to ring us and let us know that Hannah and the baby are safe at home.'

'Blasted families,' muttered Sam. 'It was all nice and quiet yesterday.'

Chapter Forty-One

The sky blackened and threatened a torrential downpour while they drove to the hospital. April said Fred should take David's car and go back to Bridie's and that they'd get a cab. Fred hated hospitals and was glad not to stay.

They sat in the waiting area for three-quarters of an hour while David fumed.

'There's people with heart attacks and things in there. Compared to them, you're not urgent,' April snapped, as his complaining got on her nerves. 'All you need is a few stitches. You won't die.'

'I'm a doctor.'

'Then you should know better.'

He collapsed into sullen silence until his name was called by a nurse with a wide, professional smile who said April could come in if she wanted to. Then they waited again, David lying on his back on a narrow couch, holding his arm which oozed steadily but which no longer poured blood.

At first the overworked, short-tempered doctor assumed there had been a fight in the street. Then he listened to their story with impassive, clinical disinterest. Fights were fights, as far as his job went.

'I'm a doctor,' David said, watching to see the effect of his announcement. A little respect, perhaps?

'Are you?' said the casualty houseman, and continued to clean the wound in his arm, making no moral judgements at all. April saw with amusement mingled relief and indignation play across David's face. He said no more until the stitching was finished. The doctor told them to wait for a nurse to come and bandage up the injury, and left.

'Wounded pride, eh?' April said, pulling her chair around to face him. 'Now you know what your patients feel like.'

He made a show of pain and stared, martyred, at the ceiling.

'Come on, it's not that bad.'

'It's bloody painful. The whole thing.'

Next door, a nurse pulled green curtains back with a jangle of rings on a metal bar.

'Why did she go for you like that?'

The nurse poked her head around their own flimsy green walls. 'I'll be with you in just a second. Are you all right?'

'Yes,' said David.

'Thank you,' added April.

He tried to shrug and pulled a pained face.

'You took against Hannah from the very beginning, I've never known why.'

'It's partly her fault. She's very difficult.'

'As a baby? Come on. You wouldn't even touch her. And then there was that business when Mum found her under the carpet. You can't blame that on her.'

'You're a fine one to talk,' he said sullenly.

'It was very hard for me, David, sending her away in the war, and then she hardly knew who I was when she came back. And you and I weren't getting on and it rubbed off on her. But I never hated her like you did. She was such an easy baby, how could you take against her like that?'

'I wished she'd stayed with the Downses in Yorkshire after the war. It would have been better for all of us.'

'She was my baby. I couldn't have given her up.'

'And what have we done for her, that's been so bloody marvellous?'

'I couldn't have.'

'I could.'

'Why?'

A man groaned nearby and doors crashed as a trolley went through hastily. Every time some other door opened, they heard the faint hum of voices from the waiting room.

'Be with you in a minute,' cried the nurse, poking her head round the curtain and disappearing again.

'Do you know,' he said, 'I've waited all these years for you to ask me that.'

'Now I have. Go on.'

'I sold my soul, April.'

Her mouth twitched incredulously.

'You cannot imagine how dreary it is to know that you won't take me seriously.'

'You sold your soul. That's a figure of speech, isn't it?'

'It is not a figure of speech, April.'

'You mean, you . . . I don't know, how do you do it?'

'Mum didn't marry my father until after I was born. I'm illegitimate. I'd never have got into medical school with that on my birth certificate, so I found someone who could change it for me, and the price was my soul.'

'You *are* joking?'

'I am not.'

'I don't believe in black magic.'

'You'd better.'

David put his good hand over hers on the edge of the couch. 'I sold hers, too,' he whispered.

'What?'

'Hannah's. I had an affair in Surrey, when we were down there during the war. You wouldn't come to me, and I was lonely, and there was this girl. Well, a cleaner found us together and threatened to tell. They'd have expelled me and you'd have found out, so I went back to . . . this person . . . and asked him to help sort it out. And he did, but I had nothing to pay him with – he already had my soul, you see, so I put an IOU on Hannah's soul. It was before she was born. April?'

'Go on,' she said in a thin, hard voice.

'I didn't know what to do, I felt so lonely and guilty and scared I wanted to run away. I think I nearly went mad. Then the night the war ended I came across this old chap who said he knew what I'd done. He exorcised me of my own evil possession, but he said Hannah would be weakened and I couldn't take the bargain back. Imagine living with that on your conscience.'

'So that's what it was.'

'Every time I looked at her, she reminded me of my own wickedness and that what I'd done would make her wicked, too. She gave me such pain, April, I couldn't stand her. In the end, I wished she was dead.'

'Ah.'

'So now you know.'

'I believe you, because it makes sense of a lot of things I never understood before.'

'I was weak.'

'You were also very wicked.'

'I was trapped.'

'By yourself, your own greed and arrogance.'

'It was more than that. I felt forced into it. And things with you were going from bad to worse. I thought if I went to Christina it would let both of us off the hook.'

Her eyes glowed with contempt. 'I don't call what you've done being forced into anything. You had the same choices as anyone else.'

'That,' he said wearily, 'is where you are wrong.'

'Rubbish. That's an evil story and if you did those things, you're an evil man.'

'Don't be too ready to condemn.'

'You demean all of us.'

David sighed deeply. 'A person like you needed a person like me.'

April got up and pushed the chair tidily to the side of the cubicle.

'I know I don't want any more of you or your psychiatric talk.'

'Couldn't we try? Please?'

She stared at him, his arm bleeding freshly with movement. 'She'll be along in a moment.'

'Please?'

'You are on your own,' she said. 'You'd better make the most of it.'

'I can't.'

'Then you'll have to do what you left me to do all these years, and try.'

'April . . .'

'Do you know, I feel free for the first time since you left me.'

'I'll never see Christina again.'

She laughed grimly. 'I don't suppose you will because she'll never see you. I'm going back to let your mother know you're doing fine, and then I'm going home with my children, and I'm going to try and see what's happened to Hannah. Perhaps we can patch something up together, even after all this time, now I know what happened.'

'What shall I do?' he cried as the nurse arrived.

'Whatever you like. When we're divorced, you can do as you please.'

'Is that still numb.' asked the nurse, touching his stitched arm gently.

'I'm numb, all right,' said David.

Chapter Forty-Two

A passer-by saw a young woman with blood on her clothes, apparently asleep in the back of Rodney's car, parked several streets away from their flat, the morning after Bridie's birthday party. The police came and forced the car open and for the second time an ambulance took Hannah into intensive care, while a social worker found someone to look after Georgina.

'Oh dear, this is dreadful,' said April guiltily over the telephone, 'I suppose a lot of it's my fault.'

'If you're talking like that, perhaps my party wasn't altogether wasted,' answered Bridie.

'I would have the child but I have to work myself.'

'We've always had very urgent reasons not to look after our eldest daughter, haven't we?' retorted Bridie, and April rang off angered, wishing she'd held her tongue.

'She's very put out,' Bridie said to Sam, 'but it's true. There's always something more important, and then you can't argue because she's quite right, she does have to go to work.'

'We could have the child here,' suggested Sam. But when they offered, the social workers said they were too old.

'What a world we live in, where you're not allowed to

look after your own,' grumbled Bridie. Lizzie pointed
out that with her arthritis and the clumsiness that was
the legacy of getting burned in the Blitz, the social
workers were probably right that she wouldn't be able
to manage.

'It's a shocking affair,' insisted Bridie. 'And what's
her father doing?'

David had left the hospital and gone home to his flat.

'Nothing,' growled Sam.

Hannah came round from her overdose and took in the
unwelcome fact that she was still alive. The staff
quickly found that she had hysterics whenever anyone
mentioned family, so no visitors were allowed and
Georgina stayed with a young and energetic foster
mother. Rodney spent excessively long hours at work
and took to staying overnight with a sympathetic secretary. He was allowed to visit his wife once she'd been
moved from intensive care to Dr Tate's shabby little
room once again.

'I want to see Georgina,' she said.

'You're hardly fit, are you?' he said, eyes bloodshot
from too many whiskies and forgetting his sorrows in
the secretary's bedroom.

'And you are?'

'I don't know what we're going to do. You can't go
on like this.'

'Don't try and patronise me.'

'I'm not. You can't carry on sticking knives in people
and swallowing bottles of pills.'

'He asked for it, and so do you. How's . . . what's
just-a-good-lay's name this time?' she demanded
savagely.

Rodney stormed out of the ward, swearing under his breath, and they gave Hannah an injection to calm her down.

'I'm sorry you are so disturbed again,' said Dr Tate the next day, looking in.

'They are a disturbing lot,' she said.

'I know. What would you like to do?'

'I haven't the faintest idea,' said Hannah. 'Who cares, anyway?'

'Some of us try to, old thing.'

'I think I'm at the end of the line,' she said.

The newspaper boy flung his bag on the end of her bed and called, 'I got just the one *Mirror* left. Anyone want it?'

'I'll have it,' said Hannah, for something to do.

'Randy lot, aren't they?' remarked the man, giving her change, nodding at the picture on the front page. 'Mind you, I mightn't say no myself,' he added, grinning. The paper lay, folded in half, on the wheeled table at the end of her bed, its main news item another scurrilous sex scandal involving Members of Parliament and two or three of the aristocracy.

'You'd think they'd realise they're just a lot of dirty buggers, wouldn't you, and take no notice? She's a real madam,' said the delivery man, and went off whistling with his empty bag. An oval-faced woman with heavily made-up eyes and long hair in a chignon looked out from the page, smiling like the Mona Lisa, thought Hannah. Then she looked more closely. Since Christine Keeler, sex scandals had been all the rage and this was just one more, except for the woman. She held the paper away from her to study the smudged photograph more clearly.

'I could swear that's Wendy Dawn Hobbs,' she muttered, reading the story underneath the photograph. It was.

Hannah lay back and thought hard. After lunch, she collected as many sixpences as she could find and shut herself in the telephone booth in the corridor. After several frustrated attempts, she got the News Editor at the *Mirror* who shouted alternately down the line at her and at other people all over his office.

'What?' he bellowed. 'Send it in but we don't pay. What? No? Oh, I can't tell you anything . . .'

Hannah persisted.

'Write it down,' he roared. 'Send me something in writing.'

'Your name?' she shouted back, as hectic as he.

He gave it to her and cut the connection. Shaking with nervous excitement, she did as he had told her and posted the letter the moment she'd licked the envelope and stuck it down, before she lost her nerve. Then she lay back on her bed once more and began to wait. Two days later, Sister said she should be thinking of going home and a woman had telephoned to say she'd visit.

'Wendy Dawn Hobbs.'

'That's her. It's a name you remember, isn't it? Very fifties.' Sister didn't seem to connect it with recent news.

'Friend of mine,' mumbled Hannah. The only real friend she'd ever had.

'She'll be in this afternoon.'

Hannah sat silent, speechless with nervous fear and hope at seeing Wendy Dawn again. What if she'd changed?

'Oh, all right, be like that,' snapped Sister. 'We do our best.'

Hannah curled in a ball on her bed and watched the minute hand on the clock above the ward doors go tick tock, tick tock.

'I couldn't believe it, when the paper rang and said you'd asked them to get in touch.' Wendy Dawn dumped an armful of flowers and greenery on the bedtable. The scent of roses mingled with expensive French perfume, drifted down the ward, out of place. 'Cat got your tongue?' she demanded tartly. 'What are you doing in here, anyway? You don't look ill. People in hospital should be in bed, and you aren't.'

'I couldn't believe it was you. Look.' Hannah pulled out the folded newspaper from under the bouquets.

Wendy Dawn giggled, the same throaty chuckle she'd always had, and it seemed to Hannah she'd never gone away.

'It's me, though not a flattering shot. I've had a deliciously scandalous time, but really I could do without the publicity. That can be bad news to a business like mine.'

'Do you really run a brothel, then?'

'And what's wrong with you, darling? Hospitals never tell you anything on telephones.'

'I'm not ill, I'm sick. But you've hardly changed at all, except for the clothes and your lovely hair and . . . Wendy Dawn, is what the paper says true?'

Wendy Dawn gave a wide, knowing smile. 'Does the press ever lie? What's sick and not ill?'

'I'll tell you if you tell me.'

'I run a brothel.' said Wendy Dawn. 'I'm a madam, and I do it very well. I have a very good house and only wish my clients would be a bit more respectful of its need for privacy.'

Hannah gaped.

'I always said my way out would be the streets.'

'You did, but I never thought you'd do it.'

'I'm not on the streets now, but I did what I had to. Now you.'

'I'm a mess.'

'You wouldn't be in here if it was all hunkydory.'

Hannah told her everything, about the baby, Ridley Manor, Joe's going away, Rodney, and sticking a knife in her father and wanting to die.

'Not so good, then.'

'Not so good. I wish I'd done half so well as you.'

Wendy Dawn chuckled. 'They put me in a bin, too, only not a fancy one like yours. More Bedlam, where they lock you all up in the belief that if you're not barking mad to start with, you will be by the time you've been in there two days.'

'They can't do that.'

'They did. Then out of the blue, my old headmaster came to visit and he and his wife got me out and took me home with them. And there I was, back in the nest.'

'You don't sound as though you stayed there.'

'I was nothing but trouble, poor nice souls. They wanted to save me from myself but I didn't want saving, so we didn't see eye to eye. I wanted to have fun. I can't abide do-gooders, darling.'

'They mean well.'

'I can't stand being meant well by.'

Hannah began to laugh.

'So there we were, them understanding me and putting up with me, and me just raring to get thrown out. So I did us all a favour and hopped it before they set themselves up for martyrdom.'

'You sound abominable,' said Hannah respectfully.

'Appalling.'

'And what did you do then?'

Wendy Dawn held up one flawlessly manicured hand and ticked off various steps on her fingers. 'I went on a diet after all those school dinners.'

'You're thin now, and you used to be podgy.'

'It took a bit of effort. Then I got some clothes. British Home Stores to start with and I worked up from there. You wouldn't believe how dozy security used to be in Oxford Street.'

'Did you get caught?'

'I was careful.'

She ticked off a third point. 'Wigs.'

'Wigs?'

'Some want a redhead, some want a blonde, some want the Asian look. I'm mouse.'

'Not . . .'

'It's streaked by Sassoon now, darling. I got a share in a room and I was away.'

'A share?'

'We booked the bed between us. One on the job, one hooking.'

'I'm shocked.'

'I'm a working girl. What's shocking? I pay my way, I have a good time, and I'm my own boss. Sounds better than what you just told me.'

'But you're still . . . what the paper said?'

'Don't let's get mealy-mouthed, darling. I'm a whore.' Wendy Dawn examined her nails and looked bored.

'How can you . . . you know?'

'How can I what?'

'Do it,' hissed Hannah.

'Professionally,' said Wendy Dawn dryly. 'How do you do it?'

She watched Hannah struggle with embarrassment. 'The papers call my place a love nest or a playpen, depending on the mental age of the editor, but it is a very tasteful brothel with a distinguished clientele,' trumpeted Wendy Dawn meanly, turning heads all round the ward.

Hannah went scarlet.

'City chaps, the odd MP . . . some very odd, darling, but there you are; it takes all sorts. Fantasy stuff, you know? It's what the poor men want, but I don't touch serious sadism,' she added severely. 'We vet our clients so finely, they'd slip through a sieve.'

'Are you rich? You look as though you are.'

'I'm careful. I want to retire, and not into Holloway Prison.'

'To think you once had nits,' sighed Hannah.

Wendy Dawn turned and looked up and down the row of beds, hearing the perfunctory chatter at bedsides, the rattle of the tea trolley coming down the ward with its big polished urn and rows of thick white cups. She put her elbows on the side of the bed in a business-like manner and said, 'Let's talk turkey.'

'Talk what?'

'What will you do, when you get out of here?'

'Nothing. Go back to sitting watching Georgina grizzle, waiting for Rodney to come home with some-one else all over him until I can't stand one more day of it, and then I'll do the thing properly. I'm no better at dying than I am at living. No bloody good at all.'

'To start with, darling, you can stop wallowing.'

'I don't wallow.'

'Of course you do.'

'I can't help being depressed. You don't think I enjoy it?'

'Ignore it,' said Wendy Dawn briskly. 'You can start by getting rid of the kid. Put it in a nursery or with a childminder or something.'

'I can't afford to.'

'Tea, ladies?' The tea trolley advanced.

'Yes,' cried Hannah, to distract Wendy Dawn.

'You stop all this nonsense,' she went on imperturbably, 'and get yourself a good haircut, a facial, a job to pay for the kid's nursery, and a decent shrink to listen to your problems. That way, your life starts to be your own, and you tell sweetiepie Rodders – did you say his name was? – to get his finger out and go . . . himself.' Wendy Dawn made a gesture with her hand and Hannah began to laugh.

'I can't do any of that,' she said.

'A vitamin supplement would work wonders. Your skin's dull. It's probably the pills. You should go jogging.'

'I've hardly ever had a job except Switzerland, and that was a disaster. Who'd give me a job?'

'Me.'

'Oh, I couldn't. Oh, no, thank you, I never . . .'

'An administrative job. I need someone to run the place. Pick up your jaw, sweetie, any business needs admin.'

'What would I tell Rodney?'

'The truth. That you've got a job in an office.'

'I can't type,' said Hannah desperately.

'You can't book-keep or manage front of house or fix linen deliveries or get rush orders from Fortnum and Mason because someone fancies doing something interesting with a bowl of something expensive, either, but you'll learn. We don't judge their little ways,' explained Wendy Dawn, 'we just charge for them. They can have bright green rubbers and reflexology, handcuffs and hair shirts. Anything they want. It'll be your job to get it. You'd be surprised,' she said, laughing.

'Condoms,' said Hannah gloomily.

'By the gross. Look, it's a doddle. I'll train you. You can go on a course or two. Typing, I suppose, and management sort of stuff. Bit of personnel. I'll invest in you.'

'Personnel? You call them that?'

'You'll have to get shot of your double standards, sweetie,' said Wendy Dawn evenly, 'if you're to work with professional women. Some of them have degrees and are more accomplished, and more sophisticated, than you'll ever be. They'll teach you, darling, not the other way round.'

'I am prejudiced. It wouldn't work.'

'You can't afford to be. I'm not prejudiced about you, and you've got a worse start on you than any of my women. You've got no business judging other people.'

A dull, angry flush crept up Hannah's cheeks. 'I couldn't sell myself,' she muttered.

'No? What else are you doing?' Wendy Dawn looked around her. 'You look to me like you're selling out. To the whole bloody lot of them, and not even getting paid. The nurses get paid, your psychiatrist gets paid, your mum and dad get on with whatever they're getting on with, and so far as I can see, darling, no one gives a toss if poor little Hannah wants to sit and earn them all their wages. You want to go on needing them?' She shrugged. 'It's nothing to me. I just thought you might like to get up off your backside and join the rest of us. I made a mistake and it's no skin off my nose, darling.'

'You are horrible,' snapped Hannah.

'It's life,' answered Wendy Dawn. 'Which is more than can be said for what you've got here.'

'I'll do it,' said Hannah, nearly crying.

'Don't start that. Not with me.'

Hannah swallowed hard and glared.

'That's better. When do you get out of here?'

'Why are you doing this?'

'I can trust you,' said Wendy Dawn flatly, 'and in my business people you can trust are thin on the ground. You'll be worth your weight in gold, on a few conditions. No more pots of pills. I can't have you doing drugs. I need someone who is so discreet they're practically invisible.'

'I've often felt invisible,' observed Hannah glumly. 'But my pills are on prescription. I need them.'

'Do they make you better?' demanded Wendy Dawn, folding her arms and leaning back to stare at her.

'I feel worse if I don't have them.'

'Do they make you better?'

'I don't know.'

'What are you doing in here, if they do?'

Hannah was cornered.

'Look,' said Wendy Dawn, leaning her elbows on the bed again, 'I've been there. Pills are for sick people and you said yourself you're not ill.'

'Did I?' said Hannah feebly.

'Messes, you clear up.'

'How?'

'You get yourself a proper shrink.'

'I've got one.'

Wendy Dawn shook her head. 'Pill popper.'

Hannah's temper boiled. 'I love him. He's saved me. Don't you dare say that.'

'I never said you didn't or he hadn't.'

'You did.'

'You wouldn't be in here if pills worked for you. You come and work for me, and you can afford an analyst.'

Hannah picked at her nails resentfully.

'Go on, you'd do it so well, darling, and I adore the name.'

'Name?'

'You're upmarket, darling, and it's real. Hitherington Mathers? You're class. I don't suppose Rodders is related to the Queen?' Wendy Dawn asked wistfully.

'Not that I know of. And, anyway, I thought you said I had to be so discreet.'

'You do,' sighed Wendy Dawn, 'but being discreet attracts class, and class is everything. Well, it's money,' she added truthfully.

'No hanky panky, ever?'

'Just looking after other people's hanky panky.'

Hannah saw her choices clearly for once. 'All right.'

'Good.'

'I can't tell anyone, because they'd all have fifty fits. But I'll put Georgina in a nursery, and come and work for you. And heaven help me, if Rodney finds out.'

'Rodders should be grateful to have his depressed wife off his hands.'

Hannah's face darkened.

'Don't be silly,' snapped Wendy Dawn. 'You sound as bad as each other. Why on earth did you marry him?'

'I was destitute.'

'That is a terrible reason to get married.'

'I'll have to tell Dr Tate. I don't keep secrets from him,' Hannah said sullenly.

'He's got his Hippocratic Oath. He can't tell anyone anything, so he doesn't matter.'

'He does matter.'

'Try not to sulk, darling, it gives you premature lines.'

Hannah didn't know whether to laugh or cry or strangle Wendy Dawn, as the tea trolley rolled to a stop at the end of her bed to collect their untouched cups.

'I take it it's not a question of your rolling in the hay yourself?' asked Dr Tate blandly, hiding his amazement.

Hannah shook her head.

'Do you want to do it?'

'Yes, I do. It'll be better than sitting around being depressed and worrying about Rodney's girlfriends and feeling so sorry for myself I want to die.' She laughed. 'She calls him Rodders, you see, and sort of makes a big joke of all the things I take seriously. Georgina will be better in a nursery. And no one else is likely to take me on, are they?'

'Not quite as readily, I must admit.'

'Then what have I got to lose?'

'Pride? Integrity? Honesty?' he suggested. 'Will it be all right, do you think?'

'Is it dishonest? If Wendy Dawn wants me to do something illegal, I can always leave. What pride and integrity is there in being in here, half dead and no good to anyone? Wendy Dawn says she runs a business. Why shouldn't I go and work in it, if I can?'

Dr Tate grinned all over his sad-spaniel face, and Hannah felt a great rush of love for him, because he would let her do it, and not judge her wanting.

'The best of luck,' he said. 'Maybe you can stop being a nuisance to us at last.'

Hannah leaned right across his desk and kissed him.

'Well, there's a dramatic improvement.'

'There's one other thing.'

'What a productive visit.'

'Wendy said I should get an analyst. She's got one, and she says he pulled her literally out of the gutter.' Hannah reddened. 'Well, I suppose some people would say that morally . . .'

'Blow morals,' said Dr Tate vehemently. 'Moralists are often the worst. I think, if you can afford it, an analyst is exactly what you want. I can't offer you that, but I've many and many a time thought that it was the thing, if you only had the money.'

'No NHS?'

'No NHS. It takes too long and too much time. I can suggest someone, though. Someone very, very good.'

'How do I do it?'

'You ring him up and tell him I gave you his name, and can you go and have a chat? He'll take it from there and you can rely on his opinion.'

She stood and held out her hand.

'Go and get better, Hannah,' he said, taking it. 'You can do it.'

'Do you really think so?'

They shook hands gravely.

'I never doubted it, not for a moment,' he said. 'If someone gave you a chance.'

'This is a pretty odd chance.'

'Cast your bread upon the waters, as they say, and see what comes back.'

'Soggy crumbs, most likely, but I'm going to have a very good try.'

Chapter Forty-Three

Joe's passion for happenings and hallucinogens began to wane, along with the seventies and the hippy paradise of Haight Ashbury, quickly and frighteningly. The area became a nightmare of horribly strung out people on a lot too many drugs, dangerous and ugly.

I'm too old for this, he told himself, the day after someone went for his wallet with a bicycle chain. That guy had eyes like catherine wheels. He mourned the passing of the good days, respectable tripping among flowers and peace signs – all gone now, like the Chinese girl and a good many others. He went house hunting, feeling vaguely betrayed. He cut off his pony tail and bought Levis, some jackets and ties, and transformed himself into a teacher. A university teacher. He packed up his apartment and put the dog-eared exercise books with Acts One into the bottom of his old travelling box, to go to his new house in the Santa Cruz mountains. I suppose I'd better try and do it their way, he thought, not minding too much.

"Play hard, work harder" brought subtle changes. As the seventies dragged towards the eighties, he had a house with a view of what might have been Eden, two cars, a small swimming pool, a dozen pairs of joggers, and a galloping case of executive stress. Workaholism and hedonism clashed; Joe had the good things of Californian life, but they had to be paid for and gradually the notebooks sank into permanent oblivion as Joe settled finally for comfort, and lost sight of himself.

Six thousand miles away, Wendy Dawn opened a second house in Notting Hill on her fat profits, and a disappointed Rodney looked at his wife through new eyes. He taunted her as much as ever; she didn't rise to the bait any more, and their splendid rows seemed things of the past. He felt let down and unloved. He sulked. In nursery school, Georgina flourished, starting proper school when she was only four, promising brilliance, her seductive sweetness only offset by shocking temper tantrums if thwarted or displeased.

'It's working mothers,' said Rodney balefully when his daughter shrieked herself sick.

'Temperament,' said Hannah bluntly. 'I wonder where she gets it from.'

They glared at each other and dissolved into shame-faced laughter.

'Quite,' said Rodney, and Georgina at length calmed down.

Hannah's work was rarely mentioned. No one ever visited her office and when Rodney tried to pry, Hannah said, all right, then, she'd come along and see what was what in *his* office. Skeletons in every filing cabinet, no doubt. Rodney gave way, and knew nothing of her secret life.

'My husband is a womaniser and a wanker,' Hannah told her analyst, a tall, plump Irishman called Ben, whom she telephoned for an appointment the same day

Wendy Dawn had told her her salary. Ben had ushered her in, sat down in silence and waited.

'What should I do?' she'd asked.

'What would you like to do?'

'I want to talk about myself.'

'Yes.'

'The trouble is, I don't know who I am, so it's hard to start.'

'Any beginning will do.'

Hannah drew a deep breath and found a beginning. 'I'm a mess.'

She quickly discovered that no session began where the last one left off. Every time was a fresh beginning. This time, the topic was ostensibly Rodney. 'Why, do you think, did you marry a womaniser and a wanker?' asked Ben, settling back in his chair, interested.

'Because I'm in love with my father, who is a . . .'

'Does it help, talking like that?'

'Not in the slightest. It's how the psychiatrists talk,' admitted Hannah, relieved at last of the pretence that saying rude things about David made her feel better.

'So even if that is the problem, we have to find other ways of looking at it?'

'Yes.'

'Tell me some of your dreams.'

Hannah told of the mad butcher dreams.

'You have a mad butcher running amok inside of you?' asked the Irishman. 'Nasty.'

'If everything in my dreams is some part of me, I have all sorts of nasty things inside of me.'

'You might start from there, then,' said the analyst cheerfully.

* * *

Besides the dreams, which were all the same, she talked about David. When she didn't talk, she cried. Once, she howled and Ben said, at the end of the session, 'What was that about?'

'I don't know.'

'You know, you always talk about your father.'

'What else do you want me to talk about?'

'When you first came, you wanted to talk about you,' he said.

She scowled and started again. About David.

The mad butcher and stone coffins nightmares were long gone. Instead, she was burgled every night, monotonously, her dream houses broken into, everything spoiled, soiled or stolen. Or she came back from somewhere and found her place ransacked.

'I need some pills,' she told Wendy Dawn. 'I'm tired and depressed and my head aches. I have panic attacks. Look.' Her fingers shook and she was pallid with stress.

'You do not need pills. You can work late, instead. Rodders can have Georgina. Tell him you're doing a stock-take or something.'

She worked late night after night, filling her mind with other things, blotting out pain, surviving.

'How long will this take?' demanded Hannah at the end of their second year. Ben shrugged and raised protruberant grey eyes to the ceiling as if to seek inspiration. 'Haven't a clue. Ask me again in six months.'

'I've got eczema,' she shouted in despair. 'Look, on my face. And you can't see, but it's in my ears and my mouth. It hurts.'

'It's horrible. I'm sorry,' he said, and really was.

'Can I come more often?' She hid her weeping skin behind dark glasses.

'As often as you need to.'

Hannah's skin broke into sores.

'I'm sore and bleeding inside,' she said, again and again and again.

'Tell me again,' he said, and she did.

'It's no good,' she complained bitterly, 'I go round and round, over and over the same things. I know it by heart and get nowhere. How can I understand it so much I am sick of my own story, and not understand anything at all?'

'You know the story in your head, not your feelings, not in your heart.'

'You do me no good. If this is a cure, I'd rather have the disease.'

'I won't fill your appointments for two months,' he promised, unmoved. She stormed out. The next week, she was back. And so it went, one step forwards, two steps back, and the months and the years rolled past.

'You can't just opt out,' cried Gladys one day on the transatlantic telephone line, 'when you're doing so well.'

'It's not opting out,' said Joe patiently. 'I'm taking a sabbatical. I've earned it.'

'How long did you say?'

'A year. Now I sit behind a desk and get pompous. I've lost touch. I want to go away and feel things again, and maybe do some writing.' He sounded clear enough to be speaking from the next room. Gladys held the receiver a little away from her ear, looking at it doubtfully. It was wickedly expensive, so she put it back by her ear and heard him say, '. . . to the rainforests.'

'You're in a forest?' she said, confused.

'Going into them.'

Gladys sighed. 'Couldn't you come home, instead?'

'Colombia. I want to go look at pre-Colombian sites and artefacts.'

'What's that? What's this pre-Colombian thing?' Gladys wished he'd make sense, watching the egg timer run through for the seventh time. Heaven knew what it was costing him.

'Ruins and remains.'

'What?' she shouted across the Atlantic waspishly. 'It doesn't sound . . . isn't that where they grow coffee beans?'

'I'll come back to this job, Mum, don't worry. I want to do some things, and if I don't get away, I won't.'

Gladys dropped her bombshell as she turned the egg timer over for its eighth run. 'I'm thinking of getting married again, Joe.' She said it too quickly, by way of revenge for his hurting her. 'If I do, I want you at my wedding. Joe?'

The receiver had a dead feel to it, as though he had cut the connection.

'Who to?'

'A man I met. He's got his own post office near Cheltenham. I'd have to move away.'

Through the curious deadness, she felt him hesitate and his breathing sounded so close she could sense his heart beating.

'You go on, then. Congratulations. That's great news.'

'Is it?'

'Sure.'

'Sure you don't mind?' she asked, disappointed.

382

'Sure, I'm sure,' he said gruffly, in his foreign, drawling way.

'You'll come?' Gladys upended the egg timer again and tried to keep count.

'I'll be out of reach sometimes but someone will forward my mail. Write me, and tell me the dates. I'll try.'

'You won't,' she said, angrily hurt.

'Mum . . .'

'I've got to go and it sounds like you have, too,' she said, seeing the sand nearly through again. 'You go to your dratted forests. Your dad was a wanderer. Tell me when you come back.' She put down the receiver. 'I want, I want, I want . . .' she said furiously at the telephone. 'Is that all they taught you at those expensive schools?'

Joe stood with the receiver clasped loosely in his hand, his head hanging. 'She'd give anything for me to go back to England,' he said to the blonde girl behind him. 'She's getting married again. I never thought she'd do that.'

Louisa sounded sympathetic. 'Not a marrying kind of mother?'

'Too much the marrying kind. It has to be perfect. My dad lived up to that by dying.'

'Are you a perfectionist? I can't say I'd noticed.'

'In a few things, maybe, like jazz. Not most, I don't think.'

'That lets you out, then.'

'Did I tell you I nearly got married once.'

'You found perfection?'

'About as far from it as you could imagine.'

'That doesn't make sense.'

'It didn't make sense, but it nearly happened.'

Louisa lifted her tanned Californian shoulders and let them drop again. 'So you didn't make the big mistake. Why worry? Be happy you didn't do it.'

'I spent most of the time having her morning sickness. Let me tell you what a passionkiller that is.'

Louisa's face narrowed and she laughed uncertainly.

'It's true,' he protested.

'You had a child? You never told me. You should have told me about that.'

'It wasn't mine and she didn't have it.'

'You had morning sickness and your girlfriend was pregnant with someone else's . . . come on, I don't believe that.'

Joe shook off a sudden fit of the spooks. 'It was a very long time ago.'

'We're happy now,' she said. 'Years ago doesn't count.'

You sound, he thought, so bloody confident. He turned away from the 'phone. 'I'll write home more often,' he promised himself aloud.

Louisa raised perfectly crescented eyebrows.

'Oh, damn,' he muttered, sounding suddenly English. 'Mum's marrying a postman.'

'I love you when you do that.'

'What? Swear?'

'Go all English.'

'What if the Englishman asked you to marry him?' said Joe recklessly. 'Would you?'

'British understatement. I love that, too,' said Louisa.

'Understatement?' he cried incredulously. 'I just asked you to marry me.'

'That's just what I mean. That is just exactly what I mean, and the answer is yes, of course I will marry you.'

'You'll come exploring with me?'

'I was, anyway.'

'You don't mind spending your honeymoon back-packing with an ageing hippy?'

'You're ageing beautifully and I don't want to spend my honeymoon with anyone else.'

'Well, I'm blowed,' he said. 'Mum and me both.'

'You weren't very kind to her.'

'I wonder what Dad said, when she told him.'

'Pardon me?'

'Nothing.'

He never told anyone except Hannah about that.

Chapter Forty-Four

Rodney, newly promoted to the Board of his company, wanted to move. 'We've been here . . .' he closed his eyes and worked it out. '. . . getting on ten years.'

So long? Hannah thought.

'It's stupid not to move. Property is rocketing and we're constantly falling behind. Wouldn't you like a house?'

Georgina sat at the dining table, doing homework.

'Not really,' said Hannah. 'I can't be bothered. It's more work.'

'Well, if we don't, we lose an awful lot of money. I wish,' he grumbled, 'you'd show some interest. A real wife would be a bit supportive, at least.'

Georgina chewed the end of her pencil, then crossed all the fingers on both hands under the table, for them not to have a row. Her mother carried on peeling potatoes under running cold water and didn't answer. Georgina let out her breath cautiously.

'I thought Highgate,' said Rodney.

Hannah stopped peeling. 'We can't afford to go there, surely?'

'I've got shares and a salary increase. We could have a look.'

Taboo for either of them to mention that Hannah had

a salary, too. Rodney hated admitting to having a working wife.

'I don't really want to go that far out. And Georgina would have to change school.'

'I don't mind. I'd like to live in a house with a garden,' said Georgina with gusto.

'You must want a house,' asserted Rodney. 'Everyone does.'

Hannah thought of all her dreams of houses burgled and broken and destroyed. Ben asked had she, herself, been plundered, by any chance? Was she plundered of joy and love, security and her sense of herself, all the good things that give life meaning? She looked the violence of her early life in the face and wept inconsolably, in the bathroom, at night, in empty streets where no one knew her, when she was alone or with Ben; never in front of Georgina or Rodney.

'I don't think I really care,' she told him lightly. 'Let's not bother.'

His thinning hair shone in the lamplight as he bent to rub out a pencil mark on the edge of Georgina's book.

'You ought to bother. For her sake.'

'We'll look then,' sighed Hannah, 'if it makes you happy.'

'Oh? It's my happiness now, is it? Since when did that concern you?'

'My mistake,' said Hannah.

And, indeed, it was. She tried again and again to face it, and quailed.

'It seems to be a case of when you divorce him, not if,' Ben observed, when they passed over that question in pursuit of other answers, to other questions.

'Maybe moving's an omen,' she murmured.

Rodney went to pick up the whisky decanter, eyeing it critically. 'Can you stock up.'

'More?' muttered his wife into the potatoes. 'You're getting a real paunch,' she said aloud. 'You should cut down.'

He poured himself three fingers and sat down to look at the property pages in *The Times*.

'It goes with the job.' He patted his stomach proudly. '. . . like a great baby.'

'What?'

'You should go on a diet.'

'If you did what everyone else's wife does, and entertained for me, I could eat better. As it is I have to wine and dine clients at lunchtime, and I can scarcely nibble a lettuce leaf while lunching with the Bank of England, can I? If, on the other hand, you'd stop this nonsense about working and be here for me, you could put me on a diet.' He peered at her over the top of the paper, to see if he had provoked her.

'You wouldn't stop boozing, and that's what puts it on,' Hannah said, bending to put a tray in the oven.

'You'd take all the pleasures out of life, if you could.'

'I could put my head in the oven and you wouldn't notice,' she murmured, sliding the tray in, hearing the high sound of the gas jets at the back.

'I let you get away with too much,' Rodney grumbled, prepared to give up the half hearted argument. He was seldom at home to bother her. Wendy Dawn always pointed out how much freedom Rodney's absences gave her, but Hannah found it hard to see it in that way.

Freedom? Depends how you look at it, she thought, and went to move Georgina's books, so that she could lay the table.

*   *   *

Over in Hackney, Sam poured a small tot for himself from his decanter. 'Some for you?' he asked, as he always did.

Bridie shook her head, as she always did. Sam's blue-veined hand clinked the cut glass against the tumbler.

'I think I'll go on up,' he said. His voice had become reedy with age. Bridie, half listening to the wireless, nodded.

'I'll bring you a hot water bottle,' she said, 'in a minute. Unless you want to wait, and I'll put it in first.'

'My bones ache,' he grumbled. 'That damn' doctor's tablets don't touch it.'

'Don't you feel well?' she asked.

'I just said . . .'

'No, you look a bit flushed, as though you're coming down with a cold.'

The old man opened the door to the dark stairs and switched on a light.

'I'll fetch you an aspirin,' said Bridie, turning off the wireless.

'I don't need no aspirin,' said Sam, and climbed the steps one at a time, carrying his toddy in front of him, with care, like a child.

Cantankerous old beggar, she thought, and went to fill the kettle for his bottle. A draught came in under the back door and chilled her ankles with February frost. She thought of Lizzie's little flat that she'd gone to when the house got too much for her. Lizzie had central heating and lately Bridie had been envious. She filled the hot water bottle, put it into the knitted cover Hannah had given her at Christmas and took it upstairs. These days the old house seemed too big and too empty and full of dark. Bridie locked the doors and put out the lights behind her.

Sam's whisky sat, untouched, on their dresser, by the side of the bed. During the war the side of the room had been blown out and there had been a tarpaulin. It had covered them the night Bridie came to lie on the mildewed old bed, to cry for Edward, dead in the Arctic, and Sam had come to her there and held her.

'Here you are,' she said, taking the corner of the sheet to slip the warm bottle in. Sam looked at her.

'Oh God, no,' Bridie said to the empty room, holding the hot water bottle tightly. His eyes gazed up, looking beyond her as though at something just over her shoulder.

'He's gone,' she said, and took his grey hand where it lay on the eiderdown. 'Oh, Sam.'

Hugging the bottle, she sat very still and gazed at him, listening to the wind picking at the windows from across the frosty park. Then she closed his eyes and crept downstairs to telephone the doctor.

April came at once and met Hannah in the drawing room, lighting a fire with rolled up newspapers and bits of coal. A box of burned matches littered the carpet.

'It's freezing in here. I've tucked her in bed, but she wants to get up and wander around. I don't know whether she's confused, or what. She's shocked, I suppose. Fancy finding him, like that.'

April was pale and her cheeks looked streaky, as if she'd been crying. 'I'll go up, then,' she said. Hannah heard footsteps in the room above, and her mother's voice persuading Bridie to stay warm until they'd got the fire going.

'It's four o'clock in the morning,' said April, coming back down.

'What time do undertakers start?' asked Hannah, and April looked slightly shocked.

'He's barely gone.'

'I only meant, to get someone who will be responsible.'

'We'll have to do most of it.'

'The doctor on call said she'd rung Dad, and that he was coming, but there's no sign of him.'

'There never was, in a crisis.' April fanned the fire with a bit of newspaper. 'I don't know how they manage,' she said.

'Mum, don't have an argument with Dad. Not this time.'

'You're hardly one to talk.'

'I won't.'

'I loved Sam, you know,' April said, putting her face close to the fire, blowing on the sputtering coals.

'We all did,' Hannah said stiffly.

'I'm sorry.' April mopped a tear with sooty hands.

Hannah sat on her heels, feeling a little warmth from the fire, and regarded her mother sadly.

'I am, too,' she whispered, and brought the fire to a flame.

David arrived in a flurry, filling the house with anxious self-importance, overlooking them all in his hurry to deal with the death.

'You don't have to go on like that,' Bridie told him, hearing him arguing with the undertaker, on the telephone, the moment the man opened his doors at half-past seven in the morning. Frost sparkled, thin and spiky on the windowpanes, like David's sharp voice.

'He's coming,' said David.

'Of course he'll come,' said his mother, 'we've known him all his life. Sam is dead, you know.'

David looked at her speculatively.

'Oh, you needn't give me that look. I'm not wandering and I'm not senile. When you've seen as much death as I have, you don't make such a fuss.'

Hannah brought in a tray of tea and complained of the cold in the kitchen.

'You can't stay here by yourself,' said April, and drew a hard, bleak look from the old woman.

'I've lived in this house all these years. Sam's not being here don't change that. Don't start bossing me, April, not just now.'

They drank tea and David eyed Sam's whisky decanter in the corner.

'Go on,' said his mother, 'put a drop in everyone's.'

He did, and then they had another. Their own doctor came and said the cause of death was simple old age and an old heart failing, and he had a whisky toddy, too, to keep out the penetrating cold. Hannah began to feel lightheaded from no sleep and spirits in the morning.

'I have to let my office know I'm not coming in.' She got up to go downstairs and stumbled.

'Here, you sit down,' cried April.

David said, 'I'll ring for you. What's the number?'

Hannah told him, without giving it a thought, and sat down next to her mother, dazed.

Bridie dozed a little, wrapped in a big old cardigan, her feet on the fender. She didn't see the look on David's face when he came back.

'Who did you say you work for?' he muttered, coming to the fireplace, frowning heavily.

Hannah's eyes snapped open. 'I didn't. I just gave you their number.'

'Someone very odd answered the 'phone.'

Hannah's heart sank. There were several numbers and some were very private indeed.

'Did they?'

'Yes. Where is this place?'

'Kensington.'

'The woman who answered said – well, what she said implied I was ringing that place that was in the news a few years back. I remember because a friend of mine at the hospital was called in to see someone or other there. The place was a bordello.'

Bridie snored softly and the fire flared and got hotter.

'What?' cried April, putting her hand to her mouth.

Hemmed in, trapped between them, Hannah turned to her father and said he must have got it wrong. April said, 'Of course she doesn't, do you?' as if she were stupid. A great urge to laugh bubbled inside Hannah and she looked up to find her grandmother watching, alert as a blackbird, from across the fireplace.

'Edward used to have some stories about what the men got up to in those places, when they docked after being at sea for weeks and weeks. We used to have some real laughs.'

'That's right. It's often funny. In fact, sometimes what people do is hilarious,' said Hannah. She covered her smile with her hands, mindful of poor Sam lying upstairs, not yet cold.

'Up in the whorehouse?' said Bridie, reading her granddaughter's expression.

'What?' bleated April.

'Upstairs,' Bridie said loftily. 'Edward called it the whorehouse. I painted that room pink and gold, before we was married, and I loved it.' She chuckled. 'But he said it looked like a tart's parlour. We fought over that something terrible. But after that, even though the gas went up and we had it all redecorated, with the rest of the house done his way, that top bedroom was always the whorehouse.'

'Oh,' spluttered Hannah, agonised by the expression on her father's face.

'You don't . . . ?' cried April.

'Brothel, Mum. I help run a brothel.'

'Well!'

'You are seldom at a loss for words, David,' remarked his mother.

'I am an administrator,' said Hannah, with dignity.

'My daughter.'

'Don't be pompous, David,' snapped Bridie. 'Hannah, are you a prostitute?'

'I am not a prostitute, Granny,' Hannah said solemnly. 'I have never been a prostitute, I promise you. I'm a manager. I have certificates to prove it.'

'You work with whores?' said David.

'It was the only job I could get. You should know why,' Hannah said calmly.

'Don't be silly,' said April.

'I'm not being. I'm efficient and competent and I do my job well. So well, no one's ever even really asked me what I do until now. So that makes me discreet, too, doesn't it?'

'My, what a list of virtues,' David growled nastily.

'And,' Hannah went on, talking to Bridie, 'I've been

394

having my head shrunk all this time, and paying for it, so if anyone feels like telling me I need my head examining, I already am, thank you.'

Out of the corner of her eye, she watched David turn slowly purple. 'What kind of therapist? You should have asked . . .'

'I don't actually see why I should ask you anything. The only time I really asked you for something, you sent me away, to die for all you cared. Mum tried to kill us that morning, and it would have suited you if she had. You wished she had.'

'Hannah, you've said enough,' said Bridie quietly.

'It's true,' said April.

They all looked at David as if waiting for him to say something.

'I've lived all my life, wishing I were dead,' Hannah went on steadily, 'because I felt I was dead already.'

'You need to understand,' he began, 'you think I'm a bad man, but I'm not. If you really understood, you'd . . .'

'How would you know what I'd think?' she broke in. 'When all you ever did was shout and hit me if I had an opinion about anything. You don't know anything about me.'

'Did you?' demanded Bridie, looking at him as though she'd never seen him before.

'What?'

'Hit her?'

'All the time,' said April.

'Discipline,' cried David. 'I was sometimes authoritarian, I have to admit, but . . .'

'Discipline isn't beating and yelling and screaming and taunting,' said Hannah bitterly. 'You're a psychological rapist, Dad, always telling the other person what they think, and what they see, and who they are.'

'You're lying.'

'Psychological rape. Any rape crisis centre will tell you that it exists and there's no difference in what it does to a person. You penetrate someone's mind enough and it doesn't matter two shreds whether you stick your . . .'

'Hannah!' yelled her mother.

'. . . up them or not. It comes to exactly the same thing.'

'What psychology . . . ?' started David furiously.

'Stuff psychology,' Hannah shouted, 'I'm talking about *me*.'

The atmosphere was explosive.

'Is this true?' Bridie's voice fell like a slow whip-lash.

'I think it is,' said April.

'No!' cried David. 'You can't listen to her. You're neurotic.' He rounded on Hannah, livid. 'You have a neurosis, d'you hear? You throw these accusations around, you have no right . . .'

'She has the right,' said Bridie.

'Does Rodney know this?' demanded April.

'Rodney and I don't tell each other very much.'

'What about Georgina?'

'I am doing my best for Georgina. I work to pay for my therapy. It's all I can do. If I sort myself out, she will be free.'

'A mother in a brothel,' said David. 'I'm sure that does Georgina a power of good.'

'Don't patronise me. I'm doing my best, and I'm doing it my way.'

'Sam always said there was something going on,' said

Bridie. 'Years ago. He said he could smell fear in your house.'

'Ridiculous!' David snapped.

'And you're the one with all the education. Sam would poke fun at me with Jewish jokes about "my son the doctor". And look at you,' said Bridie sadly. 'He was right all the time. You are rotten.'

David turned away and went to the window, drumming his fingers on the glass. Outside, the long black hearse drew up at the kerb.

'They're here.'

'They already know what to do,' said Bridie. 'It's all paid for. He was particular about that.'

'Well, I don't know what to say,' said April nervously.

'No, you don't,' snapped Bridie. 'And you should have said something a long time ago.'

April sniffled.

Shivering, Hannah let in the undertakers in a blast of icy air. Bridie listened to their feet coming up the stairs, boots banging, and felt tired to death, envying Sam his last, great peace. 'Put some more coal on, will you?'

David picked up the scuttle and shook it.

'You were always a lot of talk and not a lot of good,' she said sadly.

He banged the scuttle down, enraged. 'You call working . . . she spreads diseases that I have to cure.'

'Rubbish! She doesn't spread anything,' his mother said scornfully. 'From what your daughter says, you're the one who spreads things.'

The undertaker knocked and poked his head round the door.

'Now, here's someone useful,' muttered Bridie, beckoning him in.

'You can telephone if you need me,' snarled David, snatching his coat and gloves from the back of a chair.

The undertaker glanced discreetly away; the bereaved often squabbled.

David heard them go on talking, indifferent to his departure, and the front door's familiar bang as he rushed out. His car's engine slurred reluctantly in the cold, then ticked loudly and caught. His hands felt frozen on the wheel, his breath plumed. He put his foot to the floor, jolting, sliding away from the kerb on a sheet of ice. The car spun, careered down the short stretch of road to the junction, and met a bus side on, going down to Stepney via the Mile End Road.

They heard the crash in Bridie's drawing room and April ran to the window to look, then snatched at the door blindly, running out and down the road to where he sat quite upright, crushed. Snow began to fall, tiny flakes, thin on the wind, biting skin and blinding the eyes with tears. There was a small crowd for a while, but no one cared to stay long in the gathering blizzard, so soon it was only a policeman and the ambulance crew who took David and April to casualty at the London Hospital. April shivered and shivered until they took her into a very warm room and made her sip tea thick with sugar.

'Your husband?' said the young nurse.

'He was,' April said, her teeth chattering.

'I'm sorry. He was dead when he came in, I'm afraid. There was nothing anyone could have done.'

'There never was.'

'It takes a long while,' said the nurse, 'grieving, you know.'

'I've done my grieving already.'

'Have you, dear?' The nurse patted her hand. 'You're a bit shocked, you know.'

'Two deaths in one day.'

'There was only one person in the car.'

'No, someone else.'

'Oh, dear. I'm sorry.'

April felt the enormity of pain and loss, the waste of it all, and stared at the girl, dry-eyed. 'I did love him.'

'Of course you did,' said the nurse, squeezing her hand.

'He was my husband, you see.'

'Yes, I see,' said the nurse, and it really didn't matter whether she did or not.

Two funerals. Christina went to both, standing apart, heavily veiled, not one of the family. She watched the four women across the graves of their men, three strong faces, bleached by tears, and little Georgina. They had each other, she thought, and turned away.

Sam, they took to Golders Green, to lie at peace in the Jewish cemetery. David lay in the great cemetery in East London, where Francis, his father, had been buried nigh on fifty years before.

'Come and live with one of us, Granny,' begged April and Hannah after it was all over. Bridie stubbornly shook her head.

'Now I know why Ethel wouldn't leave in the Blitz,' she said. 'You don't want to go. You just want to stop home, where you've always been.'

'You could get a flat like Lizzie's?' suggested Hannah hopefully.

'When I can't get up the stairs, I'll think about flats,' said Bridie, unmoved. 'I can't be thinking of everything now.'

'It's not so nice round here as it was,' April argued. 'You aren't safe any more. You used to be able to leave the doors unlocked, but now you hardly dare poke your nose out.'

'Leave her,' said Hannah.

'I remember when there weren't all those horrible tower blocks and all this dirt and noise,' persisted April, 'when you never heard of muggers or people getting murdered in the park. All these black people . . .'

'What rubbish!' snapped Bridie. 'What about Jack the Ripper? The East End was always violent. Look at those Krays. I used to go all down their road, when I was lending.'

'Let her be,' said Hannah to April later. 'Leave her her house and her memories. If we take those away from her, we might lose her, too.'

'I couldn't take another funeral.'

'There's been quite enough drama,' said Hannah firmly, 'and I've got Georgina to think about, as well as Rodney's wretched house.'

'I hope Georgina is going to be all right,' cried April fervently. 'After all . . . you know.'

Hannah eyed her mother with a small, sceptical smile. 'Why shouldn't she be?'

'Well, your father told me something I think you should know, now.'

'I thought we might have scraped this barrel of secrets clean.'

'It's a bit silly.'

'Don't tell me, then.'

But April did, about the soul selling and the IOU on Hannah's own. 'All gobbledygook, probably.'

Hannah thought about it for a long time, sitting in

Bridie's gloomy kitchen, her feet tucked under her for warmth.

'What are you thinking?' asked April, rubbing chilblained fingers.

'What I think is, that maybe I need a priest as much as a shrink.'

'You don't mean you believe it?'

'Every word. Whether he did it literally or not doesn't matter. He sold himself to something and we all paid.'

'Well, I suppose you could look at it . . . what will you do?'

Hannah turned the gas down under their pan of potatoes. 'Have supper, go home and back to work tomorrow.'

'I mean, about this soul business.'

'Oh, that.'

'That!' cried April.

'It's just as well my shrink is a priest as well as a shrink, isn't it? He always says that those who need people like him, find them.'

'You never told me,' April accused.

Hannah speared a potato to see if it was done. 'Five minutes. Why would I tell you anything?'

'I do my best,' said her mother mournfully.

Hannah put plates under the grill to warm. 'You never did much to help, did you? You never stopped Dad.'

'I couldn't have.'

'You could have said something.'

April shook her head. 'You don't know what it's like, living with a man who can't keep his hands off women, who's angry all the time and you don't know why.'

'Don't I?' demanded Hannah, looking her mother

straight in the eye. 'You think I don't know what that's like?'

'Rodney doesn't . . . does he?'

'Rodney will jump on anything that moves.'

April's face went tight, and Hannah thought, she's scared I'll mention sex outright; that we'll stop tiptoeing round it.

'He doesn't touch Georgina, though, does he?' April said timidly.

'If he touched a hair of her head, I'd kill him.'

'Ah,' breathed April.

'And, of course, he knows that when women in our family talk about killing, it's not metaphorical. Doesn't he, Mum?'

April went very pale and sick-looking but she stood up to Hannah bravely. 'I've told you I'm sorry. You know perfectly well he drove me to it, and I wouldn't have harmed you if I hadn't thought leaving you would have been worse. I did care, even though it was in a misguided way. Getting bitter won't help.'

You always sound so bloody righteous, thought Hannah.

April put down the jug of mint sauce and rested her head in her hands. 'I thought we got on all right, all things considered,' she said through her fingers tiredly. 'I do with the others.'

'You do not.'

April sniffed, just like Eileen used to do.

'You tell yourself so many lies. Why do you think they've all gone away?'

'Jessie hasn't run away. It's her husband's job. And Scotland isn't away. Fred had to go there, to get work. Ingrid's only in Colchester.'

'And Precious Peter buying a house with a miner? Open your eyes, Mum, and see what's staring you in the face.'

'Peter has some nice friends.'

'Every one of them is a man.'

April rubbed her hands together and said nothing.

'You and Dad were impossible.'

'I tried, I really tried.'

Hannah felt tired and defeated. 'So do I.'

'You aren't going away, are you?' said April anxiously.

'Only to Highgate. Did you like your mother?' asked Hannah.

April stirred mint sauce with a tiny, silver spoon. 'Sometimes I didn't like her, but I loved her. Why?'

'I just wondered.'

'She had a hard time, too. My father was a very domineering man.'

The potatoes began to boil over and Hannah emptied the pan in a cloud of steam, wondering whether April ever really understood anything at all, or whether, maybe, she was much smarter than she seemed. There was no way of finding out, so Hannah mashed the potatoes instead.

Chapter Forty-Five

Wendy Dawn perched one side of her cashmere-clad bottom daintily on Hannah's desk, exposing a hint of silk suspender. 'That's three small orgies.' She pulled a big appointments book towards her. It was full of her scrawling handwriting and Hannah's flat scribble. 'I've told Chloe and . . .' she ran her finger along the page '. . . Matilde and Rosy.'

'Chloe's got a smear appointment coming up.' Hannah rummaged in a pile of papers, glancing at the ledger absently. 'And she wants two weeks off in July.'

'I've already said she can . . . what's the matter?'

Hannah's hand froze on the tidy pile of envelopes. 'Who took that booking?'

'Which? I just said, I did.'

Hannah pointed to a name. 'This one. Does his ID check out? Has he been before?'

'You should know. Regular. He checks.'

'That,' said Hannah in a freezing voice, 'is Rodney's new boss, and Rodney went out all togged up this morning because they had a big, big business meeting on. This afternoon, Rodney said.'

Wendy Dawn nearly fell off her chair. She couldn't stop laughing. She rolled and shook with mirth, eyes streaming mascara. She spat on her handkerchief and wiped under her lashes, chuckling. 'Oh dear, poor old Rodders.' She started off again as Hannah sat with a face like thunder. 'I wouldn't be in his shoes . . . oh, stop looking like that, darling, you look like bloody Lot's wife . . .'

Wendy Dawn thought it was the funniest thing ever. Hannah was fit to be tied.

'You can't say anything, you see,' cried Wendy Dawn, 'without admitting you've been here all this time. What a joke!'

'He can't come.'

'Don't tell Rosy that.' Wendy Dawn gave her throaty laugh and for a moment, Hannah hated her.

'We'll have to stop them.'

'You can't. You're hoist with your own petard, darling.'

'He's my husband!' yelled Hannah. 'He can't come here and . . .'

Wendy Dawn sobered up, but the corners of her mouth kept trembling with amusement.

'I'll tell you what,' she offered generously, 'I'll take care of him myself, and get him off the premises so fast, he'll barely notice me.' Hannah looked at her friend and employer's sweet oval face, big brown eyes and cunningly painted skin. She looked fresh and womanly and expensive and once Rodney . . .

'Oh, no.'

'You'll have to swallow this one, or get out and leave him, won't you?' said Wendy Dawn, fully serious, understanding how high the stakes had risen. 'This time it isn't just the office dolly.'

'I shouldn't care about this, should I? I know the girls here have no relationship with the men,' said Hannah miserably. 'They're less of a threat than the office dollies, but this is calculated, and I hate it.'

'Men come here for a reason. They're lonely, or angry, or they think they can't get it anywhere else. A lot are sad and we make them feel better.' She winked. ' 'Course, we dress it all up to look like something else, so they think they're the ones doing us a favour.'

'I know all that, but I don't feel better.'

'Instead of feeling bad, you'd better decide what you're going to do about his wanting this.'

'He just does,' said Hannah sadly. 'He thinks it makes him look big and important to all the other fat, grey men who come here. They can afford it, buying women, and now he can afford it . . . it makes him one of the big boys.'

'So it makes a sad little man feel better. Why should you care?'

'Because this one is my husband.'

'Well, it's a personal thing,' drawled Wendy Dawn. 'There are plenty of wives who are only too pleased to hand Mr Important over to us.'

'Not me.'

'Aren't you just the teensiest bit dog in the manger?' asked Wendy Dawn shrewdly. 'You aren't exactly in love with the poor man, are you? It isn't as if there's some big betrayal going on.'

'There is,' shouted Hannah, 'you don't understand, it's under the surface. It's why he's coming here that hurts.'

'And why is he?'

'The truth?'

'Uh huh.'

'It's been over between us for ages. He married me

because he liked what I looked like, and he was jealous of
Joe. He never even bothered to ask who I was or what I
would like.'

'Have you ever bothered to find out what he likes?'

'I'm going to leave him,' Hannah went on, hardly
hearing her, 'and take Georgina with me. Let him keep
his pathetic orgies.'

'Don't drag George into it,' warned Wendy Dawn.

'I'm going to drag us both out of it,' snapped Hannah.

A bell rang in the distance.

'Shop,' said Wendy Dawn, and straightened her
suspenders.

'Men and their stupid orgies stink,' shouted Hannah
as the office door closed behind her. 'I'm leaving.'

The doorhandle turned and Wendy Dawn's face
peeped round the door again. 'Two months' notice,' she
said, all trace of humour gone.

'You can't do it,' yelled Hannah, 'not with my
husband.'

'Customer, darling.'

'Whore!' screeched Hannah.

'Bitchy,' said Wendy, unruffled.

'Out!' Hannah threw her inkbottle uselessly at the
door as Wendy Dawn vanished smartly. Washable blue
Quink splashed all over the worn grey office carpet.
Hannah swore worse than some of their clients.

'Ouf!' groaned Rodney, manacled to a four poster by
silk ties. Wendy Dawn snapped closed a safety pin and
fastened a Harrington Square appropriately.

'Now,' she said archly, 'who's going to be a good boy
for nanny?'

'I'm whacked,' gasped Rodney.

'You are, indeed, sweetiepie.' Wendy Dawn straightened the skirt of her uniform, belonging to the most prestigious brand of nanny in the land, and settled herself firmly on black-stockinged feet encased in sensible black lace-up shoes, tapping two ping pong bats gently against her thigh. Her tone changed. 'You are a fat, piggish little man, and a walking cliché. You have a nice wife and a nice daughter and you come here. What does that make you?'

'A swine,' suggested Rodney eagerly.

'I mean it!' she snapped.

'So do I,' he groaned eagerly.

'And what else does that make you?'

She helped him find words. Then she gave a deep, throaty chuckle and moistened her lips.

'You need punishing,' she said, pushing back her beige sleeves. Rodney's eyes glazed with adoration.

The removal men had piled tea chests in their hall, so he could hardly squeeze his way in to the flat. He struggled past heavy wooden boxes and bundles of newspaper, hollow-eyed, desperate to lie down and sleep. 'Hannah,' he called, finding no lights on.

She'd left things strewn everywhere; half open drawers in the bedroom, a pile of old clothes on their bed, and Georgina's room was empty.

"Gone to Gran. Not coming back," said the note, when he found it, propped against his pillow.

'Bugger her!' groaned Rodney, threw himself down on the bed, dresses and all, and fell sound asleep.

Hannah and Georgina arrived at Bridie's house in a cab.

'I've left him. We've come to stay here, if you'll let us.

I'm sorry I haven't had time to ask,' said Hannah, standing on the doorstep, holding Georgina's hand. 'I haven't had time to do anything.'

Bridie made way for the cabbie to bring in the bags.

'I don't mean to go back, so I'm afraid I've brought a lot of things.'

The cabbie took his tip. His engine revved then died away towards the end of the road.

'Gran, I'm sorry . . .'

'I can't say I'm surprised, from what I saw of you and your husband. I walked out on my father and then left David's father, just like you, took my bags and went. He walked out on your mother. It seems walking out runs in the family.'

'It does, rather, doesn't it?'

'Come in the kitchen and tell me what's happened,' said Bridie. 'Or don't tell me. It's up to you.'

Hannah pulled Georgina on to her lap and hugged her fiercely, her cheek on the child's hair.

'I will tell you, but another time.'

'There's plenty of that, please God.'

'I don't know what I'm going to do.'

'When I was in your shoes, that's when I started lending. I managed, but it was very hard. It's all mortgages and giro cheques and social security now, isn't it?'

'I want to do better than social security. For her.'

'That's what I wanted for your father and I often wonder whether it was what I did that made him go wrong.'

'Does she have to go wrong?'

Georgina was eating biscuits now, out of earshot.

'She's a lovely child. I don't see why she should go wrong.'

'Can I use your telephone?'

'You know where it is.'

'Well, now,' said Ben, when she'd calmed down, 'we knew it couldn't go on forever. We just couldn't foresee exactly how the break would happen.'

'I'm scared stiff of what I've done.'

'That'll pass. Can you stay with your grandmother?'

'She says I can. I don't know how we'll get on, though. I don't know anything.'

'Yes, you do.'

'What?'

'You know that last time you were left on your own, by your mother and father, you had nothing, and you were a child. This time, you have yourself, your grandmother, maybe your mother, Georgina and me. That's quite a difference.'

'I've nothing secure,' she wailed, unwilling to be comforted.

'You have the possibility of handling a similar situation differently. That's not having nothing, even though it may not feel like much.'

'I'm homeless.'

'But not friendless. And if your grandmother can take you in, you're not homeless.'

'I feel it.'

'That's different.'

Hannah held the receiver silently for several moments, gazing unseeing at Bridie's front door. 'It's not nice.'

'Nice would be asking too much. Let's settle for not a disaster. Rodney isn't your father and he may in fact treat you well. He might be as relieved as you, to get it over with.'

'Rodney's not bad. He's really just a fool.'

'That is judgmental as can be. You have never been foolish?'

'I can't help it, it's true.'

'I don't question the truth of it. I just wonder whether you could see that truth without so much anger.'

'That is too much to ask.'

'One thing at a time,' he said equably.

Hannah giggled. 'I called Wendy Dawn a whore.'

'She'd be appreciating that.'

'She didn't.'

'Is it the pot calling the kettle black, by any chance?' he suggested, chuckling. 'You listen to your friends, now.'

'I can't go back.'

'Is anyone asking you to?'

'Two months' notice, she said.'

'I think she'd find that hard to enforce, in her line of business. I'll be seeing you tomorrow?'

Hannah said he would and rang off. She sat on the bottom stair, her head in her fists, wondering what on earth they were going to do, now going back to Wendy Dawn was impossible. She had no job and no money.

'I'll have to begin all over again,' she told herself, and went to take the biscuits away from Georgina.

Chapter Forty-Six

'We've got to stop meeting like this,' announced Rodney.

Wendy Dawn winced and kept her face perfectly straight. 'I would be sorry to lose you.'

'I wasn't thinking of your losing me at all.'

He sat on a small, button-back chair at the foot of the four poster where he hardly ever wanted to be tormented any more. These days, he came to talk. Wendy Dawn sat in a pink and white cotton track suit, cross-legged on the floor, her delicate ankles held one in each hand. She looked up at him and sighed inwardly. He had on a suit so pressed it was sharp, a shirt so buttoned it chafed his short neck in the most uncomfortable way, and an Old Boy tie with something discreet embroidered in the middle of it, where his fingers played nervously as he summoned his courage. Rodney was making an effort to please like he had never done before. She felt sorry for him. His face flushed brick red, his eyes bulged, and she wondered if maybe he was about to have a stroke. She eyed the bell, hidden behind the velvet folds at the head of the bed. It would be embarrassing but it had happened before; they would overexcite themselves.

'You weren't?'

'Would you marry me?' blurted Rodney, going a darker shade of brick than ever.

Her face remained perfectly impassive.

'We get on frightfully well,' he gasped.

'I'm a whore,' she said. 'People don't marry whores.'

'Oh, you'd give up work.' Rodney ran a finger around his collar, which pained him seriously, sweating.

'Give up work?'

'I never liked Hannah working. I need a wife, a proper wife.'

'You think I'd be a proper wife?'

'Absolutely proper.'

'What does a proper wife do?'

Rodney gulped. 'Knows what a chap likes, you know? And entertains for a chap. You've got taste and things like that. You know how to talk to people. I need a woman with sense. A business woman, who knows what it's about.'

'I can do all those things.'

'Better than any women I know. So, what do you think?'

'I think that I might have entertained some of your friends here. How is that going to go down, do you think, at your dinner parties?'

Rodney pulled at his lower lip. 'I did think about it,' he admitted, 'and I thought it didn't matter. The wives won't know, and no one will say . . . they'll be frightfully envious, you know. The chaps.'

'It could harm you,' Wendy Dawn said flatly. 'They'd use it against you if it suited them.'

'And we could use it back, couldn't we? If anyone plays that game, you can bet they've probably been here, too, so it's stalemate. We all look after each other's backs, since we all know so much.'

'That doesn't follow.'

'They'd forget.'

'I wouldn't bank on that either.'

'It won't have to matter,' he said firmly, his colour beginning to fade, 'because I want to marry you. I can't live without you and I don't want to have to come here, sharing you. I want you to be my wife.'

I want, I want . . . she thought. Always *I* want.

'You could sell this place.'

She uncrossed her legs and rested her arms across her knees, under her chin. Rodney thought she looked like a little girl, and felt damp and weak all over, with tenderness.

'And run your house instead.'

'Yes.'

Mrs Hitherington Mathers. Wendy Dawn's heart tightened.

'What about love?' she asked casually. 'People are supposed to love each other, when they get married.'

'Love you? I adore you,' yelped Rodney, whose declaration of undying devotion this had been. He was offering her his soul, his all. He looked down at her anxiously, the faintest of doubts nibbling at his solar plexus, in case she should somehow not quite . . .

'All right.'

'What? All right? Is that all?'

Wendy Dawn sidled across the carpet without getting up and knelt before him. 'I mean, yes, I'll marry you. Yes, please,' she said.

Rodney whooped like a schoolboy.

'Have you told Hannah?'

'Why would I? I hardly ever see her.'

'Georgina?'

'She comes to stay. But I just pick her up in the car; I don't go in.'

'I haven't seen either of them, since you split up.

Hannah might object to my having Georgina for visits. There could be problems, you see.'

'I doubt it.' Rodney was a normal colour again, his old, confident, self. 'Hannah's not spiteful, and it suits her for me to have George at weekends, because she's got other fish to fry.'

'A man?' asked Wendy Dawn, curious.

'A man, I don't know about. But she's studying like billyo. Psychology.'

Wendy Dawn studied her own beautifully pedicured feet, and nodded. 'Psychology would make perfect sense. That's good.'

'Does it?' said Rodney, uninterested. 'When shall we tie the knot?'

'I want a big, big, big white wedding with hundreds of guests and a six-tiered cake,' said Wendy Dawn, to try him out. She wouldn't have minded if he'd said no, but he said, 'Only six?' in a serious way that half touched and half dismayed her.

'Six will do,' she said faintly.

'White?' queried Rodney doubtfully. 'You're quite sure, white? Not whatever they call it, off-white or something.'

So he did have some vague, undeveloped sense of something or other, a streak of sensitivity, after all. Wendy Dawn got up off the floor and took her lover in her arms, cradling his bald spot tenderly. She thought that with a bit of luck and hard work, she and he might make something of each other, in spite of everything.

'Cream,' she said, making up her mind there would be no going back.

'That's what I meant,' he said blissfully.

'I thought it might be,' she said, and planted herself in

his lap. 'With a long train. I always envied Princess Margaret. You remember the train on her dress?'

Rodney pulled his ear. 'Can't say as I do. No.'

'She was a fairy tale,' said Wendy Dawn dreamily.

'You're my dream,' murmured Rodney, sliding his hand underneath the track suit. She slapped it away, stinging him.

'What did you do that for?' he cried.

'Not until we're married, sweetiepie,' she said, smiling the sweetest smile he'd ever seen. 'Not before the wedding.'

Rodney had a strange, falling sensation, but it passed as quickly as it came. He pulled his hand away obediently.

'Let's get married quick, then.'

'As quickly as the arrangments will let us,' agreed his affianced generously. Over the top of his shoulder, she smiled a smile of pure triumph. Wendy Dawn's ship had come in at last, and she was well content.

Chapter Forty-Seven

February in Bogata was dry and cold. Sitting next to Louisa on a stone bench, Joe shuffled through a pile of letters from the Poste Restante.

'Well,' announced Louisa, tucking her own letters into the back of a guide book, 'there's the old quarter. I suppose we could go and look at that. It says here it has narrow streets and massive mansions boasting barred windows, carved doorways and tiled roofs extending over the sidewalks. We can do the Museum of Colonial Art, the Presidential Palace, and there's a Coin Museum and the Gold Museum, with any number of old churches on the way. Posh in the north, horrible slums in the south, and it says, hold on to your bag and your money because practically everybody is a pickpocket or a mugger or a thief. Sounds depressing. Do we have to stay here?'

'I want to go to the shop in the Hotel Tequendama and see if I can find this bloke Errazuriz. He's got all the Tumaco stuff.'

'Artifacts,' sighed Louisa. 'Haven't you seen enough? Peruvian artifacts, Ecuadorian artifacts, Brazilian artifacts, and now the bloody sacred pre-Colombian artifacts. Haven't you had enough?'

'No. Would you like to go see the Salt Cathedral?'

'What I would like,' said Louisa longingly, 'is a shower, things that are clean and smell nice, and a hamburger with fries – and to have all of them at home.'

'You can get those things here.' She looked around her at the crowded sidewalks, the mestizo faces, the gamines, graffiti, beggars, street businesses, bootblacks, lottery vendors, busetas, thieves, robbers and drug dealers, and said tiredly:

'I don't want them here.'

'Tequendama Falls?' suggested Joe. 'Of legendary beauty. And I'll take you in the cable car to Monserrate, of the fabulous view.'

Traffic, jammed solid, roared and belched. Orange and white buses, relics of World War II, ran alongside green and yellow updates of themselves, the new as slow as the old in the chaos.

'Tequendama Falls of legendary stink,' retorted Louisa. 'Half the time it's so dry, there's nothing there, and when there is, it comes off the most polluted river in the world. Who wants to go there?'

'Let's go look for gold in Guatavita, then. El Dorado. The Muiscas believed that if you dived in, you received god-like powers. I've always fancied that,' Joe said enticingly, putting his arm around her shoulders, which had slumped. 'Come on, cheer up. It's the altitude. You'll get used to it.'

'I don't want to . What are all those?' she asked, pointing to the letters.

Joe sat up straight and took his arm away. 'You and Mum between you . . .' he said, half annoyed. Louisa reached over and pulled his hand around, resting her chin on his arm.

'There's a lot,' she said, tugging at the bundle. 'Let's see.'

Joe showed her.

For six months, Gladys showered letters like confetti upon the Poste Restantes of South America. Innumerable pleading letters and then one very angry letter, the writing of which left her shaken and upset but determined that Joe would come home for her wedding because, if he didn't, she'd stop loving him with that complete, unconditional love he took for granted, and judge him wanting. It frightened her and she wrote and told him so.

"You are all I've got and it might be the fashion in America, going off and getting married in that hole-in-the-corner way, without inviting your mother, but I've got this old-fashioned idea that weddings are for family. Are you still family?" she went on indignantly. "Have you forgotten us? And I take it that one day you'll do me the favour of bringing your wife home?" For Gladys, to whom putting pen to paper did not come easily, it was strong stuff. "I want you here and I won't fix the date until I know you are coming," she ended.

'Wow,' Louisa said, following her mother-in-law's regular, large hand across several pages of pale blue paper, 'she means it. She means for you to go to England.'

'She does,' he said shortly.

A hand jostled her from behind and she grabbed her bag angrily, hugging it to her. 'I can think of worse things,' she said, as crowds swept and divided around their bench in endless streams. 'Like those kids.'

'Los escombros,' he said absently. 'There's nothing you can do.'

'The throwaways,' she said sadly. 'I want to go

away from here. The whole place is a nightmare.'

'It will cost a fortune,' observed Joe gloomily.

'We'd save on not being here.'

'I like being here.'

'I don't,' she raised her voice furiously, 'and you ought to care what I want. I'd rather go to England and meet your mother than wait around for weeks while you sit in more museums. I'm bored and tired and these places scare me.'

'You could come with me, to the museums.'

'I don't know about grubbing about in archives. You know I don't.'

'This isn't a holiday,' said Joe. 'I warned you. I came here to explore and to think.'

'I've had rain forests and leeches and the shits,' Louisa said sullenly, 'and dirt and poverty and ugly men with guns and sitting on smelly old trains until my bottom is numb. I'm fed up being scared and told I can't go places because they're full of Mafia or guerillas. If we have to go somewhere, let's go to England and give your mother the wedding present she wants – us.'

He turned the little heap of letters over and over, thinking of the narrow streets of East Ham, the cold, wet days, the overcrowded houses, the claustrophobia of matchbox plots of land.

'I dread going back. You don't understand.'

Louisa knew she had nearly won. 'I promise you can come back here,' she said. 'I know how much you love it, but I don't, and I won't make you bring me again. Colombia is the scariest place in the world and you are welcome to come back next time, without me, if you must come at all.'

The jaws of a trap closed over Joe.

'It would make Mum happy,' he said. A coach careered past, blowing their hair around their faces and dust into their mouths. A child lit a tiny silver pipe of cocaine and closed its eyes. Its mouth was a spreading sore around the silver paper shape.

'Let's get out of this horrible place today.'

He followed her gaze.

'There's more to Colombia than that. You can't hate a place because it has beggars.'

'Beggars,' she cried, 'they're not just beggars, they're children. Don't you mind?'

'Of course I mind.'

'How about minding about me, and your mother? Doing something real.'

He gave in.

Two weeks later, Louisa looked out of the window at the oil refinery at La Dorada, a collection of neat grey boxes becoming smaller and smaller as the plane climbed steadily into the cloudless sky. On their way back to San Francisco Joe was resigned but evil-tempered, and passed the flight in angry silence. Louisa, overjoyed to be going home, and to be going to England, bubbled with excitement. He tried to tip the cramped airplane seat back far enough to sleep in comfort.

'I'm going to sleep.'

'You don't need to snap.'

'You reckon?'

The Colombian coast passed beneath them, miles below, and she felt for his hand.

'I'm sorry.' She leaned across to try to see his face, but the stewardess brought up her trolley.

'He's asleep. I'd like a coffee.'

The engines droned, the stewardess smiled and the moment passed. Joe slept and Louisa looked out of the window at the brilliant glare of space. She pulled a comic face at Joe's hostile back, opened a magazine and settled down to read.

London was as bad as Joe had feared; Gladys and Louisa got on like a house on fire, leaving him feeling left out and outnumbered. The old days, when he and Gladys would sit chatting together, were gone. Joe listened with lonely foreboding to their voices murmuring non-stop in the kitchen. They went over the wedding arrangements together and he thought, you'd think they'd been doing it all their lives, and went down the pub for a beer, to drown his misery, but there was hardly anyone he knew any more and no one recognised him. He had several beers and decided he had become a stateless person, belonging nowhere, staying all over the place, an emotional nomad. He didn't go home until after closing time.

In the week before the ceremony, they did London from Buckingham Palace and the Tower to Petticoat Lane. Joe sat upstairs on topless buses and shivered, his body still adjusted to steamy rain forest country, bewildered at coming home too soon, too unexpectedly. He felt strange. It was all so familiar, outwardly had changed so little, but for him was no longer home.

'If it weren't for the buses, we could be in Poland,' he said, pacing round and round the top of the Monument, going again and again to the top of the stairs by way of suggesting they should go down.

'It's cute,' breathed Louisa, enchanted, looking out over London.

'It's not cute,' snarled Joe, 'it's depressed and depressing. Look at people's faces.'

'You should look at your own, if you want to see something really depressing,' she snapped.

Gladys and Harry got married in the register office. Gladys wore dark blue, carried yellow and white roses, and was radiant.

'She's lovely,' chirped Louisa, throwing herself joyously into the spirit of the occasion. Joe retreated further into misery and looked surreptitiously for ghosts. That would show them. But his father couldn't have disapproved, or else had lost interest, since no whiff of ectoplasm appeared.

Gladys tucked her arm into Louisa's and said, 'Take no notice of him.'

Joe folded his arms and ignored them. They might have got through the bad patch, and Joe might have got over what he later recognised as grief, if the Mothercare catalogue hadn't brought it all to a head. The real end came with babies.

'Oh,' cried Gladys happily, after several sherries and some bubbly white wine, at the reception, 'he was a bonny baby.' She brought down the photograph albums from her bedroom and the two women sat knee to knee on the hard little sofa, cooing. Joe tried hard to make conversation with his new stepfather, but Harry was nervously monosyllabic, watching Gladys all the time, sipping at a glass of warm beer.

'One of the perks of getting married late in life, you can keep it quiet. No relations,' he observed, lapsing back into silence.

'Indeed,' said Joe and got a fresh beer. Pension books

and the Post Office . . . he wondered how Gladys would ever stand it. He said to Louisa, 'I'm going to have a nervous breakdown,' and she trilled with laughter.

He went out and walked the length of the road and back to clear his head. When he got back, they'd put aside the albums and were going through a Mothercare catalogue.

'She's never pregnant, he thought, panic-stricken. He felt ill. 'Where did you get that?'

'Mothercare, of course,' said Louisa, turning pages, not looking up.

'Why did you get it?' he said, summoning courage.

'Just to look.'

Gladys came in, bearing potatoes, a red pinafore over her wedding suit, flushed from all the sherry.

'You're never going to make chips on your wedding day,' cried Joe.

'Fries. You make the best fries in the world,' cried Louisa.

'Californian overstatement,' snarled Joe. 'And they're chips.'

'Louisa said she really fancied some of my chips. Why shouldn't I make some?' Gladys was very merry.

'You're being a bear,' said Louisa.

'I was saying, when are you going to give me a grandchild?'

'I don't like being picked to bits by you two.'

'Oh, come on . . .' drawled Louisa.

'All right!' he shouted. 'You tell me. What are you looking at that thing for? Why do you suddenly want chips?'

Louisa grinned. 'I fancied them, and so does Harry, don't you, Harry?'

'Are you pregnant?'

'I'm not.'

He was shaken by his own relief.

'Really,' cried Gladys, 'you don't have to . . .'

'Kids are not part of it. Not for a long, long time, if ever.'

'We didn't ever agree that,' said Louisa.

'We never bloody agreed anything different, either.'

'Well!' said his mother, arms akimbo, her wedding finery spread over the backs of two chairs, not to crease before she went away that evening, like a borderline between him and them. He looked at Louisa. Gladys was on her side; they all were.

'No,' cried Joe bitterly, 'I never reckoned on kids.'

'I wanted . . .' she began.

'What you wanted was in when you felt like it, and then when you didn't like it, you wanted out. Just like that.'

'Joe,' said Gladys tightly.

'Mum,' he mimicked.

Then the rage drained out of him and he felt cowardly and trapped and angry, all at once.

'I was only joking, really,' said Gladys. 'Anyone would at my age. It's natural I'd look forward to grandchildren. I never meant any harm.'

'We haven't faced it ourselves.'

'I took it for granted we'd have children,' said Louisa, looking ill.

'We took a lot of things for granted,' said Joe drearily. 'It was stupid.'

In Gladys's shabby kitchen, his wife was too tanned, too bright, in a curious way, too large. California and East Ham didn't mix. He had been right all along; they should never have come.

'I took it for granted we loved each other,' she said.

Gladys flushed.

'We'll go out and walk round the block,' Joe told her. 'Louisa, please.'

'It's my wedding day,' cried his mother, 'you can't fight. Not just now. Joe, you can't!'

He looked across the room at Louisa. 'There's nothing to fight about,' he said, seeing the unbridgeable gulf between them, thrown like some demonic magical trick.

'Not if that's how you feel.'

'I do.'

Gladys wrung a dishcloth in her hands. 'It's a tiff. It's that jet lag. You haven't stopped anywhere five minutes for so long, I shouldn't think you know if you're coming or going.'

'Don't worry, Mum,' he said.

Harry coughed unhappily and wished there was a telly to watch. Gladys tried to laugh.

'You shouldn't upset the bride,' Louisa rallied bravely.

'Whew!' she said, when they were alone later, in Gladys's best bedroom, overlooking the noisy street.

'I'm sorry,' said Joe, 'you don't know how much.'

'We'll manage the rest of today,' she said dolefully.

'And after that?'

'I'll go home,' she said simply.

Harry and Gladys left for a week in Torquay. Gladys tossed her flowers to Louisa and then made as if to take them back again, confused.

'Goodbye,' called Louisa, waving the little bouquet bravely. 'Goodbye.'

'She's gone,' said Joe.

'I'll never see her post office in Cheltenham,' said Louisa sadly.

'What shall we do now?'

'How like a man, to want to be told what to do,' she said softly.

'I can go to Brighton alone, if you'd rather go straight back.'

'Meaning, you'd rather I went straight back and left you alone.'

'I suppose that is what I mean.'

'Can we work through this, do you think?'

Joe thought of sitting in some bright counsellor's room, talking it through, working it out, facing things like the meaning of loneliness, and of love, things his whole life had avoided.

'I don't think so.'

'It seems just so final, so sudden.'

'I can't see my life including children.'

'We should have talked about it more.'

'I don't think it would have done any good. I only just really found out I've made promises I can't keep.'

'Why?'

'I don't know in any way that makes sense.'

'I knew in Bogata, only I didn't want to believe it.'

He nodded.

'You want a divorce?'

She always thought quicker than he did.

'I'll give you everything,' he said.

'Except a child.'

'I never meant to hurt you.'

She shook her head.

'You'd better pack,' he said. 'I've got a reservation in an hotel.'

'You were that sure I'd go?'

'Yes.'

She packed. It all happened too fast to take in. On the tube to the hotel in Leicester Square he held her hand, trying to comfort them both.

'Don't come any further,' she said at the hotel entrance. He watched her go inside. It was over. He walked the darkening streets under a low, cloudy London sky, turning at random, sick at heart, then made his way back to his last night in Gladys's little house, where he'd lived as a child, and where he would never stay again.

'Less than one year,' he said, in the tiny, deserted kitchen Gladys had left spotlessly clean, for the landlord to come in to, in the morning. Unshaded light bounced off scrubbed formica surfaces, blue and cold, like him. Outside, all night, rain fell softly on green English gardens, bringing exquisite scent from Gladys's scattering of night stocks, drifting through the open window with small night sounds and the unceasing distant traffic roar. Drops ran down guttering and splashed lightly on gleaming slate roofs, making haloes around street lamps.

At first he sat with his elbows on the table, listening to water running in the gutter. Gladys had left a pile of folded brown paper on her draining board, left over from wrapping china. It was neat and smoothed and tied with string; as Louisa wanted his life to be, neat and smooth and tied with string, to her; as Gladys's love and pride, her motherly hopes, had tied him to her dreams, to her frightening love for a ghost father who never died. The little knot in the string seemed to sum up his life, tightly tied, wanting to be free. Memories passed, hallucinatory in their vividness, of Arthur and his teddy bear, of the big boys beating the daylights out of a smaller one, of Rodney Hitherington Mather's moon face staring from a corner, where he'd been unseen. Rodney had followed Joe around, hero worshipping, for months, on the unfounded belief that he had defended Arthur. He remembered the attic room, stifling in summer, freezing in winter, where he'd made his den, to get away from the rest, from the overbearing presence of too many men, all cloistered together in expensive seclusion. He remembered the homecomings, the changes of speech, the careful hiding of half of himself, wherever he was. At school, he hid the Joe he was at home. At home, they'd have crucified the Joe from school. Never himself.

Anger squirmed in him, until cold, bitter rage broke through his self-pity. He took the pile of paper, cut the string and spread the brown sheets flat. Life used you like a plaything, profoundly purposeless unless you made something out of it. He found a pen in his pocket and bent over the paper, sick with the need to make something out of his own, hurling words across the thick, square sheets of wrapping paper. At last, passion brought words in a flood. Before, he had tried to find them. Now they came of their own accord, out of pain. He wrote all night.

In the morning, red-eyed, he looked in the telephone directory for Jenny's number and caught her leaving for work. 'I can manage lunch,' she said delightedly.

'Charlotte Street?'

'Twelve-thirty.'

'You're a stranger. How many years is it?'

'I haven't changed.' As he spoke, he realised it was no longer true. He put down the telephone, utterly weary, feeling somehow, obscurely, ashamed.

*   *   *

'You have changed,' Jenny said, thinking he looked appalling, as though he'd just witnessed a road accident, or a murder; something awful. He had a bundle under his arm wrapped in string, a bundle of paper that he kept in his lap, like a tramp, as if it was precious.

'You haven't.'

'You look like something the cat dragged in. You want to say what happened?'

'Life happened.'

'Tell me.'

He told her about getting married, about travelling in remote places, exploring; about the freakish place, Bogata, that Louisa hated; how they'd flown to Gladys instead, and Gladys's wedding to a stepfather to whom he had nothing whatever to say. He told her that after Louisa had gone, he'd looked at the Mothercare catalogue, cover to cover, trying to see a dimpled baby through Louisa's eyes and seeing instead, in his mind's eye, a dead end, a graveyard of dreams.

'I knew it would be a disaster, whichever way I went,' he finished.

'No good way out,' she agreed. 'What will you do?'

He thought of what he had written. Her prettily painted face was poised over the coffee cup, expectant, sharp. He didn't want to tell her.

'Get a divorce. Go back to work. Just start over, I guess.'

'Sounds easy, and never is.'

'Are you happy?' he asked, glancing at the ring on her finger.

'So-so.'

He felt rebuffed.

'Do you ever see Hannah?'

Jenny scraped the bottom of her coffee cup with a plastic spoon and considered. 'Occasionally.'

'Why do you say it like that?'

'Because you're going to ask me where she lives, and go off to see her, and I don't think you should.'

'Why not?'

'She's had a bad time. The thing with Rodney was a mess and they gave each other hell for a while, though I think they are back on speaking terms now. He divorced her for desertion and then married again, someone she'd known for ages, and I doubt whether she'll ever get over how unfair that was. She's only just back on her feet.'

'So?'

'I think you'll knock her off balance again.'

He shook his head.

'Yes. You'd only hurt each other.'

'Is she with her family? They never sounded much good.'

'I think she's got part of her grandmother's house or something.'

'Does she work?'

'Rodney pays her enough to let her study psychology. She wants to move into that when she's finished.'

'Psychology,' Joe ruminated. 'That would suit her.' He thought of the old days. The good old days.

'They weren't,' said Jenny, reading his thoughts. 'They were pipe dreams.'

'Maybe not all.'

'Most.'

'That's our own fault.'

'Hair shirts aren't my line,' she answered briskly. 'And I have to get back to the office.'

431

'I'm going down to Brighton. Sentimental pilgrimage. I was going to take my wife, only . . .'

'Go and look at the sea. Cheer yourself up,' said Jenny, rising from her chair. 'Look, I'm sorry, I have to get back.'

'I shall go home in a few days and I don't suppose I'll see you again. Will you tell Hannah I asked after her?'

Jenny smiled.

Brouhaha ran and ran, in London and on Broadway, to rave reviews. Many years later Joe Masters, playwright, recluse and millionaire, asked Hannah whether Jenny had been right.

"Would I have hurt you, if I'd come?" he wrote. "What she said made sense at the time. I wanted to show you something, but maybe it would have been selfish. I wanted to show you the manuscript of my first play."

Yes, you would have hurt me, she thought, reading the bold, black writing, and I would have hurt you; that is how it was with us, and how it was meant to be. It could never have been any different.

Chapter Forty-Eight

Hannah was obliquely aware of Joe's celebrity from a great distance, with wry amusement and the occasional pang. In the early days of his fame, Joe's high profile lifestyle was well chronicled and Hannah, glimpsing it from time to time in the press, followed his rise to eminence. When his plays came to London, she went to see them, and thought she saw in them something of the Joe she'd known, but changed, grown beyond her, a stranger now. When he made the cover of *Time*, she sat studying his face for a long time, remembering, and wondering what life would have been like if she'd stayed at his side. After a while, the stories in the press became rarer, describing him as solitary, a recluse who never gave interviews. There had been no new plays since his appearance in *Time*.

'He somehow doesn't look very happy, does he?' Hannah had said, showing the picture to Georgina.

'Perhaps it's true that really contented people can't write good plays. Perhaps he needs to suffer, do you think?'

'How depressing. I'm sure that can't be true.'

'A cliché, creative misery in a garret. Not that he's in any garret. Why don't you ask him? You knew him really well, didn't you?'

433

'He'd hate me to do that, I'm quite sure.'

'Why ever should he?'

'I behaved badly. We hurt each other and it would be embarrassing to reopen old wounds.'

'You're not so unforgiving as that, are you?'

'Me? I hope not.'

'Then why should he be?'

'I hadn't seen it like that.'

'Go on, Mum, don't you fancy a millionaire?'

'Don't be silly,' said Hannah.

There was occasional gossip about Joe's women. Hannah came across pictures of several of them in some glossy feature about contemporary theatre, and none were great beauties. Rather, they were homely, with degrees rather than looks. For a long time he was linked with a deeply tanned blonde ecologist with lines on her face. She disappeared in tragic circumstances in Australia, found half eaten by coyotes in some distant part of the bush while on field research. Hannah wondered how anyone got over such tragedy, and thought that Joe's life seemed dogged by it. For a very long time, no one heard anything more about him.

Then a new play and a new woman hit critical headlines. Hannah wondered if one inspired the other and felt unlooked-for stirrings of jealousy. She told Ben, who laughed.

'You laugh at everything,' she said crossly. 'You could at least treat my embarrassment with decent respect.'

'Thought of getting in touch with him? Knock the thing on its head with a dose of reality?'

'You're as bad as Georgie.'

The scandal, when it came, was delicious; Joe was photographed with what appeared to be a prominent politician's wife in a compromising situation.

'Your man is crazy,' remarked Ben, unsmiling.

'He isn't my man,' retorted Hannah. But she read the ugly story, sick at heart, seeing the Joe the press painted, a brilliant fool, playing with words like an angel, flawed by misjudgement and immature hedonism.

'He isn't so stupid,' she cried.

'Can be led by the nose? Sexually?' asked Ben.

'I don't believe so.'

'Literary licence?'

'Artistic misbehaviour? That's bullshit.'

'You care, don't you?' Ben observed kindly.

'I suppose.'

Ben looked quizzical and kept an open mind. Some of Joe's plays were, viewed in certain ways, politically contentious. He said nothing to Hannah, but wondered if someone, somewhere, had it in for the playwright.

The story was a nine days' wonder. Joe, depressed and lonely, left the politician's wife and the jackals to invent what they pleased. Wealth bought anonymity and he vanished once more into South America, avoiding the cities, mostly alone, until one day he ran out of money and had to go into Guatemala City, to do business at his bank. His wallet stuffed with travellers cheques, he walked the streets of that wretched city until in late afternoon he passed the end of a pot-holed alleyway and stopped to stare. At the far end, several small children squatted by a row of wooden trolleys, folding and smoothing and bundling a mountain of cardboard and paper, ready for roping and selling. Two urchins slumped against a wall, unconscious; the stench of the slaughterhouse on the other side of it seeped into the air, as blood seeped into the gutters. A dark figure appeared at the far end of the alley, holding something heavy. The children scattered like rats. Seeing Joe, the figure paused.

Very deliberately Joe walked up the alley and shook the children. One fell sideways, comatose. The other, flies crawling in her eyesockets, lifted an emaciated hand to brush them away and touched his sleeve. Her eyes half opened and even in semi-consciousness, she began to beg.

'They are rubbish,' said the figure. 'Vermin.' It raised its gun.

Joe lifted the girl in his arms and backed down the alley.

'Fool,' said the policeman.

'Bastard,' said Joe.

The policeman grinned knowingly and shrugged. 'She'll give you something you won't forget.'

The girl snored and dribbled into Joe's shirt, lice crawling across her red-brown, Indian skin. He heard the shot from several hundred yards away and knew the body would be left to lie by the slaughterhouse wall. He slapped at fleas on his arm.

'What's your name?' he asked, shaking her awake.

'Amy.'

'We are going to find your parents and then we are going to my home.'

She groped in her dress and he pulled her hand away, kicking the little package she held into the gutter.

'No more of that.'

Amy snarled and bit like an animal. Joe held her jaw in one large, leathery hand.

'No,' he said.

Her parents were glad to agree to adoption. Joe flew

back to Santa Cruz with a furious, mutinous cocaine addict who did not want to come off. They fought for weeks, even after papers were signed and she was installed, cleaned, disinfected, all sores treated and healing, in his home. The battle for Amy was long and grim. He hired a nurse to watch her, but she was cunning as a sewer rat. They found needles and pipes and packets and Amy lolling like a rag doll, overdosed. Enraged, Joe bawled and threatened and cursed. She didn't want to be saved; she wanted to die. Passionately he kept on, furiously forcing her to live. She fought him with silence and cunning and fury and hate. He fought her with yelling and cunning and fury and a determined, deepening love. Joe won his daughter by sheer persistence and she filled the empty place in his heart.

Chapter Forty-Nine

Hannah ran down the few shallow steps in front of the East End college where she taught psychology part-time to undergraduates, to meet Bridie and Georgina, waiting for her outside on the last day of the summer term.

'It's good,' shouted Georgina, fourteen years old and leggy as a colt, waving the narrow green booklet that held her school report. 'I've done brilliantly.'

'I expect there's room for improvement,' observed her mother.

Bridie carried Georgina's satchel of books and Hannah frowned. 'You shouldn't let Granny carry that lot.'

Georgina flapped the booklet and cried, 'Read it, read it.'

'She carried her books all the way here. She's desperate for you to look at that,' said Bridie.

Hannah stood on the pavement and read it, then saw the reason for the excitement.

'They think they'll put you in for twelve O levels next year. Oh, Georgie, that's a lot. Do you want to go in for as many as that?'

Georgina hopped up and down on the bottom step and said yes, yes, yes, she really did.

Hannah looked to Bridie with a wry smile. 'They

don't change in this family, somehow, do they?'

'They do not. But I don't think she'll misuse that bright brain of hers like some have.'

They walked round the corner towards the swimming pool. Bridie would sit and watch while they swam, Hannah to keep fit, Georgina to show off to herself and everyone else. She went ahead because Bridie was slow, then ran back. 'Mum? Wendy said I have to have a complete sunblock. I forgot.'

'She didn't forget,' said Hannah, watching her strut ahead, pigtails swinging, her head held high and perky, Bridie still carrying her satchel. 'She does it to annoy.'

'If you had a yacht off the Greek coast for a month, you could afford to annoy. He spoils her.'

'I suppose it's envy, really. I could do with a month in the sun.'

'You've got other things to do,' said her grandmother. 'It's your own fault you haven't got a holiday.'

Hannah smiled. They both had other things to do.

Cajoling and wheedling and downright bullying had at last yielded results and Bridie had agreed to get the builders in. Hannah had paid for her future comforts readily enough by hours of listening to Bridie reminisce, tales sparked off by the prospect of change, about the first time Bridie got the builders into that house, when the gas blew up. Then about the time the roof and one wall came off, in the war; about how Edward died, and Sam Saul came to find her weeping in the ruins of their bedroom. Then about how she'd stood in her porch, coming back to London after being hurt in the Blitz, nearly crying with disappointment because she'd lost her keys, and April had laughed and Bridie had rounded on her crossly until April had pointed out they could walk straight in through the missing wall at the side.

'I think gas central heating would be best. Cheaper to run.' Hannah tried to stem the flood of memories with facts and figures. She spread brochures on the kitchen table, worn into a shallow dip at one side by years and years of vegetable peeling and the scraping of sharp knives.

'Lizzie says it dries her skin.'

'She does.' Hannah had learned the art of not arguing.

'It'll do.'

'And the rewiring?'

'It'll all be yours when I'm gone. If you spend it now, you won't have it then.'

'You will be much more comfortable.'

'I was comfortable as I was,' snapped her grandmother. 'But I can see you aren't. People these days expect more. But they do say it dries your skin.'

Hannah had also learned the art of diplomacy. 'We'll have it on sparingly, then. Just when you feel cold.'

'Lizzie says it does her arthritis good.'

'All right, you put it on whenever you like.'

'You don't sound very sure whether you want it or not. Can't you make your mind up?'

'*My* mind? *Me* make up *my* mind?'

'Let's not be hasty and impatient.'

'I am not hasty and impatient,' protested Hannah, exasperated.

'See,' said her grandmother smugly.

Somehow, the work got done. While Georgina sailed round the Greek islands with Rodney and Wendy Dawn and their loud friends, and made eyes over the side of the yacht at Greek gods of sixteen or so, men tramped in and out of Bridie's house and reduced it to a shambles. Then, they built it up again, with half its chimney breasts gone, several walls knocked down, a new roof, new bathroom, new kitchen, and everything painted magnolia. Except the whorehouse and Bridie's sitting room. She refused to have them touched.

'You can do what you like elsewhere,' she told Hannah, 'but you don't come in my rooms.'

'Some heating. Like Lizzie has. She's got sense,' pleaded Hannah. 'Just ask her.'

They compromised. Bridie accepted radiators and new carpets in her own rooms. The rest stayed just as it was.

'Do you know how the value of property is rising? This house will be worth a fortune,' Hannah said, trying to make her feel pleased. Bridie seemed waspish and said she didn't care.

Lizzie listened to Hannah's complaints.

'You tell her she's old, don't you see? You look to the future, with all your changes, while we hang on to our past. You could be kinder, though I know you mean well.'

'I'm sorry,' cried Hannah that evening. 'I've been selfish. I didn't mean it.'

'Don't be silly,' said Bridie gruffly. 'That Lizzie don't know what she's talking about.'

But Hannah cleared away her pots of paint and toned her enthusiasms down, being more careful; there was more harmony after that. She spent a lot of time in Lizzie's flat as summer turned to autumn and the holidays drew to a close, so the two women drew closer, building bridges of understanding and deep affection, from one generation into another. Georgina came home, burned nearly black with her long hair frizzed yellow and split by salt and sun.

'Look,' she announced one evening just before the start of term, 'I had to do something with it. D'you like it?'

Hannah shrieked.

'You do make a fuss, Mum.' said Georgie patronisingly, preening her radiant pink crop. 'It'll wash out. You don't mind if I go punk, do you?'

'I might not, but your head teacher will,' said Hannah meanly, hoping the beastly child would get trounced.

'They like it at school,' trumpeted Georgie when she came home after a day of admiring comments.

'It's what comes of living in the bloody East End,' complained Hannah. 'You can't go around looking like that. You'll have to grow it out.'

'You never had a teenage, did you? Daddy says,' cried Georgie, hitting below the belt.

'Nor will you have, if you carry on like that. Go and do your homework.'

Georgina gathered up her scattered books. 'Miss Rattle said it's individualistic,' she said triumphantly. 'She said, she rather likes it, providing I don't put a safety pin through my nose. Do you think that hurts? Do you think . . . ?'

'Upstairs,' yelled Hannah.

Georgina fled.

'She's impossible,' cried her mother, looking for sympathy, but found none from Bridie, who wouldn't take sides and only said, 'She'll do all right for herself.'

'And to think I never dared say a word at her age,' Hannah fumed, thinking how different life might have been if she had. 'Georgina's an arrogant brat and

Rodney encourages her. I bet Wendy Dawn doesn't help, either.'

'She's bright and lovely and gets on well with everyone. I don't know what you're complaining about,' said Bridie.

'And she's from a broken home,' Hannah went on. 'It's supposed to make them insecure, but I never met a more secure child in my life. So much for psychology.'

'Huh,' snorted Bridie, who didn't believe a word of it. Hannah owned up to jealousy of her own child and was ashamed of herself.

Amy Masters and Georgina Hitherington Mathers, who knew nothing of each other, were separated by thousands of miles, different cultures, skin colour and accents neither would easily have understood, nevertheless had much in common, being teenagers. While Georgina sported day-glo socks and matching hair after the garish fashions of the East End, Amy cut her wiry black hair into a chin-length bob, had a collection of cashmere sweaters and practised baton twirling in her bedroom. Georgina sucked in her stomach and lay flat on her bed, the better to drag skintight jeans over a suspicion of hippiness. Amy, barely five feet tall, had wide, flat hips, sturdy legs and still, impassive features until she laughed, when her black eyes sparkled, almost disappearing into high, chestnut-coloured cheeks. Their styles were different as chalk and cheese, but they watched the same films, listened to the same music, danced the same dances and both had a way of giggling, blushing and provoking. They especially provoked boys. Hannah watched with cautious patience and was wise.

She only commented when asked. Joe, trying to be both father and mother, protective and possessive, irked Amy by laying down the law.

'You're too young to date,' he said, as though that made it final. Her inscrutable face stared back at him, and at the closely written pages on his desk in front of him. The bold handwriting marched across the white paper like he marched across her feelings.

'If I were at home, I'd be married quite soon.'

'Married? Who's talking about married? You're still a child.'

'I'm not a child.'

'Fifteen is a child.'

'Fifteen is a young woman,' said his secretary, popping his head round the door, and staying to listen. 'Isn't it, Amy?'

'Yes.'

Joe pushed the manuscript carefully into a pile, playing for time. 'We didn't call it dating,' he remarked, 'it was going out.'

'I want to go out,' answered Amy obligingly.

'Going out, stepping out, walking out, dating. Words,' said the secretary, grinning.

'If you have nothing to do, you might get started on these.' Joe gave him the pages.

'OK,' said the young man cheerfully.

'He's not making eyes at you, is he?' demanded Joe, as the door closed.

'Of course not.'

'Then who is?'

Amy went to the other side of the long, high room and gazed through the great glass wall that ran the whole length of one side. The mountain dropped sheer away, forcing her eyes into the far blue distance, across the top of forests that went on forever.

'Isn't it beautiful?' She sat on the arm of a chair and swung one leg.

'Yes.'

'It's a boy in my class. You've met him a couple of times. His name is Raoul Rees.'

Joe stiffened. 'He's asking you to go out on dates with him?'

'Joe,' she said, rolling her eyes with exaggerated patience. One thing Amy had never done was call him Dad, or Papa, or Pop. He was always Joe. Now, he found himself wishing she had, wondering if it meant there was not a distance, a rejection, in not being Dad. He sighed.

'He's coming this evening and we're going to a movie. I said you'd let me.'

Something nagged at the back of his mind. 'Did you, now?'

'Joe, everyone dates. We go to the movie, have a soda, come home, and you have to be nice to him, please.'

'I know what people do on dates.'

'Some people do, but not me.'

The nagging refused to go away. 'You met this boy's family?'

'At school. They come by sometimes because Mrs Rees helps with the math programme and the computers. You've seen her.'

Memory brought Mrs Rees's beautiful, sculpted features into focus, her full, carved lips and prominent, appraising eyes. Joe lifted a finger and held it up, as if overcome by an extraordinary thought.

'Ah,' he said, 'Raoul is black.'

'So am I, nearly,' said Amy, still staring out at the view. 'He's African black and I'm Indian black. We aren't much different, really, though he's darkest. His skin is beautiful. It glows. You should feel it.'

'Good heavens.'

'What?'

'You, talking like that.'

'How should I talk?'

Joe shook his head, confused by the storms breaking over him, in the face of her innocent, moving self-acceptance. He got up and went to sit in her chair, suppressing nostalgia, a longing to turn time back to the unselfconscious child, passionate and imperious and a pure delight. He leaned back and looked up at her, still swinging her leg.

'OK,' he said, 'you bring him in when he fetches you, and I'll come on a bit heavy and lay down a few ground rules, just to let him know where we stand, and then you can go.'

She kissed the top of his head.

'All right,' he said gruffly.

The secretary came in with the typing an hour later, and to see whether Joe wanted some tea.

'You look tired,' the young man observed. 'You feeling OK?'

'I just got old,' said Joe.

'You got old?'

'First you bust your guts trying to avoid commitment, and you lose out. Then you get committed and bust your guts trying to handle the thing; you try to love them enough, try to figure them enough, give every bloody thing you've got, including your heartstrings, and then

446

they come in one day and do something that makes you realise you have to start all over, busting a gut to give it all up and let go again. And they call that life.'

'Amy's got a date, huh?'

'How did you know?' said Joe gloomily.

The secretary stacked typescript in a tray and thought about it. 'They say, the more you let go, the more they come back,' he offered.

Joe stretched his legs and yawned. 'You're young. Do you believe that? Does it work?'

'Sure. At college, I read your plays until I was word perfect, and I went to typing classes, and then I came and badgered you for a job, and when I had sat out on your doorstep for a week, you got curious and let me say my bit, and here I am. And my parents thought I was crazy, plain, simple crazy, but they never tried to stop me.'

'I suppose there's a moral somewhere,' growled Joe. 'You're an excellent secretary.'

'I'm an excellent secretary on excellent terms with his mom and dad.'

'OK, OK, I give in. Where's the tea?'

'I'll get it.' He went to the door and turned. 'How did you fly the coop, if you don't mind my asking? Don't you have family in England?'

'Not a lot,' said Joe and the young man went out, then stuck his head round the door again. 'What about the grandchildren?' he asked, and vanished.

Grandchildren, thought Joe, closing his eyes. They'd belong all over the place, an amazing mix of race, culture, colour and parenting. They'd belong all over the place and one of those places was England and one of those parents was Gladys. Joe sat and thought about that until his secretary brought in the tea.

'I was thinking,' he remarked, seeing that Joe seemed disinclined to speak, 'that she's a real credit to you. You don't need to go worrying about Amy.'

'OK, OK. I got the message,' muttered Joe, and helped himself to a bourbon biscuit, brought over from London by a visiting friend. 'I got the message, all right.'

'Ah, take no notice,' said Lizzie. 'Would you take me to the window? Look at that, now.'

Hannah held her arm as Lizzie hobbled to her favourite chair. Her flat overlooked a small, cobbled courtyard where once costers had kept their horses. The picture window facing due west caught the sunsets that she loved to watch.

The sky was yellow-streaked and stormy looking, the sun blood red, sinking slowly.

'Perhaps one day I'll love the East End like you do,' said Hannah, watching with her, 'but I haven't got that feeling of belonging that you have. I never really belong here.'

'Your father used to say that. It's a shame.'

Hannah mulled it over. 'Perhaps you never put down roots, if you didn't when you were a child.'

'Is that what psychologists say nowadays?' asked Lizzie critically.

'Different psychologists say different things.'

'What does your Ben think?'

'Ben seems to think belonging is a feeling that comes from inside a person and doesn't always have much to do with places. But he's hard to pin down on opinions.'

'I think that's right. You belong to yourself first, then you can share yourself with other people.'

Walking home in the dark, Hannah wondered about

the lives of the two old women, about their long, deeply lived lives, and the men they'd loved. They'd had children and wars, catastrophes and heartbreak, poverty and uncertainty. Some would say they had been oppressed. Yet they had lived fully, lives filled with mysteries she knew little about. Hannah found, against all rational argument, that quite often she envied them.

'Why not?' observed Ben. 'They are women at peace with themselves. Of course you envy them.'

'They've paid their dues,' she said. 'To life.'

'They have.'

'I haven't.'

'I would have said you had at least partially paid up.'

'I think Georgina is growing up without my handicaps.'

'Georgina is doing splendidly.'

'Yes.'

'Don't you think that that is somewhat to your credit?'

'Yes.'

Sometimes their silences stretched and sagged like familiar garments. 'What I think I'd really like to do, if I could afford it, and if you think I'd be suitable, is what you do,' she said finally.

'Sit on this side of the fence, you mean?'

She nodded. 'I like academic things, but I'll never earn a good living at it. There aren't the jobs. I only manage because of Gran and Rodney and I don't want to depend on other people all my life. I want to pay my way.'

Ben laughed and said money was a great motivation for getting on with things, but his eyes studied her all the while, without smiling.

'What do you think?' she asked nervously. 'Would I be any good at it, do you think?'

'Why not expand the teaching?'

'I'm not a particularly good teacher and there are very few opportunities.'

'Go back to an office?'

'I couldn't bear it. Not for the rest of my life.'

'So it's not just money.'

'It is important, but it's how I earn the money as well.'

'Oh, yes.'

She felt blood creep up her cheeks until she was scarlet. 'I'd like to give to others what you have given me.'

'What have I given you?'

She sought for words. 'A chance to tell my story, even though I didn't know what it was. You never hurried me, or made me make sense when I couldn't. You were never afraid of not knowing what the story was going to be.'

'We both stuck with that.'

'I suppose, I could say, you weren't scared of the dark.'

'Pitch black, all right,' he said, grinning. 'I spend my working life groping for light switches inside other people's heads.' He laughed. 'And then they wish they hadn't found it, because what they see is awful.'

'The darkness in me was terrifying and sometimes it still is. The difference is, I know it better and I think I can handle it now.'

Ben nodded.

'Do you think I'd be any good at this kind of work, if I had some training?'

He got out of his chair and opened his filing cabinet.

'What are you doing?'

'Looking for an application form, for you. Of course,

450

they will ask you, do you want to be a psychotherapist to be like your father?' he said, holding the paper in one hand, sliding the drawer shut. 'But we can talk it through before your interviews.'

'You think I'll get as far as interviews? Maybe I do want to be like my father. Does that mean I shouldn't do it?'

Ben chuckled. 'No. But it'll give you and your supervisors something to worry at. Keep the lot of you on your psychological toes.'

'I wouldn't dare argue about it.'

'When you dare, you'll be ready to start,' said Ben, handing her the paper.

'I'm thinking of training as a therapist,' Hannah told Marcus, who was doing postgraduate studies in psychology and coached Georgina in maths for her GCE exam. He was a small, prematurely grey man with curly hair and a thick, full, speckled beard. He wanted help with his statistics, and they both watched the Apple's screen drawing lines and columns of numbers.

'That's a wacky way to earn a living.'

'No wackier than what I do already.'

Marcus tilted the terminal away from a ray of sunlight and said, 'I saw my wife last week.'

'You should have used an unrelated T test for that data.'

'She wants a divorce.'

He tapped the keyboard and numbers flashed up and down the screen.

'You've been saying she would ever since I've known you.'

'I didn't believe it.' He put his fist on the keys and

figures ran frantically across the screen, unscrolling.

'What did you say?'

'I said I'd like to choke her,' he said, sounding choked himself. She put her hand on his worn jacket, feeling his soft, plump shoulder underneath the old tweed.

'You don't, really.'

'I do. Didn't you ever want to choke Rodney?'

'All the time,' said Hannah, 'but not so as I'd do it.'

'I could do it. She has ruined my life, taken my kids, and now she wants to get rid of me and marry what used to be my best mate. Strangling her would be such a pleasure, it would almost be worth losing twenty years of my life for it.'

'Marriage,' said Hannah sadly.

Night after night, she had nightmares. Marcus throttled Iris, a faded red-haired woman the wrong side of thirty-five, with mottled, fat arms and an anxious smile. In the dreams, Iris turned yellow and black, like the flower, until Hannah woke up, sweating.

'It's bringing something back,' said Ben.

'Say you don't mean it,' Hannah said, next time she saw Marcus.

'Mean what?'

She couldn't tell him.

He came to teach Georgina and she could not leave them in the room together, wound to a feverish pitch that she tried to relieve by apologising. Georgina sulked and Marcus grew offended.

'You're a bit off, these days,' remarked Bridie. What's the matter with you?'

Neither Hannah nor Ben could make it out.

* * *

Bridie found her sleepwalking at three in the morning, huddled on the landing half way up the stairs, her head in her arms. The old woman pulled her dressing gown around her and sat down on the step.

'Hannah,' she whispered, wondering if it was true that you shouldn't wake sleepwalkers. She might fall down the stairs.

Hannah seemed to wake up. 'He's going away,' she whispered, still dreaming, 'and they'll die.'

'Who is?' Bridie whispered back.

'They'll die.'

'You're having a nightmare.'

'He wants her to die.'

'Who does?'

'Dad. Wants us to die.'

'No,' said Bridie, 'that was April.'

'Mum? No, he wanted us dead. He wished I was dead, they all wanted me dead.'

'Your dad is gone.'

'It's Marcus.' Hannah came fully awake. 'He wants his wife dead.'

'People say these things, but they don't mean them,' said Bridie. 'It's cruel, but they don't mean it, except for David and April.'

'You thought they were cruel? You never said that.'

'I thought it.'

'They couldn't help what they did, could they?'

'Edward couldn't help drowning. Rosa couldn't help dying. My dad couldn't help getting drunk. Just because people can't help it doesn't mean to say you can't still be furious with them.'

'You?'

'I was angry with Edward for getting himself

drowned. I was angry with him for a very long time. I once met a priest,' Bridie went on, beginning to feel cold on the stairs, 'a Salvation Army man I bumped into a while after Edward died. I didn't know him, but we spoke, for some reason, and he said my anger was all part of my grief, and it needed someone to receive it. So I said, in a very bad temper, that he was welcome to it. And the funny thing was, I did feel better after that. Not over it, but a bit better.'

'I hate Mum.'

'I'm not surprised.'

'Everyone said what a terrible time she had, and how I ought to understand. No one ever asked what it felt like to be me, or Jessie, or the others. Always poor Mum.'

'Sam did. We used to talk about it, but we felt helpless.'

'It was so lonely, feeling that there was no one there at all.'

'Like they died?'

'Yes, only worse, because they wanted to go away and stay away. I used to wish they had died.'

'I'm not really surprised,' said Bridie, 'and if I sit here much longer, I'll get stiff as a board. Let's go down and put the kettle on.'

'Tea. The answer to everything,' Hannah said, trying to smile, blotting tears with the edge of her nightgown.

'It saw us through.'

'If you'd been there, to say, "Put the kettle on" Mum would never have done it, would she?'

'She wasn't a good coper. You'd better leave that Marcus alone if he gives you bad dreams.'

'I'm glad we've said what we have,' said Hannah.

In the chilly kitchen Bridie lit the gas on the hob, and

then realised for the hundredth time that Hannah had bought an electric kettle.

'You can get stuck in the past,' she said to the empty room, while Hannah went to put on a dressing gown. 'It don't do no good, though, so I'd better learn to use this dratted thing.' She plugged Hannah's shiny white appliance in and got out her old brown teapot. 'But a few things, I don't change.'

She pinched tea from its caddy and waited for the water to boil.

'I'm glad you don't change,' said Hannah, coming back.

'Good,' said her grandmother, 'then come and get your tea.'

Chapter Fifty

'You ought to get married again, Mum,' said Georgina, when Hannah sometimes brought men friends home. Hannah laughed and said once bitten, twice shy, and she was used to being on her own, now. Ben said wait and see; time, after all, was still on their side. Hannah took out her old diaries, going over the years in her mind. Time, it seemed, slipped away faster and faster, like sand through her fingers. Georgina was taller than she was, and combed Marks and Spencer for the kind of underwear Hannah had never been allowed.

'There were still war shortages when I was your age. Well, I think there were. When did they give up rationing?' she said, dismissing Georgina's yearnings, remembering April giving her five shillings for her fourteenth birthday. Buying pink satin suspenders had left just enough for a pair of stockings to go with it. But that had been before . . .

'Oh, Mum, look,' cried Georgina, fingering pure silk camiknickers next to racks of cotton bras.

'Absolutely not. Where do you think money comes from?' snapped Hannah, dragging her away.

'Trees?' suggested Georgie rudely. 'Dad will let me.'

'Wendy Dawn, no doubt, has a cupboardful you could raid.'

'I thought you'd given up being jealous,' cried Georgie slyly.

Hannah looked at black silk trimmed with lace and sighed. 'So did I,' she said, and they both smiled.

'I love you, Mum,' said Georgie.

'More than black silk bras?'

Georgie hugged her in the middle of the lingerie department, even though Hannah hadn't bought her anything.

'Much, much, more,' she said.

Hannah found grey in the front of her hair. April, who came to see them very occasionally, was thinner and sparser than ever since David's death, her eyes haunted in a way that stirred uneasy memories in Hannah, who was glad when she went away again. They were stilted with each other, too conscious of mutual disappointment to be easy.

'She's got as joyless a life as I ever saw. It's such a shame, because when she was young, she was quite gay,' observed Bridie.

Hannah tried to imagine a young, pretty, gay April, who had nothing to do with this dry, betrayed mother who lived all alone. The rest of the family played safe, living well away, seldom going home, having children Hannah never saw, much younger than Georgina, leading different lives.

'She's a raving beauty, you know,' said Lizzie, coming by taxi for a rare day out.

'I told you,' said Bridie, satisfied.

Georgina blushed and grinned.

They spent their pensions on their telephone bills and wrote notes in spidery, wandering handwriting, but they didn't see each other very often any more. Lizzie walked with a frame but her mind was sharp as ever. Some days Hannah was oppressed by living only with women, only old women and herself, growing older. It depressed her, despite Georgie's bright, noisy presence, and her streams of friends.

'One day, soon, she'll up and go. It will be hard to let go,' she sighed, caught by Bridie in a moment of loneliness.

'I'd like to see you married again, before I die.'

'I don't want to marry again.'

'I mean you should enjoy yourself.'

'I do,' said Hannah. 'I enjoy my work, the training, and I have friends.'

'And you live with old women,' said Bridie. 'Half the time you're over with Lizzie. It's a waste.'

Hannah pushed aside a pile of marking from college, rested her elbows on the kitchen table and pulled back the skin of her cheeks. 'Perhaps if I had a facelift, do you think?'

Bridie parked her stick by the side of the table and sat down opposite. 'You have to be a film star for them.'

'I'm no star,' Hannah answered moodily.

'You're shining a bit dim just now.'

'It's hard to twinkle while you work for the gas bills and what have you. Stars don't have brown envelopes on the door mat.'

'Hasn't Rodney sent you your money?'

'He always does, but it's Georgina's. I can't live on it. Without you I couldn't live at all.'

'You'd manage. Women do.'

'Not half so well. I'd probably be living in two rooms or something. This is luxury.'

'Put that fiddly kettle in the plug,' ordered her grandmother, 'and make us some tea.'

'Death by tannin. What a price to pay,' sighed Hannah, getting up to obey.

Age and too many cups of strong tea, which Bridie flatly refused to give up, were behind her grandmother's nocturnal trips to the bathroom that occasionally disturbed Hannah.

'If she'd be sensible, she'd get a better night's sleep,' said their doctor. 'It's only her age. She wanted water tablets, but they'll do no good.'

'She's pickled in tea,' said Hannah. 'You'll never get her to change her ways, not now.'

'Then she'll have to keep on getting up to go,' said the GP.

They got used to finding each other around the house at odd hours. At first Hannah grumbled, and then she just said, 'Are you all right?' and went back to bed. The changes that came with growing older were so small, so natural, almost imperceptible, so that Lizzie and Bridie joked about getting a hundredth birthday card from the Queen.

'I'll be there first. I'm older than you,' cackled Bridie triumphantly. Hannah wondered if she realised what that might mean, and her heart sometimes ached.

Sounds came through the light sleep that comes with first daylight creeping round curtain edges in summertime. Birds cheeped, starting to wake, and dew lay thick on the grass leading down to the canal. Doves called somewhere in the park, while milk bottles rattled and chinked on the swaying back of a cart making its way past the chestnut trees from Unigate in Victoria Park Road. Through these sounds Hannah heard the soft fall, like a toy tumbling lightly from a child's hands.

'Oh,' came Bridie's voice, as though she'd had a great surprise.

Hannah leapt from her bed.

'How could you?' cried Lizzie, peering at the figure in the hospital bed, unsteadily balanced on her own feet; so upset, she was angry.

'She wouldn't ask,' muttered Hannah. 'Oh, no. We were so bloody independent, we'd never ask, would we?' She marched up and down at the end of the bed, glaring at Bridie, close to tears.

'Mum,' protested Georgina, 'you shouldn't shout.'

'I'm not shouting,' Hannah snapped, her eyes burning. 'Why couldn't she have asked? I'd have carried her down, or made her bloody tea for her. Oh, damn.'

'Mum,' cried Georgina, 'stop it.'

Lizzie hooked her stick round a chair leg and Georgina rushed to push it forwards. A nurse in a pale blue overall came to work the blood pressure machine hanging from Bridie's arm. She made a note on a bit of paper, smiled at them and went away. Bridie lay with her mouth open, snoring.

'That's the anaesthetic,' said Lizzie, settling down. 'It always makes you snore.'

'Why is she that horrible colour?' whispered Georgina.

'You'd be a nasty colour if you'd just had what she's had.'

Georgina retreated, deflated by everyone's anger, when she felt eager to be kind and helpful. They were both in ugly moods when you'd think they'd care. She fidgeted, unhappy and at a loss as to what to do.

'Stop it,' said Hannah. 'Please.'

'You are being horrid,' whispered Georgina.

'I . . .' said Hannah, and Georgina felt it was her fault, as tears spilled down her mother's face. 'I'm sorry.'

'Three pins in her leg. It's going to lay her up a bit,' muttered Lizzie. 'A very nasty break.'

Hannah wiped her face with the back of her hand and straightened the cover over the cradle that humped across Bridie's broken leg.

'I'll ring Mum,' she said. 'She'll want to come.'

Lizzie spoke calmly. 'As a nurse, I'd say you'd better get her to come fairly quick, then.'

'The doctor seemed to think she was doing fine,' cried Hannah, looking for the bell, to ring for someone.

'I've seen that look before. It means they're on their way out,' said Lizzie stubbornly.

'Oh, God,' cried Hannah.

'I'll ring,' offered Georgina, grateful for an excuse to leave them. So it was she who told April; 'Come quick. Great-granny has fallen down the stairs and she's got pins in her leg and Lizzie thinks she's going to die.'

'I'm coming,' cried April, and ran.

Late that evening, Bridie stirred and realised that the pain was her own.

'She's come round?' said Lizzie, waking up herself. The nurse stood in the door of the waiting room.

'If you'd like to go in, very quietly, you can. The doctor says, just for a minute, though.'

They filed in. Lizzie hung on to April's arm, shuffling on the shiny hospital floor. They stared. There didn't seem anything else to do. Bridie was saying something, but her mouth was so dry, the whisper hardly reached her lips.

'. . . a nuisance.'

'Oh, no,' cried Hannah, bending close. 'You're not. You have to get better, that's all. You just get better, and . . .'

'Here,' said April, pulling tissues out of a box and giving them across the bed to her daughter.

'It hurts,' murmured Bridie.

A nurse appeared, carrying a silver dish. She swished the curtains closed behind her and stood waiting.

'For her pain,' she said. 'She'll be asleep before she knows it and then she won't remember. You can come back in the morning.'

They looked back, from the ward door, at the little oasis of light around Bridie's curtains. White beds stretched away into gloom. The nurse stood immovable, wanting them out. It was the nurse's territory and Bridie belonged to it now, no longer to them. They went back together to her house and made pot after pot of weak tea, sitting, hardly speaking, around her kitchen table.

'I think you all ought to go to bed,' said Georgina at last. 'You'll never get up to go and see her in the morning. It's already morning. I'll make the spare beds.' Exhausted, the three women did as they were told.

They had propped Bridie up on a great pile of pillows. She looked tiny.

'Here,' cried Georgina. 'Look at these.' She put roses

on top of the hump over Bridie's leg. 'Does it hurt a lot?'

'A lot,' said Bridie in a papery voice, quite dry and hoarse and not like her own at all.

Hannah kissed her cheek. It was soft and yielding like the bruise on an apple, and much too warm. 'How do they say you are?' she asked, trying to make light of it.

'Do they say anything?'

'I'll ask the doctor. Is there anything you need that we could pop out and get? Would you like Perrier or squash, or something?' Hannah gabbled because she was afraid she would blurt out "Are you going to die?" and disgrace herself and hurt Bridie unspeakably.

'Yes,' said Bridie in a stronger voice. 'You could ask the priest to stop by.'

Lizzie was expressionless.

'Is that for last rites?' asked Georgina, round-eyed. 'Do they really pour oil on you?'

'Georgina,' hissed Hannah.

'I want him, can you make sure he comes?' Bridie seemed to come back to herself and a deep flush crept into her cheeks.

'I'll ask Sister to get him.'

'I will,' said April. 'I know what to do.'

Hannah bit her lip, unwilling to let anything out of her own hands.

'Let her,' said Lizzie, rubbing her knees, in a hard chair next to Bridie's pillows. She took her friend's hand and patted it. 'She'll have him here in no time.'

Georgina began picking petals off a rose, smelling their heavy scent.

'I want to confess,' said Bridie.

'I can't think you've got much to worry about.'

463

Hannah was startled to see sudden purpose in Bridie's eye.

'You don't know my conscience,' she whispered. 'I've had something on it many, many years.'

'Had what?'

'Birth certificate,' breathed Bridie.

'What birth certificate?' demanded Hannah. 'Do you know about birth certificates?' she appealed to Lizzie.

'That,' said Lizzie inscrutably.

'April—' said Bridie feebly.

'April's birth certificate?'

'No, I want her to know.'

'I already do,' said April, appearing silently. 'They've called the priest and he's on his way. I know about the certificate. David told me before he died.'

Bridie looked feverish. 'What did he do? Tell me what he did, so that I can ask forgiveness.'

'What are you all talking about?' demanded Georgina.

April came forward and crouched beside the bed, speaking clearly to Bridie, as though the rest of them had gone.

'He thought he sold his soul,' she said, 'to get a new certificate, so that he could go to medical school. He promised his soul in exchange for being a doctor. The optician who did his glasses dabbled in black magic and persuaded David to go through some sort of bargain.'

Hannah laughed nervously.

'He got into trouble in college, during the war,' April went on, 'and he tried to bargain himself out again, but he couldn't. I don't understand how he thought it worked, but he bargained Hannah, instead. Before she was born.'

'Aaah,' Bridie breathed out a great sigh, and closed her eyes for a moment, 'that was how it was.'

Hannah stared at her mother.

'It preyed on his mind for the rest of his life and I suppose you could say that was possession. It was why he was always so angry and harsh. He couldn't forgive himself, and he couldn't forgive you for reminding him every day of his life of what he had done. He hated what he had done, and so he hated you.'

'He hated me.' Hannah agreed bleakly.

'That's how it started. It went from bad to worse.' April folded her hands and bowed her head. 'I'm sorry.'

'It was Brother John, wasn't it? I always wondered.' Bridie lay, putting two and two together, exhausted. 'He never said how he got into that college. I should have insisted he tell . . . it's been on my conscience. I should have insisted. Sam wouldn't touch it. It wasn't there when you got married, was it?' she asked April.

'That he was illegitimate?'

Bridie fell back against the white pillows.

'No, he never said a word, until he died.'

'But you never let the bargain stand, did you, Hannah, love? You never agreed to the selling, though God knows it's been so hard, there must have been times . . . Look at Georgina. No, it didn't go through.' She sank back, closing her eyes.

'Who was Brother John?' asked Georgina.

'Her cat,' said April.

Bridie repeated, 'That bargain never went through.'

April put a hand to Bridie's cheek. 'You are hot. You shouldn't be talking about dying and working yourself up like this.'

'I want that priest. Where is the man?'

Georgina nudged her mother. 'She wants you to hurry up the priest. It sounds like we all need one, with black magic all over the place. Do you think it's real?'

'It doesn't matter. However you look at it, the effect was real enough. My father sold out to something, whether it was himself or the devil, we'll never know.'

'You're here,' Bridie said, some of her old vigour in her words.

'Yes,' said the priest, looking at the circle of faces. 'You wanted me.'

'We all need you,' muttered Hannah. 'You've no idea what's been going on.'

He winked at Bridie. 'I'll be after seeing to you first,' he said, 'if these other ladies wouldn't mind.'

The other ladies went to the waiting room again, and sat lost in their own thoughts.

Twenty-four hours later, the 'phone went at midday.

'Pneumonia,' the Ward Sister said to Hannah, 'I think you should come.'

'Thank you,' she said, with a bleak sense of relief that it was going to be over soon, and telephoned for Georgina to come home from a friend's house. Then she called April.

They went by taxi, to collect Lizzie, and then to the hospital.

'She's not really with us,' said the doctor, a young woman with tired lines on her face and a ready smile. 'We've put her in here.' She took them to a cubicle, apart from the rest.

'Mrs Saul,' she called gently, touching Bridie's shoulder, 'your family are here.'

Lizzie, against all her best intentions, burst into tears. She sobbed, trying to manage her stick and a handkerchief at the same time. The doctor fetched a chair and lowered poor Lizzie on to it, near the side of the bed, crying: 'Don't go, don't go,' as if Bridie might change her mind and stop after all.

'She isn't in pain,' whispered the doctor to April. 'I think it will be easy.'

'Old man's friend.'

'Pneumonia. Yes.'

Bridie hardly seemed to breathe.

'Gran?' cried Hannah. 'Granny?'

Bridie opened her eyes, looked at her very fiercely and cried, very suddenly, with tremendous joy: 'You broke it, darling, you broke it.'

'What was that?' cried Georgina, tears running down her nose.

'She's gone,' said the doctor.

'I think she just told us we are free,' muttered April, who knew more than the rest of them and kept most of it to herself.

Sunlight streamed in through tall, dingy windows and the lunch trolley banged into the lift to go back down to the kitchens to be refilled for supper. Life flooded back around them, letting the dead go and the living live on. Hannah stayed by the bedside, weeping until her eyes ached and her face felt raw. Georgina put her arms round Lizzie, and they sat out their little vigil, half seeing the sunlight move over the wall as time ticked quietly past. Then people came and covered Bridie decently, with white sheets, and the four women who had loved her thanked the priest, who came again, and went away for the last time.

'It's over,' said Hannah, tired out, tears still creeping from her eyes.

'It's all over,' said her mother, looking at her oddly. 'Georgina will be safe. You will be all right, too.'

'I can't let Lizzie go home alone now,' said Hannah, too numbed to pay attention. 'She'll have to stay.'

'I shall go now,' April decided. 'You don't need me.'

'Don't I?' said Hannah drearily.

'I don't think so.'

They put Lizzie in the spare room and sat in Bridie's sitting room, disorientated.

'What shall I do?' asked Hannah, too tired to do anything and too shocked to do nothing. 'Shall we open a bottle of wine and get rather drunk?'

'I know what I'm going to do,' said Georgina, feeling she'd all of a sudden grown up.

'What?'

She left her mother sitting there. She picked up the telephone and when someone answered at the other end said simply, 'Granny has just died and Mum needs you. Will you come, right away?' and put the receiver down without waiting for a reply.

Wendy Dawn and Rodney swept into the unlit room, scattering flowers, bottles and French perfume.

'Oh, no!' cried Hannah, and Wendy Dawn opened her arms. Hannah burst into tears again, weeping and weeping into fake fur that smelled of wonderful things full of life and living: cigar smoke from theatre evenings, garlic snails, musky perfume and fresh flowers; all these things hung in the soft coat that wrapped itself all round Hannah, who shivered and shivered, and cried, 'She's gone, she's gone.'

'Shhh,' said Wendy, rocking her, nodding at Georgina to help Rodney pass round the wine. 'Do you remember, in the police station, it was you who held me when I cried? Or was it me who . . . ?'

'It doesn't matter,' cried Hannah, pulling her scarlet face out of the coat. 'I just want you here now.'

'Here,' said Rodney gruffly, 'and there's something a lot stronger, in the car, if you want it.' He gave her an awkward hug. 'I'm sorry.'

'What's that?' asked Wendy Dawn, looking up.

A banging, muffled by carpets, sounded over their heads.

'It's Lizzie,' cried Georgina. 'We've woken her up from her doze.'

'Help her down, would you?' Hannah asked Rodney, who went up and brought Lizzie down some minutes later.

'A glass?' he said, looking for one more, 'and why don't you light the fire, George? Keep old bones warm.'

Rodney opened bottles, fetched coal and helped Georgina make sandwiches out of yesterday's bread and tins of pink salmon.

'This is what they call a wake,' he told his daughter, spooning fish on to crookedly sliced bread. 'You're just like me, can't cut straight. Look at this.'

'Aren't wakes after the funeral?'

'They are after anyone's died, who you are going to miss like mad,' said her father, watching out of the corner of his eye.

Georgina put down the butter knife and howled.

'I thought so,' he muttered. 'Come on.'

He held her like the little girl he'd once had, and had

not understood how to love enough. 'There, there, have my hanky.'

He shared it with her, until they pulled faces at each other in mutual disgust, and managed weak, tearful smiles.

'That's better,' said Rodney, scarlet with emotion. 'You bring that.' They took the picnic up and sat round the flames, sipping their wine. Hannah's head ached and swam and buzzed.

'You'll inherit everything, I should think,' remarked Rodney. 'There must be a fair bit, what with Sam's money and all. It all went to her, didn't it?'

'She said she'd left me what there was. How much she had, I certainly never asked. She wasn't short.'

'You won't be badly off, I'll be bound.' He sounded pleased.

'Quite rich, in fact,' murmured Wendy.

'You won't need me any more.'

Wendy shot him a warning look and said, 'Not now, Rodney.'

'She was the richest person I ever met.' Hannah wiped her eyes.

'Oh, yes,' said Lizzie, finishing her glass and feeling better.

'Mum is a lot like her,' said Georgina, flushing because it was a soppy, honest thing to say.

They all stared at Hannah, red-eyed and blotched with grief.

'You got her spirit,' said Lizzie.

'You'll make me cry again,' cried Hannah. 'Please don't.' Rodney refilled her glass.

'I'm so glad you're all here, I don't know what to say.'

'That's family,' said Wendy Dawn solemnly, folding her arms as though defying anyone to argue.

Hannah began to laugh, half crying. 'That is exactly what Bridie would have said,' she cried. 'Isn't it, Lizzie?'

'That,' said Lizzie, 'is exactly what she would have said, God rest her.'

'Amen,' they murmured, quite certain that, in Bridie's case, He most undoubtedly would.

Chapter Fifty-One

Hannah's legacy from Bridie was large. Other people had small mementoes, left with love; things they'd particularly liked when she was alive. But Hannah had everything else.

'It doesn't seem quite fair,' April complained, when the will was read after the funeral, but Lizzie fixed her with a gargoyle face they'd never glimpsed before.

'She wanted to make up for David. Don't you dare start making trouble and jealousy. She meant to look after those two if it was the last thing she did.'

April recoiled, shaken by Lizzie's anger. 'Don't take it out on me,' she protested, 'it wasn't my fault.'

'Hannah is your daughter and Georgina is your granddaughter but I don't recall as you ever did much by way of showing it.' Lizzie snapped her false teeth together alarmingly, then softened just as quickly. 'I'm not saying it was all your fault. The war did funny things to all of us. You might have done more than you did, since, is all I'm saying.'

'That blasted war,' muttered April. 'Don't bring that up again.'

'It's what did it,' insisted Lizzie querulously.

'How do you decide where things start?' asked Hannah, pale from broken nights and quiet weeping.

'You can always find someone to blame when things go wrong, but then you go back to their parents, or the war before, and you find it's the same story, over and over. It doesn't help.'

'I always felt blamed,' April said.

'Eileen did a lot of blaming,' said Lizzie. 'And before her, there was the first April, and she left nothing but trouble behind her. Like you say, it does no good handing out blame, but you can't start on Bridie for wanting to help set it right.'

'I didn't mean to,' said April feebly, crushed by the old woman's vehemence, 'I made it up with my own mother, you know, and I loved her, though she wasn't an easy woman. She'd have been the first to admit that.'

'Mothers and daughters. Is it ever easy?' murmured Hannah.

Georgina just listened, looking wise.

'I suppose you can do what you want, now,' April said to Hannah. 'You don't have to work so hard.'

'I'll be able to do the things I really want to do, like my therapy training, without having to worry all the time about how I can afford it.'

'Will you go into private practice?'

'If I can. It's a long haul. I might find I'm no good.'

Lizzie snorted loudly and thumped her stick. 'You do that, and she'll come straight down and haunt you. Just because she's dead, don't mean she's gone.'

They all wondered whether Lizzie's marbles had gone, along with Bridie. She was getting very, very old.

The winter of the year Bridie died, Lizzie came to stay. Hannah and Georgina both argued with her that it took so much time, them going back and forth to her little flat to look after her, it would be better if she came to them, at least until the weather was better. Georgina helped bring her over, and then complained.

'She goes on and on about what they used to do,' she said. 'She's boring, but it would be rude to say so, wouldn't it? She's started repeating herself an awful lot.'

Hannah loved her daughter for listening to Lizzie's ramblings at all. 'It's age,' she said, stating the obvious, 'she's not senile, but she's not quite all there, either.'

'What will you do, if she gets bedridden? It's going to be awfully inconvenient.'

'I don't know.'

'And I've got my A levels to do.'

'My, we're virtuous. I know you've got your A levels,' answered her mother repressively. 'I don't see what that has to do with looking after a very old woman whom we love.'

Georgie sighed and said she'd go and stay at Rodney's house to revise, if Hannah was difficult.

'Self, self, self,' screeched Hannah, furious. 'Why don't you go and live there? I'm sure they'd be delighted.'

'They wouldn't mind,' shrugged Georgina. 'It's my life.'

'I didn't mean it. I couldn't bear you to go away. You can go and revise, if you want, though we're not talking about now, are we? It's a year away.'

'You do over react, Mum.'

When Hannah calmed down, she thought it over and decided that, for all the callousness of youth, she could see her daughter's point of view.

'At your age, I wish I'd been more like that,' she said later.

'Like what?' asked Georgie, who had already forgotten.

'Myself. Knowing what I wanted and able to fight for it and not be ashamed,' said Hannah wistfully.

'Well, that's all right, because you are now, aren't you?'

Hannah looked around at her lovely house, her books, her possessions, her daughter, who one day would leave her.

'In a way. But it's not enough. There is something missing and it may be too late in life ever to have it.'

'Now who's being ungrateful?'

'That's not the issue,' said Hannah.

Lizzie took to her bed in early spring, bent double by arthritis, wearied by a persistent cough that would not go away. Her stories wandered and repeated themselves, until Hannah and Georgina knew by heart the tale of Sam's charabanc trip to Ipswich, to see Bridie in the Blitz, how they decorated Bridget's birthday cake with condensed milk in a toothpaste tube and how Mrs MacDonald, the midwife, had made the parson sing in St Dunstan's Church when Bridie got burned by the first of Hitler's bombers. Lizzie's son had died after the war, in a prison camp, but she rarely spoke of that. Bridget went with the WAAFs to Australia and never came home again.

'It was Edward,' said Lizzie. 'She never got over him.'

'Edward?' Hannah was incredulous. 'You never mean Edward was two timing Bridie with Bridget?'

'I don't think it was a question of two timing,' said Lizzie, and refused to explain.

'Well, I never.'

Lizzie dozed for a while and then took up her tales again.

'You miss having Bridie to tell, don't you? Do you mind that I'm not the real thing,' said Hannah, sitting in lamplight by her bed one evening. Her arms ached with carrying shopping and lifting Lizzie in and out of bed.

'Don't be silly.'

They both knew it wasn't silly and that with Bridie no longer there to share the history of their lives, Lizzie felt she'd lost a part of herself that she was trying to recover again. After the question, she fell into a reverie that lasted until Hannah brought up a bit of supper on a tray and asked her if she wanted anything.

'Only to go on talking. It's what keeps me going,' she said in a moment of clarity. 'Memories, you know. We had such extraordinary lives.'

Hannah sighed.

'No, I won't go on.'

Hannah rubbed her eyes. 'I don't mind. But I have reading to do.'

'That Mrs Trump could come in more often,' suggested Lizzie. Mrs Trump sat in when Hannah had to be out, which was more and more.

'I only need to read. We'll manage.'

'I tell you what you ought to do,' said Lizzie, her face like crumpled old lace.

'What's that?'

'You ought to write it down. I can tell you a thing or two.'

'And how!' said Hannah, amused. 'I can't write stories. You can certainly tell them, though.'

'How do you know?'

'What?'

'That you can't write stories. Have you tried?'

'No.'

'Well, then.'

'I'd be embarrassed.'

'You wouldn't have to tell your story. Tell Bridie's, and mine, and all the rest of us. That's not embarrassing.'

'The writing of it might be. I'd make a pig's ear of it.' Hannah laughed, not for a second seriously considering it.

'I mean it,' insisted Lizzie.

'No.'

'It would stop you missing her so much.'

'How do you know what I miss?'

'I'm not stupid,' wheezed the old woman, coughing, 'and I'm not deaf, neither.'

Hannah flushed and was still cross when Georgina came home.

'I don't know why you've got the hump, Mum,' said her daughter, so nearly a woman. 'I think it's a brilliant idea.'

'I wouldn't know where to start,' muttered Hannah sulkily.

'That really ages you, that expression.'

Hannah sulked harder, feeling babyishly that more was expected of her than she had ever bargained on giving.

Lizzie coughed and coughed and leaned back wearily on her pillows. 'It's not difficult,' she said, her skin milky and damp, 'you start at the beginning, like I tell you.'

The more Hannah felt angrily that this was something outside her scope, something she didn't want to do, the more Lizzie persisted. The idea seduced and repelled and frightened her. Then, one morning, rushing to get to college on time for a morning seminar, she remembered Miss Sheaffer, right out of the blue.

"Go and write, Miss Holmes," she'd said; the words they'd all wanted to hear, every one of the English students a secret, budding writer. But the words had been said to her in her wilderness, and she had changed. Miss Sheaffer might not say them to the Hannah she was now. Hannah remembered, dismissed the idea, then remembered it again. It wouldn't go away. The typewriter began to tap at odd hours and Lizzie listened from her bedroom, expectantly. Furtively, even resentfully, Hannah began to see if she could do it.

She began the story of the O'Neill family, in a village near Dublin, of how widowed Sean O'Neill raped his daughter one drunken night and how she had come to London, alone and afraid, and all that had happened since. Hannah began, painfully, slowly, doubtfully, but with secret excitement, to write down Bridie's story, just as Lizzie told it.

Chapter Fifty-Two

Lizzie was laid to rest just after Bridie's story was published. The weeks before the finished copies arrived in the morning post, she was so frail, Hannah thought she must go at any moment. A nurse came in to help, and took over most of the work during the week but Hannah and Georgina looked after her at weekends.

'It'll feel very funny, not to have a house full of old ladies,' remarked Georgina, 'and when I go to university, you'll be all by yourself. Will you mind?'

'Yes,' said Hannah shortly, not wanting to think about it.

And so Lizzie held on and held on, until the book came. Then she made Georgina sit by her bed and read it aloud, because her eyes were too filmy to see.

'Ah, that's it,' she murmured, as Georgie turned the pages. 'Oh, yes.' And then, when she'd heard it, she died. To Hannah and Georgina, it was simple and right and very peaceful, but it took the edge off Wendy Dawn's ringing up on the day the book was finally in the shops, shrieking excitedly and saying she must buy copies for everyone she knew.

'You are so clever,' she cried. 'I don't know how you do it. I couldn't.'

'It was hard work.'

Georgina yelled from the kitchen that Mum was going to be a bestseller, and both women laughed.

'It's all right, then?' asked Wendy Dawn. 'You like it?'

'I think I do.'

'Why shouldn't you? When's the next one coming out?' asked Wendy Dawn.

'What next one?' Hannah coloured, caught out in her dream.

'You've done your grandmother's story. Now you have to do your mother.'

'Do I?' asked Hannah guiltily, who already had a pile of pages by the typewriter.

'Definitely,' said Wendy Dawn. 'And then, you can do us.'

'Must I?'

'You can't leave *me* out.'

'The biggest nits in the world. Wouldn't you mind?'

'No, lice,' corrected Wendy Dawn. 'Nits are the eggs.'

'You crack them between your finger nails. Yours exploded.'

The former and the present Mrs Hitherington Mathers instantly scratched their heads, and laughed.

'What about Joe?' asked Hannah, when April's story was nearly done, and her thoughts turned to her own. 'I can't write about me without him.'

'Where is he?' asked Wendy Dawn.

Georgina, packing to go to Greece with Rodney, after A levels were over, pricked up her ears.

'I have no idea,' said Hannah, turning the strange thought over in her mind. 'There's not often anything in the papers and if there is, it's usually about plays he's doing. Not where he lives or anything personal.'

'The love of your life?' said Georgina, who by now knew something of their story. 'And you've lost track? That's careless.'

'Perhaps he's like Emmanuel, the playwright in Elizabeth Jane Howard's story, who didn't live anywhere except hotel rooms and temporarily rented houses. I can imagine Joe might be like that. He was never exactly a homey person.'

'Well, if you're going to write about him, you'd better find him, hadn't you? It wouldn't be hard, surely. He's so well known.'

'Go to Greece, and leave me alone,' Hannah cried.

They went, but the thought of Joe did not.

While they went to Greece again, Hannah went to France with friends, wandered the long beaches of Brittany, letting her story take shape. The thread of her life ran through it, and with it, even though she hadn't seen him for more than twenty years, Joe. She stood among standing stones, feeling the ancient presence of them, daydreaming of how life goes on and on, carried through generations, an unbroken chain.

'Life?' said one of her friends over dinner. 'What do you mean? Genes?'

'I mean everything, not just genes. The way we are, the things we do. What decides what the next generation is and does. What we give our children, and I don't mean just blue eyes or brown eyes, and the kind of people they are. Genes can't make good or bad, happy and unhappy, decide whether someone is creative or destroys things. We pass on more than we know.'

'Ah,' they said knowingly. 'Philosophy and psychology. That stuff. It's all been said, hasn't it? Freud and that lot. All comes down to your Oedipus complex or something, doesn't it?'

'I don't think so. What about good and evil and which side you are on?' said Hannah.

'You and your in-depth psychologising. It's too hot for that,' they cried, and went for a post-prandial plunge in the hotel pool.

But Hannah knew there was much more to it than that.

'I think he's in America,' said Rodney, who knew people who used to know Joe.

'He always said he'd go back to San Francisco. He's been in California a lot of the time.'

Someone said they thought he might be in Canada. Hannah thought that unlikely.

'How do you find people? And what do you do if they'd much rather you didn't?' Hannah asked Wendy Dawn.

'Salvation Army?'

'Don't be silly.'

'You're serious about finding him, aren't you?'

'I think I am. I don't know. I don't really want it suddenly to happen, after all these years, but I can't use him in a book without asking. He'll know that better than anyone.'

'If you really want to get in touch, it's obvious.'

'Not to me.'

'You buy a copy of one of his plays and write to his publisher. They send it on and if he wants to get in touch, he will.'

'Ah,' said Hannah, the sudden ease with which the dream could be realised startling.

'The past,' said Wendy darkly, 'have you thought that it might be better to leave him there? He's probably fat, balding and on his third wife. Why spoil a good fantasy?'

'He wasn't fat or balding the last time I saw a picture of him, and I don't think I'd mind about that.' She smiled. 'So far as I know, he's not married, but if he is, the third wife might mind about me.'

'Right. Then go for it,' said Wendy Dawn.

Joe's publishers were helpful. 'I can't give you an address, but if you'd like to write to him via me, I'll send it on,' offered the woman at the other end of the telephone. 'He gets a lot of letters, though, so I can't promise anything. But if you say you're an old friend . . .'

'I'll write to you,' said Hannah.

Hannah saw clients who came to her for psychotherapy in her consulting room at the back of the house, where Bridie had once had a cold, little used, dining room. When they had gone each day, in the early evening, she pulled her typewriter towards her and sat sunk in thought. Then she straightened up and began to type.

Georgina's going off to university brought a sense of loss and confusion. Hannah wandered her house, desolate and restless. Even outings with Wendy Dawn didn't fill the void and, when her work was done, Hannah often found herself sitting staring at the television with aching eyes. She rang Ben, friend and colleague.

'I've had enough of dying and death,' she said miserably. 'Everyone's gone and now it's Georgie. I miss her desperately.'

'Empty?'

'I don't feel empty, just lost without her.'

'And the new book?'

'The book is within me. That part of me isn't empty.'

'There you are, there's your new baby. That'll keep you busy.'

Hannah grinned. 'I'd better give birth to it, then, but it's going to be a long labour, and Joe really ought to be there to share my pains.'

'Hannah, you don't have to look backwards for nice feelings. There are plenty around in the present.'

'Is that what I'm doing? Looking back for happiness?'

'I have a feeling you may be and you don't need to.'

'I've read somewhere that novelists are people in search of lost love,' she said wryly. 'Perhaps I'm a cliché.'

'Joe is a fantasy.'

'No, he isn't. The Joe I imagine now is a fantasy and so is the one in the book, but the Joe I knew years and years ago was real, and I loved him.'

'Be careful. He is not that person now, and, to be fair to him, nor are you the same.'

'I know. And I am careful.'

'Maybe not careful enough, but there's only one way to find out, so go and write your story.'

'I shouldn't write what I want to write, unless he says I can.'

'You want to pin him down,' chuckled Ben. 'But he might not let you, so one way or another, that's a risk you're just going to have to take.'

The nine o'clock news droned from the sitting room as she put the receiver down. Fire and devastation filled the screen and the presenter said something about the Richter Scale. Earthquake, thought Hannah automatically.

another one. Are we really coming to this Apocalypse?

'. . . San Francisco . . . the San Andreas fault. Scientists said tonight that they do not think this is the big one that the West Coast has been waiting for.'

Hannah watched a bridge, collapsed upon itself, killing dozens on the motorway underneath. People spoke facing cameras with hysteria in their voices.

Think of standing holding a camera, focused on all those cars squashed like bugs, with people inside. It's ghastly, she thought, depressed by the image. We come, we go. No sense to it.

She switched off the set and went to bed.

Gladys and Harry had the trip of a lifetime. On the first-class Pan Am flight Gladys, stiff with nerves, had quaffed free champagne like lemonade and ended up quite tight, an overbright-cheeked, withered English rose wrapped in the lace of an easycare Marks and Spencer's two-piece.

'My son is a very famous writer,' she said, too loudly, to the stewardess.

'Do I know his name?'

'He's Joe Masters,' said Gladys proudly.

'The Joe Masters who writes plays?'

'You know him?' Gladys was delighted. '*First Person Plural, Mo-Mo, Brouhaha, Priestly Habits* . . . that's the one about two clerics who . . .'

'For goodness' sake,' muttered Harry out of the side of his mouth.

'Why?' Gladys wiped her eyes with a handkerchief because things looked a little funny.

'Because she doesn't want to know. You're boasting,' he hissed.

'I've seen *All Fall Down*,' said the stewardess. 'I loved it. You must be so proud.'

'Oh, we are.'

Harry found magazines in a pocket on the seat in front of him and began to look through them.

'Do you think she's coming round again with this?' asked Gladys, waving her empty glass. She watched the pretty young woman with the ready smile move slowly down the plane. Businessmen stretched out and put blindfolds over their eyes, trying to sleep. Above their heads, the in-flight movie flashed noiselessly into life.

'I don't think you should have any more of that. Why don't you put these on and watch the film?'

Harry fitted in his earpieces, determined to enjoy his flight too. 'I like this,' said Gladys happily.

'I can see that,' he remarked dubiously, and settled down to watch.

'You know something?' said Gladys triumphantly, after watching with him for five minutes.

'What?' Harry eased one earpiece and pretended to pay attention.

'That's one of Joe's movies. It's got his name at the end where it says what play it was based on.'

'I know.' Harry sighed inwardly.

The stewardess cast an experienced eye over her elderly charges, and went off to the galley.

'I'll take the old girl a cup of tea,' she said to the steward. 'She's going to go pop if she gets any more excited. Sweet, really, isn't it? Imagine going abroad for the first time, at that age.'

'Ask her if she wants to see the cockpit,' grinned the steward. 'Give the captain a treat.'

The co-pilot went to the gents and let Gladys sit in his chair while he was gone.

'I flew a jumbo jet,' she said squeakily, accepting another tray of tea, back in her seat.

Harry complained about his. 'How do you make this thing go back?'

Gladys grinned conspiratorially at the stewardess. 'He's not used to travel, you know.'

'How about a blanket and a sleep, so you get there fresh?' suggested the stewardess. 'That's what most of our regulars do.'

Gladys looked round at the wide seats full of men dozing or pretending to work, with drooping eyes.

'You know, I think I will,' she said graciously, and they tucked her up like a baby for the rest of the crossing.

'Of course,' she said afterwards, 'I got terrible jet lag, but he slept all the way and never noticed nothing.'

Joe and Harry caught each other's eye. 'At least I never took my teeth out,' muttered Harry vengefully. 'She had the girl running up and down something dreadful because they hadn't got any steradent.'

'You'd better get used to flying because we're going to Disneyland,' said Joe, amused, 'but everywhere else we'll go by car.'

'Just listen to him,' said Gladys to Harry, beside herself with pride. Joe looked out over the steeply falling hillside below his sprawling home. Massive redwoods shielded it from the sound of cars climbing a winding mountain road that ran deep into rural northern California, and from prying eyes.

'If I'm a real anything, I'm a real recluse,' he said lightly. 'Amy will take you anywhere you want to go, but most of the time, I'll be working.'

'You aren't coming with us?' cried Gladys, disappointed.

'Amy will show you much better than I can. I gave that kind of thing up a long time ago.'

Amy, a dark-haired young woman with a soft, lithe walk and inscrutable Indian eyes, nodded. Gladys got flustered with her at first, but Amy was impervious to her nervousness, having learned determined American kindness.

'Adopted daughter, eh? That means you're her grandmother,' commented Harry.

'Of course, ever since he wrote and told us.' Amy, Joe had said, was his family, his American roots.

'Do you mind he never had real children of his own?' asked Harry.

'Yes. He had his chance, though, and let it go. Poor Louisa.'

'You'd have enjoyed grandchildren.'

'Indian great-grandchildren will be very nice. I expect we'll get used to it,' said Gladys sadly.

'Joe has only made plays. He tripped over me by accident,' said Amy, not at all put out by their guarded questions.

'Plays aren't children,' mourned Gladys.

'I think they are, for him.'

They did get used to each other and Gladys became very fond of Amy. She drove them everywhere they wanted to go and left them to sit by the pool in the shade when they didn't want to go anywhere. Disneyworld transfixed and exhausted them. Afterwards Harry retired to the poolside, and put the newspaper over his face, complaining he was too old for that kind of thing. A trip to Sa

Francisco and Oakland, down the mountains and across the Golden Gate Bridge, he said, was beyond him.

'You go,' he said stubbornly, when Gladys nagged. 'I'll stay and doze out there. I don't want to go traipsing around all those people and all those motorways.'

'We'll stay in the car. You wouldn't have to walk. It's a wonderful sight,' she argued.

'I don't feel right, seeing all those people in doorways. I don't want to see. You go with Amy and leave me here by the pool.'

The people in doorways scared Harry. Sometimes young, and sometimes not so young, they frightened Gladys, too. She's never seen junkies and drunks like it in London, but she outfaced her own fears.

'All right, I'll go by myself,' she said.

She and Amy went sightseeing to Oakland, to cross the Golden Gate Bridge and see the Marin Headlands rising, wild and lonely, from the Pacific. It was a long drive. On the way back, Amy turned up the car radio.

'It's the World Series final,' she explained. 'Baseball. That's why the roads are so clear. Everyone's home already, to watch.'

'Rounders,' muttered Gladys.

The voice of the commentator rose excitedly as they approached Bay Bridge on their way back. Warm air rushed in the window as Gladys pushed the button for it to slide down. She sighed with happiness.

'It's been a lovely day. Thank you, Amy,' she said, enjoying the breeze.

'Here come the San Francisco Giants . . .' screamed the commentator against the background of feverish cheering that was shaking the stands in Candlestick Stadium.

'It sounds like a cup final between Liverpool and Everton,' observed Gladys.

'It's two local teams,' explained Amy, accelerating to overtake a truck, speeding down a clear lane. 'It's the first time two local teams have made the final. Everyone is real excited.'

Gladys said, 'That's funny.'

Amy said 'What . . . ?'

Freeway 880 fell in upon itself, mangled concrete debris flattening cars and the people in them to less than twelve inches high. Floodlit pylons over Candlestick Stadium swayed like palm trees in a storm as the earth trembled, shook and shivered itself into mud, rubble, chaos and chasms. Six point nine on the Richter scale, screamed worldwide headlines the next day, the second worst earthquake ever to hit the United States. Baseball players hugged each other in fear in smudged newspaper photographs, the clocks over the stands stopped at four minutes past five, and not one of the sixty-two thousand spectators in Candlestick Stadium was hurt.

Joe and Harry watched the build up to the game on television with a couple of cans of beer. As the screen seemed to shiver strangely, so did the walls and then they were in the air, bouncing, hurtling hither and thither like demented dolls. Joe fell to the floor in an eerie second of calm and the dishwasher slid by on smooth wheels, straight into the piano, which lay on its side in a jangle. Breaking free from its foundations with an earnumbing crack, the house slid down the mountainside, scattering itself in a thousand pieces while its roof slid off and came to a stop five hundred yards downhill. Harry sat in Joe's white, hide-covered sofa at the bottom of a cliff, untouched, transported as if by some monstrous poltergeist. Joe sat bolt upright, unconscious, in the roots of a giant redwood that stood on its topmost branches, delicately balanced against the steep side of the mountain. Harry eased himself up, moaned, and collapsed sideways on to the spotless leather seat, his eyes rolling up in his head. Neighbours found the two of them when they clambered down the ruined road from further up, trying to find a phone that worked. Joe and Harry woke up side by side in hospital.

'Ah, fuck,' groaned Joe, regressed by pain, feeling his right arm plastered up, broken in several places.

'Where's Gladys?' quavered the old man.

'Amy?' blurted Joe, coming to his senses.

Someone told them there was a car on the bridge, whose registration said it belonged to him, with two women found inside. After that Joe didn't swear again. For a while, he couldn't bring himself to say anything at all.

Chapter Fifty-Three

Whatever Joe's virtues, thought Hannah, letter writing was not one of them. She'd written to his publishers, a business-like note, asking them to forward a letter to Joe in which she asked if he'd mind if she invented a character whom Joe would recognise as based on himself. She wanted, she said, to write a novel. There had followed a resounding silence.

'Maybe he hates the idea and doesn't want to hurt your feelings by saying so,' suggested Georgina, rummaging in the washbasket for clean clothes.

'I think he more likely doesn't care enough one way or the other, to bother,' said her mother, handing her a pile of crumpled skirts. 'Here, you can iron them yourself.' As Georgina set up the ironing board she added, 'The man I remember would have bothered to say so, even if he did hate the idea, if you see what I mean.'

'Perhaps he's not the man you remember. Maybe he's dead.'

'Don't be ridiculous, they'd have said so in the papers,' snapped Hannah, then caught herself and grinned sheepishly.

'You're all worked up, aren't you?' cried Georgina, surprised.

'I am not worked up.'

'You jolly well are.'

While San Francisco pulled itself together again after the earthquake, Joe and Harry tried to pull themselves together, which was harder. Their shared grief was bedevilled by conflict about what to do with Gladys, unable to see eye to eye about where to bury her. Since Joe's house was uninhabitable, they stayed in a hotel in a little-damaged area of the city, where Harry scowled and his mouth set in a stubborn line that Joe had grown to know and dread every time they brought the subject up.

'I'm taking her home.'

'She's squashed like a bug,' roared Joe, venting his grief and frustration in the endless crude argument that ricocheted fruitlessly between them. 'How can you take a person all across the United States and the Atlantic when they are practically flat as a hamburger? It's obscenely unnecessary.'

'So is your tone. I wish you wouldn't keep saying that.' Harry rattled the little box of tranquillisers the doctor had given him.

'You are the next of kin. You only have to say and she'll be buried over here next to Amy, in a nice grave, everything done as you want. No fuss, no gruesomeness. That's how Mum would have seen it.'

'She's going back home to the East London cemetery, where she always said she wanted to go when her time come. She's got her plot there and I'll put her in it,' Harry jabbed a finger in the air, 'and I'll see her done right by, like she wanted, if it's the last thing I do.'

Joe slammed his good fist on the back of a chair and winced with pain in his broken arm. 'She's my mother.'

'She wouldn't rest easy here, son.'

'You might as well say I should bury Amy in Guatemala City, just because that's where she came from. It doesn't make sense,' snarled Joe, enraged by his own fathomless misery and his inability to do anything about it.

'If you say so,' agreed Harry. 'I know when I go, I want to be buried at home, and I wouldn't do no less by Gladys. I'm sorry there's Amy for you to worry about as well. I'm sorry for both of us, if you must know.'

'It will be an administrative nightmare.' Joe began to give way, half envious of the old man's dignity, when all *he* could do was get angry.

Harry rattled his pills miserably and said never mind that and blow the bits of paper, they'd deal with that as it came.

'I'm used to paperwork,' he said proudly, 'running a Post Office, you know.'

'It all has to go through the East London coroner,' Joe played his last card, 'and there'll probably be two autopsies, and she'll go into a deep freeze for months and you won't be able to bury her for ages and ages.'

'They said all that, at the police station when we . . .'

'I would have liked her here, you know? Just to have her here, by Amy. It's all my family.'

'She's my wife.'

Joe heaved a noisy sigh and nursed his shattered arm. 'I'll come with you, when they let her go.'

Harry fingered his pill box. 'Take her back to England together?'

'Yes. I'll help you.'

'You've gone grey,' remarked Harry sadly.

Joe answered drearily that if hair was any indication of the wreckage of his life, he should be bald; that he had nightmares and couldn't write; that his home was a heap at the bottom of a canyon; that his mother and adopted daughter were neatly crushed sardines; and that his stepfather was driving him crazy. His arm ached intolerably.

'I'm sorry,' said Harry humbly, having got his way. 'Here.' He took the box of tranquillisers out of his pocket and sat looking at it. Then he pressed it into Joe's hand. 'I never took these before, and I won't start now. You want them?'

There was a time when I would have, he thought, and pushed the box back into the old man's fingers.

'No thanks, Harry.'

It took two months to get permission from the coroner to take Gladys's body back to Britain. One wet December morning, in driving rain, men in dark overalls hurried the coffin into the hold of the plane after everyone was on board; people didn't like knowing there was a body travelling with them. Joe and Harry fastened seatbelts and heard the engines engage, then the runway flashed past and by some miracle the jumbo lifted itself into the air and flew up into low cloud, the ground vanishing in seconds.

The flight was long and dull, the purpose of it wretched. Harry, waking grumpily for meals, slept most of it away. Joe sat with his eyes closed, feeling Amy in his arms again, in that squalid alleyway where the policeman had shot the other child, wondering if there were such a thing as purpose in it all and whether the pain of it would ever go or leave him any kind of peace.

They flew in over a London hiding underneath a downpour of cold rain that bounced off tarmac and drove passengers, shivering, into terminals and tube stations. The undertaker would fetch the coffin and deal with it. Joe hustled Harry out of the airport into the tube. They travelled without speaking, all the way to Embankment, where they got out and walked hurriedly, dripping, to the Savoy, where Joe was welcomed as an old and cherished guest. Harry, exhausted and uncomfortable in such a place, and with the beginnings of a bad cold, went to bed early to sleep off his jet leg. He left for Cheltenham the next day. Joe said he'd see the formalities were done, and anything that might need signing, they could send on.

Well, I brought you home, Mum. What do I do now? thought Joe, having seen the coroner's assistant in East London. He caught the tube to Oxford Street, for want of anything better to do, needing to do something to ease the ache in his heart, and walked down to see the lights. Up and down the rainwashed streets, traffic belched and snarled. Christmas decorations, strung across the road, dripped on to passing cars, hanging dull and tarnished in weak winter daylight. Selfridges' windows glowed like magic lanterns in wintry gloom and Joe paused, his collar turned up, watching fairies flap gauzy wings around a Dickensian scene of Merry Yuletide, fingering an envelope in his coat pocket. The letter inside was dated the day before the earthquake and had been kept back when news of the disaster came, then forwarded to the hotel when his secretary let his publisher know he was in town.

'Someone said it isn't fan mail. We were told it's from a friend? Something about copyright.' The secretary, following from America in his and Harry's wake and now installed in the Savoy, had handed him the letter and he'd stuffed it in his pocket. Now, in the light from fairyland, he pulled the page from its envelope and read it. He stood lost in thought for a long while, smelling chestnuts roasting over a streetvendor's fire, then turned on his heel and made for Oxford Circus tube station, battling his way through dense and jostling Christmas crowds to get a tube to Bethnal Green.

Chapter Fifty-Four

Carol singers had been round and when the bell went again, Hannah put down the icing gun she was using to decorate her Christmas cake and took her purse to the door. At first, she didn't recognise him, though he seemed familiar. She hesitated.

'Hello, Hannah,' said Joe.

She knew his voice instantly, and then she saw it was him. He was not as tall as she remembered, very grey and much thinner in the face than his photographs had shown. But his eyes were the same bright brown, only tired and rather sad.

'What a wonderful surprise.'

She was smaller and thinner than he had remembered, fined down by age; it suited her. In her face was steadiness, a serenity that had not been there before. They stood in the light spilling from the hallway on to the garden path. Fine rain drifted down, misting his hair.

'Can I come in, Hannah?'

She stood to one side and gestured him into the bright house. It smelled of spice and sugar and burning logs, and somewhere a radio played carols.

'I have your letter. I'm sorry. We had an earthquake and I didn't get it until now.'

'You were in that earthquake?'

He followed her down to a basement kitchen and she pulled out a chair and took his wet coat to hang behind the door.

'My mother was killed on the bridge that collapsed. I expect you saw that on the news.'

'I'm sorry,' she said, at a loss for words.

'And my daughter was with her.'

Hannah sat opposite him at the table. 'That is terrible. I never heard you had a daughter. This is dreadful.'

'I brought her home for burial. Mum, that is. That's why I'm here.'

Hannah pushed aside her half iced cake. 'Would you like a cup of tea? A glass of something?'

'Could you manage whisky?'

'Of course. Where are you staying?'

'The Savoy.'

'You're not over here often, are you?'

He shook his head. 'I have an agent who handles things. I've often thought of you. Wondered what you were doing, you know? And then I find you're writing too. Funny, that.'

'How many years is it?'

He had thought about that on the tube. 'Twenty-four.'

'You've changed.'

'So have you. A lot.'

She glanced at his ringless finger. 'I was once married, but it didn't last long. It was years ago. And you?'

'I'm divorced.'

'I heard ages ago, from Jenny, that you were.'

'You see her?'

'Just that one time, after my wife left me. I wanted to find you, but she said I would only hurt you, so I didn't. I don't know whether she was right, but I know what she said felt right at the time.'

She refilled his glass and he pulled out her letter, flattening it slowly on to the tabletop with his thumbnail.

'What are you writing?'

Hannah blushed. 'Not like you; I'm not in your league. I don't write literature. It's a novel, a family saga. I wanted to put someone like you into it.'

He smiled and she thought it made him look so bone weary, it hurt her to see it. 'Of course you can. Write anything you like, short of defaming me.'

'It isn't easy.'

He gave a short laugh. 'It never is.'

'It wouldn't be you, just a character based on you, but you'd know yourself.'

'Can I see?'

She smiled and said, 'No.'

'Whodunnit? Autobiography? What?'

A flush even deeper than the first ran up her cheeks to her hair. 'It's a story about love, I suppose. I don't mean just romance.'

Joe stared into his glass. 'They sell well.'

'Yes.'

He put his elbows on the table. 'Tell me everything. What you've been doing.'

'You go first,' she said, like a child.

'I asked first.'

'I'll tell you while I finish my cake.'

'It's too long,' he said later, beside the fire in Bridie's old sitting room. 'We can't get through twenty-five years or so, in one evening.'

'Could you come back? Are you staying? Would you have time?'

'I have nothing to hurry home for.'

'No,' she said sadly.

'What time shall I come?'

Hannah smiled and said, 'Breakfast? Isn't breakfast a social event in California?'

'Lunch,' said Joe. 'I want to sleep. I haven't slept, not really slept, for months.'

'Since the earthquake?'

'Since the earthquake.'

'I'll see you for lunch, then.'

He left a message for his secretary to take all calls, and not to wake him for anything at all. Then he curled up in a tight foetal ball in the middle of the wide double bed and slept like a dead man. The nightmares were stilled for the first time since Amy died.

'I shall tell her all about Amy,' he said into the bathroom mirror, shaving the next morning. On the way to Bethnal Green, he bought three dozen red roses and a bottle of wine.

'I thought I'd given up impulses,' he grinned, handing them to Hannah awkwardly.

She held the flowers like a barrier between herself and her own impulses. She stood on the doorstep, wind gusting her apron round her skirt, pink with cold and suppressed impulse, her eyes shining.

'Would you like to stay and spend Christmas with us?'

Joe said, yes, he would.

'Georgina will be home from university, and Wendy Dawn and Rodney will come over. We're rather quiet, I'm afraid.'

'Quiet is just what I need.'

When he went home, to oversee the clearing of wreckage from his canyon and the rebuilding of his house, Georgina and Wendy Dawn teased her.

'He's fascinating,' cried Wendy Dawn. 'Is he coming back?'

'I don't know. I don't know anything about it,' sighed Hannah, 'but he does write.'

''My house is pretty well finished,'' he wrote six months later, ''but it is terribly empty without Amy. The more full it is of people, the lonelier I feel.'' Hannah read his letters, laid them to one side, and worked on her book. He never again asked to see it. His tact touched her. At last, after a good deal of rewriting of the first draft, it was done. She put the manuscript in a jiffy bag, addressed it to her publisher, and went for a brisk walk. Then she made a transatlantic call and woke Joe up, to tell him it was done.

'All right. Glad you finished it.'

He just put the 'phone down on her, on the other side of the world.

'Well, there's manners for you,' she said, mortified.

She was still angry with him when he turned up outside her front door, holding yellow roses.

'I have some affairs to see to, to do with my mother and some odds and ends she left, so I came over myself.'

'Why didn't you let me know?'

'I didn't know myself. This is a surprise from me to me.'

She took the roses and led him through to her little study at the back, and pointed silently to a pile of photocopied paper. He picked it up, shoved it under his arm and left without a word.

'You are so rude,' Hannah called after him as he banged her gate, but he didn't seem to hear.

He let her worry for two whole days. Then he rang her up and said he wanted to see her.

'I'm at home.'

'I want to take you somewhere. I'll pick you up.'

'I can't just drop everything and go away. I have patients. Things to do.'

'Cancel them. We go this afternoon.'

'Oh, really!' cried Hannah. 'That's impossible.'

'One o'clock. We'll have lunch on the way.'

'Of all the nerve.'

'And . . .'

'What?'

'. . . I like it very much,' he said, sounding oddly angry, and rang off.

'I think this is a bit much,' she said sharply, getting into his hired car nonetheless. Joe drove like a demon and hardly spoke, tearing down the A23, up over the Downs, then a long crawl on to the coast through heavy traffic. They arrived at Brighton Pier, turned right and went slowly along the edge of the promenade until Joe found a parking space.

'Why are we here?' demanded Hannah, looking out over the grey sea.

'For a walk.'

'This is where we used to play ducks and drakes. Is that why you've dragged me all this way, for a nostalgic trip down Memory Lane?'

Joe got out of the car, came round and opened her

door. Dark clouds were moving in from the horizon and a chill wind blew off the sea, bringing fine mist that would turn to rain. Joe got an umbrella out of the boot and opened it. It was brilliant orange, like the sun.

'Come on,' he said.

They walked where they had walked more than twenty years before, and leaned on the same railings. Raindrops splashed their feet and darkened the brown pebbles on the beach.

'Do you think,' Joe asked, leaning on the railings with his back to the sea, the umbrella behind him against the lowering sky, 'that we are the same people we used to be?'

'Yes and no.'

'I read your book,' he said abruptly, 'and I had no idea.'

'The book is a story. It is not our story.'

He looked at her closely. 'It might be.'

'We are not those people.'

They began pacing again, along towards Hove, with the wind at their backs.

'Did you really love me like that?'

Hannah thought before telling him the truth. 'That much is true.'

'Ah,' he growled, and seemed sunk in thought. They were half way to Hove, the rain falling steadily, before he spoke again.

'You think I loved you that much? That stuff about the box and what have you?'

'You did in the book,' said Hannah calmly. 'I told you, it's not our story.'

They walked on, huddled together under the orange blaze of the brolly.

'Well?' he said brusquely, looking out to sea with rain in his eyes.

'Well, what? I'm soaked.'

'Do you think we could do better, this time?'

Hannah smiled with rain and tears on her face.

'Do *I* think we could do better, this time?' he muttered to himself, still watching the misty horizon where it touched the rainclouds. A shaft of sunlight broke through and turned the sea, far out, to molten gold.

'Look, it's beautiful!' cried Hannah.

They tipped their heads back to follow the rainbow towards the Downs.

'Yes,' he said. 'I do.'

'Perhaps.'

'There's no one else in your life?'

'No one lasting. There never was, really. I didn't love poor Rodney, but Wendy Dawn does, so that's all right. And you?'

He thought for a long time and she watched the rainbow fade. 'I was a coward,' he said at last, 'and I have paid for it. There's no point in guilt and apologies, is there?'

'Would you have come back, ever, if it hadn't been for your mother and Amy?' she asked quietly.

'No.' They turned and began pacing back towards Brighton.

'I was heartbroken. Maybe it took that to make me stop and think what I've been doing. I can't put it into words, but things are changed.'

Hannah began to laugh. She took his hand and led him down some steps on to the stony beach.

'What are you laughing at?' he asked, bending down to pick up pebbles, weighing them in his hand, as he always had, to test if they would spin on the water and bounce. The tide was far down, the water's edge too far to go to.

Hannah turned to him. 'I'm laughing because they will all be so delighted and so smug, and they will all say "I told you so" and tell me I'm the luckiest woman in the world. And they'll be so pleased with themselves, because they're right.'

'Are they? You think they're right?'

'Oh, yes.'

'This is the happy ending?'

She tucked her hand under his arm and they began to walk back up the slope of the beach. The rain stopped and the sun peeped out from behind the clouds, promising a fair and lovely evening.

'This will be our happy ending,' she said.

His eyes met hers.

'Yes,' he said.

They turned and walked back towards the town.